MW00323029

Dire Destiny of Ours

Book Ten of the Overworld Chronicles

John Corwin

Copyright © 2014 by John Corwin. All rights reserved. Except as permitted under the U.S. Copyright Act of 1976, no part of this publication may be reproduced, distributed, or transmitted in any form or by any means, or stored in a database or retrieval system, without the prior written permission of the publisher.

ISBN- 978-1-942453-00-0

Printed in the U.S.A.

RAVEN
HOUSE

The characters and events in this book are fictitious. Any similarity to real persons, living or dead, is coincidental and not intended by the author.

THE END IS NIGH

The last battle with Daelissa took a tremendous toll on the resistance. Elyssa is hanging onto life with the help of a preservation spell and Daelissa has new elite troops ready to conquer Eden. Justin realizes the only way to save the woman he loves and his home realm is to travel to Seraphina and ask the Darklings for help.

But the Darkling nation, Pjurna, is embroiled in its own war with the Brightlings and its leaders believe Justin is an enemy. His back to the wall on two fronts, Justin decides to take the gloves off and kick some ass.

If he doesn't, Elyssa will die and Daelissa will rule Eden.

Connect with John Corwin online:
Facebook: http://www.facebook.com/johnhcorwinauthor
Website: http://johncorwin.net/
Twitter: http://twitter.com/#!/John_Corwin

Books by John Corwin:

Overworld Chronicles:
Sweet Blood of Mine
Dark Light of Mine
Fallen Angel of Mine
Dread Nemesis of Mine
Twisted Sister of Mine
Dearest Mother of Mine
Infernal Father of Mine
Sinister Seraphim of Mine
Wicked War of Mine
Coming Soon: Destructive Destiny of Mine

Stand Alone Novels:

No Darker Fate
The Next Thing I Knew
Outsourced
Seventh

To my wonderful support group:
Alana Rock
Karen Stansbury

My amazing editors:
Annetta Ribken
Jennifer Wingard

My awesome cover artist:
Regina Wamba

Thanks so much for all your help and input!

Chapter 1

Elyssa has one week to live.

The thought bounced back and forth in my mind as I listened to Chancellor Frankenberg drone on and on about the history of Science Academy.

I forced the thought from my head and returned to the present. "We need everyone to help us. If Eden falls, Science Academy falls with it."

The short, dumpy man shook his head. His long gray hair extended in all directions as though constantly subjected to insane amounts of static electricity. "Science Academy has always maintained neutrality in political affairs of the Overworld. We let those *magicians*"—he harrumphed and waved a hand in the general direction of Arcane University—"tend to their own business while we tend to ours."

I looked around the audience chamber at the other professors seated at a long, semicircular table partially surrounding the lectern where I stood. I felt like a student in the hot seat. "Does he speak for all of you?" I waved my hand around the room. "If Daelissa defeats us, she'll shut down the academy to eliminate any threats to her rule. It's time to put aside ancient rivalry and join forces." I looked at Frankenberg. "It's time to come out of our shells and face reality."

The chancellor rose to his feet, face red. "I believe we've heard enough of this nonsense." He looked at the other professors. "I forward the motion to deny this boy's request."

A bony man with a crooked nose stood and spoke in a haughty voice. "I second Chancellor Frankenberg's motion."

One of the younger professors pshawed. "Of course you would, Newton. There's nothing you'd like better than to see Arcane University destroyed even if it meant the end of the world as we know it." He stood. "I vote no."

Shelton stood from his seat beside me and raised a fist. "Hell yeah."

I gave him a stern look. He shrugged and sat down.

The other council members, most of them resembling every kind of mad scientist stereotype I'd seen in the movies, voted. The final vote was eleven to two in favor of shutting me up.

Frankenberg shot me a caustic smile. "Science Academy will tend to itself, boy. Why don't you run along, now? The magicians need you."

Anger surged. My fists clenched so tight the knuckles cracked. *How do people like this exist?* "I think you should reconsider." My Elyssa had nearly died to protect idiots like Frankenberg and Newton. Instead of immediately setting off for Seraphina as I'd planned, I'd come here in a last-ditch effort to convince them to join us.

"Or what?" Frankenberg leered and looked around the room at his fellows. "Will you throw a tantrum?" He snapped his fingers and two human-sized battle bots marched from behind the council table and toward me. Each of them bore an array of deadly weapons, complete with missiles, death rays, and other crazy gadgets I didn't recognize.

"Are you threatening me?" I said.

Shelton tugged on my sleeve. "Justin, we should go. These geezers ain't interested in helping."

I ignored him and bared my teeth. "Brave people have died to protect Eden. Now I see you're nothing but cowards who hide behind the very technology that might help us."

"These bots are magically resistant," Frankenberg said. "If you attack them, you'll only embarrass yourself."

"You think I'm an Arcane?" A laugh burst from my throat. "Challenge accepted."

The bot to my left raised an arm equipped with lasers. Before it could fire, I thrust out my hand and encased it in a cube of Murk. The laser fired, but was too weak to penetrate the shield. These particular bots were smaller and might be protection against conventional magic attacks, but it was obvious the scientists hadn't accounted for Seraphim magic.

I saw the other bot aiming for me and fired a torrent of Brilliance. The magic-resistant armor held up for a couple of seconds before melting into slag. I clenched my left fist. The Murk cube compacted around the first bot and crushed it like a tin can. A couple of mini-missiles exploded. The impact sent a shock up my arm, but the Murk barrier held.

Gasps rose from the professors.

With a sarcastic smile, I opened my fist and let the crushed bot fall to the floor with a loud crash. "Imagine facing an army of Seraphim with powers like mine." I leaned forward on the lectern. "After you clean the crap out of your pants, maybe you'll reconsider my proposal."

Frankenberg's face pale face turned purple. "Out! Out! We will hear no more of this!"

Some of the other professors recovered their wits and banged on the table with their fists. "Out!" they chanted. "Out, out, out!"

The young professor who'd supported us gave me a sad look. He pushed back his chair and left the room.

My inner demon strained against my will as the professors continued to chant.

Kill! it commanded. *Destroy!* It was even worse at diplomacy than me. Resisting the urge to rake the room with destructive rays, I turned and stalked out.

"Well, that sure went to hell," Shelton said later as we rode the rocket ferry over the valley back toward Arcane University.

I looked down at the city of Queens Gate far below and tried not to feel sorry for myself. As usual, time and distance had given me plenty of time to rethink every aspect of my failed attempt to secure another ally.

Shelton blew out a breath and rested his arms on the railing. "What now?"

"I'm going to La Casona."

3

"Elyssa wouldn't want you moping around her all the time." Shelton paced around the deck. "She'd want you figuring out a way to beat Daelissa."

"Well, I'm out of ideas." The rocket ferry docked.

Shelton got off and stepped onto the flying carpet we'd ridden here. He looked back at me. "You coming?"

I shook my head. "I'm going to take a portal to La Casona from here."

He gave me a long concerned look. "Okay, man. I'll be at the mansion if you need me." The carpet rose, and he flitted off toward the Dark Forest and the hidden tunnel to the mansion.

After he was gone, I paced around, wondering if there were any other potential allies I could talk to. None came to mind. "There has to be something I can do!" A glow emanated from my right side. I looked down and saw a sphere of Brilliance coalesced around my hand. My temper was getting the best of me.

On a whim, I drew in Murk with my left hand and wove creation and destruction into a ball of gray Stasis. I'd been practicing my Seraphim magic as much as possible lately. It would take all my abilities to do what had to be done. I released the weave and let the fuzzy gray orb float in front of me and then channeled Murk and Brilliance directly into it. A crystalline beam speared from the other side and into a nearby boulder. It simply splashed against it.

"What am I supposed to do with this?" I wondered aloud. I'd been testing this strange fourth element, but it apparently did absolutely nothing.

I'd made plenty of use of the other elements. Brilliance, aka destruction, performed as advertised and blew up stuff. Murk—creation—was great for shielding myself from destruction, though I hadn't even come close to tapping its full potential. Stasis, a mix of the other two elements, could literally freeze magical attacks. I wasn't nearly as proficient with it as Fjoeruss, the Seraphim I'd once called Mr. Gray because of his affinity for the gray magic.

All Seraphim had an affinity for Murk or Brilliance. From what Fjoeruss once told me, it was like being left or right handed. You could learn to write with your left hand if you were right handed, but it would take an awful lot of work.

I, on the other hand, had felt no particular affinity for either element, though I'd experienced an overwhelming urge to decide. Instead of selecting one, I'd chosen all of the above. Not only was it a great way to cop out of a difficult decision, but it had also revealed to me that mixing the two primary elements together created the third one—Stasis. To make matters even more confusing, once I blended them into Stasis, I could channel new streams of Murk and Brilliance into Stasis to create a fourth clear element. Why it operated that way, I had no idea. Then again, nobody ever said magic had to make sense.

Since none of the Seraphim I'd asked knew anything about it or what it did, I named it Clarity. What I should have called it was useless. I'd channeled it against magical attacks, but it went right through them. I'd tested it on wood, stone, and even on my pint-sized hellhound, Cutsauce. It hadn't so much as singed a hair on his hide.

I sighed and released the energy. The gray sphere faded away. I'd eventually figure things out. For now, I had something far more pressing to attend.

I sent the La Casona omniarch operator an image of my surroundings. A portal opened a moment later. I stepped through, nodding at the Templar as I left the control room. A few steps later I entered the doors leading into the La Casona pocket dimension and walked the short distance to the healing ward. Nobody stopped me as I marched upstairs to Elyssa's room.

I stared at the still form of my girlfriend. She lay on a small wooden bed, barely more than a cot, beneath what looked like a glass shield. The barrier was part of a preservation spell—the only thing keeping Elyssa alive after Qualan, one of Daelissa's revived Seraphim, had speared her through the chest with a beam of Brilliance.

It had been a week since I'd killed Qualan in an all-out battle with Daelissa's Brightling army. I'd overextended myself and, even now, wasn't back to a hundred percent.

"I'm afraid we can't do anything to help her," Meghan Andretti said from behind me.

Nightliss entered the room and hugged me. "I'm sorry, Justin." Tears spilled from her eyes.

"Science Academy won't be joining us." I wasn't sure what made me say that right then. Maybe it was because I didn't know what else to say. Maybe it was my way of piling more pity on my shoulders. I felt like I was suffocating beneath a massive pile of crap. I felt directionless. We had to stop Daelissa, but we needed more troops. We needed more troops, but nobody else was willing to join us.

The logic took me on a downward spiral to hopelessness. *Elyssa is out of options. The world is out of options.*

There was nobody else in Eden who could help us unless we recruited the nom military. Thomas Borathen was firmly against that.

There was one last glimmering jewel of hope, and it wasn't in this realm. Unfortunately, nobody wanted me to risk it. It was time I took the bull by the horns no matter what the others said.

I looked at Nightliss. "I'm going, and there's nothing you can do to stop me."

"It will be too dangerous, Justin!" She gripped my arm as if to keep me from walking away.

I wasn't going anywhere just yet. I freed my arm and pressed my hands to the barrier around Elyssa. The color was already fading from her full red lips, her fair skin necrotizing to a greenish tinge. A fat tear splashed on the barrier and ran down the side. I wiped my eyes and took deep breaths to keep from completely losing it. I felt my chin quivering and looked away.

"Nightliss, I'd like you to come with me." My words sounded hoarse.

Green eyes filled with moisture, she nodded slowly. "It is the only possibility left to us. I do not think you should go, but I know you will not be talked out of it."

"I don't think Elyssa would want you to risk everything for her," Meghan said.

I felt warm wetness streaming down my face. I turned to her and said, "Elyssa *is* my everything. Wouldn't you do the same for Adam?"

Meghan looked uncomfortable at the question. As a healer, she was used to seeing death. She'd been there when my Aunt Vallaena died at the Grand Nexus. She'd nursed my father back to health after he'd taken two shots to the chest intended for me at Thunder Rock. Elyssa was lying here because she'd taken one in the back meant for me.

"That's not a fair question, Justin," Meghan said at last. "I would do everything in my power to save Adam, as I do for all my patients."

Her response seemed cold and I wondered if it was the truth or not. It didn't matter. I couldn't waste another minute doing nothing.

I had to go to the Darkling Empire on Seraphina.

The sight of Elyssa filled me with a sense of purpose. The war with Daelissa could wait. We'd destroyed most of her army in our last battle at the Ranch, the now-deserted Templar Compound. Our army was still licking its wounds after the tough fight. We were in turtle mode. Despite my inability to recruit more allies, the resistance could survive a week without me.

I took one last look at Elyssa. "Pack light, Nightliss. We're leaving today."

The petite Darkling said nothing and simply nodded.

We left the healing ward and stepped into the streets of La Casona. Row houses with terracotta shingles lined the cobblestone road. The pocket dimension housing the city was slightly larger than the Grotto, maybe ten square miles. Elyssa and I had planned to have a date here just before the battle that almost claimed her life. I swallowed hard to fight back the lump forming in my throat.

I entered the second house on the left. A familiar female Templar looked up from a book on sword fighting and smiled.

"Justin!" Katie Johnson gripped me in a tight hug and kissed my cheek.

I returned the hug and backed away. Katie wasted no time hugging Nightliss and then backed away with an uncertain expression.

"Is it okay to hug the Clarion of the Templars?" Katie asked.

Nightliss smiled. "Life would be unbearable without hugs."

Katie laughed. The smiled faded as she turned back to me. "You look so sad. Are you okay?"

I disregarded the question. "What are you doing in La Casona?"

"I'm part of the nom recruitment team." Her chin rose like a proud kid who'd just made her first poo-poo in the potty. "You wouldn't believe how many volunteers we have for the Darklings to feed from now."

"That's great." I tried to muster more enthusiasm, but I'd really just come to get my own serving of human soul essence to help speed my recovery and amplify my Seraphim abilities.

Katie seemed to sense that and touched a pendant on the collar of her Templar uniform. "Please send in two volunteers."

"Confirmed," someone replied from the other end of the communicator.

A door opened a few seconds later. A man and woman entered.

"I am Beatrice, and this is Horace," the woman said in a Spanish accent. She stood about a head shorter than Horace.

"Would you prefer to sit?" Horace motioned toward several leather divans that were set up to face each other for easier feeding.

"Sure." I sat down in the closest chair. Beatrice sat down across from me while Nightliss paired up with Horace.

Nightliss magically adhered a pyramid-shaped prism in her right hand. "Thank you for volunteering, Horace." She held out her hands. Horace's rose to meet hers. An oily smoke-like substance drifted from his left hand into hers while a thin trickle of milky white drifted from his right hand and into hers.

"I should be thanking you," Horace said as he looked with interest at the soul essence pouring from his fingers. "I was dying from terminal cancer, but your healers cured me."

Beatrice's eyes flashed wide as I began feeding from her. "I knew you looked familiar. You are Justin Slade."

I forced a smile. "Yes."

"I heard about Elyssa Borathen." She looked as if she wanted to gesture with her hands, but the feeding process locked them into place. Instead, she motioned in the direction of the healing ward with her head. "How is she doing?"

From the corner of my eye, I saw Nightliss give me a troubled look. "She'll be better soon." I wasn't lying. I would make the Darkling healers in Seraphina help.

Katie's hand rested on my shoulder. "I just know they'll figure out a way to patch her up."

I changed the subject. "How are Ash and Nyte?"

"They're helping recruit noms." Katie stood behind Beatrice and leaned on the divan. "A man named Abe has been taking them around to veteran hospitals with a couple of healers."

"I know Abe." I'd met him in El Dorado. "How many new volunteers have we gotten so far?"

"Two hundred and twenty," Katie said. "The batch of revived Darklings from a few days ago are already looking like teenagers."

"And Melea?" I asked.

Katie flinched at the name of Fjoeruss's sister. "She's aging more quickly."

Melea wasn't Seraphim. She was what I referred to as a siren, a member of the race we theorized built the arches and possibly the pocket dimensions. Fjoeruss had agreed to ally with us if we revived his sister. What he hadn't told us was that she was his adopted sister. She'd been the one to cause the Desecration during the first war against the Seraphim by removing the Chalon from the Grand Nexus without properly attuning it.

I felt a slight change in the quality of the soul essence coming from Beatrice and knew I was nearing her limit. I stopped feeding. "Thanks, Beatrice."

She beamed a smile at me. "No problem at all."

Nightliss finished feeding from Horace a moment later and thanked him with a kiss on the cheek.

He blushed furiously. "It is a pleasure to be kissed by a beautiful woman. Please call on me anytime you desire."

Nightliss smiled. "Goodbye for now."

After the volunteers left the room, I hugged Katie. "We've got to go. I really appreciate everything you've done with recruiting."

Her arms tightened around my waist. "Justin, be careful. I know you've backed Daelissa into a corner, but that might just make her more dangerous than ever." Katie released me and stepped back. "And if you ever need a friend to talk to—I know this sounds crazy"—she

9

put her thumb and finger to her ear and mouth like a phone—"but call me, maybe?"

I managed a smile. "I will."

Nightliss and I headed back outside and went right. We went about a block to where the street ended in a large set of double doors. We opened them and stepped through to the La Casona way station. An Obsidian Arch loomed in the middle of a huge warehouse. Minders, creatures that looked like floating brains with long tentacles, drifted around the interior, keeping guard. I followed the left wall and entered a door to the main control room.

A huge world map spanned the slab of carved rock forming the front wall. A raised pedestal ran the length of the map. In the middle sat a pedestal with a large gray orb called a modulus, the control device for the Obsidian Arch.

We walked across the raised platform and turned left to view rows upon rows of small black arches with Cyrinthian numbers imprinted on the floor in front of them. Across a wide aisle to the right stood several slightly larger arches without numbers of any kind. Three of them were marked with green paint to indicate they worked. A Templar operator manned each one. We called them omniarches because they could open a portal to anywhere without requiring an arch at the exit.

A group of blue-robed Arcanes, Blue Cloaks, stepped through a portal in the first omniarch while a column of Templars vanished inside a portal between the columns of the middle arch as they headed to parts unknown. Nightliss and I dodged around the line of Templars and went to the last omniarch.

"Queens Gate mansion, please," I told the Templar.

He saluted. "You may enter the circle, sir."

Nightliss and I stepped inside the silver band around the omniarch. The Templar pressed a finger to the circle. The air seemed to fill with static as the circle closed, trapping magical energy within it. A look of concentration came over the Templar's face and a portal winked open within the arch. Nightliss and I stepped through and into a large, perfectly square cavern. The portal closed behind us.

We stood in a yellow square painted on the smooth stone floor. Another Templar stood outside the travel zone.

She saluted. "Welcome back, sir."

"Thanks." I offered her a brief nod since I wasn't much for saluting and headed toward a large mansion. Although giant stone golems were still constructing the west wing, the building was nearly identical to the mansion Daelissa had destroyed almost directly above this cavern.

The caverns themselves were part of a network of tunnels and old dungeons called the Burrows by those who attended Arcane University. Thomas Borathen's Arcane engineers had enlarged a section of the former dungeon in order to fit the mansion inside. The omniarch that had been in the old mansion's cellar was now on the same level as the new mansion and only about fifty yards away down a wide corridor.

Several yards in front of the mansion, Shelton sat across a table from Bella as they played a game of Scrabble and idly watched the stone golems build the house. Shelton looked to the side and spotted us. "The mansion's looking good, ain't she?" He grinned.

Bella perked up when she saw us and ran over to distribute hugs. "How is Elyssa, Justin?"

"The same," I said, trying and failing to keep a grim note out of my voice. "We just came to pack."

Shelton's eyes narrowed. "You're going, aren't you?"

I nodded. "As soon as I pack a clean change of underwear and a toothbrush."

He grunted. "I had a feeling it would come to this. That's why we packed our toothbrushes just in case."

I felt my forehead scrunch. "Say what?"

Bella squeezed my hand. "We're coming, Justin."

"That's a bad idea." I gave them stern looks. "There's no telling how friendly they'll be to us, much less humans."

Shelton looked affronted. "We ain't no ordinary vanilla noms, bud."

"Even Seraphim who haven't fed on human sustenance are still strong." I shook my head. "It's just a bad idea all around."

11

"I must agree with Justin," Nightliss said. She took Bella's hands. "I also believe it would be too risky for you to come."

Shelton slashed the air with a hand. "Tough butt nuggets, honey. We're coming whether you like it or not."

I sighed. "Your funeral." Without another word, I headed for the finished east wing of the mansion to pack. I hadn't gone far when Shelton appeared at my side.

"You're pissed off and sad about Elyssa." He shrugged. "I get it, man." Shelton gripped my shoulder and stopped me. "But you'd better get your head in the game if you want to win the Darklings to your cause. You've been a real sourpuss all week and it showed when you were talking to those muckety-mucks at Science Academy."

I felt my hackles rise. "Do you expect me to jump for joy with Elyssa about to die?"

"No, but if you go begging for help with the attitude you've had lately, they're gonna throw you out a window just like Chancellor Frankenberg wanted to do."

I hated to admit it, but I knew he was right. I'd been all doom and gloom this week. Since managing the magical equivalent of tearing a muscle after overextending myself during the battle at the Ranch, recovery had been painfully slow, giving me plenty of time to brood and wallow in a huge vat of self-pity.

I ran a hand down my face. "Do you have a happy pill I can take?"

He slapped my back. "Nope, but I can give you a swift kick in the ass if that helps."

"Nothing cheers me up more." I managed a smile. "Let me grab my things. I want to leave as soon as possible."

The mansion buzzed with activity as smaller construction golems installed aether-powered light fixtures and put the finishing touches on the east wing. Shelton, Bella, and I were the only ones living here. Mom, Ivy, and Dad were living in El Dorado for the time being, but planned to move into the mansion when it was ready. Most of our troops were still stationed there or at La Casona. I knew I should tell my parents today was the day I was headed to Seraphina, but Mom had already tried to talk me out of it several times and I didn't want to hear another argument against going.

I jogged upstairs, threw the essentials into a backpack, and grabbed a couple of the high-performance flying carpets the Templars had given me. Shelton met me outside with his and Bella's bags. A part of me still didn't like the idea of them going, while the other part felt relieved to have more friends watching my back.

We headed back to the table where Bella packed her Scrabble set. She pushed it inside the pink backpack I assumed was hers and picked up a broom. Unlike most household sweepers, it had a leather saddle and stirrups affixed to it.

"Are you seriously taking Scrabble with us?" Shelton asked her.

She smiled sweetly. "Perhaps if they imprison us, they'll at least let me play Scrabble to pass the time."

Shelton face-palmed. "Just what I need—an eternity of losing that stupid game to you."

"What's with the broom?" I asked.

Bella's face brightened. "It's an old flying broom I found in the Burrows. I used to race these things long ago. I thought it might be nice to take with us."

Shelton gave it a dubious look. "We have flying carpets. They're a heck of a lot more comfortable than stinking brooms."

"We need to pack light," I told her. "Why don't we just stick with the rugs?"

She gave me a sad look, but set it in a corner. "Very well. I guess it's not practical anyway."

I looked around. "Where's Nightliss?"

"She said she'd meet us at the omniarch." Bella slung her backpack over a shoulder. "She's retrieving her things from El Dorado."

Nightliss was just stepping back through a portal in the omniarch when we arrived. She had a small rucksack on her back and wore black Nightingale armor. I'd opted to wear jeans and a T-shirt, but wore a thin belt of the armor beneath so I could extend it if necessary. Nightliss closed the portal behind her.

13

"Do you think five pairs of underwear will be enough?" she asked me.

Shelton snorted.

Her innocent question brought a smile to my face. "It'll have to be."

"All right, cowboy, what's the plan?" Shelton asked.

I knelt and sealed the circle around the arch. "Pjurna is the Seraphina version of Australia, so using the Alabaster Arch at the Three Sisters will be the quickest route." Forming a vivid image of the tunnel mouth that led down to the way station in the Down Under, I willed a portal to open. The air within the omniarch flickered to reveal the mouth of a cave covered partially by vines about fifty yards away from us.

I stepped through the portal and into the jungle. Humidity and heat greeted me since it was still summer in this part of the world. My companions stepped through right after me. Shelton quickly shed his leather duster, but kept the hat even though the trees provided ample shade from the sun.

"This place is almost as creepy as the Dark Forest." Shelton ran his gaze over the thick foliage.

"No tragons in this place," I said. The words were hardly out of my mouth when shadowy figures stepped out of the cave. Shelton went for his staff, but I stopped him. "They're Templars."

"Scared the crap out of me," Shelton said.

The Australian Templars had taken control of the way station deep underground, but given our current shortage of healthy troops, I hadn't been sure how many were guarding this place. I raised my hand and opened my mouth to shout my identification.

Blurs of white streaked from above. Lightning crackled, and several of the Templars went down. My jaw dropped open as winged Seraphim swooped to the ground, swords drawn, and attacked the survivors.

14

Chapter 2

"Justin, watch out!" Nightliss dove into me and sent me tumbling over the jutting roots of a nearby tree.

I spun onto my back as a Seraphim flew past and slashed a hunk from the tree at the height my head had been. Shelton and Bella ducked behind the tree with us.

I watched as the attacker soared higher. "Is he really using his wings to fly?"

Nightliss looked as shocked as I felt. "I don't know how it's possible. We can levitate through channeling, but our wings are not solid."

"Save the scientific debate for later," Shelton growled. "We've got unholy terrors attacking one of our bases."

The last Templar guard went down beneath the onslaught of a lightning-wreathed sword. The Seraphim bearing the weapon stood at least six feet tall and wore sleek blue armor with a blazing white sun symbol on the front. The other flying Seraphim sported red armor that shimmered by the light of their swords. They all wore helmets with wings jutting from the sides.

"Their armor doesn't look the same," I said. The Seraphim we'd beaten before wore translucent crystal armor. This stuff looked almost like rugged but flexible plastic or carbon fiber.

"Looks like something from a galaxy far, far away," Shelton murmured.

I heard the Seraphim who'd attacked us shouting at his comrades on the ground and pointing our way. "We're about to have company."

"Christ Almighty in a walrus suit." Shelton pointed to our right.

I caught glimpses of another formation of Seraphim a hundred yards away as they flew through the trees. Beneath them marched infantry wearing armor similar to their flying buddies, though it was less ornate.

"This is not the same army we fought last week," Nightliss said.

"I have a feeling Daelissa must have received reinforcements." Bella had her wand in one hand and staff in the other.

I couldn't help but draw parallels to my LARP—live-action role-playing—days. "They're like knights and infantry."

"They're our death if we don't run like hell soon," Shelton said.

I stared at the opening to the cavern. Any other Templars below might be completely unaware of the army about to march down their throats. They'd be slaughtered. It didn't take a lot of brainpower to understand why Daelissa's forces were attacking the Three Sisters way station. It was one of only a few such places that had Alabaster Arches—the only arches capable of opening a gateway between realms. She undoubtedly knew about the Darkling Empire's location in Seraphina. Once she super-powered her army with human soul essence, they could march through this arch and lay waste to the Darkling nation.

I looked at my companions with grim determination. "We can't run. If we do, we'll lose a lot of good people and give Daelissa the perfect backdoor to attack Pjurna."

Shelton wrinkled his forehead. "We sure as hell can't fight."

I gripped him by the shoulders. "Nightliss and I will distract them and try to get into the way station. I need you and Bella to escape so you can have someone open a portal for you. You have to warn Thomas about this new army so they can reinforce our positions."

"I don't gotta run back to base." Shelton gave me a strange look and pointed at his arcphone. "I already sent a video of the invasion back to headquarters. It's the twenty-first century, man."

"Oh, um, yeah." Something about fighting sword-bearing angels sometimes made me forget we had magical cell phones. "I still want you and Bella to escape while Nightliss and I try to make it inside."

"They're coming," Nightliss said before Shelton could answer.

Sure enough, I looked up to see the small surprise attack force walking toward our hiding spot. I counted four of them. I unrolled our two flying carpets and stood on one. I felt the carpet's enchantment bind my feet to it. Nightliss got on behind me and wrapped her arms around my waist while Shelton and Bella boarded the other one.

"We're not leaving you," Shelton said. "Lead the—"

A bolt of lightning speared from the sword of the enemy leader and exploded against the tree. Two of the Seraphim in red armor blurred to our right. Shelton's carpet rose and zipped back away from us to escape the attack. The two Seraphim extended their huge ethereal wings. Their eyes glowed bright white and their misty, vaporous wings seemed to solidify into brilliant flames as they leapt from the ground and flew in pursuit

I directed our carpet to the left to avoid attacks from the other two Seraphim. The angel in blue wore a confident smile on his face as he angled his sword toward me. I wasn't feeling a hundred percent, but I wasn't helpless either. I shot a tendril of Murk and latched onto the decorative wing on the side of his helmet and gave it a hard jerk. His helmet twisted sideways and he lurched forward as my tug pulled him off balance. The sword speared into the dirt and his companion tripped over it.

I was actually surprised my trick worked. "The armor didn't repel the attack."

Nightliss lanced an ultraviolet beam at the Seraphim in red armor. Her attack crystallized a spot on the breastplate before punching through. The man—the seraph—gurgled and went down.

"Foul Darkling magic!" the seraph in blue armor cried out at us.

I shot him with a beam of Brilliance and knocked him back a few feet. "Here's a whiff of foul Brightling magic, jackass!"

I wanted to finish him off, but saw the rest of the army quickly closing the gap. "Where's Shelton?"

"I don't see him or Bella anywhere," Nightliss said.

A huge explosion erupted in the jungle behind us. I craned my neck and saw flaming boulders rolling through the trees. "That's one of his spells!"

17

Someone roared. The blue seraph lunged at us with his huge lightning sword. Swinging the carpet like a surfboard on a huge wave, I narrowly avoided the deathblow and sent a wave of Murk at him. He leapt into the air with one beat of his huge wings and avoided my attack.

I wanted desperately to go back for Shelton and Bella, but the enemy forces were almost on top of us. I had a choice to make. *Should I go after my friends, or should I go to the aid of the Templars in the Three Sisters way station?* More explosions rocked the jungle in the direction Shelton had fled. *Please forgive me.* I had to help the Templars and hope Shelton could escape.

"In the name of the Divinity, I, Primarion Arturo, commander of the First Battalion of the Seraphim Empire, will end you!" The blue seraph dove toward us, sword extended.

"In the name of me, Justin Slade, commander of the butt monkey legions," I shouted, "tell Daelissa she can shove it up her fat ass!"

"Yes, into her stinky bottom!" Nightliss said and launched a volley of ultraviolet spheres at Arturo.

The seraph barrel-rolled out of the way. His eyes widened as if suddenly recognizing someone. "How is this possible? You look identical to the Divinity!"

Nightliss didn't have a chance to answer because in that instant we made it into the cave. I saw Arturo pull out of his dive and swoop after us. He pursued us into the dimly lit tunnel only a short distance before coming to a halt. He obviously didn't want to risk chasing us before his army arrived.

I immediately withdrew my arcphone, Nookli, from my pocket and called Shelton. No answer. Ice-cold dread filled my heart. Had I lost two more friends? A surge of anger and grief tore a shout from my throat. I spun the carpet around and angled back toward the cave mouth.

"Justin, what are you doing?" Nightliss sounded scared.

Emotion choked me. "Shelton. Bella." What had I been thinking? Why hadn't I gone to help them instead of people I didn't even know? *Because they're your responsibility.*

18

"You can't save everyone, Justin." Nightliss pressed her head into my back and sniffled.

It wasn't the first time someone had told me that and it wouldn't be the last. Even if I were at full strength, it was too late to race after Shelton and Bella without plowing through an army. "We need to close off this tunnel." The corridor was carved through solid rock and spanned about thirty feet across.

"Even together it would take us too long to collapse it," Nightliss said. "Perhaps the Templars have explosives."

"It's the only way we'll have a chance of defending this place." I whipped the carpet back down the slope and urged it to full speed. We were about two-thirds of the way down when I spotted a group of black-armored figures racing up the tunnel.

"Halt!" the leader of the squad called out.

"I'm Justin Slade." I leaned over to reveal Nightliss. "I have the Clarion with me."

The lead Templar gazed at her. He saluted. "I apologize for a less than cordial reception, but we've lost contact with our people up top." His voice had a heavy Australian accent to it.

I didn't have time to mince words. "They're dead."

"Dead?" a young female shouted. "But Kurt was up there."

The leader looked back at her and turned back to me. "Are you certain?"

"There's an army of Seraphim about to march into this way station." I jabbed a thumb over my shoulder. "We think Daelissa got fresh reinforcements from Seraphina. If you thought the ones we fought at the Grand Nexus were bad, these look even tougher."

"Oh god, not Kurt," the female said. Tears poured down her face and she slumped to her knees. "He just asked me to marry him."

My heart knotted with sorrow. *We've all lost loved ones in this damned war.*

"He just told me last night that we never know what day will be our last." She broke into fresh sobs. "And now he's gone."

"Get on your feet, soldier. You're a Templar, not a child." The Templar leader looked mildly embarrassed. "I'm sorry, Clarion. She's a new recruit."

19

Nightliss leapt from the carpet and helped the woman to her feet. "There is no shame in sorrow. I have shed many a tear over this war and there will be many more to come." She wiped a tear from the woman's face. "You must draw upon your love and strength to fight for his memory. He would want you to survive."

The woman sniffed. "I will do my best, Clarion. Thank you."

I thought of Shelton and Bella again and felt like crying. Now definitely wasn't the time. Just as I'd done many times before, I had to dig deep and push forward. "Do you have anything we can use to seal off this tunnel before the Seraphim reach us?"

"We have emergency protocols in place." The leader motioned at the tunnel. "This entire section is enchanted to implode if need be."

"Then by all means, let's clear this area and do that," I said. "We don't have a lot of time."

As if in answer to my commands, the sounds of hundreds of marching feet echoed down the tunnel.

"Templars, retreat!" the leader shouted.

Nightliss released the weeping female and hopped back on the carpet. Our group took off at top speed down the tunnel. We reached a red line painted on the floor. The Templar leader went to the closest wall and seemed to reach his arm through solid rock. A portion of the wall vanished as he turned off an illusion hiding a wooden panel with five runes carved into it in a circular pattern. At the center of the pattern was the outline of a hand.

He traced each rune with his finger, choosing the next one in no particular order I could detect, and pressed his hand against the outline. "Templar Nelson hereby confirms this order," he said. The runes flashed red. Nelson looked at us. "We should clear out of here."

White light shone from around the bend in the tunnel behind us. Seraphim soldiers appeared, their swords held at the ready. There was a scant fifty yards between them and us.

"How long until—" I hadn't finished my sentence when the rock walls and ceiling on the other side of the red line began to crumble. Rubble showered down along what I estimated to be a thirty-yard span of tunnel. I backed away as boulders and earth began to fill in the tunnel with a tremendous roar.

20

"This is only the first section," Nelson said. "We have another section we can collapse twenty meters from here."

"Let's go," I shouted over the rumble.

We ran back to another red line.

"This will collapse it all the way back to the other line," Nelson explained as he traced the runes. "Unless they have some heavy earth moving equipment, they won't be making it through anytime soon."

"What about omniarch portals?" I asked.

He shook his head. "We're using portal-blocking statues here."

"Which means we can't escape via omniarch without disabling a portal blocker." I ran through all the alternatives at our disposal. Shelton had warned Thomas about the new army. We could still keep a token force of Templars here to maintain the portal blockade, but what if the Seraphim broke through the collapsed tunnel sections?

"Sir, we're prepared to stay here as long as necessary, but I'm not sure there's much we can do against a force of Seraphim." Nelson looked back at his squad as he jogged alongside my carpet. "We have only thirty more soldiers back in the way station."

"Daelissa must have used the Obsidian Arch near Sydney to transport her army," Nightliss said. "I hope the Australian compound wasn't also attacked."

"Doubtful," I said. "It looks like she just wanted the Alabaster Arch. I also doubt she used the Obsidian Arch near Sydney. A Seraphim army marching across the countryside would've been noticed and reported on the news. I'd bet they used omniarches."

"Either way, they're here," Nelson said. "How should we handle it, sir?"

It felt strange having this older man call me sir, but his tone of voice sounded as though he trusted my decisions. "Set up a perimeter of ASEs to keep watch on the tunnel, the control room, and the way station." By this time, we'd reached the main way station. Looming in the middle of the large cavern stood an Obsidian Arch. It looked large enough to admit a jumbo jet without wings.

A small statue of an obsidian obelisk sat on the floor between the arch columns. Two statues with an asterisk design stood guard against omniarch portals within the way station. Each portal-blocking statue had an effective spherical radius of about three hundred yards. We headed toward a large door in the back wall and entered the control room. It looked virtually identical to the control room at the other way stations, complete with the world map, modulus, rows of numbered arches, and a niche with omniarches. The big difference was the large Alabaster Arch, obsidian with veins of alabaster running through it, sitting in front of the numbered arches.

A statue shaped like an angel sat on the floor beneath the Alabaster Arch to prevent any portals between it and Seraphina from opening. Other statue designs could block portals from different realms, and each one required a musical sequence to toggle them on and off.

Nelson met with all of his Templars and ordered them to distribute a network of ASEs—all-seeing eyes—to record and transmit video back to our primary headquarters beneath Queens Gate. Each of the small, marble-shaped devices could hover in the air and keep discreet watch.

I stared at the arches in the room and pondered how I could best handle this. If we sent away all the Templars, there would nobody here to reactivate the portal-blockers. We could keep a token force here, but it seemed like a waste of manpower given this new Seraphim threat.

Once Nelson was finished giving orders, I motioned him over. "Nightliss and I have to go through the Alabaster Arch to Seraphina. If things go well, we'll be back in less than a week."

He nodded. "We'll hold the line for you, sir."

I almost shook my head to tell him no, but it suddenly occurred to me that this mission was far more than one of mercy. This new Seraphim army looked far stronger and more disciplined than the previous one. *They have flying angels, for crying out loud.* Even if all our revived cupids were ready to fight, that wouldn't be nearly enough. We needed an army with a chance of countering them.

In short, we needed the Darkling nation to help us.

If things were to go well with my request to get help for Elyssa, I planned to broach the subject of an alliance. Now I had to make that my primary mission. I had to put my obligations to this realm, Eden, above my personal desires.

My heart ached as images of Elyssa, Shelton, and Bella flashed through my head. Life would hardly be worth living without them, but just because I felt that way didn't mean I could condemn everyone else to slavery beneath Seraphim rulers.

I nodded. "Contact Thomas Borathen and inform him of the situation. Tell him we need to hold this way station at all costs. Hopefully, I can bring back a Darkling army with me."

Nelson's eyes flashed with hope. "Godspeed, sir. We won't let a single one of those bastards in here unless they walk over our dead bodies."

I placed an arm on his shoulder and looked him in the eye. "I won't let you down." I hoped I could live up to that promise. I walked over to the Alabaster Arch, picked up the portal blocker and gave it to Nelson. "Disable this and turn it back on after we're through. Deactivate it again in two days and each day after for one hour in the morning, and one hour in the evening." I checked my arcphone, Nookli for the time. Overworld timekeeping didn't account for time zones like the noms did. "Do it at ten hundred and eighteen hundred hours."

He took out an arcphone and tapped in the information. "Anything else, sir?"

I took one last look around the room and shook my head. My heart felt unbearably heavy. Nookli chimed. I looked at my arcphone and saw a text message.

Justin, did you make it? We got away and portaled back to Queens Gate.

The message was from Shelton. I threw up a fist and whooped. "They made it!" I turned to Nightliss, hugged her, and spun her around. "Shelton and Bella are alive!"

Tears formed in her eyes. She buried her face on my shoulder and sobbed with what I knew had to be relief. I set her down and wiped at the tears forming in my eyes. "Nelson, please deactivate the portal blocker."

I tapped out a quick text to Shelton. *I knew the universe wouldn't let a jackass like you die. Nightliss and I are fine. We're about to take a portal to Seraphina. Be safe.* Truthfully, I knew I could open an omniarch portal from here and have them here in a jiffy, but having almost lost them I wasn't about to risk it on this journey. I sent the text.

"Are we ready, then?" Nightliss asked, her green eyes bloodshot from crying.

"We're ready." We stepped into the silver circle around the Alabaster Arch. I knelt and willed the circle to close. The static rush of aether filled the air. There were no controls to the arch. I simply concentrated on it and willed it to activate. I could almost sense another world an instant before the air within the arch columns began to flicker between ultraviolet, gray, and white. A klaxon bellowed as the energy within the arch built with a loud hum. The smell of ozone filled my nostrils. With an electrical crackle, a gateway split the air vertically before blinking open horizontally to reveal a blue sky and a wide plain covered in reddish grass.

I turned to Nelson. He and the other Templars flashed a synchronized salute. I gave them a thumbs up and stepped through the portal with Nightliss.

Hello, Seraphina.

Chapter 3

Aside from red grass and blue-tinged trees, Seraphina didn't look a lot different from Eden. I willed the Alabaster Arch to deactivate. It blinked off behind me. A warm breeze rustled the tall grass surrounding the obsidian slab upon which the arch sat. I looked around for other arches but saw none. Either the builders hadn't constructed Obsidian Arches and omniarches here, or if they had, they were elsewhere. It was strange enough seeing an Alabaster Arch aboveground.

"We're on a skylet." Nightliss pointed to a bank of clouds drifting just past the end of the plain.

I walked through the grass toward the clouds. Before reaching the end of the grass, my foot found open air. I shouted. Nightliss grabbed my arm and jerked me back. Heart pounding, I took a closer look at the grass and realized it grew out from the sides of the cliff, giving the illusion I had several more feet before the edge. I dropped to my knees and looked over the precipice.

A clearing in the clouds revealed a huge water vortex swirling in a green ocean far below. The cliff face angled backward beneath us and vanished into mist.

"I don't see where the cliff enters the water."

A smile graced Nightliss's lips. "As I said, a skylet." She drew in a deep breath. "Oh, how I've missed you, Seraphina." She looked at me. "Until this moment, I didn't realize how much that was true."

I was too busy trying to understand her first statement. "Are you saying this chunk of rock is floating in the air?"

She nodded and pointed at the vortex. "There is a tremendous updraft of aether beneath us. Sometimes it creates these whirlpools, while other times it merely makes the sea appear as if it's boiling."

I looked back at the arch. It must require a great deal of aether to power. In Eden, the arches usually sat above ley lines, magical power conduits, which provided them with ample energy. Apparently, the aether vortex beneath us was the provider of aether to this arch. It might also explain why there were no other kinds of arches here.

Another very important question occurred to me. "How in the dickens are we supposed to get down from here?"

Nightliss looked around. Her eyes lit on something and she motioned me to follow her. A waist-high stone pedestal with a gray gem the size of my palm on top of it sat near the cliff edge. "This is the skyway. I hope it works." She held a finger toward the gem and zapped it with a burst of Murk. The gem glowed. As if someone had unrolled misty gray carpet, a cloudbank formed a path into the sky.

I felt my stomach lurch at the thought of stepping onto clouds with nothing but thin air between me and a vast, sucking maw in the ocean thousands of feet below. Nightliss tested the skyway with a foot. She grunted with satisfaction and rested her full weight on the clouds.

"It appears to be working." She stepped onto it all the way.

Butt cheeks clenched tight enough to crush a soda can, I gripped a handful of the red grass like a tether and gingerly placed a foot onto the cloudbank. It felt as solid as the ground beneath me. "How long does the charge in the skyway last?"

"Once activated, it cannot turn off while it has passengers," Nightliss said. "It gathers aether from the air around it for power."

"Could someone turn it off at the other end?" I imagined a cartoon version of me running in midair before plummeting a thousand feet to my doom.

She shook her head. "We can only turn it on, not off from the gems."

I just hoped there wasn't a roadrunner waiting to pull the plug the minute I stepped onto it. My other leg didn't want to join the first on the cloud. I tried to move it, but my stomach knotted. I wasn't

26

particularly scared of heights, but looking down at such a distance while having to rely on otherworldly magic would probably make anyone think twice.

Elyssa needs me!

Just a single thought of her was enough to vanquish my hesitation, though my butt refused to unclench. I stepped onto the skyway. Several seconds passed. I didn't plunge to my death, but we didn't move either. "What now?"

"You simply will it to take you to a destination." She looked ahead. "I believe this will take us to the capitol city of Tarissa.

Take us to Tarissa! I thought without hesitation.

Like the moving pathways at Science Academy, we commenced moving forward, even though the cloud path itself didn't seem to move at all. The breeze in my face accelerated into a stiff gust, which grew into a howling gale.

"You must have given it a very urgent command," Nightliss yelled above the noise. "I suggest you turn on the wind buffer."

Wind buffer on.

Nothing changed. I looked at her. "Um, how?"

She laughed. "I'm sorry, I forgot to tell you. You must think the words in Cyrinthian, or visualize your intent."

I'd learned to speak some Cyrinthian during my early days of Arcane tutelage. In other words, I was about as fluent as a toddler. *Mommy. Daddy. Poo-poo!* I took out Nookli and opened a translator program I'd installed long ago. It quickly provided me with the words I needed. I transmitted them with my mighty brainwaves and the ghostlike cries of the wind abruptly vanished.

"Much better," Nightliss said. "It is important you learn as much as possible before we arrive."

I moved to sit down on the skyway and a cottony puff of cloud rose to meet my posterior. It felt as plush as it looked. A backrest formed and allowed me to lean back. I laughed like a kid. "This is cool!"

Nightliss smiled and sat down. Another cloud chair met her posterior. "It is a rather nice way to travel."

I looked down with a sudden desire to see the landscape beneath us, and the cloud beneath my feet vanished. I yelped, and jerked up my feet before realizing the transparent area was still solid as ever. "I visualize my intent or command it in Cyrinthian?"

She nodded. "I believe this particular path is part of the Imperial Skyway Daelissa ordered built after she overthrew the Trivectus government. It is a little faster with better options."

Her comment made me think of something. "Does Seraphina have Obsidian Arches or omniarches?"

"There are ruins of arches scattered across this realm, but they are not organized like the ones on Eden." She touched her chin thoughtfully. "I vaguely remember there being talk of functioning arches, but that was so long ago, I can't be sure."

"It's almost like Seraphina was the first place where they built Alabaster Arches, and by the time they got around to making them on Eden, they'd refined the process and maybe invented a few new arch types."

"You are probably correct." Nightliss didn't seem all that interested in the subject.

I took in the view beneath me where the green ocean waters met the verdant land of a small island. Thick mist rose in the distance, obscuring the horizon. "Is there any way to tell how far away we are from Tarissa?" I pulled up the maps feature on my arcphone. "Nookli, where are we?"

Nookli flashed a big question mark after a moment to show it didn't know what in the hell was going on. "Justin, you are lost," my phone said with absolute certainty. "There are no Indian restaurants nearby."

I shook my head at my poor confused phone and stuck it back into a pocket. *We ain't in Kansas no more.*

"I cannot say." Nightliss turned her gaze forward as mountains appeared in the mist ahead. Rather than go over them, the skyway went between them and into a wide valley where the air was clear. A sparkling river wound its way through a forest of blue and green hues. Flocks of brightly colored birds soared beneath us.

I whistled. "Beautiful."

Nightliss abruptly stood. "I remember this place." She looked at me with wonder. "This is the Ooskai Valley. My family was forced to move here during the Great Exile."

I turned back to her. "The Great Exile?"

"After my people, the Darklings, rose up to demand representation on the Trivectus, they were banished to this continent, Pjurna." She waved an arm as if to encompass the land. "Daelissa and I were very young at the time and hadn't yet discovered our affinities."

"Were your parents Darklings?" I asked.

She nodded.

"What did they do during the Seraphim War?"

Nightliss looked down. "They died long before the war."

I grimaced. "I'm sorry."

"There is nothing to be sorry about." She sat back down. "When Daelissa discovered she was a Brightling, she demanded they return her to the Brightlands—that was the term the Brightlings gave to the lands they controlled."

"Wow, she was a bitch even when she was a kid."

"She was always the difficult one." Nightliss rested her chin on one hand. "When my parents refused to send her to the Brightlands, Daelissa ran away. My parents wanted to go after her, but feared they would be imprisoned for breaking exile."

I patted her shoulder. "Your poor parents."

Nightliss blew out a breath. "They had hoped the Trivectus would grant them an exception due to Daelissa's affinity as a Brightling. They hated living here." She shuddered as if the mere thought was too unpleasant to bear. "My parents were no angels."

I snorted. "Technically, they were."

She gave me a cross look. "You understand my meaning."

"Your parents were willing to callously use Daelissa's Brightling affinity to escape exile."

She nodded. "Daelissa didn't want them going with her because she didn't want to admit she had Darkling parents."

I shook my head. "That's awful. I guess a lot of Darkling parents have to deal with that kind of garbage from their Brightling kids."

"Actually, that's not true." Nightliss gazed into the distance as we reached a towering waterfall at the end of the valley. "Two Darkling parents or two Brightling parents almost never have a child of the opposite affinity. Daelissa was one of the rare exceptions."

"What about if a Darkling and a Brightling mate?" I asked.

Her lips peeled back in horror. "That was not allowed."

I narrowed my eyes. "Hang on. Are you saying you'd never be attracted to a Brightling?"

"It simply is not the way things are, Justin." She shuddered.

I groaned. "Nightliss, I love you to death, girl, but that's gotta be the most prejudiced thing I've heard you say."

She stood, eyes blazing with ultraviolet. "The Brightlings treated us like servants and animals! When we tried to claim basic rights, they killed protestors and exiled most of us to Pjurna! You will excuse me if I think mating with our oppressors is disgusting!"

I thought of Lanaeia, an elfin Brightling with silvery white hair who'd defected from Daelissa's side. She was a kind gentle soul from the little I knew of her. "Do you like Lanaeia?"

Nightliss slumped a little. "She is different."

"How about my mom?"

She pressed her lips tight and gave me a cross look.

I pressed the attack. "You told me yourself there were Brightlings who joined your cause. They aren't all bad."

"Yes, and there were Darklings who fought against us." She folded her arms. "Unfortunately, there are very few Brightlings who consider us as Seraphim as they are."

The skyway crossed over a mountain and entered a new bowl-shaped valley that stretched as far as I could see. I blinked with amazement at what I saw. A giant island floated above the bowl, almost as if it had been carved from a mountain and cast into the sky. I looked for a whirlpool or other supernatural phenomena keeping it afloat, but couldn't find anything that stuck out. Sand with an ultraviolet hue carpeted the valley. Trees and other foliage dotted the land. From what I could tell, there were no houses below.

The island was another matter.

Shiny ultraviolet spires literally reached into the sky since the floating chunk of land was already on level with the skyway and us. I magnified my super vision and oohed at the organically twisting buildings and alien designs. I spotted dozens of Seraphim floating on skyways in all directions from the city in the sky.

"Tarissa?" Nightliss said in a questioning tone. She turned in a circle as if uncertain about her location. "The city was little more than a collection of hovels and small houses when I last saw it."

"I guess they've had time to modernize," I said. "It has been a couple thousand years or so since your last visit."

She stared with open wonder. "It is so beautiful."

"And really purple." Depending on the way the sun hit the buildings, it looked almost like black chrome in places.

"I suspect Murk was used almost exclusively to build the structures." A smile lit Nightliss's face. "It would be lovely to tour."

I sighed. "We're not here to tour. First thing we need to do is find their equivalent of a healer and convince them to take a little trip with us." I touched Nightliss's shoulder to draw her attention back to me. "Do you know where to go first?"

She gave me a helpless look. "Everything has changed, Justin." She looked back at the city. "I don't even know where to begin."

"Where did you go in the old days?"

"There was rarely a need for gifted healers until the Eden War."

I gave her a confused look. "Eden War?"

"Your people called it the Seraphim War." She continued before I could get in a snappy comment. "We selected a core group of Darklings to hone their healing skills. During the course of the war, the group grew as our needs increased."

A horrific thought crossed my mind. "Were they all caught in the Desecration?"

"No."

Relief melted the sudden knot in my stomach.

Nightliss offered me a smile. "We sent some home to help with a new uprising against the Brightlings in the hope that the war had weakened them here at home. That was shortly before the Desecration."

31

"Surely they've expanded their knowledge over the millennia." A new hope suffused me. If that was true, we could definitely find someone to heal Elyssa quickly. The positive thoughts had barely entered my mind when Nightliss gripped my arm.

Her green eyes filled with worry as she looked ahead. "Oh, dear."

I turned toward the city where a large pearly gate guarded the end of the skyway. Shimmering walls extended about a hundred yards to either side of the gate. The gate looked about twelve feet tall, and wouldn't have been an issue for the two of us to scale.

The large squad of stern-looking Seraphim in black armor, however, were a different matter.

Chapter 4

The skyway slowed as we neared the gate. I looked to either side of it and wondered if Nightliss and I could levitate to the wall and run for our lives. I willed the skyway to remove the wind barrier and felt a breeze on my face.

"Think you can levitate to the wall?" I asked Nightliss.

She shook her head. "The skyway safety measures won't allow it."

I wrinkled my forehead. "The wind barrier is off." I reached to the side of the skyway. My arm hit resistance about three inches out. "An invisible barrier."

Nightliss sighed. "It's to prevent anyone from accidentally falling to their death."

I looked back at the gate and was met by several glaring guards. We were less than fifty feet away. "We're probably stronger than they are since we've fed on humans. Maybe we can bulldoze our way through."

"Perhaps it would be best if we didn't antagonize them." Nightliss smiled sweetly at the soldiers. "Let's see what they want."

Several soldiers drew shiny black swords that emitted a dark glow. "Judging from the way they're holding those swords, they don't want to hug us."

Nightliss began talking in Cyrinthian under her breath. She made a frustrated noise and spoke again. It sounded as if she was practicing her old language.

I didn't even know how to ask where the restroom was, much less carry on a conversation.

"I will tell them you're from Murika," Nightliss said. "That should keep them from wondering about your poor Cyrinthian language skills."

I blinked. "From where?"

"During my youth, Murika was a powerful province that refused to adopt Cyrinthian as the official language." She sighed. "They were once the most powerful province in terms of commerce, but their dominance faded as power shifted to Zbura."

"Murikan?" Panic gripped me. "How do they talk? How do I act?"

"Just use your broken Cyrinthian and you will be fine." Nightliss made a nervous noise. "I just hope Murika still exists after all this time."

I planted a friendly smile on my face and hoped for the best as the skyway came to a stop. Meanwhile, my eyes searched for escape routes.

A soldier with a set of wings on the breast of his black uniform said something in an angry or scolding tone as he approached the gate. I assumed he was the leader. He touched something I couldn't see. An ultraviolet light flashed and the gates swung open. The leader pointed back the way we'd come and said something else.

Nightliss replied to him and gave me a sad look.

A couple of the guards rolled their eyes at me and shook their heads. Some of them looked at my clothing as if they didn't know what the hell I was wearing. It suddenly occurred to me I wasn't exactly dressed to blend into the crowd. Nightliss's Templar uniform, however, almost fit right in, though the native uniforms had an interesting honeycomb armor. I just hoped my guise as a Murikan made the jeans and T-shirt seem normal.

The leader looked me up and down and addressed me.

I didn't have a clue about what he'd said, so I improvised. "I from Murika," I said in broken Cyrinthian. "You are leader?"

The soldiers burst into laughter.

Nightliss gripped my arm and whispered, "Why did you say he was pretty?"

I felt my eyes widen with horror as I looked at the seraph. He didn't seem amused with my mistake.

The leader jabbed a finger at the skyway and spoke again.

Nightliss's eyes widened with innocence. She shrugged and replied.

I felt completely lost and wished I had a universal translator handy. I remembered that Nookli's translator program might help me understand some of this gibberish, but didn't want to pull out an arcphone in front of these people.

A pleading tone entered Nightliss's voice but the leader turned and spoke in a commanding tone to his soldiers. Before I knew what was happening, two of the soldiers gripped me while a third wrapped a glowing strand of what appeared to be Murk around my wrists.

"Son of a goat," Nightliss said angrily as they secured her. "Apparently, travel on this skyway is forbidden. They are taking us to a holding facility until we can be sentenced."

"I'm not putting up with this." I noticed curious looks from bystanders as the soldiers marched us down a walkway toward the edges of the city. "Let's break free and make a run for it."

"Perhaps there is a better way," Nightliss said. "If you feign an injury, perhaps they could bring a healer to us. Then we could escape and take them back to Eden."

Her idea wasn't bad. "Won't they think it's suspicious if I suddenly act like I'm hurt?"

"Perhaps we could pretend to fight."

Fighting under these circumstances wasn't practical. "If most Darklings have healing abilities, won't they just patch up my scrapes?" I shook my head. "You'd have to cut off my arm to get a super-skilled healer."

Nightliss lowered her head. "Then we have no choice. We must fight our way free and find someone."

I actually thought about letting her cut off my arm or severely injuring me in some other way. If it brought me a Darkling that could heal Elyssa, it'd be worth it. Just as I was about to say this to Nightliss, I thought back to a trick I'd once used while hiding from vampires by covering a deep hole with the illusion of solid stone so the vampires looking for us would fall into it.

I'd gotten a little better with illusion during my time at Arcane University, but hadn't used it for any practical applications since. This might be one of those times. I typically needed a wand or staff as a focus for Arcane spells, but simple illusions could be done without their aid. I pictured a stain of blood spreading across my T-shirt. I looked down and saw a pinpoint of illusionary crimson spreading across the fabric.

One of the guards did a double take when she looked at me. She called ahead to the leader and pointed out my bloody shirt. I knew they might want to see the wound itself, so I created the illusion of a huge gash across my stomach, and threw in a bit of protruding bone just for the hell of it. If they touched the fake wound, the gig would be over.

The leader halted the march and said something to me.

"He wants you to lift your shirt," Nightliss said with a confused look on her face.

"I'm gravely injured," I said, putting a pained look on my face, lifting my shirt with bound hands.

Nightliss hissed when she saw the wound. The soldiers merely looked at it, but didn't react much. I could only assume they'd seen some gruesome injuries in their time, or else they just didn't give a crap. Despite the horrors I'd seen fighting the Brightlings, I still hadn't grown used to death and destruction.

My primary mission here was to score a healer for Elyssa. But that wasn't my only mission—we needed the Darklings from Seraphina to help us. I considered telling these soldiers the truth and hoping they'd take me to their leader. Then again, they might not believe that I'd come from Eden. With the Alabaster Arches dysfunctional for over two thousand years, they might think I was just crazy.

I pulled down my shirt and groaned to buy a little more thinking time. An idea finally came to me.

"Nightliss, tell them that I was attacked by a Brightling who was inspecting the arch at the other end of the skyway." I resisted the urge to wink at her.

"I don't understand." Worry flashed in her eyes. "Why would I tell them such a thing?"

"From what Lanaeia told me, there's a stalemate between the Darklings and Brightlings." I feigned another wince of pain to make it look like we were talking about my injury. "If it looks like the Brightlings are trying some new tactic, the Darklings might take us to someone in charge."

Understanding dawned in her eyes. "So you can speak to them of an alliance."

"Exactly." I cried out in pain, causing several of the soldiers to look at me with concern.

Nightliss translated the story. Judging from the looks of worry and disbelief in the eyes of the soldiers, my story had hit home.

The leader narrowed his gaze and spoke.

Nightliss turned to me. "They want to know why we were out there."

I grasped at the first thing that came to mind. "We're lovers. Tell them we went out there on a bet to do the deed."

A look of horror crossed Nightliss's face. She took a breath and translated. Her cheeks turned bright red as the soldiers broke into laughter and made universally rude gestures. The leader didn't laugh. He asked a few more questions which Nightliss handled without asking me for advice. I just hoped she knew how to fib as well as I did.

We stood just outside what looked like a maze of towering buildings much like the skyscrapers on Eden. The designs here curved and spiraled in ways that looked impossible by nom standards. The only detraction was the homogenous dark purple material. I had a strong suspicion the Darklings relied heavily on channeling Murk to create this city.

The leader remained silent for a moment before touching a gem on the collar of his uniform. Ultraviolet light sparked from his fingertip and into the gem. He spoke a few sentences. Another voice replied.

"He's speaking some kind of military jargon I don't understand," Nightliss said. "I think he's contacting a superior."

"Hopefully someone way up the chain." I caught a pair of bystanders gawking at me and wondered if it was due to the fake blood on my shirt, or just my clothes in general. I felt like the one guy dressed in street clothes at a science fiction convention. Civilian attire seemed to consist of dark skin-tight uniforms with very moderate variation in colors. "Why does everyone look so grim?"

Nightliss looked at the gathering crowd of citizens. "I imagine centuries of oppression forged this society. If Brightlings truly control much of Seraphina, the Darkling nation is but a speck in the grand scheme of things."

I leaned on her as if I needed her support to continue the fiction of my wound. "I'd bet every person here learns to fight from birth."

She nodded. "It would stand to reason."

The squad leader barked a command. The soldiers pushed us forward.

"Where are we going?" I asked.

Nightliss repeated my question in Cyrinthian. The leader replied. Nightliss gave me a troubled look. "We're going to the Intelligence Ministry."

I didn't like the sound of that. "The Darkling version of the CIA?"

She gave me a confused look. "I'm not familiar with that term."

I clarified. "A spy agency."

"It would appear so."

A finger of mist from a cloudbank above touched a grassy patch of land between two of the towering buildings. The soldiers corralled us into the alcove. The leader sent a charge of Murk into the mist. Clouds billowed beneath our feet and shot us into the sky so quickly I hollered with alarm. The soldiers looked at me as if I was an idiot. One of them motioned at me as he spoke to Nightliss.

She gave me an apologetic look. "He said you looked as if you'd never used a skyway before."

John Corwin

"Tell them it hurt my injury." I didn't want them knowing this was only my second time riding a skyway.

Nightliss relayed the message.

The skyway carried us just high enough to skim the tops of the buildings. I spotted dozens of patrols in the streets below, though, soldiers perhaps, or maybe ordinary citizens. The clothing was hard to tell apart from this distance. A building of massive proportions in the center of the city seemed to be our destination. It looked as if someone had taken a cylinder, slightly flattened it, and twisted it into a spiral. Crystalline spikes protruded along the edges. Arcs of ultraviolet electricity ran up the spikes like something from a mad scientist's lab.

My apprehension grew stronger and stronger as we neared the building. What if they locked us away and I never had a chance to speak with a real decision maker? We might end up thrown into a dungeon and forgotten about while Elyssa died and Daelissa rampaged across Eden with her new troops.

Overpowering the soldiers and making a run for it seemed like a better idea every passing second. Unfortunately, I didn't know if we could commandeer the skyway to take us elsewhere or if it would deliver us to our destination first.

We passed over a wall of skyscrapers to an area clear of all other buildings except for the ministry building and, to my disbelief, giant pyramids resembling something straight out of Egypt. Eyes engraved on all sides of the top third of each pyramid stood sentinel, their outlines blazing with ultraviolet light as the top section rotated like the lamp in a lighthouse. I had no idea what they did, but knew for certain I didn't want to find out the hard way.

Platoons of soldiers marched along wide pathways between the pyramids. Some of the groups fragmented into smaller squads and walked through a flowing sheet of mist that outlined the large square plaza around the ministry building.

Our cloudbank broke from the skyway and abruptly descended at an alarming rate. I managed to hide my fear with a grimace and pressed my hands over the fake injury. We reached the ground just in front of the flowing sheet of mist.

One soldier led Nightliss through to the other side. Another took my arm and walked me through. There was a tingling sensation. The mist faded to light gray and a basso note ruptured the air. I hardly had time to be surprised before every soldier in the platoon was on top of me.

I caught a look of horror from Nightliss. "Justin, they said the mist identified you as a Brightling!"

Judging from the looks on my captors' faces, they were about to make my fake injury very real indeed.

Chapter 5

The soldiers whisked me and Nightliss toward the ministry building. As we neared the structure, I realized it also had a sheet of mist guarding the doorless entrance. The minute I passed through it, a stain of white spread across the mist as if someone had thrown a can of paint on it. A high-pitched alarm wailed briefly before a guard near the entrance sent a burst of Murk into a nearby gem and silenced it.

"I'm not your enemy!" I struggled in the grip of my captors. "I swear I love puppies and kittens."

They didn't even glance at me.

The hallways had a slight curve to them probably due to the odd shape of the building. We reached an intersecting corridor. The group of soldiers guarding me took a left while the ones with Nightliss took a right.

"Justin!" she called out before vanishing down the corridor.

I had a feeling things would only get worse from here. After all, they thought I was a Brightling. They thought I was an enemy spy attempting to infiltrate their city. It was time to get out of this mess.

The cord of Murk around my wrists was a problem. Thankfully, Elyssa had taught me a few ninja tactics to get out of certain situations. I flattened the palms of my hands against each other to brace my arms and tucked my elbows to my sides. The guards at my sides snuggled up to me as I'd hoped. I thrust my elbows hard into their sides. Before they could react, I delivered a crushing roundhouse to the first, turned to the other and head-butted him hard enough to send him crashing against the guard behind him.

I ducked beneath a punch from another guard. Bracing my hands against the floor, I swept my leg beneath his. His back slammed to the floor. I lifted my foot and brought it down hard on his head. He grunted and went still.

Three guards remained. Each one drew black steel, or whatever their swords were made of. A tall seraph held his sword high and brought it down as if to slice my skull in half. I took a gamble and thrust my arms up so the Murk binding my wrists met the blade. Ultraviolet sparks exploded from the impact. The aether rope arrested the swing of the sword just before snapping and vanishing in a puff.

Wrists free, I slapped the sword aside. I blurred forward and gripped the sword hilt. Before the surprised guard could react, I planted a foot in his abdomen and pushed him away. I spun and threw up my newly acquired sword in time to intercept a sword strike from the female guard. Her male companion circled me in a flanking maneuver. Before he completed the move, I charged him.

He threw up his sword. I batted it aside and slammed the flat of my blade on his wrist. His scream of pain echoed in my ears as he dropped his weapon. I rushed forward, buried my shoulder in his chest. He slammed into the wall. A crack ran up the material. I backed away and let him topple forward onto the floor.

The woman—the sera—said something in a frightened but determined tone of voice. I looked at her, bared my teeth, and said, "Take me to your friggin leader, lady."

She, of course, didn't understand me any better than I understood her and directed a flurry of attacks at me. She was supernaturally fast, but I was hyped up on human soul essence, the equivalent of angel steroids, and easily blocked her strikes. I disarmed her with a quick flick of my wrist. Fear shone in her eyes. I put the point of my sword to her neck and resisted the desire to say something witty. Anything I said would be lost on her thanks to my awful Cyrinthian.

A light bulb pinged on in my head. I took out Nookli and turned on the Cyrinthian translator app while my prisoner looked at it with a mix of curiosity and dread. I flicked through the settings and activated a feature that sent sound directly to the user's ear. I didn't see an option to send it to everyone and hoped a voice command would do the trick. "Nookli, transmit all audio directly to the ears of those nearby." I expected my phone to reply with at least one reference to an Indian restaurant, but apparently, it knew I was all business right now.

"Translated audio will be broadcast to the auditory sensors of nearby entities," Nookli said. Whoever had programmed that app had obviously earned a degree in nerdology.

I put the phone back into my pocket and spoke. "Where did they take my friend?"

After a brief pause, a startled look entered the sera's eyes. She spoke in Cyrinthian. A split second later, a slightly robotic voice sounded in my ear. "Your friend in the holding cell is. Taken grass not far away."

I cringed at the awful translation, but it was better than nothing. Keeping my words as plain as possible, I said, "I am not a Brightling."

The sera narrowed her eyes at me and replied. "Security gracious nuts barrier otherwise says."

I blinked a couple times and wondered what mistranslated words equaled gracious nuts. "Lead me to my friend." I pointed the sword down the hallway.

Her lip peeled back in a sneer. "A song of justice to be mishandled I am not, beggar of destruction."

By now, I was ignoring the Cyrinthian she spoke and focusing on the translation instead. She'd obviously used an idiom because it didn't make a lick of sense to me. Instead of talking, I simply gripped her by her uniform and shoved her down the hall. "Lead the way, song of justice."

She muttered something and moved forward. By the time we reached the intersection where they'd split off with Nightliss, I realized the sera's help wasn't really necessary to find the holding cell in question, namely due to the contingent of guards standing near a doorway a few feet into the hall.

My prisoner cried out. I sighed and clunked her on the head. She dropped to the floor as six guards came my way. They held their swords in a similar fashion to Brightling soldiers, arms extended, blade diagonal to the floor. The stance was a median between aggressive and defensive. I visualized the quickest way to take them all down.

They stood two abreast. The corridor was wide enough for three bodies if swinging swords weren't involved. That meant I had a slight bottleneck to work with. Unless these guards were significantly better with steel than their unconscious compatriots, putting them out of commission shouldn't be too difficult.

Even so, I tried a little diplomacy first. "Your comrades are unconscious. Free my friend and we will leave peacefully."

Looks of shock passed over their faces as my phone transmitted the translation to their ears. The first two guards looked at each other with confusion.

The one on the left spoke. "A Brightling claims a Darkling as friend?"

I nodded. "She is one of my dearest friends."

"Used her to gain entrance you did," he shot back.

"Free her now, please." I put on a fierce scowl. "I won't ask again."

"There is no <untranslatable> in the dark sugar bowl!" Even the robotic translation voice seemed befuddled by whatever the guard said.

Unfortunately, the time for translating was over. The guards charged. The first one made a chopping motion with his sword. I intercepted his wrist. Bent it back with a quick flick and heard bones crunch. He cried out and dropped the weapon. I spun him around and used him as a meat shield. His companions held back, unwilling to risk his life. I shoved him forward into the second guard, sending them crashing into a heap. Before they could recover, I thwacked them both in the head with the hilt of my sword and sent them to dreamland.

The last four guards sheathed their swords. At first, I thought they'd given up. Instead, they gripped each other's forearms. A sphere of Murk formed in the palm of the seraph on the end. He extended his arm and a bubble of Murk shot toward me. I threw up an ultraviolet shield. The two forces collided so hard, the impact sent cracks racing up the walls, across the floor and ceiling.

The Seraphim looked absolutely astonished as my shield began to slowly push theirs back.

My opponents had linked themselves to make a single channeler more powerful. I didn't know if that gave him power equal to four Seraphim or simply amped him to some lesser degree. Either way, I could tell it wasn't nearly enough to beat me.

One of them shouted something. "How are you channeling Murk?"

"I'm not a Brightling!" I decided to take a risk and threw in a postscript to my declaration. "I can channel both sides." To back up that claim, I speared a beam of Brilliance into their Murk bubble. Sweat broke out on their foreheads. One of them stumbled as my attack drove their efforts straight back at them. The seraph channeling collapsed to the floor.

I immediately stopped my attack, keeping a sphere of creation and destruction flickering in either hand. "Free my friend and take me to your leader."

Before they could answer, a tall Seraphim stepped into the hallway. His inky black hair was combed straight down Roman style. He wore a black cape embroidered with what looked like glowing strands of Murk. The seraph held up his hands as if to ward off further attacks.

"I am Cephus." He offered me a confident but friendly smile. "You may deal with me."

I regarded him suspiciously, but relinquished the hold on the aether coursing through my body. The energy vanished from my palms. "I am not your enemy. I am here on a mission of mercy."

He looked me up and down. "We can discuss that if you will follow me." He gestured down the perpendicular hallway.

"Not until you free my friend." I pointed to the door.

He nodded and spoke to the guards. One bearing a badge with wings, similar to the one I'd noticed on the leader of the soldiers who'd originally captured us, sent a charge of Murk into a gem next to the door. The door dissolved into a cloud of mist. Nightliss emerged a moment later, eyes uncertain.

I motioned her to me. She came and stood by my side without uttering a word.

"Do not try to trick me," I said.

Nightliss started to translate, but flinched as the translation reached her ears. She looked at me with a puzzled expression. "What magic is this? Why is the translation so bad?"

"I don't think my language dictionary is geared for speaking." I shrugged. "At least I can understand what's going on."

Confusion flashed across Cephus's face. My phone was still broadcasting to everyone present.

I approached the seraph carefully where he stood at the intersection of halls. Aside from the defeated guards nearby, he didn't seem to have reinforcements. I knew better than to take that for granted. "Are you alone?"

He shook his head. "Never alone. Thirty more soldiers there are waiting in the atrium." He pointed back toward the entrance. "Take you prisoner, we could but"—he looked from side to side at the unconscious and defeated guards—"the bloodshed worth it might not be."

Even though I knew he was right, I put on my best poker face. "I'll beat them like rented mules if they try anything."

His forehead wrinkled with confusion. I could only imagine how my idiom translated to Cyrinthian.

"I don't think they could take me," I said to clarify my statement. "Are you truly the one in command?"

"A member of the Trivectus I am." He gave me a meaningful look.

"I know of the Trivectus that used to rule the Brightlings thousands of years ago," I said. "Do you use the same form of government?"

His eyes flared with astonishment at my statement. "How do you know of this?" He held up a hand. "Wait. Improve our communication, I must. Will you allow me to call in a specialist?"

"Nightliss can translate," I said.

His eyes grew even larger at this statement. He quickly regained his composure. "I have a better method in cranium."

I gave him a suspicious look but nodded.

He motioned me toward hallway. "Come. We will go to a better meeting place."

"Where?" I wasn't about to walk into a trap.

He pointed up. "The minister's office at the top." He held out his hands, palms up, as if to show they were empty. "I promise trickery befall you will not."

I really hoped he had a better way to translate because the random word order was really starting to get on my nerves. I couldn't imagine listening to someone talk like this all the time. I looked at Nightliss. "What do you think?"

"It is our best hope," she said. "Perhaps our last hope."

I snorted. "No need to get melodramatic."

She offered a wan smile. "I am female, Justin. This is the perfect opportunity to be dramatic."

A laugh burst from me. "Fine." I offered my hand to Cephus. "My name is Justin Slade." He gave it a confused look but eventually extended his own. I gripped and shook it. "Let's do this."

Cephus looked at his hand after I released it, as if looking for some sign that I'd cursed him. He recovered, smiled reassuringly, and led us down the hall.

We took a right and headed toward a glowing shaft of light in an alcove. Cephus stepped inside. Nightliss and I joined him. Our host charged a gem on the wall and we zipped upward on an invisible platform, other floors blurring past until we neared the ceiling at the top of the shaft. When our momentum ceased, Cephus simply stepped forward and into a room.

I looked down at the long drop and quickly followed him.

We entered a wide, empty room with no furniture or walls aside from the curving windows along the exterior of the building. The shiny black floor rippled like water beneath our feet as we walked across it, giving me an uneasy feeling. I wondered if we could sink into this material, or if it was some sort of special effect. Cephus charged a gem inset in the floor. A holographic image sprang from the floor displaying an organically curved piece of furniture that only slightly resembled a desk. Cephus flicked past it and several other interesting designs until settling on a plain circular table with tufts of cloud floating around it.

He charged the gem again, and ultraviolet mist rose from the floor in front of us, slowly forming into the image we'd just seen. Within seconds, a floating table with cute little clouds as chairs hovered before us. The color of the table changed to a deep mahogany while the clouds turned white.

It was a nice change from the homogenous color of Murk. I mean, I liked purple as much as the next guy but had begun to wonder if these people lacked appreciation for any other hues of the rainbow.

"Impressive." I ran a hand along the table. It felt like wood. "You made this with Murk?"

He nodded. "The force of creation." He touched his ear. "How are you sending words to my ears?"

I noticed the word order from the translation had improved marginally and wondered if the translation program had made adjustments as it heard more and more speech. I took out Nookli and showed it to him. "This is an arcphone. You can talk to people with it."

He raised an eyebrow. "Can you not use your mouth to talk to people?"

I chuckled. "If another person has an arcphone but is across the city from me, I can call them." I made a show of dialing a number and speaking into the handset. "It is like a communicator."

"Ah." He touched a gem on his collar. "We also use long-distance communication magic." Cephus looked at my phone. "Is this Brightling magic?"

I shook my head. "No. The Brightlings don't have this sort of technology."

He looked a little confused and I had to wonder if technology translated into Cyrinthian.

Nightliss said something and Cephus nodded as if she'd cleared it up.

"What is the language you speak?" He looked at me. "I know you are not speaking Murikan."

This was officially the point where I had to tell him I was from Eden. Either he'd believe me, or things would get really weird and he'd think I was crazy. I'd seen enough movies with people claiming to be aliens to know how this usually worked out. Unfortunately, I'd have to convince him sooner or later.

"Cephus, I am not from Seraphina." I gave that a moment to sink in. "I'm from another realm called Eden. The language I speak, English, is one of many from there."

Surprise registered on his face, though it was mild compared to earlier. "The legends are true."

It was my turn to look surprised. "You believe me so easily?"

"I have read the histories from those who have lived since the ancient days." He looked at Nightliss. "Many have removed themselves from society, though a few still participate."

A warm sensation blossomed in my chest as hope made a comeback. "You know about the Seraphim War, about Eden? You know about Daelissa and her quest for world domination? Holy crap, this is great!" I almost leapt from my cloud seat but managed to resist the urge.

Cephus's forehead wrinkled with confusion. "I'm sorry," Nookli translated in my ear, "but I did not understand much of what you said." He motioned toward my phone. "It would be beneficial to all of us if I could help you with your Cyrinthian. To do so, I must examine your mind."

Chapter 6

Allowing a stranger to get inside my head sounded like a risky proposition. He'd seen me take down a squad of guards without breaking a sweat. If I allowed him inside my head, he might be able to knock me out without a fight.

Nightliss touched my hand. "I believe he means to imprint you with knowledge of the language. I do not think he means you any harm."

I did a double take. "Wait a minute. If that's possible, why didn't you do that to me before we left?"

Her facial expression turned apologetic. "I am good at healing mind trauma, but I am not very good at imprinting knowledge unless it is simple." She looked at Cephus with wonder. "If he is capable of such a thing—"

Cephus held up his hand to stop her. "I am only marginally capable." He motioned at the room around them. "This building is enchanted with spells from the most gifted among us. I will use one of those spells to help." He continued to speak, but the translation grew worse. "Intelligence…dietary fiber…brain midget experiments."

I deactivated the translation routine to get rid of the nonsense words and turned to Nightliss. "What did he just say?"

"He lapsed into a very technical explanation, some of which even I couldn't understand." Nightliss said something to Cephus. He chuckled and nodded.

"Should I take him up on the offer?" I asked.

Nightliss turned her serious green eyes on me. "I will not allow anything bad to happen to you."

"You know I trust you with my life."

She smiled. "It is mutual." She spoke to Cephus in Cyrinthian.

He nodded, turned, and sent a charge of Murk into a gem located on the window next to the levitator shaft. His eyes closed as he continued to channel. After a moment, he opened his eyes and spoke to Nightliss.

"He found the spell and is about to channel it into you," she said. "It will take some time."

I gave Cephus a thumbs-up and nodded. "Go for it."

He raised an eyebrow. Nightliss translated and he nodded.

Cephus channeled into the gem. He raised his other hand and channeled into me. My head tingled as if a ghost had just passed through it. I felt myself growing sleepy. As I closed my eyelids, images and letters danced through my mind so clearly, it was as if I was seeing them projected on a screen. Glimpses of memories flickered through my mind's eye.

I see the outlines of my parents in a doorway as they hand baby Ivy to Jeremiah Conroy. I see my old bike, the neighbor's cat, someone mowing their lawn. I witness a fast-forward account of middle school. Kids making fun of me, the fat boy. A teacher paddling someone in the hallway. Blood on my knees after falling off my bike.

My memories reach high school. I see Katie Johnson, tears in her eyes. Brad Nichols, her former boyfriend, frozen in the act of punching me. Stacey, my felycan friend, hitting on me in the gym when I was still a pudgy nerd, desperate to improve my looks.

I feel a smile stretch my lips as Elyssa laughs at a corny joke I just made. We hardly know each other at this point in time. Her lips press against mine for our first kiss. My heart leaps as memories of her flicker past. I see us playing Kings and Castles. Feel warm blood on my neck after Elyssa attacks me, eyes filled with tears when she realizes I am no ordinary human.

Shelton tries to apprehend my father and me. He is kidnapped by vampires. I see Elyssa dead in my arms as a horde of vamplings lumber in for the kill. I am a mindless rampaging demon, killing everything in my path. The sight of Elyssa's body brings me back. Somehow, I breathe life back into her still form.

Events accelerate. I see Thunder Rock and a dark pool of water as Elyssa, Kassallandra, and I swim to the bottom seeking escape. El Dorado is next. Shadow beings swarm me. Husked Seraphim reach for me, desperate to drain the light from my soul.

The cruel face of Vadaemos flashes past. Leviathan leyworms rumble toward Elyssa and me, scooping dozens of husked angels into their maws. History leaps forward. Maximus leers over me, fangs red with my blood. I fight gun-wielding vampires. Watch helplessly as Ivy channels a spell that will kill every vampire near Maximus's old hangout in Little Five Points.

Arcane University looms before me. I fight with Mr. Bigglesworth, Ivy's deceased Flark protector. I see my sister crying after others make fun of her. Laugh with her as we eat ice cream. The memories blur faster until I can make out only bits and pieces. A giant golem attempts to immolate the Arcane Council. The tragon tries to eat me but Elyssa knocks it out with lancers. I rescue Mom from Maulin Kassus. I am trapped in the Gloom with my father. We escape. Templars engage Nazdal in bloody combat. The Shadow Nexus drops into a pit. I reunite with my parents and they come to live in the mansion.

I see the Grand Nexus. Two massive armies collide in battle. We are pushed back as the Brightlings surge through the arch. I manifest to demon form and channel Brilliance. Unholy rage explodes as my inner demon revels in the destructive power. It wreaks devastation and nearly takes control of me. I push it back at the last instant and retain my sanity.

I am running for my life. Elyssa screams. White-hot Brilliance bursts from her chest. I fight Qualan on a damaged flying carpet. Fury burns through me as I pierce him through the chest with destruction.

Recent history flashes past. I see Seraphina for the first time. I am arrested by Darklings.

I look at Cephus and allow him to look into my mind.

Darkness.

I gasped and opened my eyes.

Cephus regarded me with concern. He might have just been constipated, but I wasn't sure. "How do you feel?" he asked.

My heart suddenly felt like lead as I realized I was back in the present where Elyssa was near death. "I'm fine, I guess."

"I'm glad to hear it." He smiled.

It suddenly occurred to me that he and I were speaking Cyrinthian. I touched my lips as if they were possessed by spirits. "How in the world did that spell work?"

"Context is often in the experience of the individual. By making you relive your memories at an increased rate, the spell was able to find the most appropriate equivalents for the spoken language including idioms and other minutia that often escape a pure translation." An excited look came over his face like a nerd at a cosplay convention about to explain starship propulsion in layman's terms.

I held up a hand to stop him. "It's not really important I know all the details. What's more important is getting the help of your people."

"While channeling the spell, I was able to give myself knowledge of English." He looked slightly embarrassed. "I also saw into your memories quite clearly." He looked between Nightliss and me. "Even though they offered only a glimpse into your life, I now know the truth of your mission."

I resisted the urge to pump my fist. "Does that mean you'll help us?"

Cephus sat back on his cloud with a pensive look. "I am merely a member of the Trivectus. While we might be able to authorize a token force to return with you, we cannot commit an army."

"Don't the Trivectus members serve as rulers?" I asked.

"In day-to-day matters, yes." He waved an arm at the city beyond the windows. "The citizens must vote on major policy decisions."

My heart began to droop again. "How long would it take to hold a vote?"

"Not long, but first you must convince the other members of the Trivectus. We must agree unanimously to hold a citizens' vote."

I blew out a frustrated breath. "Sounds redundant."

"It can be, but it is an improvement on the old form of Trivectus government under the Brightlings."

"Can you decide one small thing for me?" I asked.

"The woman from your memories." He looked quite sad. "She was struck down in a battle."

I nodded. "I need a gifted healer to mend her heart."

"Centuries of war with the Brightlings have molded many Darklings into superb healers." He gave me a thumbs-up. "I will dispatch someone at once to return with you."

I almost cried. "I can't tell you how much that means to me."

"Believe me," he said, "I know."

I kept forgetting he'd been in my head. "Do you know everything about me now?"

"The memory imprint is already fading," Cephus said. "It was like watching a theatre performance in fast motion. Soon, all that will be left is the language. The glimpse I had into your memories was enough, however, to give me excellent insight." He touched the gem on his collar. "Please have Pross report to the ministry chamber."

"At once," someone on the other end said.

"Also, please notify Thala and Uoriss that the Brightling situation is resolved and they may join me in the chamber as well."

"Yes, Minister," the subordinate replied.

"Will you allow us to travel back to the Alabaster Arch on the skyway?" I asked.

"Of course." Cephus's forehead pinched with a troubled expression. "We will dispatch a squad to guard the arch. Once my fellow Trivectus members arrive, I request that you give us a full debriefing on the arch and its capabilities. I may also ask you to demonstrate certain things to overcome their skepticism."

"Can't I just show them my memories again?" I asked.

He shook his head. "The memory imprint process is still working in your mind. To do another so soon after would risk severe brain damage."

I couldn't afford to lose any more brain capacity. I backed up to one of his other requests. "Don't you already know about the arches? You said there are Seraphim who were alive during the first war."

54

"This is true, though many of them were quite removed from the conflict." He looked out of the window toward the mountain peak in the distance. "Our history tells of the twin sisters banished to this land with their parents. How one of the sisters denied her Darkling family and returned to the Brightlands. How this Brightling sister overthrew the Trivectus and installed a regency that enslaved our people. How her Darkling sister led an insurgency against her." His eyes snapped toward Nightliss. "You are the Darkling sister they spoke of."

Nightliss's head jerked back as if he'd struck her. Eyes downcast, she nodded. "I am the sister of Daelissa."

He stood and bowed deep. "You were the one who led the first uprising against our oppressors. There are many legends about what happened to you when you vanished after the Brightlings crushed our insurgency."

Nightliss slowly shook her head. "I knew we couldn't hope to defeat Daelissa without discovering how she'd grown so powerful. I went to Eden with as many of my people as I could. Once there, we joined with the humans and the demons in their war against the Brightlings."

Cephus's eyes brightened. "Humans and demons? Our history only whispers about such creatures. Do they truly exist on the other side of the arch?"

"There are more wonders and horrors in the universe than you could imagine, Cephus." Nightliss shook her head. "Even after so long, my mind is still incomplete. I remember only generalities, in most instances."

"Our historians have long theorized that the closing of the Alabaster Arch was the precise moment when we lost our longevity." A look of profound regret shadowed his face. "Those who were far away at the time maintained their immortality while others were cursed with mere centuries of life."

"We refer to it as the Desecration," Nightliss said. "A being named Melea removed the Chalon, the key, from the Grand Nexus. Her action closed the nexus and disrupted every Alabaster Arch within Eden. The backlash drained the light from any entity caught in its massive wake. While it did not kill them, it husked them—turned them into shadow creatures that would drain the light from any creatures they touched."

Cephus's eyes widened with horror. "Was Eden overtaken with these horrors?"

I shook my head. "No. They couldn't survive in daylight. We found a way to resurrect the cherubs—that's what I call husked Seraphim. As for the Flarks, humans, and other entities that were husked, they don't survive the resurrection process."

"Flarks?" Our host touched his chin in a thoughtful manner. "Those were the shape-shifters mentioned in historical records. To the best of my knowledge they have not been heard from or seen in our time."

I shrugged. "Won't see me crying about it. They're extremely hard to kill and mean as hell." Ivy's former bodyguard, Mr. Bigglesworth, claimed that he was the only Flark to survive the Desecration, at least in Eden.

The sound of rushing air echoed from the levitator shaft. A young woman appeared a second later. Unlike most of the other Darklings I'd seen, she wore a long red dress that somewhat resembled a sari. It was certainly the most colorful article of clothing I'd seen so far.

"Please state the nature of the medical emergency," she said with a bright smile as she looked around the room. Her eyes caught on me. "I certainly sense a fashion emergency. What sort of clothing is that?"

"Hipster," I replied. "I haven't managed to grow a thick beard yet."

She looked even more confused. Since *hipster* hadn't translated into Cyrinthian, I'd apparently said it in English.

Cephus indicated me with his hand. "Chief Healer Pross, this is Justin Slade and Nightliss."

Pross's forehead wrinkled and her eyes twitched as if her train of thought had just hit a semi-truck. "Who would dare name their child Nightliss?"

I held up my hands. "Whoa, don't get so upset." I turned to Cephus. "There's a law against naming your child Nightliss?"

He returned an affable smile. "There is a great deal of debate about her role in our history."

Nightliss turned a confused look at Pross. "It is truly my name."

"She is *the* Nightliss," I added.

Pross stumbled back a foot. Her eyes flicked to Cephus. "She is truly the one?"

He nodded. "She has returned."

I was starting to feel positively bubbly about our chances of securing an alliance now. With Nightliss's status as a returning war hero, she might be able to single-handedly raise an army to take back to Eden.

"Who else knows of her identity?" Pross stared at Nightliss with a slightly disturbed look.

"Only those in this room." Cephus held up a hand. "I know what you will say, but perhaps I can convince the others she was not at fault."

"Not at fault for what?" My jubilance took a shot to the ribs.

Cephus leaned on the table. "The religious among us believe in a single deity, the Primogenitor, who built the heavens and the earth and also created the arches. It was believed we were once his direct servants and used the arches according to his will to aid his other creations."

"This was not the belief in my day," Nightliss said. "We believed other beings created the arches, but it was a mystery. There was no religious aspect to it."

"The Schism—Desecration, as you call it—shortened our lifespans to centuries and caused us to age. Primogenesis spawned from the desperate minds of those seeking answers and finding none. They wondered why they were being punished and prayed for redemption." Cephus seemed to deflate. "History became legend and legend became myth. History was misinterpreted, lost, rediscovered, or simply fabricated to support popular beliefs. Now there are those who cling to such corrupted stories as religion."

"Some would kill you for that statement," Pross said with a troubled look. She turned to Nightliss. "Primogenesis blames you for the shortening of our lifespans. It was said that after your failed uprising against the Brightlings, you joined them in the Promised Land and desecrated it. This led to the Schism, the great punishment

57

which revoked our immortality and separated us from the Primogenitor."

"Preposterous!" I shook my head. "Nightliss went to Eden to fight Daelissa and keep her from destroying it. Melea, a member of the siren race that probably built the arches, is the one who closed off the nexus and caused the Desecration that took away your immortality."

"It isn't me you have to convince," Pross said. "The other two members of the Trivectus are both believers in this *god*." She loaded the word with contempt.

I crossed my arms. "In other words, they'll look at Nightliss as the enemy."

"I'm afraid it may be worse than that," Cephus said. "They will likely order her immediate execution as a sacrifice to the Primogenitor. They believe this is one way to heal the Schism."

"What other ways can they heal the Schism?" I asked.

The levitator shaft whooshed and two females dressed in tight, drab uniforms stepped into the room.

The rest of the Trivectus had arrived.

Chapter 7

"Chief Healer Pross, it is good to see you," said the first female, a sera of ebony skin and bright hazel eyes. Silky black hair hung loose around her shoulders.

Pross nodded. "A pleasure as always, Minister Thala." She repeated her nod to the other sera. "You as well, Minister Uoriss."

Uoriss stood as tall as Cephus. She wore her dark blond hair in a tight bun and gazed around the room with piercing gray-blue eyes. "What is the meaning of bringing these accused Brightlings to this chamber?"

"I have determined they are not Brightlings," Cephus said. "This is Justin Slade and his companion—"

"Tibbs," I said, thinking of the first name that came to mind. I'd met Nightliss while she was in the form of a cat. I'd named her Captain Tibbs until learning her real name from my felycan friend, Stacey.

Cephus raised an eyebrow, but didn't call me out.

Uoriss's lips peeled back. "What bizarre names."

I almost told them we were from Eden, but my unfamiliarity with their religion froze my tongue.

"I think they're wonderful names," Thala said with a broad smile. She turned to Cephus. "Please explain the nature of the false alert. I'm also curious why you brought our…guests here once you determined they were no threat."

He relayed the story, including how I'd defeated two squads of guards. The two seras looked me up and down. Thala seemed delighted and amazed while Uoriss clearly viewed me as a threat.

"I find this story hard to believe," Uoriss said. "Surely he had aid."

"I assure you he did not," Cephus said.

Uoriss narrowed her eyes and turned to me. "Where are you from, young seraph?"

I saw no point in disguising my true nature and lifted my chin. "I'm not a full seraph, Minister. I am from Eden."

Thala jumped back a step. "Eden? The Promised Land? Is this seraph troubled, Cephus?"

"He speaks the truth," Cephus said. "These two came through the arch on Malkiss Island."

"They came through a Sacred Arch?" Uoriss's gaze turned to steel. "This cannot be true."

"The Primogenitor disabled his gateways until we atone for the sins of the betrayers," Thala said, her friendly tone fading.

"How does one atone for the sins of the betrayers?" I asked.

Uoriss regarded me with a level stare. "Blood."

"The Brightlings betrayed the creator." Thala's smiled reappeared. "They must repent or die."

These people are crazy! "What if I told you there was another way to find penance?" I dug deep in my memory for the few times I'd gone to church with friends since my parents had never taken me.

"Who are you to know such things?" Uoriss said. "Do you claim to be a prophet?"

"No." The last thing I wanted was to be labeled a religious icon. These seras were nothing if not zealots, judging from my brief interactions with them. I had to keep this as cold and logical as possible while still coming across as non-threatening to their beliefs. "I'm simply a person who's interested in helping your people by ridding them of an ancient enemy."

Uoriss pursed her lips. "Explain."

I looked at Cephus for guidance in case I was about to enter dangerous waters.

He smiled and motioned toward the table. "Perhaps we should sit down."

"May I first have permission to send Tibbs and Pross to help my friend?" I asked.

Thala paused in the middle of sitting down. "You have friend who requires a healer?"

"Yes." I doubted going into detail was for the best, so I didn't elaborate.

"Pross already has the required information," Cephus said.

"I see no harm in the request," Thala said. "Proceed."

I gave Nightliss a meaningful look. "Please go with Pross. Return when you can."

Worry flashed across her face, but she nodded. "I will see you soon."

The pair stepped into the levitator. Nightliss's troubled face dropped from view.

"Now, back to your claims about other ways to atone for our sins," Uoriss said.

I felt like an English teacher who'd just been told to lead a math class. The only thing I had at my disposal was the truth. Judging from the reactions so far, these two seras didn't want to deal with the truth. I decided to stall for time, primarily to give Nightliss and Pross plenty of time to reach the skyway to the arch. That way if Uoriss and Thala decided I was a threat, they wouldn't have time to send soldiers after them.

"What do you know of Daelissa?" I asked.

Uoriss and Thala exchanged a look. "She misused the gift of the Primogenitor and traveled to Eden. Her sister, Nightliss, tried to seize control of the government. While some think she did so to free our people from Brightling rule, others believe she simply wished to rule in her sister's place."

I felt sick about the way history had been twisted here. "Is that what you two believe?"

Thala shrugged. "It is up for debate. The Atharis denomination believes Nightliss wished to do good, but gave up and betrayed the creator."

"This is where the Catharis disagree," Uoriss interjected. "We believe she was always in league with her sister."

"There are even sects which contend that Nightliss gave her life to kill her sister and ascended to be with the Primogenitor," Cephus said.

Uoriss scowled. "They are nothing but cults with dangerous beliefs."

I sensed an opportunity for further delay. Anytime I'd witnessed a religious argument at school, it had revolved around denominational quibbles. "Which denomination is the largest?"

"Immaterial," Uoriss said.

Thala spoke at almost the same time. "Atharis has slightly more members."

I scrambled for another question. "Do either of you think dancing is evil?"

Thala's forehead scrunched. "There is nothing forbidden about dancing."

"Only fools would ban such a thing," Uoriss added.

My hopes of driving a wedge between them fizzled as they turned scrutinizing gazes on me. "Interesting." I desperately tried to think of some other way to waste time.

"Are you truly so ignorant of this realm, or is this an act?" Thala asked. She turned to Cephus. "I'm hesitant to believe his claims about Eden. Either he is a liar, or he has discovered some devious way to activate a Sacred Arch."

"I wish to know how he defeated two contingents of guards," Uoriss said. "The more I hear his asinine questions, the more I doubt the truth." She directed her iron gaze on Cephus. "What is truly going on here?"

"Everything is precisely as I said." Cephus's face hardened. He turned to me. "Perhaps you should show them some proof. A display of your other half, perhaps."

I figured he had to be talking about my demon half. The only bad thing about spawning was it would ruin my clothes. Thankfully, the belt of Nightingale armor beneath my jeans would grow to fit my new form. "Give me a moment." I reached into my pants and touched the hem of the armor. Like paint poured over a canvas, it spread to cover my waist and legs.

"Are you touching yourself?" Uoriss said.

I felt my cheeks heating. "No. I'm adjusting something."

This only caused the seras to look even more disturbed. They gasped as I pulled off my jeans. I extended the armor over my torso and pulled off my shirt.

"Calm down." I held up my hands in a placating gesture. "I'm just switching into a new uniform."

Cephus seemed highly amused as he sat back and watched my clumsy efforts to impress these religious zealots.

I stood back from the table, stretched my lips in what I hoped was a reassuring smile. "Now, don't freak out. I'm about to spawn into my demon form. I might look scary, but I won't hurt anyone."

Uoriss and Thala burst into laughter.

"He's delusional," Uoriss said. Her fingers brushed against a blue gem on the sleeve of her uniform. I didn't know if the gem on her sleeve functioned like the one on her collar, but it made me wonder if she'd just done something I wouldn't like. I noticed Thala had a green jewel on her sleeve while Cephus's was red.

Thala's laughter stopped abruptly. "While entertaining, this has been a colossal waste of time." She rose from her seat. "This seraph belongs in a mental institution, not in an audience chamber with the Trivectus."

I was really getting sick of their attitudes. I decided there was only one way to shut them up. Reaching inside me, I uncaged my inner demon. Muscles coiled around my body like snakes. My body swelled and gained height. My forehead grew heavier as large horns spiraled upward while my backside counterbalanced the new weight with a long tail. The armor stretched to accommodate everything.

Uoriss and Thala froze, astonishment plain on their faces. It quickly morphed to horror.

"He is truly a demon!" Thala shouted.

Uoriss channeled a sphere of Murk and flung it at me. "He is an evil one from the Nethers!"

63

The two seras ran in opposite directions, each trying to reach one of the six levitator shafts encircling the room. Before they'd gone far, every shaft was suddenly full of soldiers. The moment the soldiers stepped into the room, mist filled the entrances to the shafts and solidified, blocking them off.

"Kill him!" Uoriss shouted.

I didn't have time to think as nearly thirty soldiers charged my position. Some hurled orbs of Murk at me. My tail catapulted me to the side as survival instinct kicked in. The channeled energy splashed harmlessly against the windows. I shielded myself with Murk against the next onslaught. I saw Thala and Uoriss shouting at the soldiers, but there was too much noise in the room to make out what they were saying. Cephus, a horrified look on his face, waved his arms frantically.

Well, that escalated quickly.

"I'm not evil!" I shouted, my voice guttural.

The soldiers were too busy attacking me to care. Escape seemed my best option. I slung a volleyball-sized sphere of Murk against the closest window. It barely left a crack. It suddenly occurred to me that the purple hue of the buildings wasn't just a side effect of being constructed from Murk—these buildings were heavily shielded. While brute force might break them, Fjoeruss had shown me that there were more economical ways to deal with such things.

I dodged another flurry of magical attacks. Five soldiers closed in from all sides. I karate-chopped the arm of the closest one. His sword clattered on the floor. I caught an attack from the neighboring soldier on a horn. My tail lashed out and gripped the disarmed soldier. I flung him hard at the magic channelers.

Using my superior height, I planted a huge demon foot in the chest of one seraph and kicked him hard enough to send him slamming into the window. I jumped back as two swords clashed where I'd stood. I gripped the soldier's wrists. Squeezed hard. Bones cracked and the seraphs cried out in pain. With a flick of my wrists, I sent them tumbling backward.

The bulk of soldiers were still picking themselves up off the floor, or trying to flank me, so I spun to the window. Murk flowed through my veins. I drew upon Brilliance and sent it coursing into my hand. Like a dog sensing raw meat, my inner demon surged as I channeled destructive power.

Gritting my pointy teeth, I pushed back as my infernal side vied for control of my body. I'd learned before that channeling Brilliance while manifested in demon form was dangerous. Unfortunately, I couldn't spare the time to cage the demon. Plus, having the extra strength was absolutely necessary right now.

I wove Murk and Brilliance into a gray beam, which I shot against the glass. The material shimmered as it resisted. Cracks sprouted like weeds in the material. Everything had taken only seconds, but my senses told me my time had run out.

Using my tail, I catapulted myself to the side just as a wave of Murk swept my former position and shattered the window. Brilliance flooded into me. My right hand flew up of its own accord and swept a searing beam of destruction across the front line of soldiers. They screamed in agony as white-hot destruction carved their bodies into ash.

Kill them all!

I clenched my teeth and struggled to bring my arm back under control, but my inner demon fought back. The world seemed to recede as my consciousness was pushed toward the back of my mind. I watched in horror as my own hand mowed down more soldiers.

No, I can't let this happen!

With a burst of will, I shoved back hard against my demon side. For an instant, I held control over my body. It was all I needed. I cut myself off from Brilliance. The moment I did, my demon side lost its grip on my mind. I shoved it back into its cage and felt my body shrinking back to normal.

I threw up a shield of Murk to block further attacks, but as I looked around the room, I realized that wouldn't be necessary. Three lone soldiers remained. One screamed as he stared in horror at the charred remains of his arm. The other two huddled on the floor, eyes wide with terror.

"Oh my god." I released the shield and walked forward.

"Please, spare me!" one of the soldiers said in a trembling voice.

The other soldier held his hands up in surrender. "You are truly a god."

I was too preoccupied looking at the carnage to say anything else. Uoriss lay on her back in a pool of crimson. Thala lay next to her, a stream of her own blood mingling with Uoriss's. Terror filled her hazel eyes.

She hissed, struggling for breath. "Help…" She coughed blood.

I knelt next to her. "I'm so sorry. I didn't mean for this to happen." I looked at the soldiers. "Call a healer! Do it now!"

Thala gripped my hand. "Not you…" her voice trailed away, her eyes went dull and cold.

"T-they are all dead," said a familiar voice. Cephus rose from behind the conference table. He looked at me. "Was this your plan all along? Draw us all into this room and murder us?" He backed away, but with the levitator shafts sealed, there was nowhere to go.

I held out my hands, palms facing him. "I swear I didn't mean for any of this to happen. Why did they attack me?"

He looked at the remaining soldiers. "Who called you up here?"

"We received an emergency signal from Minister Uoriss," the soldier said.

The other soldier looked up. "My signal came from Minister Thala."

The third soldier with the burnt arm had thankfully passed out.

"You saw everything, did you not?" Cephus said to the soldiers. "He has killed the ministers. He is powerful beyond belief."

"He is the Destroyer as foretold in the prophecies," the first soldier said. "We have taken too long to atone."

"We are doomed," the other said in a quavering voice.

Cephus dropped to his knees and bowed deep before me. "Please forgive my doubts about the Primogenitor, almighty Destroyer. We will drive the Brightlings from our lands as the prophecy said we must do to atone."

Destroyer? What prophecy? "I'm not the Destroyer!" I backed away from the bowing seraph.

Cephus remained bowing. "Justin Slade, the Darkling nation is at your mercy."

Chapter 8

I hadn't come all this way to murder the Trivectus and take over the Darkling nation by force. I stared at the blood on my hands where Thala had touched me. I looked at the lake of blood on the floor and knew without a doubt a terrible monster lurked inside me.

What have I done?

I backed away from the others as my mind tried to comprehend this turn of events. Just then I remembered the injured seraph unconscious on the floor. "Can you unseal the levitator shafts?"

One of the soldiers stood and charged the gem on the wall. Nothing happened. He looked at me. "It requires a command override."

Cephus walked to a gem near him and touched the red jewel on his sleeve to it. The opaque barriers sealing the shafts turned to ultraviolet mist and vanished. "I have a healer on the way."

"How does this levitator work?" I asked him.

The minister gave me a confused look. "Why?"

"I need to get out of this room." I couldn't stand looking at the bodies one second longer. The smell of blood filled my nose. Nausea clotted my throat. "Get me out of here this instant."

"At once." He led me into the levitator and charged the gem with his finger. Within seconds, we were back on the ground floor. Cephus motioned with his hand. "We can step outside. Perhaps the fresh air will do you good."

I let him lead the way. As we stepped into the courtyard outside, I saw a seraph standing a few feet away. The gem on his collar was projecting something a few inches from his face. From this angle, it looked like a sliver of light. Curiosity piqued, I stepped behind him. The sliver resolved into a three-dimensional hologram. It only took me a second to realize I was the star of this particular film. I watched with horror as my demonic form burned my attackers to ash, but this time it was from the perspective of my victims. The gems everyone wore must record video, I realized.

"This is how the people are informed," Cephus said in a calm voice.

I looked at the courtyard. Ranks of soldiers stood in silent lines, each one watching the same scene from their gem. As I turned in a circle, I saw every eye glued to the video playing from their gem. I stepped closer to the first person I'd noticed and detected faint audio emanating from it. I watched the scene where I shrank back to normal size and knelt next to Thala. I heard Cephus surrender and bow to me. My image stood and looked at the blood on my hands just as the video flickered off.

The seraph turned to face me. His eyes widened with recognition.

"You will bow before the Destroyer," Cephus said.

The seraph dropped to his knees and placed his face to the ground. "The Primogenitor has sent our deliverance and destruction at last. I am ready to follow."

I saw other Seraphim looking my way. Soldiers broke from their ranks and converged on me. I started to back away, but Cephus gripped my arm. "You must let them acknowledge you."

I felt sick to my stomach. Shame gripped my heart. Another contradictory feeling rose in my guts—pride. The religious zealots, Uoriss and Thala, would have denied me the help I needed. I'd single-handedly taken the power necessary to do what needed to be done. All that remained was claiming this victory and leading an army to Eden.

Murderer. Savior.

Which am I?

Before long, I was surrounded by Darklings, all bowing and scraping as if I were the best thing since sliced pickles. Beyond the throng of supporters, however, I saw dozens of Seraphim staring at me, dark looks in their eyes. Some of them clenched swords as if they wanted to use them.

"There will be those who do not believe," Cephus said. "You must force them to follow."

"Force them?" I shuddered at the meaning behind his words.

Already, those among my new followers were taking notice of the nonbelievers. A group pushed a seraph to his knees. Two crowds burst into a loud argument. Some among them thrust their swords into the air. This place was about to catch fire.

My guts knotted. Without really thinking, I waded into the throng. The crowd parted before me, giving me wide berth. I reached the closest skirmish. "Stop!" I bellowed over the raucous noise of clashing swords and screaming people. At least two dozen Seraphim were either fighting with swords, or punching the living daylights out of each other.

Either they didn't hear me, or they ignored me.

I shouted again to no effect.

A seraph screamed and went down with a sword in his guts. Another went down hard as his opponent slammed him with a wall of Murk.

Rage inflamed my blood. I spawned. This time, the change hit me almost instantly and I burst into my half-demon form. More experienced Daemos like my father could pull off such a quick transformation, but I'd never managed it before. Though it was a pleasant surprise, I didn't have time to high-five myself.

"Stop fighting!" I roared. My guttural demon voice echoed throughout the courtyard.

As if they were charged by dying batteries, the soldiers slowed their attacks and backed away. Two seraphs continued to slash at each other, completely ignoring me. I tromped over to them, gripped their arms, and shoved them hard to the ground. A growl rumbled deep in my throat. As I looked around, I saw every eye on me. Even those on the disbeliever side looked like they were about to crap their uniforms.

The believers dropped to their knees and started the bowing thing again. Some of the Seraphim on the flip side fell to the ground. Only a few remained standing. One gave me a defiant look.

"This is mere trickery," she said. "You are nothing more than a charlatan."

Anger surged in me. I blurred to her position and towered over the sera. "Test me."

She gulped. Her hand rose toward my face. I bent over. The sera ran a hand along my horn and gave it a tug. Her eyes widened. "How is this possible?"

"I am not from Seraphina. I come from Eden." I straightened and let my body melt back to normal.

The sera shrank back from me, eyes flaring. "I must say, you are very convincing."

"If you can't trust your eyes and your hands, what can you trust?" I noticed all eyes were on me. "There will be no more fighting! Put away your weapons and go about your business peaceably."

The crowd thinned, though many stood and stared at me. Either they were in shock, or just plain rude.

I turned and walked back to Cephus where he spoke to a small group of people. I had to admit I was at a loss for what to do next and he seemed to be the best person to ask. I pulled him aside and walked back toward the ministry building.

"How may I serve?" he asked as we walked.

"You surrendered to me. Does that mean I'm in charge?"

He nodded. "All that remains is a formal announcement by the Trivectus—" he cleared his throat. "I mean, by me. Although all citizens have seen the news by now, I must still legally transfer the power."

We entered the building. I stopped and turned to him. "After that I'll have full control of the military?"

"Indeed."

"The moment I do, we march for the Alabaster Arch." I noticed a handful of people in the lobby staring at us as we spoke.

He raised an eyebrow. "That is not what was promised."

"Promised?" I gave him a confused look. "I didn't promise anything."

"According to Primogenesis, the Primogenitor will send his Destroyer if the faithful do not purge the Brightlings from the land." He seemed to struggle with what he was saying, as if he couldn't believe these words were coming from his mouth. "Only then can we travel to the Promised Land."

It took a moment for his meaning to register. "Eden is the Promised Land?"

Cephus nodded. "I will draw up the necessary papers and make the announcement tonight. Tomorrow you may inspect our troops and tell us what we must do."

"Just like that?" I simply stared at the seraph, unsure what to make of all this. "I murdered two members of the Trivectus and killed dozens of soldiers." My mind hardly knew what to make of the unfolding circumstances. "I should be arrested for what I've done, but here you are, eager to give me control of the entire country."

His eyes flared with alarm. "Please don't speak like that." He pulled me into a corridor well away from curious eyes. "Primogenesis is a cancer to my people." His lips peeled back in distaste. "The believers will blindly follow you. Unbelievers are in the minority—"

I stopped him right there. "Wait a minute, you proclaimed full belief in me a few minutes ago."

He shrugged. "I simply do not know what to believe right now."

"Or else you never believed."

Cephus's nose wrinkled with distaste. "Whether I believe or not is immaterial. You are powerful beyond belief and thus the only one who can drive the Brightlings from Pjurna and back to the very capitol itself."

My stomach lurched at the thought of how long it would take to follow through on a campaign of such magnitude. My strength would fade the longer I was here without feeding from humans. The more power I used, the faster it would diminish. I had to convince my new army to follow me to Eden.

For now, I'd play along. "I need to know what capabilities the soldiers have before I can plan anything."

71

"As I said, there are several things I must do before you can inspect the troops." The worried wrinkles on his forehead smoothed out. "You should eat and rest."

My stomach grumbled at the thought of food. "I don't need to see the troops right now, but I do want all available information on your military."

"I will send you the information." He touched the gem on his collar. "Kalissa, report to me at once."

A female voice replied. "At once, Minister."

Cephus led me to the levitator. At first, I feared we were going back to the ministerial chamber, but we stopped a few floors below the top. My guide motioned me toward an open doorway down the corridor. After charging a gem in the wall, steaming water began to pour from a slit in the ceiling like a miniature waterfall and into a pool. The clear water filled a T-shaped section of the room all the way up to the window, giving the impression of a sheer drop. Much like the ministerial chambers, the room held no furniture.

"This chamber is used by visiting dignitaries from other provinces." Cephus pointed to the small gem on the wall next to the door. "You may choose furniture of any configuration by simply thinking of what you want and directing a charge of Murk into the gem on this wall."

I imagined my bedroom from the house where I'd grown up and zapped the gem with Murk. Ultraviolet tendrils of mist rose from the floor. They wove together like thread, forming cloth, wood, and even metal until every bit of furniture from my old bedroom stood before me exactly as I'd remembered it, including the spaceship bed.

"How is this possible?" I asked.

Cephus seemed pleased at my astonishment. "The city hovers over a massive aether vortex. We trap this energy in crystalline structures we call aether wells." He held up his thumb and forefinger and wove two threads of Murk into a strand of cloth. "Individually, we do not possess enough power to weave Murk into such intricate configurations. By channeling directly from the aether wells, we're able to entwine the complex patterns necessary."

The rush of nostalgia from seeing my old bedroom was almost enough to help me forget I was a stranger in a strange land. *Almost.* "How long until I have the information about the military? I want to go home tonight and return in the morning to sign whatever documents you require."

His eyebrows rose. "Home? To Eden?" Cephus shook his head. "The way station you left was under attack. It would be unsafe and unwise to return."

I was about to counter his assertion when I realized I hadn't told him about the attack. "How do you know that?"

His cheeks reddened a bit as if from embarrassment. "I still retain some memories from looking into your mind."

"Some of my memories?" I'd seen my entire life replay during his brain scan.

He shrugged. "It takes some time for the memories to fade."

"Whatever." I waved away the unimportant topic. "I want to see Elyssa the minute Pross heals her."

"You must speak with several provincial leaders," he said quickly. "I may even have the documents ready to sign today." He waved his hand around the room. "Relax and enjoy yourself. It will likely take Pross quite some time to heal your beloved. If you stay here, we may finish the formalities with plenty of time to spare for your return."

I stared at the flowing water as I considered his proposal. If he could really get me the papers ready today, it'd be a lot better if I stayed. "How do I contact Nightliss?"

He touched the gem on his sleeve. "Pross, please reply."

There was no answer.

Cephus tried again a couple more times, but failed to reach Pross. "They are likely on the skyway over the ocean by now." He gave me a reassuring look. "There is a great deal of interference to communications out there. I'm sure they are fine."

"Don't you guys have something like cell phones?" I asked.

He raised an eyebrow. "Cell phones?"

"Long-range communication devices."

"The gems are also for long distance." Cephus's expression turned regretful. "I wish we could contact them, but I'm afraid it will be impossible for now."

At least they're almost back to the arch. I hoped with all my might that Pross was as good at healing as she claimed. I couldn't wait to hold Elyssa in my arms again. Violent images of the carnage from earlier interrupted that blissful thought. *My god, what have I done? What will Elyssa think of me?* My guts twisted and knotted painfully. I'd never liked killing in the first place. I could rationalize what I'd done as self-defense, but my conscience laid bare my guilt.

I am a murderer.

"I must go now." Cephus backed out of the door. "You shall have the requested military information within the hour." He closed the door and left me alone with my thoughts.

I paced around the room for several minutes, stopping a couple of times to touch my old chest of drawers and to feel the fabric of the science-fiction themed blankets on my spaceship bed. I even found a copy of the *Princess Bride* video sitting next to my laptop. Unfortunately, my laptop didn't work. In fact, when I tapped it, it sounded like a hollow shell. The chest of drawers held a pair of my favorite superhero underwear inside the top drawer. They were several sizes too small since they'd been my favorite when I was nine.

Even magic has its limitations.

I took out my arcphone and tried to contact Nightliss for the hell of it. Amazingly, I heard ringing. It sounded as if someone answered, but all I heard was static before the line went dead. Arcphones used ley lines to transmit communications, so it made sense my phone might be able to contact another phone in the same realm. Then again, maybe not. I tried twice more, but failed to elicit even a ring.

Having run out of entertainment options, I touched the ankle of the Nightingale armor I wore. It retreated from my feet. I dipped a toe into the bubbling pool water and found it to be nice and warm. "Might as well get my feet wet." I shrank the armor down to something resembling bikini bottoms since it didn't have a setting for long shorts. Despite being alone in the room, I felt silly. Even so, I didn't let it stop me from slipping into the pool. The frothing water massaged my aching muscles. I leaned back and closed my eyes.

Tortured screams tore from the distorted faces of burning Seraphim as I raked them with Brilliance. Thala and Uoriss's eyes flashed wide as bloody blades burst from their chests. I looked at my hands. Blood seeped from every pore in my skin. I backed away in horror. My heart turned to stone in my chest. *No, this can't be happening.* "This can't be happening!"

A massive explosion shook every bone in my body. I jerked awake as the water in the pool swept me toward a gaping hole in the window and the empty air beyond.

Chapter 9

"Holy crapballs!" I shouted as the current of the draining water tumbled me head over heels toward a long plunge to the hard ground below.

A light flashed in the room and an alarm chimed.

Survival instinct overcame my shock. I flung a strand of Murk at the wall. Instead of adhering like a web, it slid off. I shot another aether rope at the glass waterfall. It refused to stick. My feet pressed hard against the bottom of the pool, but the tiles were so slick they couldn't stop me from sliding. My hands grasped for the side of the pool, only it was too far away.

I had once last chance. The jagged edges of the hole in the window loomed close. I grasped a shard jutting in my path. My feet flew out from beneath me and into the dusky sky. I cried out in pain as the glass sliced my hand all the way to the bone. My back slammed against the building and I dangled at least a hundred stories over the streets below.

A group of four Brightlings hovered in the air about a hundred feet from the building, white wings blazing behind them. One of them thrust his hand forward and a white meteor streaked toward me. I watched helplessly as death closed in. I couldn't let go with either hand. It was all I could do to maintain my grip on the slick, bloody glass. That meant I couldn't protect myself. *Or does it?* Seraphim could channel from any part of their bodies. That was what made levitation possible. Unfortunately I didn't have a full grasp on that ability just yet or I'd simply let go.

On the other hand, I knew how to channel from other parts of my body. Back braced against the unbroken glass, I stuck out my bare foot and channeled a burst of Murk from it. The shot intercepted the meteor. A halo of sparks showered from the impact. The Brightlings didn't seemed deterred. They spread out and launched a volley of fireballs my way. I desperately tried to shoot down the projectiles, but my hands slipped further. Blood dripped on my head and trickled down my arms. Agonizing pain seared my palms. I hit one fireball. Missed the next. By the time I adjusted my aim, it was too late. I was about to be fried bacon. There was no choice.

I let go.

Fear clawed up my throat as wind rushed into my face. I'd avoided becoming bacon, but I'd simply exchanged it for another breakfast food like, say, a pancake or a fast-food breakfast burrito. I'd nearly plunged to my death after my fighting Qualan on a flying carpet. At the time I'd been in demon form which in and of itself wasn't particularly strange, at least not in my world. What had been odd was when I sprouted wings. The only other time that had happened was during my short stint at Arcane University.

I'd been able to reinforce the wings with aether and use them to slow my fall before hitting the ground. I just had to figure out how to manifest them first. It had only taken me a few seconds to reach this conclusion, but mere seconds remained before I wrecked the walkway a few hundred yards below with my face. I thought back to the fight with Qualan and what I'd done just before the wings appeared.

I channeled both Murk and Brilliance at the same time.

I unclenched my bloody hands, formed a sphere of creation in my left hand and destruction in my right. No wings. I channeled through my feet and willed myself to levitate. It seemed as though I slowed ever so slightly. This tiny deceleration wouldn't make much of a difference since my body was still traveling at terminal velocity.

"Where are my damned wings?" It suddenly occurred to me that my Seraphim side was a lot like my demonic side. To get the most use from my inner demon, I had to will it free from the psychic cage I locked it in. Manifesting into my half-demon form was like utilizing muscles I didn't use a lot. Just like my former classmate, Bucky

Jergens, who could flare his nostrils and wiggle his ears on demand, I could make myself grow horns and a tail.

But all the demon powers in the world wouldn't make me fly, and so far, the only muscles responding right now were my tightly clenched butt cheeks as the ground loomed. Drawing upon more aether, I sent it coursing into every pore of my body until my skin glowed. I felt an itch in my shoulder blades. Concentrating on that itch, I sent more aether into that spot and imagined the pain that occurred the last time I'd grown wings.

A stabbing sensation pierced my back. I saw the tips of wings in my peripheral vision as they unfurled. The left was ultraviolet while the right was snow white. They flamed like pure energy. I sent every ounce of power into my new appendages.

The ground was less than thirty yards away. Horrified pedestrians looked up at me. Wind caught my wings. Twenty yards to impact. I shouted with effort. People scurried back and forth as they cleared the impact zone. Ten yards. "Fly you stupid bastard! Fly!" I drew on all the aether in the air around me and squeezed my eyes shut as the ground rushed to meet me. The wind tried to tear out my wings by the roots.

The only sound was my terrified scream.

A few seconds passed, and I suddenly realized my feet were standing on something. I opened my eyes and my cries of terror faded to a whimper. Wide-eyed spectators stared at me. I looked at the coagulating blood on my sliced hands as they slowly healed, at my bikini bottom armor, at my huge wings. They spanned at least twelve feet. My skin glowed with aether.

I look like a male stripper in angel drag.

Frightened murmurs rose from the crowd as a bright spotlight shined down from above. I glanced up and saw the flying Brightlings diving straight down, hurling deadly spheres at me. I pinched my back muscles and felt my wings respond. With one hard thrust, I flew up a couple of feet. I just as suddenly dropped right back to the ground with bone-jarring impact. Darklings screamed and ran from the path of the spheres. A group of girls, or whatever they called young seras, fell over themselves trying to run. I ran to their position and threw up a bubble of Murk just as the first volley of spheres hit with tremendous explosions.

The girls screamed.

"Everything's gonna be okay!" I shouted as the ground shook.

Cracks raced up my protective dome. I reinforced it as the next wave of destruction slammed into it. Even though the attacks weren't nearly as strong as Daelissa's, the sheer number made them a force to be reckoned with.

The Brightlings swooped low, spearing my shield with death beams before climbing high into the air. I released the barrier. "Run!" The girls dashed for cover. I clenched my fists tight, stretched my wings, and flapped them. I felt the wind catch in my aetherial feathers. My body simultaneously sent a burst of aether through my feet and into the ground even though I hadn't consciously commanded it to do so.

Instinct.

My Seraphim side knew what to do even if I didn't.

I flapped my wings and let my body do the rest. I felt a rush as aether jetted from my feet. I flew several feet into the air. The next thrust sent me even higher. Within seconds, I was high above the ground.

"I'm flying!" I pumped a fist. "Whoo-hoo!" I was so exhilarated, I almost forgot the bastards trying to kill me.

A white beam sliced the air just over my head. I dove between two skyscrapers as a flurry of attacks splashed against the building to my right. I glanced over my shoulder and saw the Brightlings right behind me. They were closing the distance at an alarming rate, making it painfully obvious that my newfound skill wasn't developed nearly enough to outpace my pursuers. I had to ground these jackasses in a hurry. I spotted a building shaped like a giant corkscrew and dove toward it.

Wind whistled past my ears. My heart raced with a mixture of exhilaration and fear. I angled up at the last second and landed on a spiral some thirty stories above ground level. The building looked as though someone had taken a rectangular building and twisted it so it formed a gently sloping spiral from the ground all the way to the top.

The entire structure was made of the ultraviolet Murk glass. Some sections were blacked out while others were transparent.

I ran toward the center mass of the huge structure. I looked down through a clear section of glass and saw a hallway. Startled Seraphim looked up at me as I ran downslope overhead. Most of them wore the drab Darkling uniforms favored by these people. I couldn't tell if they were working, or if they lived here.

I heard thuds and turned around. The Brightlings had landed.

"Did Daelissa send you?" My heart felt tight as I considered the possibility that she'd taken control of the Alabaster Arch at the Three Sisters and sent through assassins.

The lead Seraphim wore crimson armor with the sigil of a barren tree emblazoned on it. She lifted her arms and aimed her palms at me. White flames flickered in her grasp. "You will not speak of the Divinity in such familiar terms."

I drew in aether and prepared myself. Baring my teeth, I leveled my gaze at the leader. "Did she send you?"

"She did not." The other three Brightlings spread out in a semicircle.

I backed away. If Daelissa hadn't sent this assassination crew, who had? "You must have seen the video of me."

The sera didn't answer. Every Brightling fired on my position. I threw up a mirrored shield and redirected the blast at a seraph to my right. He screamed as two of the beams burned holes in his armor.

The other three Brightlings ceased fire. I lowered my shield and sent a blast of Murk at the dying Brightling. His body sailed off the building and vanished from sight, leaving a trail of black smoke. I saw two cloudbanks rushing my way and spotted Seraphim in familiar drab uniforms. The Darklings were finally coming to my rescue.

The assassins drew swords and rushed me.

I formed a shield with my left arm and threw it up just in time to intercept a vicious slash from the lead sera. I rolled right. Swept the feet from beneath a seraph. His wings splayed out and stopped his fall, leaving me in a very vulnerable position. He drove his sword straight down at my face. I caught it on my shield and drove my foot straight up into his crotch.

"Catch this with your wings!" The impact sent the seraph flying into the air.

Unfortunately, it seemed his armor saved him from a life of sterility because he didn't even scream in a high-pitched voice. His wings spread wide and caught air. I rolled away and flipped to my feet as two swords clashed against the roof where my neck had been.

The cloudbank reached the building. A group of Seraphim in Darkling uniforms piled off of it.

"Thank god!" I shouted. "These jackasses ruined my bath. I hope you can arrest them for that."

The lead sera smiled and went to the head Darkling. They clasped forearms. The Darkling leader drew a blade. His other five companions did the same.

My sense of elation dropped like a lead stone and played pinball with my guts. "Who are you people working for?" I shouted. "What Darkling in their right mind would join with Daelissa's cronies?"

They formed ranks. The second cloudbank reached the roof and more Darklings joined the others. I looked more closely at their uniforms and realized they were actually quite different from the ones worn by the Darklings in the hallway beneath me. These uniforms were pitch black with crimson striations running along them like muscle fibers. A deep red gem on the sleeve of the lead Darkling sparkled by the light of Brilliance coalescing in the hands of the Brightlings. The other combatants had similar gems on their sleeves.

A thudding noise beneath my feet drew my attention. A Darkling on the other side of the glass pointed frantically down the sloping hallway she stood in. It didn't take a lot of brains to understand her meaning. *Run!* I faced my enemies and considered spawning into demon form. I flashed back to the carnage from the ministry chambers and shuddered.

What if I completely lose control? A thin barrier of will was all that kept me in control of the raging beast lurking inside me. That was why I only manifested into a half-demon form. If my inner demon had his way, I'd spawn into a raging monstrosity destroying everything in my way. Since my demon seemed to thrive on Brilliance, that made it even more dangerous.

81

Killing these assassins wouldn't be pleasant, but I could live with it. Unfortunately, my demon side wouldn't stop there. It would happily kill innocents as well. A simple moment of misunderstanding had resulted in the murder of too many people already. I'd have to save my demon side as a last resort.

The Brightlings thrust their hands forward. Blinding light speared toward me. I threw up a shield. The Darklings charged while I was pinned down. I felt thumping beneath my feet and saw several Darklings shouting and pointing downslope.

Refocusing the shield into a mirror, I redirected the deadly energy and sliced off the leg of a charging enemy. The Brightlings stopped their attack. I decided it was the perfect moment to follow the advice of the Seraphim in the building.

I turned.

I ran.

Shouts echoed behind me. I turned and saw the Darklings charging after me but, compared to me, they were slow as dirt, and I quickly left them behind. The Brightlings were nowhere to be seen. I ran down the spiral a couple of turns and suddenly saw where they were. The Brightlings had simply flown down a level and waited on me.

They thrust their hands toward me.

I jumped high into the air over their attacks, extended my foot, and slammed a seraph in the face. Before his companions could respond, I gripped his neck and squeezed until I felt something crunch. The sera screamed and slammed into me. We rolled down the slope. Her knee slammed into my crotch, but the armor protected my man parts. I finally got a bit of leverage and punched her in the face.

She reeled back. I threw her off me and stood just as her remaining companion dove and slammed into my stomach. I tumbled backward. He stood and spun. His wing slashed my chest. Searing heat bit into my flesh. I cried out and jumped backward. Blood trickled from severed pectoral muscles. My arms suddenly felt limp and useless. I could move them, but it took immense effort.

The seraph bared his teeth and slashed with his wings again. I turned on instinct. My ultraviolet wing caught his thrust. Holding my arms tight against me to keep from tearing my muscles further, I wove Brilliance and Murk into a fogbank of gray Stasis. It enveloped the seraph and froze him in place. The pursuing Darklings rounded the corner and skidded to a halt as the seraph's wings crackled and shattered like white ice.

The sera watched with open horror. "Monster!"

"You people are the monsters!" I shouted as I backed away. Every step cost me in blood and pain. My supernatural healing struggled to clot the chest wound, but all this fighting had overtaxed my system. I looked toward the Darklings. "And you all should be ashamed of yourselves. Who are you working for?"

"Primogenesis is a blight," the leader said. "We will not stand for your perpetuation of myths and fallacies. By killing you, we purge the cancer from this land."

I didn't know if I should laugh or cry at the absurdity. I'd killed the two super-religious zealots on the Trivectus and spared the non-believer. Now I was suddenly at the epicenter of a culture war.

"Primogenesis is fake!" I shouted. "I don't want to promote it; I just want to save Eden."

"Liar!" the Darkling leader shouted.

The Stasis mist faded and dropped the unconscious seraph to the ground. The Brightling sera rushed to his side. She looked up at me, hate burning in her eyes.

"Why would you ally with Brightlings who follow the Divinity?" I asked.

I felt thumping under my feet and looked down. The same group of Darklings were frantically motioning me to run again. I desperately wanted to untangle this strange mystery. Unfortunately, I couldn't adequately defend myself. I took another step back. My feet slipped on blood.

I looked down at my bikini bottoms and cursed my stupidity. I'd been so busy surviving I hadn't even thought to extend my armor. I touched the hem and sent Nightingale armor creeping over my body. The armor gave me a firm grip on the building despite the blood on my feet. I was too injured to fight and it was obvious talking wouldn't accomplish anything. Once again, I ran.

83

Grunts of pain hissed through my teeth with every step. My arms hung by my sides since moving them only invited agony. I probably looked as ridiculous as Gus Gurtzky in third grade P.E. class when he tried to run like an ostrich. I looked down at the hallway beneath me, but my group of faithful Darklings had fallen behind. Startled looks from others in the hallway greeted me almost every step of the way.

It made me wonder if Darklings had nine-to-five jobs, or if they just lounged around in pajamas all day coming up with the most bizarre building designs possible. I looked over my shoulder and saw no signs of pursuit. That didn't mean anything. I hoped the two remaining Brightlings didn't try to cut me off at the pass again. I could probably fight them, but it would hurt me about as much as it hurt them.

I angled toward the edge of the building and saw the ground only about ten stories below, though I doubted the height of this building could be measured by such human terms. When I looked up, all hope vanished.

A veritable platoon of soldiers stood in my way. Someone shouted a command and the soldiers drew swords.

Chapter 10

These people left me no choice. I had to spawn or dive off the building and hope my wings could still hold me. Even if I let my inner demon rampage, I didn't stand a chance against a platoon of soldiers.

"Destroyer Slade, we are here to protect you," said a seraph with a blue gem on his sleeve. "I am Legiaros Ketiss."

Despite the use of my new cringe-worthy name, I almost melted with relief. "Are you absolutely positive you're not here to kill me?"

He raised an eyebrow. "Yes, sir."

The enemy Darklings and two remaining Brightlings charged around the curve. They saw the force of enemies and nearly fell over themselves in an effort to reverse course. The platoon of defenders rushed the enemy.

The Brightlings dove off the building and glided through the air.

I ran to the side of the building and shook my fist. "Run all you want, cowards, but I'll get you if it's the last thing I do."

Their flight pattern wobbled. The strain on their faces made it obvious they'd overextended themselves and were exhausted. The sera glanced down and a look of hopelessness erased the determination from her face. I followed her gaze and saw more soldiers gathering in the plaza at the base of the building. The Brightlings might be able to glide to the ground, but there was no escape for them now.

The sera flashed a furious, defiant look at me. "I have failed today, but others will come and they will succeed."

"You will die, monster," her companion declared.

The Brightlings gripped hands. A look of acceptance came over their faces. Their wings flickered away and they fell without a single cry toward the ground far below. The crowd parted like a sea of ants. I saw splashes of crimson paint the ground and looked away.

The enemy Darklings furiously fought my defenders. The cloudbank the attackers had arrived on hovered into view. Some tried to leap to it before it reached the building. Two made it while three others plunged to their deaths. The enemy leader rushed toward the cloudbank, but my rescuers surrounded him.

"Surrender," Ketiss called to him.

"Never," the seraph hissed back. Sword held high over his head, he loosed a battle cry and ran at Ketiss.

Blasts of Murk caught the seraph's charge. One slammed him in the shoulder. He dropped his sword. The next blast hit him in the face. His legs flew from beneath him and his back thudded against the glass. He groaned once and lay still. I heard shouts of fear and looked toward the cloudbank with the only remaining enemies. Ultraviolet beams speared into it. The billowing clouds dispersed, leaving only thin air between the escapees and the ground.

Biting back pain, I shot strands of Murk at them. I missed one, but caught the other and willed the aether rope to bind him. The strand contracted and brought him into the waiting arms of my protectors who immediately secured him. The enemy leader was also bound. Apparently, they'd knocked him senseless with their attacks instead of killing him.

"Are you injured, Destroyer?" Ketiss asked me.

The black Nightingale armor was soaked with blood, but it merely looked wet since it hid the red. "I've been better." I tried not to groan and hoped my supernatural healing would be able to do something.

"I'll have a healer attend you." He snapped his fingers and a young sera came forward.

"Yes, Legiaros?" she said.

He motioned toward me. "The Destroyer requires your services, Flava."

Her bright blue eyes looked me up and down. "Are you wounded, sir?"

I lowered the armor to display the slice across my chest. It still wasn't healing and I abruptly remembered why. Seraphim wings were pure aether. When the Brightling had sliced me, he might as well have hit me with a blast of magic. Unlike physical wounds, magical ones typically took longer to heal.

"Goodness, this is quite awful." She touched it.

I flinched. "I agree. It's awfully awful."

She blinked a couple times as if what I'd said hadn't translated, shrugged, and leaned forward to examine the wound. "This will take a few moments." Fingers extended, she sent gentle pulses of Murk into my wound. At first, my tissue seemed to resist the procedure, but suddenly began to seal shut like a zipper. The pain melted away and my body relaxed. I stifled a yawn.

"Wow, that was really good." I sounded like a stoner who'd just eaten a bag of cheesy poofs. With the chest wound gone, aches from other parts of my body gave notice that I had a lot more healing to do. It was also evident that my demon side was ravenous from the clawing sensation in my guts. I switched to incubus vision and saw the glowing auras of the Seraphim around me.

They glowed much brighter than humans. Healer Flava's halo shone bright and golden. A psychic tendril from my aura automatically quested toward this tempting source of sustenance. She flinched the moment it touched her aura.

Eyes wide, she backed away. "What are you doing?"

Ketiss raised his eyebrow. "What is the issue, healer?"

Forehead pinched, she stared at me. She felt her head. "He touched me."

I felt my face burning. "I'm sorry. There's a part of me that needs to feed."

She held her hand flat and splayed her fingers, demonstrating the way Seraphim fed. "You did not indicate you were feeding."

I shook my head. "My demon side feeds differently."

"Healer, you will assist the Destroyer in any way he requests." Ketiss gave her a sharp look. "Do I make myself clear?"

Her big eyes flared wide with fear. She looked down. "As you command, sir."

Ketiss surveyed the bodies and shook his head. "None of them are wearing gems. They must have known this would be a suicide mission."

I was about to ask him what help the gems would've been when a large cloudbank drew even with the roof. I felt vibrations beneath my feet and looked down to see a crowd of Darklings inside the building. Some seemed to be cheering and shouting something at me, but I couldn't hear them through the protective glass.

Ketiss motioned toward the cloudbank. "Destroyer, this will take you to a secure location. Flava and a contingent of guards will accompany you." He gave me a gem. "Press this to your uniform wherever you wish and it will adhere to the surface. Should you need to speak anyone, simply think of them and it will put you in touch."

"I need to question the captives later," I said. "I need to find out who sent them."

"They were obviously sent by the Heretics," Ketiss said.

"Even the Brightlings?" I was still having a really hard time wrapping my brain around that one.

"It is likely Brightling spies learned of your appearance from our information feed." He tapped the gem on his sleeve. "They realized you are the Destroyer of legend who has come to drive them from our lands and attempted to assassinate you."

"But the Heretics seemed to know them." I shook my head. "I think this goes deeper."

He gave me a curt nod. "I assure you, we'll get to the truth."

I looked at other nearby soldiers. Many of them wore open looks of fascination and admiration as they gazed upon me. I took Ketiss by the arm and led him a distance away. Once we were hopefully out of eavesdropping range, I faced him. "Which denomination are you affiliated with?"

He stiffened ever so slightly. "Atharis, sir, but my unit is mixed as required by law."

"Even those who don't believe?" I asked.

He nodded. "Heretics are treated as equals so long as they do not impede the teachings of Primogenesis."

How sweet of them. "I killed Thala and Uoriss. I assume you've seen the video."

Ketiss looked down. "I have. It fills me with shame to know we have failed for so long. The Primogenitor must be very displeased with us." He almost looked as if he wanted to cry. "Our leaders have not done enough to drive the Brightlings from our lands. The enemy has been allowed to live for too long." He knelt before me. "I swear, Destroyer Slade, we will purge the Brightlings or be annihilated in the attempt."

These people are cray-cray to the max.

I managed not to cringe at his fanatical words and decided to play along for now. Thankfully, my days of Kings and Castles, a live-action role-playing game, had prepared me for eloquent speeches. "Brave words, Ketiss. Rise and go forth in the name of the Almighty. We will soon embark on an epic journey to the Promised Land and drive the Brightlings into the land of the dead."

He stood and gave me a sharp salute. Joy lit his face. "At once, Destroyer."

I pinched my lips tight to avoid snickering at my ridiculous declaration and walked with him back to the cloudbank. Flava and several guards waited on it. I stepped aboard, graced Ketiss with another nod, and turned to the crowd on the cloudbank with me. "Let's go."

A seraph on the other side saluted and the cloudbank moved out. We flew over a sea of people gathered in the square below. Even from here, I was able to see imagery from my battle with the Brightlings playing back from the gems the Darklings wore. I wondered how such recordings were transmitted to everyone so quickly and who was in charge of deciding which news people could see.

"Is there an agency that decides what news is published on the info feed?" I asked.

Flava raised an eyebrow. "The people decide which news is transmitted, Destroyer." She brushed a hand across her gem. "The more citizens who record and declare something as newsworthy, the more likely it will be seen by others."

"They upvote it?" I could tell she was confused by my internet lingo, so I clarified. "In other words, they give it a positive vote and once it hits a certain threshold, the gems automatically replay the news."

She nodded. "Yes, they...upvote." Flava said the word a couple more times as if practicing it.

Humans had made an art of murdering the English language by fusing words into almost unrecognizable mutants. It felt kind of nice that my magically acquired Cyrinthian skills allowed me to genetically modify this language as well. More importantly, I began to see that these gems were the analog to arcphones back on Eden. This info feed of theirs was like a social network on steroids.

I wanted to know more. "How long after something happens can a person go back and replay the event?"

Flava touched a finger to her chin and her gaze grew distant. "I am not sure, Destroyer. Things that are very important to me are always available. I simply think of what I wish to view, and it appears."

These gems sounded like an identity thief's wet dream. Despite the dozens of other questions I had about the magical gadgets, a towering monolith caught my eyes. The designer had created the structural equivalent of a neighborhood bully. Wide at the base and narrow at the top, this structure was built to intimidate. Several pyramids like the ones I'd seen at the other ministry building bordered the perimeter of the building's wide plaza, their eyes rotating to watch the surroundings.

"What is this place?" I asked.

Flava answered. "The Ministry of Defense, Destroyer."

"Will you stop calling me that?"

Her eyes filled with uncertainty. "What shall I call you?"

"Justin would be fine." I smiled.

"Is this a word from Eden?"

I managed not to laugh. "It's my first name."

Her eyes widened. "Oh. It would be improper for me to call you by such familiar terms."

"The Destroyer commands it," I said in what was hopefully a commanding voice.

Flava looked down. "As you command, Des—Justin."

Some of the other Darklings on the cloudbank cast jealous looks at Flava, as if I'd bought candy but only given it to her.

Our cloudy chariot docked at a circular platform jutting from halfway up the side of the building. The contingent of guards escorted me down a wide corridor devoid of decoration. The black floor and dark gray walls did nothing to alleviate the monotony. Flava charged a gem on the wall and a portion of it melted away to reveal a similarly bland room on the other side. She and I entered while the guards remained outside.

Unlike my previous residence, this room already had furniture, most of it in shades of white or black. On the right stood a table with four cloud chairs, and to the left, a floating cloud.

"Is that my own personal icloud?" I asked.

Flava's forehead wrinkled and abruptly smoothed over as if she'd just remembered I was a noob in these lands. "It is where you sleep."

"Really?" I made a beeline for it and touched the billowing surface. It was incredibly soft. I lay down felt it mold to my contours. It was almost like lying on thin air. "This is cool."

"I'm glad you approve, J-justin." She stumbled over my name as if afraid to say it.

My demon stomach growled. I stood and motioned Flava to a chair. "I need to feed."

She sat in a cloud chair and folded her hands in her lap. Eyes wide, she looked up at me. "Will it hurt?"

I couldn't help but feel sorry for her. "No, it won't hurt." I touched her hand. "I promise."

She made a whimpering sound, but quickly stiffened her back. "I am ready."

It was all I could do to keep my questing aura from lunging at hers. As before, she flinched, and suddenly it was as if I'd hit a wall. My father had told me that feeding from Seraphim was very difficult if they didn't want you to. Even though, in their natural state, they weren't as powerful as those who'd fed on humans, I wouldn't be able to sneak past her defenses.

Flava unclenched her teeth and took a deep breath. As she blew it out, her barriers relaxed and melted away. My questing probe latched onto her halo. Warmth seeped into me. I sensed fear and uncertainty from Flava along with a healthy dose of awe. She really did seem to think I was this Destroyer dude everyone was talking about. My inner demon sensed something different about my current victim and strained against its leash like a male dog sensing a French poodle in heat.

Her eyes widened. She licked her lips and looked me up and down. I felt the change in her attitude immediately and gave my demon side a good hard shove back into its kennel. Sexual tension oozed up the link from Flava. She moaned and stood. Her heavy-lidded gaze appraised me as if I were in the display case at a butcher shop. This only encouraged my demon. I tried to sever the link, but it felt as though Flava's aura held it fast. I pulled at the link again but she had me as much as I had her.

Flava launched herself at me and knocked me onto my back on the cloud bed. My demon pushed. Lust surged through the bond and it was all I could do to maintain control over my carnal urges.

An internal battled raged for control of my body and I was losing.

Chapter 11

I hadn't been out of control of my demon feeding abilities since my days in high school. It had become almost second nature to me at this point. But ever since my Seraphim side had fully awakened, my demon side had become very unruly. Coupled with Flava's ability to maintain a grasp on my essence, I was in unfamiliar territory, without an instruction manual.

Flava pressed her hands to my bare chest. She leaned down and kissed my face. I pressed my lips tight and struggled to avoid her lips, but it was nearly impossible. Despite my predicament, I was feeding at a healthy pace and strength flooded into me. Feeding from a Seraphim tasted far richer than it did with humans.

My body responded to her touch. My second brain joined my demonic side, urging me to take this succulent creature and enjoy her fully. In the most physical sense, it was almost unbearably tempting. But my love for Elyssa was even stronger.

I gripped Flava's wrists, held them together, and pushed her back on her feet. She stumbled backward. "Stop!" I yelled. "This is a side-effect of the feeding."

She moaned. "I do not want to stop. I want you."

I rolled backward and dashed to the other side of the table. I tried freeing my essence from hers, but it was like tugging on tangled yarn. "Let go of my aura."

She traced a finger down the front center of her uniform. It peeled open and fell away from her nude body. "Give me more, Destroyer." She moaned. "Show me your power."

What is this, a low-budget adult film?

Flava circled the table. I dodged around it to keep the amorous angel well away from me. Unfortunately, my inner demon was fanning the flames of passion the best it could. Anger flared, heating my face. Thanks to my infernal side, I'd murdered a roomful of people. Now it was about to cause a female to do something she wouldn't under normal circumstances. If I gave in, I could add rape to my capital offenses.

Flava flinched and her gaze turned uncertain.

She just sensed my anger. I'd been so angry it had overridden the lust. I thought back to the ministry building. I visualized the soldiers bursting into the room. The burned bodies. The lake of blood. The pain and guilt I'd felt.

The sera gasped. Her eyes filled with tears. "How could I?" she said. "So many bodies. Burned alive."

I felt my demon side recede. Tears pouring down her cheeks, Flava dropped into a chair and buried her face in her hands. My essence untangled from hers and snapped free. I nearly fell over backward. Sweat dribbled down my nose and my heart pounded. *What in the hell is wrong with me?* "Hell" was an appropriate word in this case because it seemed to be the primary problem with me. My demon side was like an unstable catalyst when combined with my Seraphim abilities.

"I'm so sorry, Flava." I stayed back from her.

She lowered her hands and revealed a tearstained face. "I don't know why, but I lost control of my sexual inhibitions." Another tear trickled down her face. "I sexually assaulted you, Destroyer."

"*Justin.*" I sighed. "It wasn't your fault. It happens sometimes when my demonic side feeds."

Flava wiped her eyes. "You caused these feelings in me?"

I nodded. "It's like a psychic link. Emotions travel both ways, but my emotional state can control yours." I ran a hand through my hair. "I've never fed my incubus side on Seraphim. Apparently it made me lose control."

"I am honored to be your first." She rose to her feet, revealing more of her naked body. "May I publish an article in our healer journals about this experience? I think it will be very educational."

I blinked at her a couple of times before an answer penetrated my confusion. "An article? Uh, sure."

She picked up her uniform and brushed a finger against the gem. A video of the incident from her perspective projected into the air. She paused it and used her fingers to spin the view around from different angles. When her uniform fell to the floor in the video, the recording went dark as a fold of cloth covered the gem. Unfortunately, the audio came through loud and clear.

Flava smiled. "I will be sure to save this."

My face heated to about a thousand degrees as I thought about the article she planned to publish. "Do the gems record everything?"

She nodded. "They are very useful."

A bell chimed. The door melted away to reveal Cephus in the hallway. His forehead was wrinkled with worry. He saw Flava's nude form and averted his eyes. "I'm sorry, Destroyer. Did I interrupt something?"

"We were performing a medical experiment, Minister." Flava hurriedly slid back into her uniform.

I cleared my throat. "All in the name of science." I quickly changed the subject. "I assume you're here to talk about the attack on the ministry building."

"Of course." He looked up and seemed relieved to see a fully clothed Flava regarding him. "May I?" he motioned toward the entrance.

"Please, come in." I leaned against the table and folded my arms, trying desperately to look casual.

Cephus looked at Flava. "May I ask who this is? Should she be here for our conversation?"

Flava stiffened and folded her arms behind her back. "I am Flava, prime healer of the Tarissan Legion."

"Ah, yes. I've heard of you." Cephus splayed his fingers toward her and held his hand out, palm down. "It is a pleasure to meet a prime healer. I assume you have tended to the Destroyer's needs?"

95

She returned the gesture. "Yes, Minister."

He raised an eyebrow. "I am curious to hear more of this medical experiment you were performing."

Her face turned bright red. "It is rather complicated, sir."

I don't have time for this. I cleared my throat. "As I was saying," I continued, "I'd like to know how Brightlings managed to penetrate your security measures. Please don't tell me they were simply able to fly over them."

Cephus shook his head. "No, the detection mist surrounds the building from top to bottom; it just isn't as visible farther up. Somehow the intruders disabled a section and went through."

The Darkling Heretics must have helped them, I figured, but I still didn't understand why. Did they really see me as a common enemy? I went to my next question. "How were they able to destroy the glass?"

"These Brightlings were members of the elite warrior class," Cephus said in a matter-of-fact tone. "They call themselves archangels."

"Archangels, huh?" *What a pretentious name.* "I fought a group of them in Eden."

Cephus hissed a breath between his teeth. "They are in Eden?"

I gave him a level gaze. "Yes. That's precisely why I need to take an army back with me to get rid of them." A disturbing thought occurred to me. "Do your people have elite warriors who can fly?"

He shook his head. "I'm afraid we're limited to using cloudlets."

I assumed he was referring to what I called cloudbanks, and made the lingual adjustment. Considering how nimble the archangels had been compared to the sluggish movement of the cloudlets I'd seen, I didn't see how the Darklings stood a chance against the super-powered Brightlings in Eden. "If the Brightlings have such an advantage, how have your people managed to maintain control of your lands?"

"We are barely holding on," Cephus said. "Brightling forces to the far north have already claimed the city of Ajarta and surrounding lands. The only reason we have managed for so long is the limited number of archangels at their disposal."

I pushed myself off the edge of the table and straightened. "Let me take an army back to Eden. I know how to make your people even more powerful—perhaps powerful enough to counter the archangels."

"We cannot spare anyone." Cephus's tone was firm. "We train all citizens to fight from a young age. We've improved our armor and weapons to match the enemy's. We have scoured the land for the brightest minds to lead our forces." He closed his eyes and pinched the bridge of his nose as if a terrible headache had just set in. "The Brightling Second Battalion is simply too large and well-trained for us to fight. If the First Battalion had not been recalled to Zbura, they likely would have taken several more cities from us as well."

"Why were they recalled?" I asked.

"Our spies were only able to determine it was some sort of emergency." Cephus walked to a niche inset in the wall and charged a gem there. "Would you like something to drink?"

I shook my head. "I want to know why—" It suddenly occurred to me why the First Battalion had been recalled. After we'd defeated Daelissa's army, she must have sent for reinforcements. The primary question in my mind was why didn't she call in more troops sooner? Considering the way her forces had crushed us like ants, she must have thought the war was won.

Cephus picked up two containers of steaming liquid from the niche and took a sip from one. "Just in case you change your mind." He placed the second cup on the table. "Our spies in Zbura informed us that the entire city guard was deployed somewhere outside the city. They were last seen taking the Imperial Skyway toward the Eternal Cliffs."

"The Eternal Cliffs?" Flava touched her gem and a holographic map appeared in the air. She zoomed in on a section of land. "A Sacred Arch is located there."

This new information sent the hamster wheel powering my brain into overdrive. "What's the difference between the city guard and their regular soldiers?"

"The difference is night and day," Cephus replied. "The city guards use crystal armor and weapons, which are highly effective at controlling other Brightlings. Such weapons are not as useful against us since we can neutralize them with Murk. This weakness allowed our people to free themselves centuries ago. Over time, the Brightlings developed new magical weapons to counter us."

My stomach keeled over backward and landed on my spleen. We hadn't fought the real Brightling army at all. Instead, we'd barely beaten the city guard. It suddenly made sense to me why there'd been almost no diversification of weapons or personnel in Daelissa's first army. The city guard wasn't equipped to fight wars and yet they'd nearly driven us to extinction. Now a real Brightling army threatened Eden and we simply didn't have the manpower to stop them.

I swung my gaze to Cephus. "Have you prepared the papers for me to sign?"

"They are still being processed." He looked at his drink and took a sip.

"Where is the real Darkling army?"

Flava scrolled the holographic map to a continent that vaguely resembled Australia but with a slightly different shape to the southern coastline. Instead of curving inland, it bulged out into the ocean. A wide river ran deep into the center of the continent and branched out into large tributaries. Mountain ranges and fields of red and blue covered much of central Pjurna. If I was reading it correctly, the geographic detail indicated the land was fertile and not desert as in Eden.

Flava pointed toward a large, northeastern section of the island continent shaded red. "This is the front line, Destroyer Justin."

I ignored her use of my distasteful title and peered at the map. It looked almost like live satellite imagery. I wasn't exactly a military genius, but even I noticed the range of mountains protecting the southern lands from further enemy advances. "I assume most of the enemy army can't fly."

"True," Cephus said. "They have access to cloudlets, as do we, but our defenses atop the mountains would easily destroy any attempts to ferry soldiers across."

I traced a finger along a network of lines that looked like roads. "What about the skyways?"

Flava pointed to several hubs with skyways radiating from them. "These skylets hovering above large aether vortexes are the power source for the skyway system." She indicated several hubs close to the conflict zone. "We shut down the skyways leading into those lands so the enemy could not use them."

I examined the coastline. "Do they have boats or ships they could sail down the coastline?"

Cephus looked confused. "Watercraft?"

I gave him a weird look. "Exactly."

"Why would they use watercraft for military purposes?" he said in a perplexed tone. "They could simply fly cloudlets over the water."

I threw up my hands. "Okay, fine. Why haven't they done that?"

Cephus motioned toward the map. "Flava, please show him the Great Barrier Vortex."

"Yes, Minister." She scrolled to the ocean just off the coast. Instead of the Great Barrier Reef, there was a cauldron of boiling ocean water. Gouts of steam flew into the air, and the air shimmered with heat.

The place looked inhospitable for sure. "I don't see a vortex."

"It is far below the water," Cephus said. "The energy it throws into the air disrupts magical patterns. The spells powering a cloudbank would come unwoven and cast those aboard into the deadly waters below."

A monstrous reptilian creature with glistening black scales abruptly burst from the water. It leapt like a giant dolphin, arcing through the air. Great wings unfurled from its body, casting sheets of water in all directions. It glided a distance before plunging back into the ocean.

"Holy crap." *It's a dragon with wings.* I could hardly believe my eyes.

"Who is this Holy Crap?" Flava asked. "Is he a deity?"

"You have dragons here?" I said.

"They are supposedly guardians created by the Primogenitor," Cephus said. "They live within the vortexes, but we rarely see them."

Considering the amount of aether in Seraphina, I should have known there'd be dragons here. I wondered if they knew Altash and

Lulu, two leviathan dragons that lived beneath El Dorado. The sighting raised tons of questions, but now wasn't the time to ask them. The Great Barrier Vortex guarded much of the northeastern coast from invasions by sea, and the mountain defenses blocked the Brightlings inland.

Flava traced a red line to the northwestern coast. "The First Battalion was supposedly making its way further west before they were recalled."

"We suspected this recall was a feint so our defenses would relax, but our spies confirmed the bulk of their forces did indeed leave our lands." Cephus set his drink on the table. "Our last reports indicate they traveled to Anjora."

Flava rotated the map to this realm's version of North America and zoomed in on an area I'd recognize in just about any realm. *Thunder Rock.*

Cephus continued. "So far, we have been unable to discover why they travelled there."

"I can tell you why," I said.

"How would you know what our spies do not?" Flava asked.

I jabbed a finger at the map. "Is there a Sacred Arch there?"

"Yes," Cephus replied.

"That arch goes to a place called Thunder Rock in my world." I gave them a super-serious look. "The First Battalion is in Eden. If you think they're powerful now, just wait until they've fed on humans. Imagine an army of Brightlings as powerful as me."

I realized with absolute horror that what I'd said wasn't true. The archangels were already powerful without feeding from humans. Once they supercharged themselves, even I might not be a match for them.

Chapter 12

Flava's already wide eyes managed to flare wider. "But you are the Destroyer. No single Brightling could match you."

I sighed. "Even I can't fight an army."

"I don't see how feeding on humans could increase their abilities," Cephus interjected. "Why would the Primogenitor"—he rolled his eyes at the word—"give such powers to the forces of evil?"

My fists clenched and I let out a frustrated grunt. "Look, I'm the Destroyer. I know what I'm talking about. That's why I need to take an army to Eden and supercharge them so they can fight the First Battalion."

"The Brightlings are stealing the power from the Primogenitor," Flava said. "They are abusing the Promised Land just as Daelissa and her minions did." She turned to Cephus. "I think the Destroyer is right. We must stop them."

Cephus shook his head. "Absolutely not. Do you not remember the prophecy?"

"There are several prophecies regarding the Destroyer," Flava replied.

"Yes, yes. They all say he is to drive the Brightlings from our lands, correct?" Cephus challenged her with two raised eyebrows.

"It is a matter of interpretation." Flava opened her mouth as if to launch into an intense religious discussion.

I'd dealt with too many prophecies, or foreseeances as the Overworld community called them, and wasn't about to let this conversation nosedive into irrelevance. I cut off Flava before she could speak. "I'm the Destroyer, so I think I know what the Primogenitor wants." It was a cheap move on my part, but I had to stop this nonsense.

"Unless you are a false Destroyer," Cephus replied calmly.

I almost punched him. "From what you've seen, do I look like a false Destroyer?"

He didn't reply right away. Despite his calm façade, he seemed to be wrestling internally with some dilemma.

"That's what I thought." I turned to Flava. "Who would I speak with about deploying a military force?"

"But, the front line is too delicate," Cephus protested. "We cannot move—"

I slashed a hand through the air to cut him off. "I'm not talking about moving front line defenders. I'll take a city legion."

Cephus shook his head. "But—"

"Will you stop with the buts?" I put a finger to my mouth. "Just be quiet if you can't say anything constructive."

His face turned bright red.

"The Tarissan Legion would gladly fight by your side," Flava said. "We can speak with Legiaros Ketiss first thing tomorrow."

"Is 'Legiaros' his first name or a title?" I asked.

"That is the term for a legion commander," she replied.

"Do I still need the documents declaring me the ruler and all that?" I asked.

Flava looked at Cephus. "I am not familiar with the requirements for assuming leadership, but there is no mention of such a requirement for the Destroyer."

"It is protocol," Cephus said in a precise, nerdy tone.

"What if I'd killed you too?" I asked him in a deadly quiet tone. "Would I still be required to sign documents?" I was done playing games with this seraph. More than anything in the world, I wanted to go home to see if Pross had healed Elyssa. Duty to Eden held me here until I could raise an army. If Cephus intended for me to lead Darkling forces all the way to the north so I could drive out the Brightlings, he had unrealistic expectations. Such a campaign would take years, especially considering the superior Brightling fighters.

Cephus seemed extremely unnerved by my question. "There are sub-ministers who would have to cede power." His voice trembled. "Signing a document transferring power to you would ensure the legitimacy of your rule."

Flava's eyes flared with something like anger. "The Primogenitor ensures his legitimacy, Minister. There is no higher authority the Destroyer needs recognize."

I narrowed my eyes at Cephus. "You'd best recognize, brah."

He tugged at the collar of his uniform. "I am not questioning the will of the Primogenitor—"

"Indeed you are, Minister." Flava made as if to touch her gem. "I must contact my religious leader and ask them proper protocol."

He held his hands in front of him in a gesture of surrender. "No, that will not be necessary." Cephus turned to me. "Do as you see fit, Destroyer. I just pray you don't doom us all." He turned and left.

I faced Flava. "Did you see the video where I killed Thala and Uoriss?"

She backed away a step. "I did." Her voice faltered. "Must I also be a sacrifice?"

"I'm not going to harm you." I almost reached out to put a reassuring hand on her shoulder, but decided against it. "Why would people willingly follow a person who assassinated your leaders?"

"They failed the Primogenitor." She tilted her head slightly. "It was not assassination, but sacrifice. They failed him for too long."

I didn't even know why I bothered to ask anymore. Guilt weighed on my guts like a sumo wrestler in a hammock, but I was desperate. "Would it hurt the city's defenses if I borrowed the legion?"

"The attempt on your life was the only Brightling attack we've suffered in this city for over a century." Flava's lips curled into a reassuring smile. "Tarissa will survive long enough for you to visit death upon the evil scourge threatening the Promised Land."

"Alrighty then." I wanted to go speak with Ketiss right that minute, but a yawn cracked my jaw and fatigue tugged on my eyelids. "I'm going to sleep. Let's meet with Ketiss first thing in the morning, okay?"

"As you command—"

"Do *not* call me Destroyer." I gave her a severe look. "From now on, I want everyone to refer to me as either Justin or Billy Joe Bob Baxter Corinthian the Third, Esquire Junior."

Her mouth dropped open a fraction. "Then I must call you Justin, because I could never remember such a complex name as the second." She touched her gem. "It is, of course, recorded. I could review it several times until I pronounce the name to your liking."

I held back a laugh. "No, that won't be necessary."

"Is there anything else you require of me, Justin?" She touched the front seam of her uniform. "I would be quite happy to experience your demon feeding again, in the name of magic, of course."

I managed a faint smile, but the thought of doing anything with any woman besides Elyssa made me sick to my stomach. "I'm devoted to another woman, Flava. You are a beautiful sera, but what happened earlier was an accident."

She looked down. "I understand. I did not mean to tempt you. If you must kill me, I understand."

"For crying out loud, I'm not going to kill you." I face-palmed so hard I hurt my nose.

"Why do you flagellate yourself, Justin?" Flava looked horrified. "Are you seeking penance for me?"

I could have face-palmed another ten times for that statement. Instead, I took her by the elbow and guided her to the door. "Go home, do three Hail Marys, and go to sleep."

She turned around, her forehead wrinkled. "What is a Hail Mary?"

I charged the gem next to the doorway and a wall closed the opening. I turned and rested my back against the wall, ran a hand down my face, and sighed. "The Darklings are every bit as crazy as the Brightlings, and it's all Daelissa's fault."

I just wanted this day to end. I should've been hungry, but I wasn't. I saw the drink Cephus had left for me and tasted it. The liquid was tepid, but mildly sweet and dark like tea.

I took the gem from my armor and set it on the table. Touching the seams of the Templar armor, I adjusted it back to bikini bottom size. My thoughtful hosts had left a stack of clothes on the table, but the armor was comfortable enough to use as pajamas.

The cloud bed called my name, but first I needed to take care of some personal business. I went into the other two rooms and found one that seemed to be the bathroom. A thick cloud of ultraviolet mist hovered in front of a mirror. I put a hand into it. It swirled, but didn't drift beyond its invisible confines. My teeth felt gross, and I really had to pee. I put my hands into the mist and wondering if it was water or something else. I suddenly felt cool liquid in my hands. Apparently, I had to imagine what I wanted. I washed my face. When the water fell back into the mist, it vanished.

"How am I supposed to brush my teeth?" I imagined a toothbrush, but nothing appeared even when I reached into the mist. Apparently, such a mundane object wasn't something enchanted into the spells here. After several more attempts to procure everything from dental floss to toothpaste, I decided to put my request in more general terms.

Clean my teeth.

I jet of liquid sprayed against my lips. I opened my mouth in surprise. The liquid fizzled on my tongue. Fighting back an instinct to flee, I let the liquid spray until my mouth was full. I closed my lips and almost giggled at the funky carbonated feeling going on in my mouth. Within seconds, my teeth felt polished and clean. I spat the cleanser into the mist where it vanished.

By now, I really had to pee. Even worse, it felt like I might have to do more and I didn't see a toilet anywhere. I regretted not having asked Flava how to take a poop in this place. The mist had absorbed the water and mouth cleanser. Surely, it would take in most other liquids as well, but what about solids? Did angels drop deuces? Did it smell like roses?

I suddenly realized I had no time to spare.

When I emerged from the bathroom ten minutes later, I had a whole new appreciation for angelic bathrooms. Not only had the mist taken care of all my scatological needs, but it had cleaned me right after. Even my Nightingale armor was clean. I smelled even better than roses.

The minute this war is over, I'm gonna replace the toilets and showers in the mansion with magic angel mist.

It had been only twenty minutes since Flava left, but my tired body felt like it had been hours. I headed for the cloud bed and let myself sink into it. It felt absolutely amazing, as if nothing were holding me up.

Just as my eyelids drooped and dreamtime tried to kick in, a sharp pain stabbed me in the stomach like an icepick. I gasped and curled into the fetal position. A sensation like jabbing needles ran up my legs, my arms, and my torso. I made it to the edge of the bed and rolled off. I hit the floor like a slab of beef. It took all my effort to drag myself toward the table where I'd left my gem. Something was horribly wrong. I wondered if I'd sustained internal injuries during the earlier fight, or if I'd completely misused the bathroom mist and vaporized my colon or something vital.

Ragged breaths rasped from my throat. I could hardly move. Every muscle in my body prickled with pain. My neck could no longer hold up my head and my face met the floor. It didn't take a rocket scientist to figure out this had nothing to do with internal injuries.

Minutes seemed to pass as slowly as hours while I lay on the floor, my breath coming in pants. Despite the panicked beating of my heart, I must have fallen asleep, or passed out. Strong hands gripping my arms woke me up. My head sagged forward as someone lifted me. I saw the bodies of Ketiss's guards on the floor, three in all.

"Kill him and pin him to the wall," a deep masculine voice said.

A figure dressed in black from head to foot was writing something on the wall. I realized with horror he was writing in blood. *No Darkness shall ever stop the Light.*

It didn't take me long to realize what that meant. The light represented the Brightlings. The murder of their new religious icon, namely me, was supposed to scare the Darklings into thinking they were powerless to stop the Brightlings. These people might very well be Heretics setting up a crime scene to pin the blame on the Brightlings, or they might be enemy agents like those that had tried to kill me earlier today.

106

I knew one thing for sure. I was never going to get a decent night's sleep with people constantly trying to kill me.

I tried to move. I tried to channel magic. I tried to manifest into demon form. Nothing happened. The person writing with blood traced a strange symbol on the wall.

"Make sure it's large enough so his body will be in the center," the voice said again.

I didn't know how long it would take to finish drawing the symbol, but it gave me a few precious seconds to think. Unfortunately, I saw no way out of this situation. My heart hammered with fear. I felt sweat dripping down my face.

"He's awake," another voice said.

A masked figure knelt before me. "Are you afraid, *Destroyer*?" He said the word in a mocking tone. "I despise what you and your kind do to brainwash the idiots among us into thinking there is a god. Every time a false prophet rises up, we will be there to kill them. Perhaps one day the believers will realize the truth."

I tried to respond with a smart-ass remark but couldn't even make my lips move.

He laughed. "From powerful to powerless. I'll give you a few more minutes to anticipate your death."

Whoever was holding me up dropped me like a sack of potatoes. My nose hit the floor with a painful crunch. If I'd been in control of my body, I would've cried out in pain. As it was, I couldn't even grunt. I imagined unleashing a torrent of destruction on these assholes.

All my rage was for nothing. I couldn't so much as twitch a finger. I would soon be dead and with me would die the hope of saving Eden.

Chapter 13

I tried with all my might to do something, anything, but my body refused to respond. I would have given anything to activate beast mode and rip into my captors like a hellhound chomping a baloney sandwich.

My inner demon stirred.

Oh, are you pissed off too?

Even though it seemed to have a mind of its own, it was a part of me, just like the man brain in my pants, leaving me to answer my own question.

A foot nudged me in the ribs and shoved me onto my side. I felt my back rest against something hard, and assumed it must be the table. The wall with the bloody symbol came back into view.

"Enjoy the view while it lasts," said one of my tormentors.

I had one trick up my sleeve that might work if I could actually move my head. I'd learned how to blink—instantly move myself a short distance—but I had to see where I wanted to go. The last place I wanted to end up was closer to the wall where they planned to sacrifice me. While a blink might take me a short distance away, it would also leave me even more disoriented than I felt right now.

All I could do was watch the man paint the bloody symbol on the wall. I realized, with disgust, he was using the blood of the dead guards. I wanted to tear out his throat with my teeth. One final option suddenly occurred to me. Not wasting another second, I went into a light trance and withdrew inside myself. Dread fought my final hope as I went to the place inside my soul that connected me with my demon half. My spirit resided partially inside my body and partially in Haedaemos, the demon realm. It was a bizarre arrangement that was common to Daemos. To maintain the connection, there was a small opening, a window in my soul to the infernal realm.

Because of my paralyzed system and sluggish brain, it took longer than usual for me to reach that inner plane of existence. I hardly dared to look. When I did, a profound sense of relief warmed me. The window was there even though I wasn't in Eden.

I sent forth a tendril of my essence the same way I usually did when feeding my incubus tummy. Instead of questing forth into the world, I sent it through the window to seek out something that would show these people they'd messed with the wrong hombre.

Hellhounds.

The moment my probe went through the window, I detected a very powerful and familiar presence.

The Abyss awaits your command, said a deep multi-harmonic voice.

I almost crapped a brick. The voice belonged to a very powerful demon known as an Abyssal. I'd first summoned this particular demon as a hellhound. The second time I'd summoned him as a flaming hand to kill off a horde of murderous demon scorps. The third time I'd called upon his services, he'd come in full glory as a massive Abyssal demon. Kassallandra had warned me never to summon him or others of his kind again.

Sorry, I just need a simple hellhound.

I sent my probe into the wilds of Haedaemos, questing for a suitable presence.

The Abyss will serve, said the many-voices of the demon.

It had been a terrible struggle to maintain a grip on my sanity the last time I'd called forth this demon in its most powerful form. I didn't want to risk losing control. I found a dog-like presence not far from my demonic probe and quickly snared it.

Even though my eyes remained open the entire time, I had to fully return to my body for vision. I focused on the floor not far from me and willed the creature to spring forth from there. Thick black tar bubbled. A skeletal head rose from the ooze. Flesh wrapped around the bones as first one foot then another strained free of the birth pool. My potential murderers were too busy watching Michelangelo paint the wall with blood to notice as a monstrous hound broke free of the infernal pool.

Remain quiet, I said using brainwaves. *Hide.*

The hellhound stared with baleful yellow eyes at me. Just because I'd summoned it didn't mean it was immediately bound to obey me, especially in my current position.

I sent forth images of me destroying the roomful of Seraphim with Brilliance. *Obey, or die in agony,* I sent to the creature.

It stiffened, and the rebellion in its eyes faded to obedience. It slunk into the small closet near the bed, its footpads silent. I didn't know how a hellhound would do against vanilla Seraphim, but two would surely be better than one, I figured. I sent my presence back into Haedaemos.

Why do you not call upon me? The Abyssal's chorus of voices sounded a hurt tone.

You're too dangerous. I could barely control the summoning last time.

We seek only to serve. If infinity had a voice, it would sound like this demon's.

Despite the ultra-scary voice, it sounded sincere. I didn't care if it gave me chocolate and flowers. I wasn't about to call on it unless it was an absolute emergency. *I don't require your services right now.* I sent my probe questing. Something immensely powerful glided past my senses. I quickly withdrew for a second to avoid attracting its attention.

When I went back, I sensed the Abyssal lurking nearby. That thing obviously didn't plan to give up. Thankfully, I found a suitable demon and leashed it with my essence. When I returned to the physical world, I felt pressure under my arms and realized my captors were dragging me toward my final resting place.

"He's in some sort of trance," someone said.

"He'll wake up when my sword enters his guts," came the reply.

I felt the demonic presence wriggling on my tether like a fish on a hook. Fueled by desperation, I focused on the floor and called the hellhound into being. As it formed, I sent a message to the other one.

Come out and kill these people!

"What is that thing?" someone shouted as the second hellhound burst from the birthing pool.

The giant hound growled. Saliva drooled from its oversized muzzle. Its yellow eyes glowed with the fires of destruction. Hellhound one—I named him Punky since he'd been such a punk to me at first—lunged for the closest Seraphim. Drooler—the second hellhound—went for a figure I barely detected in my peripheral vision.

My captors dropped me. I landed on my butt, back against the wall. It was the perfect spectator position. One seraph swung a sword at Punky. The hellhound ducked under the sword and viciously chomped the attacker's arm. With a loud snarl and twisting motion, Punky tore the arm free and threw it to the ground. The seraph screamed. Blood spurted from his newly formed stump. Eyes wide with horror, he stumbled backward, feet slipping on his own blood.

Drooler tore another seraph's throat to shreds. Apparently, the clothing my captors wore was no protection against hellhounds.

Light flashed off metal as a sword bit into Drooler's hindquarters. He yelped, spun, and clawed his attacker. The seraph screamed as razor-sharp nails gouged skin.

"Kill the target!" shouted a deep voice.

Two figures charged me, blades held high. Punky sped across the room and bowled into them. The seraphs slammed hard against the window on the far wall. Drooler finished off another seraph and ran to join Punky.

Wait, I sent to them. Teeth bared, basso growls vibrating in their throats, the hounds stopped feet away from the survivors.

Straining with all my might, I managed to speak. "Who sent you?" I could barely move my mouth, but managed to make the words intelligible.

The larger of the two seraphs slid back his mask to reveal a handsome face with a square jaw and large, straight nose. "We may die, but others will come."

"You sound just like the Brightlings." I had trouble with the 'B' and felt slobber on my lips. Just like the other attackers, these seraphs wore no gems of any kind. It made sense now that I knew how the stones worked. An assassin would have to be pretty stupid to wear something that recorded his every move.

My lips regained a little more movement. "I just want to save Eden. If you let me do that, I might be able to help you with the Brightlings."

The seraph sneered. "You mistake us for loyalists to the current regime. Our *people*"—his spat the word—"have proven they are not fit to govern themselves. They've allowed religion to corrupt everything. We would rather live subservient to the Brightlings than allow this cancer to eat us alive."

"You must not be familiar with Daelissa." I felt my legs and arms start to respond and managed to push myself up. "She has declared herself the Divinity. Her people now worship her like a goddess."

The man's sneer faltered. "Lies."

I shook my head. "I'm not lying. If you're helping the Brightlings, why don't you ask one of them?"

"We do not serve the Brightlings." Squarejaw countered me with a defiant look. "You are already a proven liar anyway. There's nothing you could say to sway me."

"I fail to see how I'm a proven liar."

"You claim to be the Destroyer." He spat on the floor. "There is no such thing, just as there is no Primogenitor."

I shrugged. "Believe what you want, but unless you tell me what I want to know, I'm going to hardcore destroy your ass." *Advance*, I told the hounds.

Teeth bared and growling menacingly, the hellhounds stepped forward, backing the two seraphs toward the balcony.

"Who are you working for?" I asked.

Squarejaw barked a laugh. "We will die before we talk."

112

The other seraph pulled off his mask. "Actually, I would be more than happy to tell you whatever you—ACK!" He made an awful noise as Squarejaw gripped his head and savagely twisted it to the side. The would-be informant's neck snapped, crackled, and popped like a bag of walnuts under assault by a midget with a mallet.

The hellhounds lunged forward. Squarejaw dropped the body and jumped back a couple of feet. "Now there is no one left to talk."

"I'm still alive," the informant rasped.

"Not for long." Squarejaw lifted the hem of his shirt and grabbed something small. Red light flashed from within his hand. "There will be no survivors." He tried to leap over the dogs, but Drooler intercepted the seraph's crotch with his teeth.

Squarejaw made a noise like a girl who just found a spider on her shoulder. Drooler maintained the grip on his junk and bulled him out to the balcony. Squarejaw's arms flailed. I noticed a flashing red gem in the palm of his hand. I didn't know what the gem was supposed to do, but felt a hundred percent sure I didn't want to find out the hard way. *Throw him over the balcony!*

Drooler twisted his head hard and launched the seraph far out into the night air. Squarejaw spun like a Frisbee and screamed like a wounded pig. For an instant, he seemed to hover in the air as he hurled one last curse at me.

The gem flashed brilliant red. Squarejaw's body stretched wider and wider as if he were made of rubber. Suddenly he shrank to a pinpoint and vanished. A spherical void occupied the place where he'd been and the vacuum of absolute silence blanketed my ears.

"What the hell was that?" I felt my mouth form the words, but couldn't hear anything.

I saw the hellhounds running in circles howling and slobbering like crazed animals. I turned and saw Flava standing in the doorway, eyes wide, mouth hanging open. She looked at the bodies, the blood-painted wall and backed away.

My earls popped and crackled as if clearing of congestion. The sound of howls grew louder and louder. The void in the night sky closed in on itself and vanished.

113

I worked my jaw back and forth. My ears popped again and seemed to clear once and for all. "Flava, I need you." Without waiting for a response, I dropped to one knee next to the seraph with the broken neck. It didn't take a doctor to realize he was dead.

"What sick ritual are you performing in here?" She looked aghast.

I suddenly realized how it must look with the hounds and blood all over the place. "These men tried to kill me. I summoned hellhounds to protect me."

"Hounds." Flava formed the words as if it was one she's never heard. She looked at the bodies and back at me. "You have strange powers, Destroyer Justin." She stepped over the blood and corpses and knelt beside me. "What do you need?"

I indicated my informer. "Can you save this man?"

She touched his neck and closed her eyes. "His spirit is long departed." She ran a hand over his eyes and closed them. "Who was he?"

"He was with these guys." I pointed out the assassins in their black uniforms with the odd red striations. "I'd hoped to get information from him." I sat back on my haunches and pressed both hands to my forehead.

Flava screamed. She simultaneously tried to jump up and move backward. Instead, she tripped over her own feet and tumbled to the floor on her butt.

I smelled sulfurous breath and realized the hellhounds were lurking directly behind us. "Don't worry, they won't hurt you."

Flava's terrified look told me she wasn't convinced. "These hound creatures frighten me."

I tilted my head slightly to the side. "Don't you have dogs here?" When I spoke the Cyrinthian term for dog, the image of something like a dog mixed with a cat flashed into my mind. Apparently, the translation spell helped my lingual centers use analogous words if it couldn't find an exact match. When I said the word "hound" I spoke it in English.

"Yes, but they look nothing like this." She inched away on her rear end until she found the far wall. "Forgive me for being weak, Justin. Some of your powers frighten me."

114

I stood up and gave the hounds a stern look. *Stop scaring the girl.*

Drooler made a whining noise and curled up on the floor. Punky went to a pool of blood and began lapping it up.

Flava gagged.

"Why are you here?" I asked.

She pushed herself up along the wall and brushed off her uniform. I noticed it was the same one she'd been wearing earlier. "Ketiss assigned me to a room down the hallway from here." She pointed out the doorway. "I could not sleep, so I went onto my balcony. I heard strange noises coming from the direction of your room so I came down here to see what it was. When I saw the dead guards in the hallway, I rushed inside immediately and saw the seraph vanish after your hound threw him into the air."

I walked to the door and looked at the dead guards. "I'm never going to get any sleep."

Flava touched the gem she wore on her sleeve.

"What do you need, healer?" said a voice.

"Legiaros, there has been another attempt on the Destroyer." Flava's eyes wandered toward the writing on the wall. "I believe we need more guards."

"I will be right there," he said and ended the call.

Flava took a deep breath and motioned me toward the table. "May I take a look at you, Destroyer Justin?"

I took a seat at the table. "Knock yourself out."

She stared at me for a moment, apparently realized my request wasn't literal, and pressed her hands to my neck. I felt a tingling sensation on my face and in my ribs.

"You were drugged," she said. "It feels like a paralytic of some sort."

"Did they inject me with it?" I asked.

The tingling sensation increased along my body. "I am not sensing any puncture wounds along your skin, but with your healing ability, it is likely any such marks would have healed already." Her hand shifted to my forehead and rested there. "The drug temporarily nullified your healing ability, but it probably didn't act quickly enough to stop your body from healing minor wounds right away."

115

"Where would someone get such a drug?" I asked.

She touched my temples and a dull headache I hadn't even felt lifted. "A drug this powerful would only be accessible to someone in the military, though there are probably dark market sources for such things as well."

"In other words, you don't have a clue." Whoever wanted me dead was obviously powerful and well connected. I had a feeling my tenure as the Destroyer was going to end in my own pain and blood.

Chapter 14

Flava bit her lower lip. "I will extract the drug and examine it, but from what I can tell, it's one that is often used for subduing dangerous enemies."

"It's used for subduing, all right." Whatever they'd used had certainly put the kibosh on my super abilities.

Flava made a circling motion on my forehead with her finger. The tingling from earlier returned along with a prickling sensation from my scalp. Brownish liquid streamed into the air where it formed a small bubble. She channeled Murk and enclosed it in an ultraviolet sphere. She took the sample between thumb and forefinger and set it to spinning on the table.

"I will have an analysis within a few minutes," she said.

The sound of rustling fabric and the step of boots on the floor echoed down the hallway. Within seconds, dozens of soldiers formed up in the corridor. I spotted a cloudlet loaded with troops move into position midair a little ways from the balcony. Ketiss entered. His eyes scanned the scene and paused at the writing on the wall.

"The Heretics have gone too far this time," he growled.

"I kind of felt they went too far the last time." I stood and approached him. "I understand these people want me dead, but I need to know one thing."

Ketiss nodded gravely. "What would you like to know, Destroyer?"

"How have these groups broken into two heavily defended ministry buildings?" I gazed at the deceased guards outside as one of the other soldiers inspected the bodies.

"They apparently have contacts on the inside," Ketiss said. "At this point, I trust no one but my people with your protection."

A soldier entered the door. "Legiaros, the Destroyer's new quarters are ready."

"Understood." Ketiss turned back to me. "I have personnel on cloudlets all around the building and will keep a contingent in this hallway. It would take a small army to break through."

"I hope that's enough." A yawn stretched my jaw. I was beyond exhausted. If Ketiss could get me through one night of sleep, I knew exactly how to solve this cycle of assassination attempts. "I was going to talk to you about something tomorrow, but there's no sense in waiting."

The seraph inspecting the bodies entered the room. "Legiaros, the guards' gems were destroyed. Something prevented them from transmitting their recordings before they died."

Ketiss folded his arms. "Begin the cleanup and notify me of further developments."

The soldier turned and went back to his duties.

Ketiss turned to me. "What did you wish to discuss?"

I motioned him and Flava into the hallway. "Where are my new quarters?"

Ketiss led us down the corridor lined by at least twenty guards. He touched his gem to the wall. A portion dissolved into a doorway.

Once inside, I noted it looked exactly like the last place, though this one also had a cloud futon near the window. I leaned back against the table and faced the Legiaros. "How would the city legion fare against the Brightling First Battalion?"

He returned a pensive look. "Many of the soldiers in the Tarissan Legion have been to the front lines. They are a match for the Brightling infantry, but would have less success against the archangels."

"Do you have anything to match the archangels?" I asked.

118

He shook his head. "So far, flight eludes us. I believe our most skilled fighters would be a match for the enemy if they had such an ability."

"What about levitation?" I asked.

"Levitation requires too much magical energy to maintain even if one hovers in place." He pressed his lips together. "Why do you ask such things? Do you mean to take us to the front lines?"

"That's exactly what I intend to do."

Ketiss stiffened. "We are at your command, Destroyer. Give me the word and we will take the skyway north."

I gave him a sly half smile. "Those aren't the front lines." I pointed in what I figured was the general direction of the Alabaster Arch. "The front line is Eden. I want your legion to come back with me tomorrow."

His eyes flashed wide for an instant. "To the Promised Land?"

"Exactly."

"We would be honored." He straightened, clapped his hands twice, and gave me a curt bow. "I must prepare the legion at once. It will require several hours to mobilize."

"How many soldiers do you have?" I asked.

"Approximately eight hundred fighters plus two hundred support, which includes logistics, healers, and a command staff of fifty."

"Sounds good." I stifled another yawn. "Please get your people ready. As soon as I wake up, I want to get a move on."

"As you command." Ketiss performed the strange clap-bow salute again and left the room.

"I cannot wait to see the Promised Land," Flava said, her voice full of joy. "We won't disappoint you, Justin."

"That's great," I mumbled, barely able to keep my eyes open.

"I will remain and monitor you in case the drug is still affecting your body," she said.

I was too tired to care. I flopped onto the cloud bed.

Soldiers howl in agony as I cut them down with Brilliance. Blades burst simultaneously from Thala's and Uoriss's chests. Blood sprays from the wounds. Crimson foams in their mouths. I kneel in a lake of blood and look into the accusing eyes of my victims. Thala says something in a faint whisper. I lean closer to her mouth, but the words die on her lips.

I jerked upright in bed and let the unpleasant dream slip away. Flava looked as though she'd fallen asleep while sitting on the futon, judging from the awkward angle of her body.

Why do I keep dreaming about swords in their chests?

I'd immolated the soldiers; cut them down with pure, fiery Brilliance. Channeled differently, the same destructive energy could be used to cut like a blade, just as the Brightling had sliced my chest with a wing. That thought took my brain by the hand and led it to another question. Why had there been blood on the floor? Uoriss and Thala should have burned like the rest.

I closed my eyes and thought back to the incident. I'd been conscious and aware of everything even if I hadn't been in total control. The only people with swords in that room had been the soldiers. I got out of bed and picked up my gem from the table. I obviously hadn't owned a gem during the massacre so there would be no recording from my point of view. Imagining the scene in my head, I willed the gem to replay the video.

The video started from the perspective of one of the soldiers. The view jumped around as soldiers fell. *Pause.* The image froze. Using my hands as I'd seen Flava do, I rotated the scene. Though I could view nearly everything in front of the recording device, everything behind the bearer was gray since the gem didn't have a clear view of it.

Show all recordings from this incident.

A list of names and pictures of faces scrolled onto the holographic image. My heart weighed heavy in my chest as the dead confronted their killer from beyond the grave. Swallowing a lump in my throat, I forced myself back to the task at hand. Touching an item in the list replayed their recording. Most of the recordings were useless since the angle showed only the back of the soldier in front of the viewer just before my white death ray cut them down.

It took some time to work my way down the list. The last three recordings showed the first-person view of the soldiers charging into the room before the playback abruptly burst into static. I reached Thala's recording. In the picture next to the description, she wore a pleasant smile. She had been a lovely sera. Despite her zealotry, she'd been mostly pleasant.

Stop guilting yourself!

I stiffened my spine and played her video. Her video played back from a similar perspective as the others. Since there were no other videos listed under her name, I assumed that meant the colored gem she wore on her sleeve was only for command authorization instead of recording. Thala threw up her hands as my demon form bared its teeth and unleashed a torrent of death on the soldiers. The view lurched and flickered. As Thala fell to the floor, the ceiling came into view.

Rewind.

I paused the video at the moment just before the flicker and rotated the perspective. Though I could see nothing behind Thala, the look of surprise and pain on her face made it clear she'd been wounded. I rotated the image again and saw my demonic shape focused on a group of soldiers on the right, all the way across the room from Thala and Uoriss. As I continued rotating, I caught sight of Uoriss's profile. Her face was locked in a grimace of pain. I let the playback move forward a frame at a time. The image flickered and suddenly Thala was on the floor.

Something was wrong. I ended Thala's recording and went to Uoriss's. Her recording showed the same exact time lapse. I briefly wondered if perhaps all the magic I'd blasted into that confined space might have damaged the gems, but since most of the other gems hadn't shown such anomalies, that theory didn't hold water. It also didn't explain why three soldiers' recordings blanked out seconds after the fight started.

I went to the last recording in the list: Cephus's. He'd been near the back and to the left. If anyone's gem had been in a good position, it would've been his. The playback started. I heard screams and saw a gout of white fire incinerate a soldier. The view shifted to the right, showing the three soldiers whose recordings weren't working draw swords. Something shifted across the view and blacked it out for several seconds. I rewound the video and examined the obstruction. It appeared to be a piece of cloth, but I wasn't sure.

I punched at the immaterial image as frustration got the better of me. "Son of a biscuit eater." I continued the video. The offending cloth went away a few minutes after the fight ended.

"Someone has tampered with the recordings," Flava said in a hushed voice. She looked down as I jerked my head her way. "Apologies, Justin. I awoke several minutes ago and did not want to interrupt you."

I waved away her concern. "How would someone edit the recordings?"

"One of my friends who works for the historical archives said that someone at a higher level could possibly alter a recording if they have access to the storage crystals." She projected the image of a vast chamber filled with glowing crystals that seemed to float in the air. "There was once a scandal involving a sub-minister who tried to erase evidence that he'd abused servants in his household."

"Could someone alter the recording before it left the gem?" I asked.

"They would have to be quite skilled at enchantments." She braced her chin on a hand and seemed lost in thought for a few seconds. "From what I know, the enchantments will notify the historical authorities if you try to tamper with them."

"What's to keep people from covering up the gems with something like their hand so they don't record?" I made a frustrated sound. "What's to keep people from just leaving them at home for that matter?"

"There are ways to rebuild a scene in its entirety even if the gem is covered." Flava stood from the futon. "You could order someone from the historical archives to do that. So long as the recording is not corrupted, they have advanced methods for reconstruction."

She continued to explain the process, but my mind was already wandering down a different path. I had been attacked in two highly secure locations. Brightlings had attacked me in a building

122

surrounded by a security barrier that could detect them the instant they crossed it, just as that same barrier had detected my ability to channel Brilliance. The second time I'd been attacked, my assailants had practically waltzed into the Ministry of Defense and killed my guards.

Whoever had engineered these feats had high-level access. Whoever was in charge of my would-be assassins bore an absolute hatred of religion. The people who followed this person echoed this hatred. If someone who worked in the historical archives held similar beliefs, they would, in all likelihood, willingly help the cause.

So far, I'd only met three people who had the charisma and power to convince so many people to follow them. Out of those three, two were extremely religious. Those same two were also quite dead. The more I thought about it, the more sense my conclusion made.

I looked at Flava. "I think I know who's been trying to kill me."

Her eyebrows arched in tandem. "Who?"

I folded my arms, narrowed my eyes, and gave ample time for a dramatic pause. "Minister Cephus."

Chapter 15

Flava's eyebrows rose another millimeter and her mouth dropped open. "Why would Minister Cephus do such a thing?"

Part of the answer had already occurred to me, but how had he known I would kill those soldiers? Had he taken advantage of an opportunity, or somehow planned this out? The conclusion hit me like a ballpeen hammer in the funny bone. My guts twisted into a hangman's noose and proceeded to execute my stomach as logic led me down a horrifying trail of cause and effect.

"When Cephus used a spell to teach me your language, he was able to see my history all the way from childhood to the present." I dropped onto the futon and gripped the sides of my head. "He discovered how volatile my inner demon becomes when it interacts with Brilliance. That was why he asked me to transform into demon form in front of the Trivectus. He knew it would frighten Uoriss and Thala and cause them to call in their guards. The minute those soldiers stormed into the room, he's the one who sealed the levitators so nobody could escape."

Flava staggered back. "He made you assassinate the other ministers?"

I shook my head. "I didn't kill them." I looked at her. "The three soldiers in the back of the room, the ones whose videos wouldn't playback—they killed the ministers." I pointed at the still-hovering holographic image of Thala and Uoriss soaking in their own blood while all around them were the smoking remains of incinerated soldiers. "Don't you see? I burned the soldiers, but the ministers were stabbed by swords."

I recounted everything, all the way back to the moment I'd met Cephus. He'd seen me beat the snot out of the soldiers who'd tried to imprison Nightliss and me. That was probably when he'd conceived the notion of using me to kill the other ministers. Once he'd read my mind, he'd known exactly how to trigger my demonic rampage.

If Cephus had tried to use me from the beginning, that meant— ice-cold panic raced down my skin—Pross might have been working for Cephus. They might have kidnapped Nightliss. They might have killed her. In all likelihood, Pross was not, at this moment, healing Elyssa.

If I was right, Nightliss might be dead and Elyssa was only days away from death.

My fists clenched tight. I ground my teeth. My body shook with absolute rage. *Cephus, you bastard! I'm going to kill you if anything has happened to Nightliss.* In the calmest voice I could muster, I said, "How do I find Cephus?" I remembered what the minister had told me about Nightliss's bad reputation with the Primogenesis crowd and wondered if it would be dangerous to use her name.

Flava seemed to sense my anger. She backed away a step. "I will find out for you." She tapped her gem.

Ketiss spoke. "Yes, Healer Flava?"

"I am looking for Minister Cephus." Her voice quavered ever so slightly.

"He is on his way to see me." Ketiss made a disgruntled noise. "Apparently, he discovered we are mobilizing and wants to dissuade us from going to Eden."

"Where are you?" I asked.

"We are in the plaza outside the building you're in, Destroyer." Ketiss cleared his throat. "We should be ready to go within two hours."

"Do you know a healer named Pross?" I asked.

"Yes, that is Minister Cephus's personal healer."

"Where does she work?"

Ketiss made a disapproving grunt. "She works for the Ministry of Research. Flava can show you where it is." He paused. "May I ask why?"

"It's nothing important," I said. "When will Cephus be here?"

"Perhaps thirty minutes," Ketiss said.

"I'm going to visit Pross." I took a deep breath to ward off more pain as thoughts of Nightliss intruded. "Don't tell Cephus, and keep him here until I return."

"As you command, Destroyer."

I nodded at Flava.

She ended the communication. "Why are we going to see Pross?"

I decided to use Nightliss's real name. Flava would find out sooner or later. I'd just have to convince them not to sacrifice my friend. "Pross was supposed to return to Eden with a friend who came here with me so she could heal someone very dear to my heart."

"I was not aware of that." Flava said. "Do you believe Pross did not return to Eden?"

I nodded. "I think she kidnapped my friend. Her name is Nightliss."

Flava's right eye twitched. "Your friend is named after the betrayer who caused the Schism?"

"She is the original Nightliss."

Her eyes flared. "Have you brought her here for us to sacrifice?"

"Absolutely not." I gripped her shoulders. "Nightliss was not the cause of the Schism. The Brightlings spread lies about her because she fought against them. The Brightlings themselves caused the Schism."

Judging from the look in Flava's eyes, she was having a hard time processing this. She took a deep breath. "You are the servant of the Primogenitor. If you say Nightliss is not to blame, I believe you."

Thank goodness the Destroyer has street creds. With that out of the way, I switched back to the troubling topic at hand. "Because Cephus lied to me from the start, I believe Pross never went to Eden with Nightliss. Either my friend is dead or Pross is holding her somewhere." My thoughts kept ricocheting between Elyssa and Nightliss. "Pross and Nightliss were supposed to go back to Eden to heal my love, Elyssa." Hot tears burned my eyes. I wiped them away and gripped Flava by the shoulders. "Can you heal her?"

She flinched. "Your love?"

"Elyssa is my heart."

A troubled look crossed Flava's face. "How severe are her injuries?"

After a few deep breaths, I was able to explain the situation. I let go of her and backed off. "Can you do it?"

"I think so, Justin." She looked down. "I have healed many terrible wounds during my time on the front lines. I will do my best."

I allowed a tiny bit of relief to warm the icy despair in the pit of my stomach. Even though it felt like I'd been trapped in Seraphina for weeks, I'd only just arrived yesterday. Elyssa still had time. *But what about Nightliss?* With a name like Ministry of Research, I didn't dare think what kind of horrors they could've committed on her.

"Let's go." I ran out to the balcony and spotted a small cloudlet with two soldiers on it. "You two, come here."

They stiffened and directed their ride to the balcony at once.

I motioned them off. "Flava and I must attend something important. We'll be back soon."

"As you command, Destroyer." The soldiers clapped twice and bowed.

I grabbed Flava's hand and pulled her after me to the cloudbank. "Take us where we need to go."

"Yes, Justin." She directed her gaze to the right and the cloudbank moved in that direction. It picked up speed until we were moving at a decent clip, though nowhere near the speed I'd managed on Templar flying carpets.

"Can it go any faster?"

She shook her head. "The skyway might move faster, but it would take us by a more indirect route." Flava pointed to wide domed structure barely visible behind the taller buildings in front of it. "That is our destination."

"Will we be able to walk right in?"

She glanced back at me. "You are the Destroyer."

I waited for further explanation, but apparently, being Mr. Destroyer gave me all the authority I needed to go anywhere. A few minutes later, Flava landed the cloudbank just outside a security perimeter similar to the one around the other ministry buildings. I walked up to the sentries. A symbol on their uniforms caught my attention. It looked like a white circle around a black void.

I addressed them. "Do you know who I am?"

The two seraphs exchanged glances. "Yes, Destroyer," the one on the left replied. "How may we serve?"

"I need to see Pross."

"Of course." The guard made as if to touch the gem on his chest.

I grabbed his wrist to stop him. "This is a surprise inspection." I motioned toward the building. "Why don't you two lead me inside?"

The two guards seemed extremely uneasy with this suggestion, but nodded.

"As you command, Destroyer." The left guard said.

They entered the security field. I followed them in, but it didn't sound an alarm. I wondered if they'd modified it to recognize me somehow. Many other guards patrolled the grounds. All of them wore the symbols on their uniforms. I put my curiosity about them on hold and entered the building behind the seraphs. They guided me to a holographic three-dimensional map of the building, including several stories below ground.

"Locate Healer Pross," the first guard said.

A light blinked in one of the sub-basements labeled *Restricted Access.*

My stomach lurched at the confirmation that she was still indeed in Seraphina. "How do I get there?" I asked.

"Sir, perhaps it would be best if I call her up here," the second guard said. "We don't have the clearance to enter those levels."

Despite eagerness to tear my way through this place, I kept my voice calm. "Who does?"

He turned back to the map and said, "Locate Neemah." An icon glowed on our level. The guard tapped his gem. "Neemah, please report to the lobby."

Someone sighed on the other end. "Coming."

A portly angel, something of a rarity, judging from what I'd seen, appeared from a nearby corridor a few minutes later. With gray hair and ample wrinkles on his face, he was obviously quite old. His eyes widened when he saw us, but he quickly covered his surprise. "How may I help you, Destroyer?"

It seemed I was more famous than I wanted to be. I turned to the guards. "You may leave now."

They each clapped their hands twice and bowed before turning and exiting the buildings.

"I want to see Pross," I told the seraph.

"She, um, is indisposed at the moment," he stuttered. "Let me notify her of your presence—"

"No." I slashed my hand to stop him right there." I pointed to her blip on the map. "Take me to her now. This is a matter of utmost importance."

Flava pulled me aside and spoke in a low whisper. "Justin, what if they capture you too?"

"Go to Ketiss. Tell him to prepare a rescue in case I don't return."

She shook her head. "I won't let you go alone. Let me notify him."

I saw Neemah reaching for a red gem on his sleeve and gripped his hand. "Don't even try it."

"I was merely scratching my arm, Destroyer." He quickly withdrew his hand. I pulled the gem from his sleeve and took another from his collar.

Flava touched my arm. In a low voice she said, "Ketiss is on the way with troops. He will be on standby in case something happens." She gave me a worried look. "I hope it does not come to that."

I could only nod. "Take us to her now," I said to Neemah in my most commanding voice.

"Y-yes, Destroyer." He led us to a levitator shaft and pointed to a gem on the wall. "You must use my authentication gem and ask it to take us to sublevel five."

I held it near the gem and willed it to take us there. We descended quickly past several levels and stopped at a long, black corridor.

129

I motioned him forward with my hand. "Lead the way."

We walked down the long hall. Rooms shielded by ultraviolet Murk lined the passage every twenty feet or so. Most had Seraphim inside. Some stared blankly into space. Others were shackled to wicked-looking chairs and other contraptions. I noticed placards on the walls outside the cells with notations in Cyrinthian. Thanks to the translation spell, I was able to read them.

Subject responded poorly to concentrated aether injections. No increased strength or abilities noted. Large tumors have formed in the body cavity and brain. Projected outcome: death.

I passed several more placards, each one with similar notations of whatever horrific experiments they were carrying on down here.

We took a left and came to what looked like a dead end with a gem on the wall.

"You must use my authentication gem on the wall," Neemah said.

Suspicion crept into my belly. I gave the seraph a long hard look. "This had better not trigger an alarm."

He shook his head and waved his hands. "I assure you, Destroyer, it will not."

I did as he'd said and the wall misted away to reveal a large, white room. Rage boiled in my veins at the sight it revealed: Nightliss strapped to a metal chair. A large orb attached to a metallic arm hung over her head. Murk and Brilliance arced from the device and into an ultraviolet band around her head. Her eyes stared blankly. Spasms shook her body at each charge of energy.

Nightliss looked as if she were almost dead.

Pross stood in front of her facing away from us. "The subject's strength is related to the mingling of unknown soul essence with aether. Attempts to extract this energy have failed. I'm hopeful—"

I didn't give her the chance to finish that sentence. Blurring across the room, I gripped her by the back of her neck and lifted her from the floor. A roar ripped from my throat. "What have you done to her, you bitch?"

Pross screeched. Her feet flailed uselessly. She tried to touch a gem on her sleeve, but I ripped it off savagely and threw it across the room.

I slammed her feet to the floor and spun her around so she could see me. I felt the sting of demon horns growing from my forehead and let the fires of Haedaemos burn in my eyes. "Release her at once."

The healer made a whimpering sound and liquid soaked her crotch. "Please don't kill me."

My voice deep and guttural I repeated my last sentence. "Release Nightliss."

I heard a scuffle as Neemah made a break for it. I held out my arm and slammed him in the back with a blast of Murk. It sent him skidding bonelessly across the floor. He twitched once and lay still.

I turned back to Pross. "Must I repeat myself?"

Tears poured down her face. She spoke in a strangled voice. "Use my gem on the straps."

Flava ran to the gem, picked it up, and ran them across the straps holding Nightliss. They parted at once. Flava pressed her hands to the small, still form. "She is very weak."

"Can you heal her?"

She nodded. "It will take several minutes." Flava took Nightliss's head in her hands. A soothing ultraviolet glow surrounded her.

Pross sucked in a harsh breath. "How did you know?"

I bared my teeth. "I discovered Cephus's betrayal. I know he tried to have me killed. He must have thought it the perfect opportunity to take control of the Trivectus with Uoriss and Thala dead."

"I meant Nightliss no harm." Pross tried to smile, but it looked more like a grimace. "I simply wanted—"

Rage erupted like an inferno in my chest. "Every step I took down the hallway leading here made it perfectly clear what you want. I may be the Destroyer, but you and Cephus are monsters." My demon surged to life. Before I even knew what I was doing, my hand clenched tight. I heard bones break and felt her windpipe crush in my grasp.

Pross's eyes went wide. Her hands tightened against my wrist. With an awful croaking sound, she went limp. I dropped her body and backed away. Acidic bile burned up my throat as horror seized me.

Why did I kill her?

I slammed a wall of will between me and my demon until it was a muted voice in the back of my head. *This is getting out of control.* How had my savage impulses controlled me? I took several deep breaths and turned away from the corpse. I had to get a handle on this. I had to understand what in the hell was wrong with me.

Nightliss gasped and sat up. She pushed Flava from her and tried to run. Her legs betrayed her and she stumbled to her knees.

I rushed over and gripped her shoulders. "Nightliss, it's me, Justin."

"Justin?" She looked into my eyes with disbelief.

Tears burned in my eyes and relief melted the knot of stress in my stomach. "I'm getting you out of here."

She hugged me fiercely and shook with sobs. "I failed you, Justin. Pross led me here after we left you. She said she needed a few things. They knocked me unconscious and when I woke up, I was bound to this chair." Her eyes lit on Pross's body. She pushed to her feet and spat on the body. "Evil bitch!" She kicked the dead sera in the ribs, sobs tearing from her body.

I pulled her back and held her against me. "It's over now." I kissed her forehead. "We need to go before someone finds us and sounds an alert."

Flava appeared at my side. "I have Pross's gem. We can use it to leave."

Nightliss slumped. "How long have I been here? Is it too late for Elyssa?"

"No," I said in a soothing voice. "We still have time."

"How will we heal her?" She looked up at me with wet eyes. "We need a healer."

"I am the best healer in the Tarissan Legion." Flava made a curt bow. "I will heal your friend."

I released Nightliss and motioned toward the healer. "This is Flava." I mustered a confident smile. "Not only is she going to heal Elyssa, but we're taking an army back to Eden."

"An army?" Hope brightened Nightliss's features. "How?"

"It's a long story," I told her. "For now, let's make like shepherds and get the flock out of here."

Chapter 16

Using Pross's gem, we were able to leave the ghoulish dungeon without further incident. I wanted to free the other prisoners in that hellhole, but for all I knew, every level was full of cells with Seraphim lab rats and it would take precious time to locate them all. I paused for a moment when we reached ground level, torn between the desire to rescue them all, and the knowledge that doing so would take time Elyssa didn't have.

I can't save everyone.

I had to return home, save the woman I loved, and win the war. Once that was done, I could return and help Ketiss clean up this mess. I owed them that much.

I led Nightliss to the exit. The moment we stepped into the plaza, a klaxon began to wail. Nightliss still looked battered and bruised even after Flava's hasty healing, so I supported her with one arm and moved us forward as quickly as possible. The same two guards were at the perimeter when we reached it.

"Sir, we're on lockdown," the first guard said. "No one is permitted to leave until the incident has been resolved."

"I have a very important meeting to attend," I told him. "Stand down."

"Attention all guards. This is a code red alert from Director Neemah." Neemah's voice emanated from the gems on the guard's uniforms. "You are to apprehend the Destroyer on sight for the murder of Healer Pross by the order of Minister Cephus."

The two guards tensed and reached for their swords.

I stared them down. "Tell me this. Why would I be arrested for the murder of Pross when just yesterday I killed two members of the

Trivectus and a roomful of their guards?" I put on a confident smile. "If I could do that, what's to stop me from doing the same to you?"

They took their hands from the hilts of their swords quickly and stepped out of the way.

Neither of them looked particularly happy about it, but I was willing to bet they'd weighed the odds and figured their ability to survive in a fight against me were relatively slim. I looked behind us and saw a platoon of soldiers emerge from the building. It was time for us to go.

I turned to the guards. "Before I go, I'd like you to tell me what the symbols on your uniforms mean." In my short time here, I hadn't seen a similar patch or insignia except for here. Something told me it was more than just decoration.

"It identifies us as soldiers for the Ministry of Research," the first seraph said.

"No other ministry requires such symbols," Flava said. "And this ministry is well known for its secrecy and alliance with the Heretics."

"One last chance," I told the seraph. "Tell me the truth, or you're coming with us."

The other guard smirked. "We'll tell you nothing, pretender."

I suddenly had a bad feeling about this burst of confidence from someone who'd looked ready to crap his pants a moment ago. I touched the security field. It wasn't mist anymore. In fact, it was solid.

"We only needed to delay you for a few seconds," the first seraph said. "You can kill us, but the rest of our people will be here shortly."

I grabbed each of them by their necks and lifted them from the ground. "Lower the shield or die."

"We die willingly," the first said.

"We serve the Void," the second said in a hoarse voice. "After our people are done with you, you will serve or die."

I didn't like the sound of that one little bit. "Is this Void your god?"

"There is no god," the second said. "Only life and the Void."

"In other words, once I kill you, you're gone forever." I dropped them to the ground. "Is that what you want? Oblivion?"

"Justin, we don't have much time." Flava pointed to hundreds of soldiers converging toward us. "We must lower the shield!"

"Where are the controls?" I asked.

"Inside the building," the first guard said. "We have no control over it."

The second guard was on hands and knees gasping after the rough handling I'd given him. He looked up. "You are trapped, pretender."

It didn't take a rocket scientist to figure out that the Darklings who'd been trying to kill me probably came from this facility. I examined the shield surrounding the plaza. Aether wells shaped like flat circular pods ringed the plaza. Each one channeled the Murk creating the barrier. I knew from experience those things were channeling more raw energy than I could match. On the other hand, this barrier had the same weakness I'd discovered in Brightling shields.

I channeled Brilliance in my right hand and Murk in my left. Holding my arms toward the shield, I willed the channeled energy to weave itself into gray Stasis. The gray beam of energy intersected the shield. Tiny cracks ran through the barrier. Gritting my teeth, I put more effort into the channeling. The surface splintered like thick ice. Fissures crisscrossed each other. With a loud crash, the Murk exploded into shards.

Flava channeled a protective barrier. The impact drove her back and knocked her to the ground. Her shield collapsed. I threw up my arm to shield my face. A few shards of Murk cut right through my armor, stabbing into my leg and torso. Nightliss and Flava cried out as shrapnel bit into them. I lowered my arm and saw a jagged gap in the shield, but it was already growing smaller. Angry shouts drew my attention the opposite way. The charging ministry soldiers were only yards away.

I jerked Flava off the ground and pushed her through the opening. She stumbled on the other side, but stayed on her feet. Slinging Nightliss over one shoulder, I ran for the exit. One of the guards who'd tried to prevent us from leaving dove after me. I kicked him in the face as I leapt through the hole. He fell on the jagged edge of the hole. Murk knifed through his midsection and exploded from his back. He screamed. His screams abruptly stopped as the shield closed the breach and cut him in half. The upper part of his torso spilled innards and blood across the smooth surface of the pedestrium.

Large cloudlets filled with legion soldiers arrived moments later. Ketiss leapt to the ground before his ride finished settling to earth and ran to us.

He grimaced at the sight of the glass-like Murk jutting from my skin. "You're injured."

"We all need healers," I told him. I didn't know if Flava could heal herself, but knew she had to be exhausted after healing Nightliss.

Ketiss shouted orders. Two healers debarked a cloudlet and rushed toward us.

"This place needs to be shut down," I told him. Something tickled my lungs. I coughed into my hand. Bloody spittle sprayed it.

"We cannot break through the shield," Ketiss said. "Not without bringing in heavy assault equipment."

The Murk shield had turned opaque, blocking our view. "Where is Cephus?"

Ketiss scowled. "He must have discovered his ruse was exposed because he never met with me." The Legiaros shook his head. "This is an inopportune time to leave the city without a legion. I fear Cephus will have a free hand while we're gone."

"What about the citizen army?" I asked.

"I will contact the citizen leaders and tell them of Cephus's betrayal." He stepped out of the way as a healer examined me. "Perhaps it will be enough." Ketiss tapped his gem and walked away as he spoke to someone.

"This will hurt, I'm afraid," said the healer as he examined the glasslike daggers protruding from my flesh.

He was right. Pulling those shards from my muscle, skin, and bone hurt hella bad. One barbed piece had lodged firmly in my ribs and refused to budge. The healer had to lay me on my other side and cut me open so he could work it fragment free. Thankfully, he numbed the area first.

Flava's shield had saved her from the brunt of the damage, and apparently, my body had been a meatshield for Nightliss, leaving her with only a few bits of shrapnel.

"Can't you just dissolve the Murk?" I asked as the healer removed one last piece that had sliced into my thigh and protruded from the back of my leg. My Nightingale armor was in tatters. The protective enchantments on had borne too much trauma over the past day and a half.

"The sort of Murk generated by aether wells is extremely dense," the healer said. "I would normally take you to a facility equipped with aether wells and equipment designed for such a purpose, but we have packed up much of our equipment for the pilgrimage."

I watched as he wove numbing threads of aether into the wound on my leg. "Pilgrimage? Is that what they're calling it?"

"It is a journey to the Promised Land." He smiled as he slid the bloody shard from my leg. "We are on a holy mission."

The minute we kicked Daelissa's ass, I'd have to sit down with these people and figure out a way to get rid of this Primogenitor nonsense.

"Once we have driven the Brightlings from Eden, we will be the guardians of humanity as was originally intended by the Primogenitor." He hummed to himself as he healed my wound.

My stomach tightened as I processed his words. *Guardians?* The Overworld Conclave was not going to like the sound of that. Then again, the conclave was in tatters. It might take years to rebuild, and even longer to regain any trust among opposing factions.

You're getting ahead of yourself. We have to win the war first, stupid.

It was a sobering thought, but harsh and true. I had an army, but it was still no match for Daelissa's troops. Her people had likely been feeding on humans all this time. She had archangels who could fly. Even the vanilla archangels at the Three Sisters had been tough for me to fight.

The healer stopped humming and stood. "You are healed, Destroyer."

I held out my hand.

He looked at it. "Is there another injury?"

I sighed. "Grip my hand." He did so. I shook it. "Thank you."

"You are most welcome." He shook my hand back. "Is this how you thank someone in your realm?"

"Yeah, which is why it's really important to wash your hands after you use the bathroom."

He chuckled. "Advice any good healer would give their patients." He retrieved a satchel. "I will rejoin the troops. I look forward to following you to victory."

I flashed what was hopefully a confident grin. "We won't fail."

Ketiss approached a moment later. "The citizen brigades are on alert against the Heretics. I think Tarissa will be in good hands for now."

I looked at the large hovering cloudlets laden with troops. "Where are the rest of your soldiers?"

He pointed to his right. "They await our arrival at the pearly gates to the skyway." He turned and barked an order. The large troop transports lifted into sky and headed in the direction he'd pointed. "If you are ready, I have your transportation waiting."

I took one last look at the ultraviolet dome protecting the Ministry of Research. *If I survive the war, this place is on my to-do list.* "Cephus will pay for what he's done."

Ketiss nodded. "At least one good thing came from his plotting. We were able to use the translation spell he modified for you and implement it on ourselves and the troops." He cleared his throat and spoke in accented English. "Now I can communicate with your people."

I managed a satisfied smile. "Excellent. I'd kind of forgotten about the language barrier."

"I will assimilate the spell during the trip to the gateway," Flava said. "I'm most curious to understand some of the strange words you have said. Perhaps I will soon understand what 'poop' is."

Nightliss face-palmed. "Oh, dear."

We rode a cloudlet across the city to the city gates. The soldiers disembarked the large troop transports and lined up on the skyway, which whisked them off into the sky and toward the skylet with the Alabaster Arch.

Flava and Ketiss left to deal with logistics, leaving Nightliss and me alone aboard the cloudlet that had brought us here.

"Though I was happy to see Seraphina, I am eager to return to Eden," Nightliss said. "My people have changed so much. They are stronger in some ways, but weaker in others."

I squeezed her in a one-armed hug. "They've done what they needed to cope with centuries of abuse and threat from the Brightlings."

She regarded me with her big green eyes. "How are you, Justin? Flava told me you've been through a lot since we arrived."

I wanted to talk to her about my demon problems, but decided that could wait. "I'm a lot better now that we're on the way home."

She leaned her head against my shoulder. "It is strange, but now I think of Eden as my home." A small sigh escaped her lips. "You and the others are my family, Justin."

"We've come a long way since you were posing as a little black cat in Stacey's hideout." I chuckled at the memories that evoked.

"Meow." She giggled.

My chuckles turned to laughter.

Flava returned and saw us laughing. "I am happy to see you in good spirits, Justin." A wan smile touched her lips. "Seraphina has not been kind to you."

"Story of my life." I nodded toward the skyway. "How's it looking?"

"The last of the legion is boarding as we speak. We should be at the gateway within a few hours." Flava motioned at a nearby seraph. He brought a small glass container filled with what looked like bread, cheese, and some strange looking vegetables or fruits. "You should eat while we wait."

My stomach grumbled at the sight. I'd been so eager to rescue Nightliss I hadn't even eaten breakfast. "Good idea."

The bread stuff was crunchy and tasted sweet. A large purple pear-shaped thing tasted like an avocado. I expected to find some mystery meat in the mix, but detected nothing unusual or disgusting.

139

A round vegetable shaped like a tomato turned out to be as dense as peanut butter and filled my tummy to the rim.

"Where's the beef?" I asked Nightliss.

She ate a small orange fruit the size and shape of a grape. "Killing and eating animals is not normal here as it is in Eden. There are several different plants bearing fruit with enough protein and nutrients to satisfy all requirements."

Ketiss returned. "Destroyer, we are ready to leave."

I walked toward the skyway. "Let's go."

Nightliss and I boarded the skyway with Ketiss, Flava, and a group of officers behind the bulk of the troops. The cloud road picked up speed as we gained distance from the city until we were speeding along.

Flava looked back at the ultraviolet city on the floating island of rock until it vanished from sight. Ketiss never looked back. I couldn't tell if he didn't care or was simply putting on a brave face.

I took Nightliss's hand and squeezed it. My heart soared.

Elyssa, I'm coming home.

Chapter 17

The hours dragged by as if determined to make me suffer as long a wait as possible. At long last, the skylet with the Alabaster Arch came into view. The floating island teemed with soldiers arranged in neat formations. When I arrived, I was surprised to see that the gateway was open.

A small group of Templars stood in front of the arch. I spotted Nelson talking with one of the soldiers and headed toward him.

"Justin!" Bella appeared out of nowhere and nearly bowled me over with a big hug. She pulled my head down to her height and kissed me on the cheeks. "We were about to launch a rescue operation."

"I haven't been gone that long," I said.

Someone gripped my other arm. "You son of a biscuit eater." Shelton gripped me in an uncharacteristically firm hug. I felt tears sting my eyes and squeezed him back. He held me at arms' length. "Looks like you're mostly here."

"It is so good to see you," Nightliss said as she and Bella hugged and cried. "I was so worried when we left."

"C'mere sweetheart." Shelton enfolded the petite angel in his arms. "I swear to god I wanted to punch Justin in the face when he made the executive decision to leave without waiting for us."

"We could have just portaled in," Bella said. She wiped tears from her eyes.

"We had to hold the arch open ever since you left," Shelton said. "You mom detected someone trying to realign the Grand Nexus to another realm. Apparently, opening the gateway prevents them from removing the Chalon or attuning the arch."

I hadn't even thought of Daelissa trying to realign the arch. She must have guessed my reason for going to the Three Sisters. I looked around and saw Flava and Ketiss standing nearby. I motioned them over and introduced them to Nelson, Shelton, and Bella.

"Ketiss, you coordinate with the Templars and move your troops." I turned to the Templars. "Nelson, you're in charge of logistics. Can you handle it?"

He pounded a fist to his chest. "I'll see to it. I've already sent word ahead."

I turned to Shelton. "I'll see you guys back at Queens Gate in a little bit."

"Off to heal Elyssa?" Shelton said.

"You know it." I grabbed Flava's hand in my right hand and Nightliss's in my left. "Let's go. We have a princess to save."

I didn't give anyone time to comment and marched straight through the gateway.

"This is amazing," Flava breathed.

I opened the closest omniarch to La Casona.

"Truly marvelous!" Flava exclaimed as I hurried her through the portal and into the busy way station. She nearly broke her neck looking around as I rushed her toward the doors leading into the pocket dimension.

"I'm having trouble keeping pace," Nightliss said, pumping her short legs furiously. "Could you slow down?"

I released her hand. "Catch up with us when you can."

"Is this the Promised Land?" Flava said, jogging along with me. "Is the Primogenitor here?"

"Nope, he doesn't mingle with us mere mortals." I led Flava onto the road lined with row houses, entered the first one on the left, and nearly ran into Meghan as she came down the stairs.

"Justin?" She looked at Flava. "Who is this?"

"A healer from Seraphina. She thinks she can help Elyssa."

Meghan pursed her lips with a doubtful expression. "I'm surprised to see you back so soon. Things must have gone very smoothly."

I burst into wry laughter. "Yeah, it was a piece of cake." I motioned up the stairs. "Take us to Elyssa?"

She nodded. "Of course." Her brow furrowed. "I must warn you, her condition has noticeably worsened since you left. I believe the preservation spell will be unable to last more than another day."

My heart turned into a searing lump of ice. I nearly bulled over Meghan in my haste to get Flava up the stairs. I took her into the room and cried out the moment I saw Elyssa. Her jaundiced skin sagged in places. Her eyes had sunk into her skull.

Flava released my hand and walked to the preservation barrier. She looked at Elyssa for a while and finally turned to Meghan and spoke in accented English. "I will need this barrier removed."

Meghan gave her a steady look. "Are you sure you know what you're doing?"

"Once this barrier is down, I will channel a new preservation bubble around the patient." Flava pointed toward the blackened chest wound. "I will then release the wounded area from the spell and regenerate it." She turned to me. "Justin, I must warn you that her skin shows advanced signs of necrosis. She may already be too far gone for me to save."

I felt my chin tremble and forced down a painful lump in my throat. "Please save her." I couldn't say another word without crying like a baby.

Flava's eyes welled with tears. "I promise to do everything in my power."

Nightliss appeared a moment later and gasped as she saw Elyssa. "Is there anything I can do to help?"

Flava shook her head. "I don't think so."

"I will wait back in the way station. If you need me, let me know." Nightliss gave me a sad look, turned, and left.

I pressed my hand to the glasslike barrier and kissed it just over Elyssa's lips. "I love you, babe. I'll see you soon." I walked to a chair in the corner of the room and sat down. My chest felt so tight it was painful to breath. Fire seemed to burn in my heart one minute followed by the cold swelling of dread. I'd never felt so powerless in my life. I'd done everything I could to save Elyssa by bringing Flava back with me. Now it was out of my hands.

I looked up at the sound of footsteps. Elyssa's brother Michael walked in followed by their parents, Thomas and Leia Borathen.

"We came the instant we heard," Thomas said. He looked at Flava. "Are you the Darkling healer?"

"I am," she replied.

"This is Elyssa's family," Meghan said. She motioned to the chairs near me. "Please stay out of the way."

For once, Thomas Borathen took an order from a lower ranking Templar. Michael sat on my left. Leia sat to my right and Thomas to hers.

Leia gripped me in a hug. "I can't believe you did it."

"A healer and an army," Michael said, a note of extremely rare admiration in his voice.

"Impressive," Thomas said in a quiet voice.

"I remember the first day we met you," Leia said.

I nodded, barely able to keep the tears from my eyes as Meghan began to dispel the preservation barrier.

"We were so unkind to you that day." Leia kissed my cheek. "Our daughter stands a chance at life because of you."

"She's here because she saved my life." My voice trembled. Tears blinded me. I couldn't hold back the pain any longer. I buried my face in my hands. "Life won't be worth living without her."

I felt a hand on my elbow. "Don't blame yourself, Justin," said a voice that sounded eerily like Elyssa's.

Wiping away the tears, I looked into the violet eyes of Phoebe Borathen, Elyssa's sister. She crouched in front of me. Though they'd been born over a century apart, the two could have been twins. Seeing someone who looked so like my beloved was more like a dagger in my chest than a salve.

"I'm trying really hard not to feel sorry for myself," I said, quelling the tears.

"When you accept the duties of a Templar, you are taking a great responsibility onto your shoulders," Thomas said. "Elyssa willingly put her life in jeopardy to save you as she's done many times. If she could speak right now, she would have no regrets about her decision."

I knew he was right, but it didn't help with the pain.

Phoebe kissed me on the forehead, stood, and took a chair next to Michael. He didn't say a word. It made me wonder how well Phoebe was integrating into the family after her time as public enemy number one when serving as Daelissa's top strategist. True, she'd been brainwashed, but that probably didn't make it any easier on her.

I welcomed the distraction of thinking about other people's problems, but it was short lived as my eyes were invariably drawn back to the table. Once Meghan finished dispelling the barrier, Flava began channeling a gentle weave of Murk around Elyssa's feet, coating her body as the old spell faded. Elyssa was soon bound in a skintight ultraviolet layer of glowing energy.

Meghan backed away and watched intently as Flava slowly rotated her finger above the area with the wound.

The Seraphim paused, took a deep breath, and closed her eyes. "I pray the Primogenitor give me the strength to heal this woman. Guide my hands and let them not waver." She opened her eyes and looked at me. "I must ask you all to remain absolutely quiet. Elyssa is so near death that it will require my full concentration."

I gulped, nodded.

"I will put up an isolation barrier," Meghan said. "I will be the only one inside with you."

Flava nodded. "A wise precaution."

Meghan waved her wand in a circular pattern and flicked it. A transparent bubble formed around them. Flava looked with interest at the wand and asked Meghan something, but the bubble blocked all sound. Meghan showed her the wand, said something, and tucked it away in a holster at her side.

Flava seemed to brace herself and bent over Elyssa. She worked for what seemed like hours as Meghan dabbed sweat from her forehead and occasionally gave her a sip of water from a bottle with a straw. At long last, Flava backed away and closed her eyes. She spoke with Meghan.

145

I jumped up from my seat and paced back and forth. From what I could tell, Elyssa was still in Flava's preservation spell. I looked at the two healers and waited for some encouraging gesture to tell me that everything was going to be okay.

Meghan sighed. She turned and saw me standing there. Tears trickled down her cheeks. Flava dropped to her knees and buried her face in her hands. Her body shook with sobs.

"No." The words emerged as a hoarse whisper. "No!" I shouted. All hope drained from me. There was no sorrow. No regret. No anger. Only a numb cold emptiness. *She's gone forever.*

Meghan flicked her wand and dispelled the isolation bubble. The room filled with the sound of Flava crying. Meghan came up to me and gripped me in a tight hug.

I stared at the still form on the table unable to make myself move.

The ultraviolet energy around Elyssa's body slowly dissipated. Her skin looked pale as ice.

"She did it." Meghan sounded as if she hardly dared believe her own words.

Comprehension seeped into my dulled mind. "She did it?" I asked.

"Elyssa will be extremely weak until she's had a chance to feed on blood and eat food, but she will live." Meghan released me. "Don't let her do anything strenuous. I'll be right back with blood."

Elyssa's fingers twitched. I dashed to her side. Her eyelids fluttered open. She stared blankly at me for a long moment, nostrils flaring.

I leaned down. "Baby, it's me."

The love of my life looked at me. She drew in a long breath through her nose. She stretched languorously, releasing a contented sigh. Her full, luscious lips peeled back in a sensual smile while she gazed at me through heavy lidded eyes.

With a hiss, she jerked my head down and buried her fangs in my neck. I felt warm liquid trickle down my skin. Euphoria rushed through my body with a comfortable weightlessness. I felt a dopey grin stretch my lips. A warm, fuzzy sensation invaded me. I understood what it must be like for a woman who'd just gone for a long walk on the beach and was just now curling up with a good book and a glass of wine next to a blazing fire.

I'd been bitten by vampires, but even that feeling paled in comparison to this. Elyssa's bite was like no other.

"Elyssa!" Leia and the rest of the family surrounded the table.

I held up a hand. "Let her feed."

Thomas bore an uncharacteristic grin on his face. "It's against Templar protocol, but I'll let it slide this one time."

Even Michael smiled as his little sister nommed away on my neck. "Don't let her drain you. If she kills you, she'll turn into a full vampire."

I widened my eyes. "Seriously?"

He nodded. "That's why Templars don't allow dhampyrs to live feed." He shrugged. "Though I'm sure most of us would have the self-control to stop."

"I very nearly killed someone like that once." Phoebe shuddered. "It was a very hard time."

Wooziness made my knees buckle. I tried to disentangle myself from Elyssa, but she'd latched on tight. I pushed on her head, but was afraid I might injure her.

Leia reached over and pinched Elyssa's nose shut. My girlfriend made an awful gagging noise and jerked her head back. Thomas pressed his daughter's shoulders to the bed. Elyssa's face was a bloody mess. She screamed like a wild animal and struggled against Thomas's grip. Michael gripped her flailing feet.

Meghan appeared at the door, eyes raking us. "What in the world is going on in here?"

"She took me by surprise and fed on me," I said. "Why is she acting like this?"

Meghan reached under the table and pulled diamond fiber straps across Elyssa to fully secure her. "Her body is in survival mode."

Elyssa abruptly stopped struggling and slumped into sleep.

"It will be at least a day or two before she is fully conscious," Flava said. She pushed herself to her feet and wiped at swollen red eyelids. "I saw inside her mind. I now see what you are to each other." Her head bowed. "I would like to return to my people now."

I hugged her and kissed her on both cheeks. "Thank you, Flava. You don't know how much this means to me."

She trembled in my grasp. "I do understand. Completely." She pushed away. "I know you would like to stay with your beloved. Can you ask someone to take me back to Ketiss?"

As much as I wanted to stay with Elyssa until she woke up, I felt the weight of other responsibilities settling on my shoulders. "Can you give me a few minutes? I'll walk you back myself."

She gave me a miserable look. "Of course." Flava took a seat in the corner.

"What's wrong with her?" I asked Meghan.

The healer set up a blood pack and inserted a tube into Elyssa's mouth so she could suck on it. "She's beyond exhausted." Meghan looked admiringly at the Darkling. "Her work is amazing. I wish I were so capable."

"Perhaps you could collaborate with the Darkling healers," I said. "Even though your magic operates on a different level, I'm sure there's plenty both sides could learn from each other."

"That's a good idea," Thomas said. "Healer Andretti, you're the official liaison to the Darkling healers."

Meghan looked as if she wanted to protest. Instead, she pressed a fist to her chest in a Templar salute. "Yes, commander."

I returned to Elyssa's side. Phoebe looked up from cleaning the blood off her sister's face and smiled. "Her skin is already looking better. I guess drinking your blood really helped."

I still felt a little woozy from blood loss. "I hope so." I kissed Elyssa on the forehead and stroked her hair. "Wake up soon, my fair maiden. I love you." I kissed forehead, her eyelids, her nose, and even her bloodstained cheeks. I could hardly wait to feel her respond to my kisses once again. I looked at Phoebe. "Take good care of her. I'll be back soon."

"I'll let you know the minute anything changes." Phoebe reached across as if to touch my hand, but seemed to rethink it and simply offered a smile.

Elyssa is alive!

148

Life was once again filled with promise, but I had an army to train if there was to be any hope of winning this war and keeping us all alive.

Chapter 18

Leia caught my attention as I prepared to leave. She handed me a fresh uniform. "I think you've gotten all the use you're going to get from your Nightingale armor."

I looked down at my tattered outfit and chuckled. "I'd kind of forgotten about that." I went into a restroom and threw on the new clothing. It felt good to be back in fresh armor again. I found Flava sitting in a chair. "Are you ready?"

She nodded and stood.

We walked in silence toward the doors leading into the way station. The Darkling seemed absorbed in her own thoughts, so I didn't bother her with all the grateful hugs I wanted to give her.

"Are you feeling okay?" I asked.

"I am just very tired." She kept her eyes on the ground. "I would like to meet the woman who has captured your heart once she awakens."

I smiled. "She'll want to meet the sera who saved her life." I felt proud of myself for not referring to her as a woman, though being back in Eden made it harder to keep the differences between races straight.

The Darkling troops were nowhere to be seen when we arrived back at the way station.

"I am still amazed by these arches," Flava said in a quiet voice. She stared in open awe at the massive Obsidian Arch in the center of the way station. "What does this one do?"

"There are arches just like it located all around this realm." I pointed toward the control room. "An Arcane in there can link two of the arches and send you instantly to your destination."

"Arcane?"

I was about to launch into a deeper explanation about all the various arches when two Templars called out my name from across the cavernous warehouse space. I recognized them instantly.

"Yo, Justin!" Ash had gone from being a thin Asian emo Goth to a muscular Asian Templar with the kind of thick black anime-styled hair that made him look like someone out of a comic book.

"Dude!" Nyte dragged out the "u" as he and Ash jogged over to me. Nyte's carrot-top was cropped close and he positively towered over Ash. He'd put on slabs of muscle and his voice even seemed deeper.

I looked at Nyte's thick red beard. "Are you a hipster Templar now?"

Ash laughed. "He thinks it makes him look manly."

I looked Nyte up and down. "I feel like I'm breathing testosterone just from being in his presence."

"He's so manly that he only produces bear hormones now." Ash elbowed Nyte in the ribs.

I noticed my two friends were looking at something else and abruptly remembered Flava. "Oh, this is Healer Flava of the Tarissan Legion from the Darkling nation."

"Hello, Healer Flava of the Tarissan Legion from the Darkling nation." Nyte grinned. "With a title like that, are you also the mother of dragons?"

Flava offered him a smile. "You may call me Flava."

"You've sure grown a lot more confident." I regarded Nyte with surprise. "The first time you met Nightliss you just about wet your pants."

Ash slapped Nyte on the back. "Since we've been helping Katie recruit noms to feed the Darklings, we've kind of gotten used to angels."

Flava tapped me on the shoulder. "I'm sorry to interrupt, but might I ask where my people have gone?"

"They relocated to Queens Gate," Ash said. He pointed across the space to the control room for the Obsidian Arch. "You can go in there and they'll portal you to your people using an omniarch."

151

"Thank you." Flava turned to me. "If you don't mind, I would like to rejoin Ketiss and the others."

"I'll walk you over," Nyte said.

I was about to suggest that all of us walk with her when I noticed the way Nyte's eyes seemed to shine as he looked at Flava. "We'll be here," I said and winked at Nyte.

As he and Flava walked toward the control room, Nyte gave us a thumbs-up behind her back.

"How's Elyssa?" Ash asked. He and Nyte had been her best friends when we'd gone to high school.

"Alive, but with some recovery time ahead of her." I filled him in on how Flava had healed her and how Elyssa had tried to suck me dry.

"Wow, Flava must be an amazing healer." Ash's smile faded to worry. "Nyte didn't want me to tell you this because he thinks you have enough to worry about already, but his dad was killed when Daelissa marched her troops through town a couple of weeks ago."

"What?" Shock jolted my heart. "I thought the area was mostly evacuated."

Ash shrugged. "His dad broke a leg during the snowstorm and his mom couldn't get him out of the house." He loosed a long sigh. "I really liked Mr. Connors. He was such a nice guy. Nyte keeps blaming himself because he didn't make sure they got out."

I felt sick to my stomach. Elyssa and I had accidentally created that snowstorm by using magical snow globes we'd found in Jeremiah Conroy's secret vault. The snowstorm had caused people to leave town and stay out of Daelissa's way when she marched her army across southern Atlanta to assault the Ranch, the now deserted Templar compound formerly run by Thomas.

"How did he die?" I asked, uncertain if I really wanted to know.

"One of those damned Brightlings blew a hole through the house. The blast missed Nyte's mom by a few feet and covered her in rubble." He blew out a breath. "I don't even think there was a tactical reason to blast the house. The Brightling was probably just bored or something."

"I'm really sorry." My fist clenched. "You know you guys can tell me anything, right? Just because we've got an interdimensional war to fight doesn't mean you can't talk to me whenever you want, okay?"

"Yeah, right." Ash snorted. "You can't do everything Justin."

"I can sure try." I looked toward the control room to see if Nyte was coming back but he hadn't emerged. "How are things with you and Katie?"

"We're back together again."

I held up a fist and bumped his. "Awesome. Last she told me, you two had split."

"Meh, she got over the whole vampire thing and decided I wasn't evil after all." He threw up his hands. "Don't ever expect me to understand female logic."

"I hear you there." Ash and Nyte had once been given a vampire serum mixed with my blood and god only knew what else. Maximus, a rogue vampire, had hoped to use the serum to build an army of vampires. Things hadn't worked out, and a spell cast by Ivy had changed all the vampires back into noms. Those who'd taken my blood serum had retained super strength and a bluish glow to their eyes.

Ash looked behind me. "Ah, here comes Romeo."

I looked back and saw Nyte running over to us, his big feet pounding the ground. "He looks like an excited Clydesdale."

"Nah, that's way too dignified a comparison." Ash put a hand to his chin. "I think he resembles a mutant-sized orangutan expecting a fresh shipment of bananas."

I burst into laughter.

Nyte gave us a confused look. "What's so funny?"

"How'd it go with Flava?" I asked.

"She said she'd get coffee with me!" His face split into a huge grin. "At first she was all like, 'What's coffee?' Then I told her and she was all like, 'Wow, cool!' I promised I'd take her to try hamburgers too."

"Just skip the spicy Indian food for a while," Ash said with a serious look. "Nothing worse than an angel with diarrhea."

We burst into laughter.

As the laughter died down, a tiny pang of sadness pinched me in the guts. This was just the calm before the storm. Then again, it might be the calm after the storm before a hurricane slammed ashore. After all, we'd already been through several serious battles. I'd lost my aunt Vallaena and nearly lost Elyssa. Too many good people had lost their lives. As much as I wanted to chat and have a good time with my friends, the pressure of responsibility prodded me in the back.

I sighed. "Guess I'd better go get our new army up and running." I gave them each fist bumps and one-armed bro-hugs. I wanted to talk to Nyte about his father, but now didn't feel like the right time. It would be better if Elyssa and I did it together and told him about the snow globe. "You two take care of yourselves."

"Stay alive, bro." Ash pressed a fist to his chest in a Templar salute. "We're all behind you."

"And hey, we just signed up another hundred nom recruits over the last couple of days." Nyte rubbed his hands together. "It's not nearly enough for this army you brought, but it's a start."

"We've got a few more people helping us now," Ash said. "We'll get our numbers up."

"Thanks, guys." I gave them one last wave and headed for the control room. I traveled through the omniarch to Colossus Stadium, which stood next to Arcane University. Members of the Tarissan Legion were busy setting up camp in the large space outside the traversion zone of the Obsidian Arch Daelissa's people had installed there. Large piles of stone rubble, all that remained from construction golems we'd fought and destroyed, had been pushed to the sides of the arena.

The last time I'd seen this place, we'd put up a barrier and left the tragon in here after I'd used it in an attack on enemy forces. Judging from the large piles of still moist dung dotting the field, the tragon had been here only recently. I briefly wondered who'd evicted him from the premises and how. Part Tyrannosaurus Rex and part dragon, the massive reptile wasn't the smartest or friendliest creature I'd encountered.

I watched with curiosity as groups of Darklings joined hands and channeled to create small domed buildings that looked as though they could house about ten people each. As with structures in Tarissa, these domiciles were such a dark purple as to be almost black. I walked through the encampment and found Ketiss near the arched stadium exit.

He saw me and walked straight over. "The Promised Land is truly marvelous." He waved an arm at Obsidian Arch towering in the middle of the stadium. "The method of transport is ingenious, and this stadium is a work of art."

"That's because it's not purple." I decided not to tell him that we were actually in a pocket dimension, location unknown. The arch builders, for whatever reason, had created these pocket dimensions next to most of the Obsidian Arches except for those way stations with Alabaster Arches.

"True, this place is full of color." His eyes roamed the surroundings. "Our buildings are built to withstand attacks should the Brightlings break through our lines and invade."

"Understandable." I looked around for Flava but didn't see her. "I know you're just getting settled in, but we need to talk about a few things that will improve your fighting abilities."

"I am at your command, Destroyer."

"Yeah, about this whole Destroyer thing—I don't want you calling me that anymore."

Ketiss raised an eyebrow. "What title would you prefer?"

"Justin."

"But that is your name." He motioned at the soldiers around us. "It would be improper for us to call you by your name."

I gave it some thought. I'd always wanted to be called Head Honcho, Kingpin, or possibly Supreme Overlord of the Elven nations. Since elves didn't—to my knowledge—exist, and since Supreme Overlord was even more pretentious than Destroyer, I decided to keep it simple. "They can call me Commander Slade."

He clapped his hands twice and bowed. "As you say, Commander Slade."

I really wanted to change this disco clap salute of theirs too, but decided it was far more important to deal with the real issues at hand.

155

I noticed a domed building that was larger than the others. "Is that your command center?"

He nodded. "Yes. Shall we go inside and talk strategy?"

"We shall." I took out Nookli and sent texts to Mom, Dad, Thomas Borathen, Shelton, and a few other people who needed to be in the loop.

Mom replied at once. *When did you get back? How's Elyssa? I'm coming right away.*

I received messages from several other people at the same time and decided not to waste time responding to all of them since it looked like everyone would be here shortly anyway.

We entered the command center. Though it was fairly spacious, I realized it wouldn't be large enough for everyone. "We'll need to relocate the meeting." I'd been itching to use the war room in the new underground mansion anyway.

"I will follow your lead," Ketiss said.

I sent out texts with the new location and had a Templar open an omniarch portal using the arch that was beneath the ruins of the old mansion. The gateway opened a moment later. Ketiss and I went through and walked down the long stone corridor to the large, manmade cavern housing the replica of the mansion once used by the original Arcane Council.

"I hope this is not inappropriate to ask," Ketiss said, "but did the Primogenitor create these arches for you? It is like having the power of god himself to be able to move instantly from one place to another."

I'd decided to stick to the truth when it came to questions like these. "We don't know much about who built the arches." I opened the large oak door to the mansion and ushered him inside. "I once witnessed beings singing an arch into existence."

He stopped and looked at me. "Singing?"

"We call them sirens." I told him how Shelton and I had once been sling-shotted into another realm after an omniarch malfunction. "These women with long living hair were singing and an arch was literally growing from a plain of obsidian rock."

156

"They must also be servants of the Primogenitor." Ketiss gave me a wondering look. "I do not think your journey there was an accident. You were meant to witness his power."

I disagreed, but didn't want to debate him on the matter. I stopped in the main room of the mansion and felt a grin spread my lips. It was good to be home. Bella's Scrabble box was on the table next to a couple of other board games Shelton had purchased so he could actually win on occasion.

"How interesting." Ketiss touched a plush leather chair and looked at the magically powered chandeliers. "I've never seen a configuration like this, though I've heard such things are common in the Brightling lands."

"We don't have aether wells or ways to create the furnishings in a room like you do back home."

"We have always relied heavily upon our magic for our survival." He ran his hand along the leather as if fascinated by the texture.

I let him have a moment.

The door opened. Mom, Dad, and Ivy came inside. Ivy rushed and jumped into my arms.

"Justin!" She kissed my cheek. "Why did you go to Seraphina without telling me?" Ivy wriggled free and gave me an accusing look. "I told you how much I wanted to go."

Mom squeezed me tight before I could answer. "I was so worried when I heard about the attack outside of the Three Sisters."

Dad slapped me on the back. "Good job, son." He nodded at Ketiss. "I'm David Slade, Justin's father. This is his mother, Alysea and his sister, Ivy."

"This is Legiaros Ketiss of the Tarissan Legion," I said.

Ketiss saluted and bowed. "It is a privilege to meet the family of the Destroyer." He cleared his throat. "Apologies. I forgot to use his preferred title of Commander Slade."

Dad chuckled. "No, I think Destroyer sums it up pretty well."

Ivy's eyes grew wide. "Destroyer?" Her chin trembled. "How could you go to Seraphina and blow up stuff without me?"

"I, uh—" No good explanation came to mind. "Let's just save that part for the meeting, okay?"

"It's a pleasure to meet you, Legiaros Ketiss." Mom extended her hand, fingers splayed.

Ketiss responded. "You are Seraphim?"

Mom gave him an apologetic look. "Brightling, to be precise."

A look of absolute shock crossed his face. Ketiss leapt back, hand reaching for his sword.

Chapter 19

"Wait!" I shouted.

Ketiss's hand froze just above the hilt of his sword. "How could your mother be a Brightling?" His jaw worked back and forth. "Why would the Primogenitor use the son of a Brightling as his emissary?"

"She's nothing like other Brightlings." I held up my hand, palm out. "Just calm down."

"I mean you no harm," Mom said. "Nightliss is a dear friend of mine. I fought by her side against the Brightling invasion of Eden."

Ketiss looked back and forth between my parents and me. With a deep breath, he lowered his hand. "I am sorry. I must learn to trust the will of the Primogenitor."

Dad arched his eyebrows. "The what?"

"I'll explain later," I told him. I looked back to Ketiss. "I'm going to tell you a story you might not like."

The Legiaros seemed to steel himself. "I've heard much to dislike over these past twenty-four hours, Commander. I appreciate your bluntness in such matters."

"Let's go into the war room." I herded the group inside the door. Aside from a long rectangular table and chairs, it was completely bare to make it harder for spies to eavesdrop. I sat on the edge of the table.

"Are you about to give him the family history?" Dad wore a mischievous smile. "You might want to get him drunk first."

"David!" Mom rolled her eyes. "Please forgive him, Legiaros. He's not much on formalities."

Ivy reached a tentative hand toward the gem Ketiss wore on his chest. "That's pretty. What does it do?"

159

"It's for communications." I waved off further questions. "Let me give him some background before the rest of the war council shows up."

Ivy looked ready to protest, but Mom shushed her with a look.

It took me a moment to figure out where to start. Seraphina seemed like the best place. "My mother and Daelissa were once the best of friends." I crossed my arms and gave Ketiss a second to absorb that.

Aside from looking as if he wanted to throw up, he handled it pretty well. "I see."

I continued the story. I told him how Mom had discovered the way to unlock the Grand Nexus by singing to the Chalon, a small orb which was the key to operating the nexus, and attuning it to different realms. "Alysea and Daelissa entered Eden, the mortal realm, and soon discovered how powerful they became by feeding on the soul essence of humans. Daelissa invited other associates of hers. Before long, the Brightlings had enslaved thousands of humans and were using them to fight wars, all for their sick entertainment."

"I left them when their dreadful games began," Mom said. "I wanted no part in it."

"This is part of our history passed down by the elders," Ketiss said. "I thought the name Alysea sounded familiar."

Mom looked away. "All this mess is my fault. Daelissa was so popular among our friends. I just wanted to impress her." She squeezed her eyes shut for a moment. "Instead, I unleashed an unholy terror on this realm."

Dad patted her back. "You got a handsome husband out of the ordeal, so I'd say we all came out ahead."

Ivy gave Mom a stern look. "You always told me peer pressure was bad."

Mom would get no complaints from me. I wouldn't exist if she'd never opened the nexus. I forged ahead without commenting on Ivy or Dad's statement. "The first human Arcane, Moses, began searching for others who could also use magic in the hopes they could fight the Brightlings. Baal, the demon overlord of Haedaemos, also thought the

160

Seraphim posed a future threat to him. My father and other demons merged with humans to become the first Daemos."

"There are mentions of such factions in the histories." Ketiss furrowed his brow. "I also remember something about humans the Brightlings mutated into creatures who required human blood to live."

"Vampires." During our effort to shut down the Grand Nexus we'd met the original vampires. They were a lot tougher than their descendants. I didn't want to go off on any tangents, however, so I continued the story. "The final battle was fought at the Grand Nexus. Darklings, humans, lycans, felycans, Arcanes, and even dragons fought against Daelissa's forces. Just when the alliance made a final push for the nexus so Alysea could disarm it, a siren by the name of Melea removed the Chalon from the nexus. The shockwave drained the light from those caught in it, reducing them to dark husks. This is what our side calls the Desecration. Your people refer to it as the Schism."

"One of the Primogenitor's builders caused the Schism?" Ketiss gripped his hair as if he planned to pull it out. "I thought you told me the Brightlings were the cause."

I felt really bad for the guy especially with the next bit of information about to hit him over the head. "Yeah, well, Melea is sort of the adopted sister of a Brightling we're now allied with."

Ketiss blinked a couple times and shook his head. His wrinkled forehead went flat, probably because it was so tired of crinkling with surprise. "This is all so confusing and troubling."

"Tell me about it," a familiar voice said. "I don't understand half of what comes out of his mouth."

I looked right and saw Shelton and Bella standing in the door.

"Oh, you'll adjust." Bella smiled sweetly as she and Shelton approached.

Shelton held out a plateful of doughnuts to Ketiss. "Try one. This is literally the food of the gods."

Ketiss took one and bit into it. "Delicious." He polished it off in a couple more bites. "Might I have another?"

Shelton grabbed another for himself and nodded. "Help yourself." He set the plate on the table.

Ketiss took a cream-filled pastry and bit into it with gusto.

Thomas Borathen, Christian Salazar, and Commander Taylor
entered the room. Despite his customary serious expression, Thomas
seemed in high spirits. The lycan Alpha, Colin McCloud came in
behind them along with a huge man I recognized as the leader of the
felycans. Though he'd never offered his real name, everyone had
taken to calling him Saber since his preferred feline form was that of a
massive saber-toothed cat.

The Templar leaders reached us. Commander Taylor shook my
hand. "You've beaten the odds once again, Mr. Slade."

"Aye," McCloud said as he and Saber joined the group. "Mr.
Slade has a knack for that."

I extended a hand toward our guest. "This is Legiaros Ketiss of
the Tarissan Legion."

Ketiss held out his hand, palm down, fingers splayed. "A
pleasure."

The others didn't seem to know what to make of the Darkling
greeting. McCloud broke the silence. "This is how we greet each
other on this side of the arch, Mr. Ketiss." He gripped the seraph's
hand and shook it vigorously.

Ketiss seemed a bit taken aback by the lycan's enthusiasm, but
quickly recovered. "Apologies. Commander Slade taught me this
greeting, but I have yet to grow accustomed to it."

Captain Takei of the Blue Cloaks entered the room. "Oh, my.
You've done it once again, Mr. Slade." He introduced himself to
Ketiss and shook his hand a bit more gently than McCloud had. "I'm
certainly looking forward to learning more about your people."

"I am very interested in learning about Arcanes." Ketiss looked at
the wand Takei wore on his side. "Is it true you channel magic
through those?"

"We cast magic." Takei smiled. "I believe we will have very
interesting conversations when time permits, Legiaros." He glanced at
the door as more people filed inside. "I believe there are others who
want to meet you, so I'll find my chair and make room." He took a
seat on the left side of the table, pilfering one of Shelton's doughnuts
in the act.

I wondered if Takei had heard anything from Kanaan lately. The enigmatic Magitsu master had departed on a covert mission for the Blue Cloaks after our last engagement with Daelissa's forces, presumably to find where Cyphanis Rax was keeping political prisoners.

Kassallandra Assad entered the room flanked by several other Daemos heads of house.

A dreamy look came over Ketiss's face. "Such beauty."

"Yeah, don't let the outside fool you," Dad said. "She's frosty on the inside."

To my great displeasure, Godric Salomon and his wife-slash-daughter entered a moment later with Yuuki Wakahisa by their side. I uttered a silent prayer that Godric wouldn't see me.

He continued to walk with the group, but once they drew near, he did a double take, as if realizing for the first time that I was in the room. "Ah, Kohvaniss, it is a pleasure to see you here. House Salomon once again stands ready to impart its wisdom and guide the alliance in these troubling times."

How about I impart a flying dragon fist punch to your face? Gathering my willpower, I decided to adhere to expected social standards. "We are bettered by your presence." I made sure to look at the others in the group while I said that so Godric, the incestuous attention whore, wouldn't think I was directly addressing him.

Kassallandra curtseyed, her red eyes maintaining contact with mine as she did. Despite our past, I respected her more than the other leaders, though Domitia Calidious ran a close second.

"Greetings, Daemas Assad." I took Kassallandra's proffered hand and pressed it to my forehead, released it. I turned to Domitia. "A pleasure, Daemas Calidious." I repeated the process with the females in the group and then offered formal greetings to the males. Although my Daemos social acumen was still weak, I remembered some of the tips my father had given me.

"Have I heard correctly that you've just returned from Seraphina?" Yuuki asked. The slit in her red dress ran all the way up to just below her hip, showing off her firm caramel colored legs. She wore her black hair in an intricate weave and heavy eye makeup enhanced her already large almond-shaped eyes.

"You have." I noticed her and the others eyeing Ketiss as he spoke with the Templar commanders. "I will fill in the details during the meeting." I could tell Godric was itching to open his big mouth again so I quickly turned and headed to the front of the room. It was kind of amazing to think about, but I wasn't even twenty and had probably led more meetings than the CEO of a major company.

Cold gray eyes met mine from across the room as Fjoeruss, aka Mr. Gray, entered the room. My friend Cinder, one of Fjoeruss's golem creations, followed close behind him. Fjoeruss was technically a Brightling, thought he preferred channeling gray Stasis. Cinder hoped to learn the secrets of creating golems from his creator. As part of a deal we'd made with the seraph, Fjoeruss was supposedly teaching such things to Cinder.

Everyone took a seat. I caught Ketiss's eye and motioned him to join me at the front of the room. Shelton stared forlornly at his empty doughnut plate. He tried to rise but Bella gripped his hand and gave him a stern look.

I knocked a fist on the table. The room grew quiet. An expectant air hung heavy around the table as curious eyes met mine. I was the first person affiliated with the good guys who'd gone to Seraphina and returned in thousands of years. Not only that, but I'd returned with an army at my back. I made me feel pretty darned gangsta, like Hannibal or Genghis Khan.

I thought of all sorts of profound things to say, but didn't want to sound like a blow-hard so I kept it simple. "I've been to Seraphina. While there, I made new friends and new enemies." I let my gaze wander over the assembled allies. "Though I've returned with an army we still have tough challenges ahead. We have to supercharge them with human soul essence, and we have to find out how to counter the new army Daelissa has gathered."

I paused to let those words seep in and then launched into my story about the past couple of days. As I described the aether vortexes and floating skylets of Seraphina, Ivy raised her hand and waved it vigorously. Mom pulled down her hand and whispered something to the young girl. Ivy pooched her lips in a pout, but I was glad Mom hadn't let my sister derail the story.

I continued with the meat of the story, reciting it as briefly as possible. I made no mention of my demonic issues or my emotional state. It wouldn't be wise to open up in front of Daemos like Godric and Yuuki, and I was also ashamed of my loss of control.

Once I finished, I summed up my thoughts. "Though Ketiss and his people are experienced veterans, I believe it's vital we invest more people in finding human volunteers."

"We now have fifty revived Darklings who have reached maturity," Cinder said in his calm voice. "The number of volunteers has been more than adequate to help them achieve 'supercharging' as you put it."

I looked at Fjoeruss.

The seraph seemed to anticipate my next question. "I can supply more prisms so Ketiss and his people can feed."

"Prisms?" Ketiss exercised his forehead muscles again with a questioning expression.

Using my arcphone, I projected the image of a Darkling feeding with a prism. "The prisms are small gems which enable Seraphim to feed from both the dark and the light sides of the spectrum."

Ketiss's face went slack with amazement. "This is truly the edge we need." He looked at me. "Do the Brightlings have such devices?"

I shook my head. "Not that I'm aware of." I turned off the image. "Darklings become nauseated when they feed from the dark soul essence of humans. When Brightlings feed, they feel an elated rush. The prisms allow Darklings to balance the flow of soul essence so they don't become nauseated. With training, those Darklings can also channel both Brilliance and Murk."

"It takes many weeks of feeding from humans to saturate a Seraphim," Cinder said. "The longer such saturation has occurred, the more powerful the Seraphim becomes."

"Daelissa is extremely powerful," Fjoeruss said. "But because she feeds exclusively on light soul essence, it has prevented her from achieving her full potential."

I certainly didn't want Daelissa figuring that out.

"Apologies if this is off subject," Commander Taylor said, "but can Seraphim feed on each other?"

"We can, but it doesn't have the same effect as feeding on humans," Mom said. "We aren't supercharged from such an exchange."

"We have hundreds of Templars who will volunteer for feeding duty," Christian Salazar said. "We just have to be sure they aren't drained too much. We don't want to weaken our fighting forces."

"Speaking of which," Thomas said, "our infantry will have a very hard time fighting the Brightling ground forces."

"They were outright slaughtered by the bloody city guard." McCloud didn't mince his words. "Those crystal swords of theirs shattered our steel."

"The First Battalion no longer uses crystal swords," Ketiss said. "Since those swords are charged with Brilliance and absorb magic attacks, we long ago discovered they broke apart once saturated with Murk."

McCloud grunted. "What are they using now, toothpicks?"

"Whatever they're using looks just as deadly." I blew out a breath as I thought about the fight outside the Three Sisters. "It's like their swords have lightning running up and down them."

"Vjaltis," Ketiss said. "Only the archangels use those blades. The front infantry use brightswords and glaives."

That caught Thomas's attention. "Brightswords?"

"They are Brilliance forged, but do not absorb magic," Ketiss said.

Thomas laid a silvery dagger on the table and pushed it to the Legiaros. "Our weapons are aether forged by Arcanes, infusing steel and silver into an alloy. How would they fare against brightswords or vjaltis?"

Ketiss channeled strands of Murk, lifting the dagger from the table and rotating it in midair. He closed his eyes for a moment. When he opened them again, the dagger settled back onto the table. "They should withstand the blows from enemy swords quite well, but because they are made of conductive material, they will be very vulnerable to aether charges."

Thomas didn't look pleased with the news. "In other words, the energy from the vjaltis and brightswords will travel through our swords and into our people. They don't actually have to strike us to win."

"I'm afraid so." Ketiss picked up the dagger in his hands. "We adapted to this by infusing our swords with Murk. The opposing charges cancel out each other for a time."

"Are you saying the energy in the swords runs out?" I asked.

Ketiss nodded. "Both their swords and ours recharge by absorbing aether in the air. During an intense swordfight, the energy output is much greater than the rate of recharging."

"How difficult would it be to infuse our swords with Murk?" I asked.

"I would have to ask our crafters," Ketiss said. "The infusion is usually done during forging. It may not be possible to do it to a finished blade."

Thomas tapped on his arctablet and nodded. "Do you have weapons to spare?"

"Not many." Ketiss set down the dagger. "Certainly not enough to equip another army."

I waited to see if Thomas or anyone else had more questions, but the room remained quiet. "I think our next steps are obvious. We need Darkling crafters to examine our arsenal, we need more volunteer feeders, and we need to determine when and where to attack Daelissa."

"Our intel indicates she's at her stronghold in Thunder Rock," Thomas said.

Shelton raised his hand. "I got an idea for upgrading the weapons that won't take any time at all."

All eyes turned to him.

"What would that be?" I asked.

"Duct tape." He motioned at the dagger. "Wrap the handle with a couple layers. It won't completely stop a strong aether charge, but it'll keep the worst from getting through."

"Duct tape?" A bemused frown crossed Ketiss's face.

167

Thomas seemed to seriously consider the suggestion. "Have you ever tested it before?"

"I had to get inventive on a few bounty hunting missions." Shelton grinned. "Duct tape fixes just about anything."

Thomas tapped on his arctablet. "I sent out a general notice about the duct tape. Perhaps it will work until we can look into Ketiss's solution." He opened his mouth to continue when the comm pendant on his uniform beeped sharply. He touched the pendant. "What's the emergency?"

A voice at the other end answered. "Sir, there is a large army moving northeast from Thunder Rock toward Atlanta."

Thomas bolted to his feet. "Daelissa?"

"Yes, Commander."

"Units?"

"We don't have a full headcount yet, sir, but they have several giant battle golems flattening the forest between Thunder Rock and the city." The voice paused. "We estimate they'll reach populated areas within the hour."

Chapter 20

By the time the Templar finished speaking, everyone was on their feet.

"Scramble the Templars," I said to Thomas. "You have full tactical command." I turned to Ketiss. "I'd like you to ride the command platform with Commander Borathen. You two can coordinate your armies from there."

"Yes, Commander Slade." Ketiss saluted in the Darkling way.

I turned to the others. "Liaison with Commander Borathen for your orders. I need every available fighter between Daelissa and Atlanta within the half-hour."

"I'm not sure how we can accomplish that," Christian said. "Even operating all our omniarches at maximum capacity, we'd be hard pressed to send through so many units."

Commander Taylor spoke. "The Grotto way station might be the answer."

"It's in a densely populated area, and too far north," Thomas replied.

"What about Kobol Prison?" I asked.

The Templar commanders looked at me.

"Is it still standing?" Taylor asked. "I was under the impression the arch there was destroyed by a malaether crucible."

"Only one way to find out," I said. "In the meantime, use every available omniarch to portal our forces in." I pulled up a map and traced a line northeast from Thunder Rock. Daelissa probably knew we'd abandoned the Ranch after her last attack. If that was the case, why were her forces on the move toward Atlanta?

Thomas issued several orders through his communications pendant and addressed us. "We have twelve functioning omniarches including three inside the Queens Gate way station." He turned to Ketiss. "We'll send your troops through the arch in Colossus Stadium straight to Queens Gate. From there, my people will coordinate your travel via omniarches."

A young Templar entered the room and saluted Thomas. "Orders, sir?"

"Escort Legiaros Ketiss to the omniarch and see that he gets to Colossus Stadium." Thomas gave Ketiss an appraising look. "Do you think your troops are ready to fight right now?"

Ketiss nodded. "The journey was long, but we're ready to fight for Eden."

"Very well." Thomas saluted him. "We'll meet you at the rendezvous point."

Ketiss left with the Templar soldier. Thomas quickly coordinated with the other factions. The lycan and felycans were encamped at El Dorado with the Blue Cloaks. Most of the Daemos were in the town of Queens Gate in the valley between Arcane University and Science Academy, much to the dismay of the local citizenry.

Queens Gate was populated primarily by Arcanes. After Cyphanis Rax had taken over the Arcane Council, hundreds of citizens had gone missing. We suspected they'd been made political prisoners and moved elsewhere. I hoped Kanaan was having luck finding where they were. In the meantime, all the empty homes were providing temporary lodging for the Daemos.

"I'll rally the Daemos and await travel coordination in the Queens Gate way station," Dad said.

Nightliss entered the war room. Her eyes were bloodshot and the color hadn't fully returned to her face. She came up to me. "Why wasn't I told about this meeting?"

"You need to rest," I said.

She poked me in the chest. "So do you."

I pulled her to the side. "Daelissa is moving on Atlanta. We don't have time to argue about this now."

Her eyes widened. "Why would she attack Atlanta?"

170

"That's what I want to know." I motioned Bella to us.

"Nightliss, what are you doing out of bed?" Bella made a tsking sound.

By now, the room was nearly empty.

"Justin." Thomas pointed to a red line and a blue line on a holographic map hovering above the table. "We're assembling at the blue line. Perhaps you should leave from the Queens Gate omniarch."

Since I didn't have an image of the destination, I couldn't use the omniarch here to reach the rendezvous. "I will." I saw how close the red line was to the Atlanta airport. "Why is Daelissa attacking Atlanta? It doesn't make any tactical sense."

"I received word that the Exorcists have activated their covert agents in Washington D.C. and other centers of government around the world. It would seem she's preparing to launch a political offensive." Thomas's eyes seemed to gaze into the distance. "I think her strategy in this attack is twofold. First, she plans to show the world what she's capable of. Secondly, she knows you and I call the Atlanta area home and will rise to defend it."

I pshawed. "We'd defend any city threatened by her."

"True, but she likely believes this attack guarantees we'll send everything against her."

I almost asked why she'd want to provoke us but it didn't take long for me to see the underlying strategy. "She probably knows something about our Darkling army. She knows we're still recovering from the last battle." I tapped a finger to my chin. "She's had over a week for her fresh Brightling troops to feed on humans while the Darklings have just arrived." I deactivated the map holograph and tucked my arcphone back into my pocket. "Daelissa knows she can beat us right now. If we had time to supercharge the troops, it might be a different story."

"That leaves us with few possibilities," Thomas said. "Either we fight her now and do our best to survive, or we prepare for the long term and let Atlanta fall."

I pondered the idea. *Atlanta is my home!* My inner demon growled like a dog defending its territory. No, I couldn't stand by and do nothing. Besides, there were other reasons to defend my home turf.

"By the time we prepare for the long haul, Daelissa's political operatives might have taken control of major governments." I shook my head. "We could be fighting the nom military before long."

"That is a possibility." Thomas gave me a grim look. "I spoke with McLean about possible Illuminati help."

"The last time I talked to him he said they had a new leader who was pulling the organization back together."

"That's why I spoke with him." He picked up the dagger he'd handed to Ketiss earlier and sheathed it. "Your father has also activated the Daemos operatives in various world governments. I can only imagine the brutal games of espionage playing out at high levels."

"One thing is for sure," I told him. "The world will be a very different place a few hours from now."

"I'm afraid you're right." Thomas sighed. "The Custodians are attempting to manufacture another evacuation, but there simply isn't time to clear a major metropolitan area."

"Fausta is going to pop a blood vessel before this is over." Once a master-at-arms for the Colombian Templars, the feisty Italian was now in charge of keeping the noms blissfully unaware of the Overworld.

"I should go," Thomas said. "I'll see you at the rendezvous."

"I'll take care of Nightliss," Bella said.

"I should be fighting!" Nightliss said.

Shelton groaned. "Great, we get to babysit a tired angel while you have all the fun."

Nightliss gave Shelton a dangerous look. "Do not talk about me as if I am a child."

"Whoa, Nellie!" He gave me a desperate look. "Please let me come with you."

"Harry Shelton, you're staying with me." Bella put her hands on her hips.

"Sorry, pal." I actually wasn't all that sorry to keep them out of danger. "Will you keep an eye on Elyssa's condition for me?"

"Of course," Bella said.

I headed for the door, paused, turned around. "If she regains lucidity while I'm gone, would you let her know I love her?"

"And then we'll hold her and squeeze her and call her George." Shelton snorted. "Go beat Daelissa to a bloody pulp, then come back here and tell Elyssa yourself."

I managed a smile. "Sure. Easy, peasy, lemon squeezy." Without further ado, I headed to the omniarch and went through the portal with Thomas.

We stepped through the gateway and into the Queens Gate way station. Darkling troops and Templar soldiers formed neat ranks stretching across the cavernous space and into the control room where the omniarches were located. The double doors leading into the pocket dimension hung open. Daemos streamed through. Most remained in human form, though several had morphed into larger half demons. A blue-skinned female, her tail swishing with agitation, strode past me, six large hellhounds panting at her heels.

Every Daemos had several of the giant hounds with them, thickening the air with a sulfurous odor I honestly found somewhat pleasant. Many Darklings looked around with confusion as if trying to identify who among them had cut the cheese. Someone shouted a command and the lines of Templars and Darklings began to move. Like a giant millipede gaining speed, they marched faster and faster into the control room.

Back when we'd had only a couple of omniarches to use, moving so many troops would've taken at least an hour. With the four in operation here, the troops sped through in a quarter of the time.

Thomas joined the other commanders and raced through after the troops. I detoured to the Templar supply depot and took a high-performance flying carpet. As I entered the control room and headed for the nearest portal, I couldn't help but feel that I'd forgotten something. I stepped through the shimmering gateway and emerged on a wide strip of asphalt outside a large dilapidated warehouse. I unrolled the flying carpet, hopped on it, and levitated it a few yards to survey the surroundings.

It suddenly occurred to me why I felt as if I'd left something behind, or rather, someone. Elyssa was almost always by my side and

173

now she wasn't. I kept expecting to feel her arms wrap around my waist, or to hear her joke about the oncoming danger to alleviate tension. The lack of her presence made me feel uncertain. Incomplete.

With some effort, I tucked away the sadness. *Elyssa is alive!* All I had to do was win this battle and I could go home to her. I was going to turn this lemon Daelissa was trying to shove down our throats into a giant can of lemon whoop-ass.

I took a deep breath and returned my thoughts to the battle ahead. Large warehouses and other industrial buildings occupied the landscape. Our forces assembled in a wide but empty parking lot. Weeds and grass grew between the latticework of cracks in the old gray asphalt. The red brick buildings around us looked as though they hadn't seen use for quite some time. According to the map on my phone, we were on the industrialized southwest side of town. The airport was less than a couple of miles to the northeast.

A cold breeze stirred the long weeds in the asphalt. Dark gray clouds above threatened rain. The thunderous sound of a jet taking off rumbled in the air.

A trumpet sounded from below. I looked down as the large rectangular command platform rose from the ground. Thomas and the other Templar commanders stood around a table in the center of it. A holographic image of the battleground hovered before them. Coordinators manned stations arranged in a circle around the core.

I looked to the southwest as a great crackling sound split the air followed by a thud. In the distance, I made out the great black humanoid shape of a stone golem wading through the forest around Thunder Rock. It looked almost like a person wading through chest-high marsh grass, except in this case, it was pushing through trees. The onyx goliath stood at least three stories high. I couldn't see the other golems the scouts had sighted, which made me think they must be walking in single file. The swath of destruction they were creating was more than enough for an army to march through.

The Darklings deployed cloudlets and hovered a few feet off the ground. Blue Cloaks rose on flying carpets. Templar Arcanes pushed hovering siege engines into place and loaded them with aether crucibles that glowed with destructive energy. Templar soldiers

174

formed lines with the Darkling infantry. Lycans and felycans split into packs mixed with feline and canine shifters. As they morphed into animal form, the packs vanished into the surroundings, ready to flank the enemy once they showed their faces. Daemos forces split in half and spread to the outer edges of the army as well. I lost count of the hellhounds and hoped they were enough.

Fjoeruss's army of gray men gathered near the back of the army. I saw their master hovering over them on a flying carpet. They divided into three platoons by specialization. He'd designed some to be proficient in countering magic while others were more deadly in the physical sense. Each one of the gray-skinned golems looked the spitting image of their creator. Fjoeruss claimed to have giant and experimental golems of his own, but they were nowhere to be seen.

I navigated my carpet to the Templar command platform and got Thomas's attention. "Do we have any giant golems to counter theirs?"

"We have construction golems, but they're not outfitted for combat," he replied. "Our Arcanes simply haven't had the time to construct anything like those."

"What about Fjoeruss's experimental golems?"

"The only way to get them here would be using an Obsidian Arch." Thomas tapped something on his arctablet. "My scouts report that the Kobol Prison Obsidian Arch is still functional, but there's a deployment of enemy soldiers guarding it. We can't spare enough people to take it."

Daelissa had been using Kobol Prison to revive husked Seraphim. Though a malaether crucible—the magical equivalent of a small nuclear warhead—had exploded there, it seemed it hadn't put her out of business.

"How large a force?" I asked.

"About three hundred units consisting of vampires, battle mages, and a few dozen Nazdal that must have survived the battle at the Grand Nexus." He shook his head. "I'm afraid we'll have to do this without the benefit of Fjoeruss's battle golems." He looked toward the oncoming monsters. "Daelissa's seem to be standard goliath configuration with what appears to be heavily modified weaponry."

He frowned. "They have some kind of crystal shards, but we're unsure of their capabilities."

As the thunderous footsteps of the goliaths drew closer, another loud noise drew my attention. I looked behind us and saw a helicopter racing toward the giants. Judging from the bright yellow decal on the side, it was a news chopper. The aircraft abruptly swooped around and rotated. A door slid open and a large camera appeared, pointing toward us. I could only imagine what must be going through the minds of the viewers.

"This isn't good," I said.

One of the Templar coordinators looked up from her console and spoke to Thomas. "The Custodians have enacted a distortion spell in this area to disrupt nom communications and to conceal a large area from outside view. The helicopter shouldn't be able to transmit back to base."

I breathed a sigh of relief. "In other words, we're not on live T.V. right now."

"Not now," Thomas said, "but it won't prevent them from recording the incident."

Still, a recording was more easily destroyed than convincing several million people they hadn't just seen a supernatural war erupt on the outskirts of town. A flying carpet with Custodians rose from the ground and intercepted the news chopper.

Several hundred yards behind us, the air shimmered and crackled with orange energy. I was about to put everyone on red alert but Thomas watched it calmly. Over the next several minutes, the event repeated itself in a wide radius around us.

Thomas seemed to sense my confusion. "That's the obfuscation spell. From the other side of the barrier, the air will look smoggy and clouded. It doesn't render everything invisible, but it should make it a lot harder to be noticed."

"Can they interdict this zone like Thunder Rock used to be?" I asked.

He shook his head. "True interdiction takes time and power to implement. What we're using now is the equivalent of magical duct tape."

"Let's hope duct tape wins the day."
Otherwise, Atlanta was in for a very nasty surprise.

Chapter 21

When the onyx goliath was a couple hundred yards away, four more branched off from behind it. Two goliaths went to its left while the other two went to its right. Each giant bristled with crystal shards I assumed were capable of firing destructive spells. Each had a distinct color—jade, gray, brown, and white quartz. When we'd invaded Queens Gate not long ago, Elyssa and I had counted at least ten of the monstrous creations. Either the other five weren't fully operational, or Daelissa had other plans for them.

Part of me was relieved they weren't here. Another part of me didn't know if five more would make much of a difference. Fighting her new army would be tough enough without these monsters to deal with.

Lanaeia, a silvery-haired sera with elfin features, flew to me on her carpet. "Is Nightliss here?"

I shook my head. "She's still recovering from her ordeal." I looked at the soft-spoken sera. "Are you prepared to fight?"

She looked down. "I am prepared to do what must be done."

Mom and Ivy swooped in on a flying carpet and hovered beside me. "Those things are huge!" Ivy clapped her hands together as if they were the bestest thing she'd ever seen.

"You realize they're about to trample us," I said.

"I know." She crossed her arms and gave me a look. "I'm just excited about blowing them up." She tugged on Mom's dress. "Can I ride with Justin?"

Mom looked at me. "I don't know—"

She jumped up and down. "Please? Pretty please? With strawberries on top?"

I didn't like the idea of my sister being in a warzone, but it wasn't like this was her first battle. She was also a lot stronger than she looked. I took her hand and helped her over to my carpet. "Come on over, sis."

Ivy gripped me in a tight hug. "Thanks, bro!"

Lanaeia regarded Mom uncertainly. "Might I ride with you, Alysea? I believe we would do better as a team."

Mom nodded. "Of course." She reached over and touched my arm. "Be careful, son."

Lanaeia stepped onto Mom's carpet and rolled hers up.

As the goliaths drew closer, I saw movement on their shoulders and realized there were soldiers piggybacking on the lumbering stone giants. More precisely, the archangels perched there. The onyx golem destroyed the tree line at the edge of the parking lot with its massive flat feet and stopped. The other goliaths drew even with it and halted.

Behind the goliaths, infantry spread into formations. Battle mages and Exorcists hovered in the air aboard flying carpets.

A lone figure in white stood atop the onyx giant. She spoke in a voice enhanced by an amplification spell. "Justin Slade, you poor stupid creature. Do you really think your feeble forces can stop mine?"

I cast an amplification spell of my own and replied. "How's your nose, Daelissa? I hope it healed crooked after I punched you in the face."

"Petty boy." She made a clicking sound with her tongue. "You were lucky at our last encounter. Now I see you've truly scraped the gutter and dredged up scum to replace all those soldiers you lost the last time you dared fight me." She made a spitting sound. "I will give your Darklings a chance to bow before me, their true goddess. If they surrender now, I will be merciful to them and their speck of land in Seraphina."

"I have a better idea," I called back. "Why don't you surrender now and I promise not to hand you over to the Darklings so they can beat the crap out of you for being such a bitch to them all these millennia?"

Daelissa raised her hands in a magnanimous gesture and ignored me. "I will extend this amnesty to all who abandon this fool child and bow before me. Simply come before me and drop to your knees. Acknowledge me as your one true goddess." She beamed a smile and stood there as if she'd just given everyone the greatest gift a person could give.

"Do we get doggy treats if we're good little worshipers?" I glanced around and saw not a single person taking her up on the offer. "Here's a clue, Daelissa. Nobody likes a narcissistic bully who thinks they own the world."

"If that's true, how did she get an army?" Ivy asked me in a soft voice.

I deactivated the amplification spell for a moment. "There's a difference between following someone out of fear and following them because they deserve it."

"Has this boy truly brainwashed each and every one of you?" Daelissa said. "I assure you he is nothing but a liar."

As Daelissa spoke, I examined the goliaths. In addition to the crystal shards, ruby-colored gems gleamed in their eye sockets and jagged teeth protruded from their mouths. Golem makers rarely went through the trouble of making mouths or noses for such massive creations. I assumed it must be for the fear factor. Intimidation could be an effective tool as evidenced by the unsettled looks on the Darklings from Pjurna. I wondered if they'd ever seen anything like goliaths on Seraphina.

I knew from experience the feet and legs were the best places to attack these monsters. Unfortunately, it appeared the engineers had thickened the legs and reinforced the connection to thick, domed feet. The golems didn't have bendable joints to attack. The magic, which animated the stone, also gave it flexibility almost like rubber. The only other weak spot would be the magic spark, which animated the golem. The spark could be located just about anywhere—the chest, the head, or even the butt. On something so ginormous I wouldn't even know where to begin looking.

Daelissa finished her little speech. I was still trying to come up with an appropriate smart-assed remark when she thrust her hand forward. The golems opened their mouths and roared. Although I knew the sounds came from magical special effects, it was still scary as hell. A throbbing hum filled the air and a sullen glow infected the crystal shards.

Archangels leapt from their high perches. Brilliant white wings unfolded as they streaked toward the Darklings on cloudlets. The goliaths simultaneously stepped forward, giant feet crushing the asphalt. The hum rose to a shriek.

Yellow light lanced from the crystal shards with a grating screech. Several flying carpets bearing Blue Cloaks burst into flames and spiraled toward the ground. A torrent of deadly energy engulfed a Darkling cloudlet, leaving nothing but ashes to fall in its wake.

Thomas shouted orders. Our catapults launched crucibles at the golems. Most of them exploded ineffectually against the stone, though a couple managed to crack the weapon shards on the jade golem. I heard the low humming noise again. When it reached a high-pitched whine, the shards once again erupted with screeching death rays.

Archangels engaged the Darklings on the cloudlets. Dark steel clashed with vjatis. One archangel ducked and spun. His wings flared wide and sliced through two Darklings. The other three defenders blocked the blow with their swords. The archangel leapt into the air and blasted them with Brilliance. The Darklings screamed and died. A fleet of flying carpets rushed to their aid. I spotted Joss and Otaleon, both revived Darklings, spearing the enemy archangels with bolts of Murk. Other revived Darklings who'd had time to feed from humans helped to shield soldiers from the brutal attacks of the archangels.

Another burst of deadly energy from the golems obliterated flying carpets and cloudlets, sending our people falling to the hard ground below. Blue Cloaks and Templars managed to catch some of the survivors amidst the ashes of those who'd not been so lucky.

A third wave of crucibles crashed into the golems, destroying one of the crystal shards on the onyx golem. At this rate, we'd all be dead before we disarmed even one of the damned things.

Thomas turned to me. "We've got to do something about those shards."

I had something of an idea percolating in my head. "Maybe if we get up close and personal Ivy and I can blast the shards apart."

"It might work," Mom said. "Lanaeia and I will assist."

"Target designations Onyx and Jade should be priority," Thomas said.

"Why those two?" I asked.

"Watch targets Bronze, Ash, and Quartz." He motioned toward the brown, gray, and white golems as they fired another salvo of death rays. One laser hit a flying carpet but didn't destroy it. "The other golems don't have as much firepower. I think their weapons spells were rushed or are incomplete."

I winced at the rain of ashes where the jade golem's attack had directly hit another target. "We're on it." I pointed to Onyx. "It's already damaged, so let's finish it off if we can." I urged the flying carpet to top speed and raced toward the goliath. Its head rotated. Twin red beams speared from its eyes. I twisted the carpet into a barrel roll over the attack.

"It burned my hair!" Ivy said in an outraged voice. "I knew I shouldn't have worn pigtails to war."

I was too busy dodging the goliath's giant fist as it tried to smack us out of the sky. The air hummed and vibrated with magic as the giants recharged their primary weapons. Judging from the pitch of the hum, they were about halfway there. Jade's massive arm swung toward us as I maneuvered away from Onyx's strike. I jerked the carpet up at the last minute and took us into a steep climb. Onyx's head rotated a hundred and eighty degrees like an owl. The gem eyes fired another blast at us. I blocked it with a shield.

I felt warmth at my back and turned. Ivy had channeled a shield to block us from Jade's eye lasers. Mom and Lanaeia swooped in behind us. Lanaeia thrust her fists toward Jade's left eye and unleashed a gout of Brilliance. The eye was nearly as tall as her and apparently magic resistant. For a second, nothing happened. Then a crack formed in the center of the red gem. Mom whipped the carpet around and flooded the crack with white light. The eye shattered.

"I can do that," Ivy said. She gritted her teeth and pummeled Onyx's left eye with white energy. Heat washed across my skin from the intensity of the attack. The eye exploded. She raked the blistering energy across the other eye, leaving a furrow of molten lava in the stone golem's face. The other eye drooped into a molten glob.

Movement caught the corner of my vision. I threw up a shield in time to intercept attacks from battle mages as they rose to stop us from crippling the goliaths. Mom and Lanaeia destroyed the second eye of Jade and turned to face the new threat.

The weapon shards erupted with another discharge. More of our people fell. I swept our carpet to the far side of the goliath to avoid more attacks from the battle mages. Lanaeia swept Brilliance across the chest of a man and cut him in half. With her other hand, she burned a hole in a carpet, sending its occupants plummeting earthward.

I took a quick glance at the battle. Nearly half of the Darkling cloudlets were either gone or empty of soldiers. Brightling infantry poured between the feet of the marching golems and into our ranks.

"Justin!" Ivy shouted.

I caught sight of a giant fist and whisked us out of the way just in time. Thankfully, the golems were big and slow with their physical attacks. I took aim at the nearest shard and blasted it with Brilliance. It glowed white hot, cracked, and splintered. I felt sweat break on my forehead from the effort. Ivy took aim at another shard with a massive pulse of energy. The target exploded, leaving a blackened crater where it had been.

I gave her a surprised look. "You've gotten a lot stronger."

"I've been dual feeding." She grinned. "I can channel Murk now too, but it's not as good as yours."

I dodged a flurry of spells from pursuing battle mages. Mom incinerated one of the attackers while Lanaeia blew the other out of the sky.

I gave Mom a thumbs up and turned to Ivy. "Your Brilliance channeling seems even more powerful than mine now."

We circled around to the back of the golem as the shards discharged again. I tried not to look at the damage to our forces, but smoke and ash rained from the sky. Crucibles exploded against the other nearby golems, but noticeably didn't target Onyx. I was glad

183

Thomas knew how to conduct a battle. Ivy and I blasted several shards on the back of the golem. Two battle mages zipped toward us. I heard a loud whoosh and slid the carpet to the side just as the golem reached over its back to swat us. Ivy flung a glowing white aether disc at the enemy carpet. It zinged through the air and sliced the rug in half. The mages fell screaming.

Ivy pumped her fist. "Booyah!"

"Great, now you're starting to sound like me."

She giggled.

Another flight of battle mages decided to try their luck.

"We'll hold them off," Mom shouted. "You take out the shards!" She slid the carpet to a sideways stop and sent Brilliance streaking toward the oncoming attackers.

I went beneath Onyx's arm and strafed around the front. Pulses of ultraviolet Murk streaked into the sky like arrows from the Darkling army. Some of the archangels fell to the ground. Deadly aether rained down on the attacking Brightling army. Their shields shimmered with hundreds of impacts.

Ivy destroyed two more shards. I sent a weave of gray Stasis at one of the crystals. It rewarded me by crumbling apart like chunks of ice. We finished off the last two shards, rendering Onyx without weapons aside from its physical ability to smash our ground troops into meat pancakes.

"Look over there!" Ivy pointed to Quartz. Dozens of gray men scaled the monster, planting gray bricks all along the golem's torso. One of its shards fired, blasting a gray man far into the air, its body burning like a meteor.

Ivy laughed. "They look like rabid butt monkeys in business suits."

"Like what?" I gave her a confused look.

"I dunno." She grinned. "It seemed like something you would say."

"The scary thing is you're probably right."

The gray men leapt from Quartz. I spun the carpet around and saw Brightlings on a carpet attacking Mom and Lanaeia. An explosion rocked the carpet forward and hot air buffeted us. I looked back. Quartz's torso was badly damaged. Nothing was left of its weapons but jagged stumps. The golem ignored the damage. The shards energized and pulsed. The crystals must have focused the energy toward a direction. With them destroyed, the energy had nowhere to go.

Quartz's torso glowed. A muffled explosion rocked the stone creature. Its forward march stopped. With a loud crunching grind, the goliath toppled toward our army. I didn't have time to watch—Mom and Lanaeia were in trouble. Two carpets, each bearing a pair of Brightlings, streaked after them.

Ivy sliced off the arm of one enemy Brightling with an energy disc. I threw up a refractive shield behind Mom as an attacker flanked them. Their attacks bounced off.

"It's the Slade boy!" a seraph shouted to his companion. He veered and charged us on a collision course. Judging from their youthful appearance, they hadn't been revived for more than a couple of weeks.

Ivy reached her arms around my waist. Brilliance burst from her fists. The seraph threw up a shield. It didn't last for long. His skin blistered red from the onslaught. A tortured scream burst from his throat as he threw up his arms in a futile gesture. The carpet swerved out of the control and slammed into Jade. Blood sprayed. One seraph fell to his death. The other was skewered by a weapon shard on the goliath. His body twitched and hung limp.

The air rumbled as if a massive earthquake had just hit. I spun around and saw nothing but a huge dust cloud where Quartz had slammed to earth. The Darkling army was nowhere to be seen. The pavement below was littered with bodies. Brightling infantry pushed through the Templar ranks with slow, bloody efficiency. Archangels flew in circles around the Templar command platform like vultures.

Our army was dying.

Chapter 22

Mom and Lanaeia glided close to us.

Mom pointed to a large formation of flying carpets and enemy ground troops hanging back from the battle. "I think they're sending in more revived Brightlings."

I narrowed my eyes and spotted Daelissa on a large flying carpet. Her face lit with a delighted smile. She knew she was winning. A swarm of carpets streaked toward us. I counted over a dozen—too many for us to handle all at once.

"There's no way we can take down these golems before they get here." I looked back at our army. "We've got to retreat."

"Justin, look." Ivy pointed to a stone tile on Jade's back that looked out of place.

I took our carpet closer. The tile was positioned between two weapon shards and probably wouldn't have been obvious except for the blood from the dead Seraphim spattered across it. Using a wedge of Murk, I pried at the tile. Ivy pitched in and we broke the magic-resistant stone. A crackling sphere of energy hovered inside the revealed space.

"Ooh." Ivy bared her teeth. "The spark." Without another word, she engulfed it in a blanket of Murk and snuffed it out.

Jade stopped just as it was lifting its rear leg to walk forward. Seemingly in slow motion, it toppled backward toward hundreds of Brightling infantry. Most of them didn't even see it coming. With the clouds covering the sun, there was no shadow and no noise but a slight rush of air to warn them. I heard hundreds of voices cry out and just as suddenly vanish in a roar of dust, stone, and confusion.

Ivy clenched her fists. "Die, you filthy bastards."

Mom's eyes flared. "Watch your mouth, young lady."

A trumpet sounded from below. Despite the heavy casualties the Brightlings had taken from the fallen golem, the Templar front was collapsing. To my left I saw the Darkling army falling back. I couldn't tell how many were left, but it looked like we'd lost hundreds. Another of the giant golems, Bronze, toppled sideways as explosions raced up one of its legs, severing it a third of the way from the ground. It hit Onyx on the way down, sending the disarmed golem stumbling sideways.

Most of the golems were down or badly damaged, but it didn't matter at this point. The bulk of Daelissa's army pressed in from all sides.

A Templar trumpet sounded again, this time to retreat. I saw a dozen portals open behind our back lines. The troops began falling back in an orderly withdrawal. The Brightlings cheered and surged forward.

"We've got to help the retreat," I said.

Mom nodded. "I say we strafe their forward ranks."

"Follow me." I guided the carpet to the far right edge of the turmoil, dodging spells and bolts of Brilliance along the way. I veered sharp left, urged the carpet to full speed, and dove to about twenty feet off the ground. Ivy and I unleashed searing beams of destruction into the second row of Brightlings. Mom and Lanaeia aimed for the third row.

Soldiers screamed as we raked their lines.

A thrown spear with a wicked black blade narrowly missed me. Enemy soldiers began to aim ahead of us, hoping to strike us from the air. I bobbed and weaved, but it took all my concentration so I let my sister do the firing.

Ivy cried out. I glanced back as she slumped to the carpet. Blood seeped from a cut in her Nightingale armor.

"Ivy!" I gained altitude to take us out of range.

"I'm okay," she said, tears in her eyes.

I looked back. We'd sown enough damage and confusion in the Brightling ranks to give the Templars space, but the Darklings were still under heavy assault.

A line of gray men, the elite fighting units, raced into the fray, inserting themselves between the Darklings and the enemy lines. One gray man leapt high into the air, flying over the front ranks of the Brightlings. Spears slammed into the golem. It hit the ground and exploded. Bodies flew in all directions.

I took us back down and razed the disoriented Brightlings. "Retreat!" I shouted to our people. "Retreat!"

I spotted Ketiss in the back ranks motioning his people into a full run. The enemy flung crackling energy and spears at us. I flipped sideways to avoid a rush of blades and death rays and flew out over our army. I looked back. For a panicked moment, I couldn't find Mom and Lanaeia. I finally spotted them guarding the Templar flanks along with other revived Darklings on flying carpets. Bolts of energy flashed back and forth in a dazzling display.

The Brightlings recovered from our delay tactics and raced after us with a roaring battle cry. My bones went limp as noodles with fright. There was no way we'd get our army through the portals in time.

I thought desperately for some way to slow down the onslaught. The Darklings had stopped running and turned to face the enemy while their fellow soldiers filed through the bottleneck: three omniarch portals. The Templars, having done this many times before, made much faster progress. Even so, allies were being cut down left and right. The remaining giant golems fired into our tight ranks.

Daelissa had a bigger army. Her forces were stronger in every way.

I couldn't see her from my current location, but I knew she was laughing. She'd drawn us out and slaughtered us. Our attempt to stop her from attacking Atlanta had been futile. Even worse, her army would only grow stronger if they built more goliaths.

I watched as the enemy cut down retreating lycans. I saw Saber in his massive prehistoric cat form savaging Brightlings in a desperate attempt to defend his people. Hellhounds swarmed around our right flank, throwing their bodies between Daemos and the attackers. The red demonic form of my father stood out. He swung a massive cobalt blade and cleaved through a Brightling. Kassallandra in her purple demoness form, spun, ducked, and weaved through enemy attacks, twin daggers flashing as she cut down infantry.

A sudden blast from the weapon shard of a giant golem slammed into the Daemos. Bodies scattered. Hellhounds yelped and squealed. As the smoke cleared, I couldn't find Dad or Kassallandra. My horror turned to an inferno of rage.

They're dying! We wouldn't escape. Daelissa would cut us down like fleeing deer. There was one thing I could do.

I closed my eyes and sent my senses into the demon plane.

I am here, said the calm many-voices of the Abyssal demon.

Jeremiah Conroy had warned me not to do this. Hell, anyone I'd told about the Abyssal demon thought summoning it again was stupid. I wanted to ask this thing what it wanted for its help. Did it want my soul? Did it want freedom from Haedaemos? I didn't have time to play twenty questions.

Get ready to fight. With that, I wrapped its presence in a strand of my essence. The demon didn't feel massive like other powerful presences, but like a brick of lead, incredibly dense, as though something tremendous had been concentrated into a much smaller space. The cold grip of fear touched my heart. Then again, it might have been the chilling touch of this demon. I couldn't sense its emotions, expectations, or anything else from it. It was a complete enigma.

And I had no choice but to use it.

I opened my eyes and focused on a bare patch of asphalt between the Darkling army and the Brightlings. The surface bubbled like a pool of molten tar. It widened as if oil were seeping up from the ground. The Brightlings backed away, uncertainty in their eyes. The Darklings used the diversion to reform their defenses.

The surface of the black pond swirled upward like a cone. A glowing red eye formed near the base. The spinning vortex seemed to turn inside out, reversing shape. The wide top morphed into a head and torso. Arms with six-fingered hands stretched from the primordial goo. The Abyssal grew in size until it was nearly half the height of the goliaths.

An immense weight pressed down on my entire being. I dropped to my knees and nearly lost control of the carpet.

"The Abyss awaits." The demon spoke in many voices, each with its own distinct tone and timbre. It was almost as if hundreds of people spoke at once.

The Brightlings didn't seem to know what to make of the creature at first. The archangels, however, attacked it immediately and the golems changed course for this new threat.

"There's Dad!" Ivy pointed excitedly to our front lines.

I spotted him as he climbed from beneath a pile of dead hellhounds and pulled Kassallandra out behind him.

The Abyssal extended an arm and raked a stream of black energy at the Brightlings. They screamed in agony as their bodies seemed to come unglued to reality and fell apart. I saw ghostly shapes flying from their remains and into the Abyssal's red eye. The weight on my concentration grew heavier and heavier as the demon killed more of our enemies.

Daelissa's battle mages were ready for such an attack. They swooped in on two large platforms, each bearing a large golden tetrahedron. They dropped to the ground and opened the vessels. The Abyssal sensed the threat and fired beams at one set of battle mages as their pyramid unfolded into a complex hexagonal pattern. Even after the mages died, I could still hear the screams of their souls as they streaked into the Abyssal.

"My god, it's devouring souls." The last time I'd summoned the creature, I'd been too preoccupied to notice this. Then again, the army we'd fought had been much smaller.

The gray golem, Ash, reached the Abyssal before the demon could destroy the battle mages with the other tetrahedron. One of the men waved his staff at the device. It unfolded into a complex pattern similar to the first. The mages directed their staffs at the infernal pattern and activated it.

Light flashed and a sonic boom vibrated the air. Crimson liquid formed in the middle of the summoning pattern. A massive red creature uncoiled from within and rose like a python. At first, I thought it was a snake but soon realized it had hundreds of legs like a millipede. Its head bore the shape of an axe without any discernible eyes.

The Abyssal pounded a fist into the chest of the attacking goliath. It seemed to be having greater difficulty with the lifeless automaton, but finally penetrated the rocky outer shell. Its hand engulfed Ash's spark and ripped it out. The golem crumbled to the ground.

By now, the Brightlings realized the perils of attacking the Abyssal and backed off to let their new pet demon engage it. This widened the gulf between the enemy forces and my allies. More battle mages appeared and activated the other demon pattern. A huge ball of tentacles rose from it and rolled toward the Abyssal. At first, I couldn't find the head of this new horror, but then I magnified my vision. What appeared to be suction cups along the tentacles were actually human faces. Round orifices filled with needle teeth served as their mouths.

"Justin, I don't like this at all." Ivy gripped my arm. "Can your guy beat up the other ones?"

"I have no idea," I said between clenched teeth. The Abyssal's weighty presence in my mind was almost unbearable. I slowly swiveled my head and saw most of our army had escaped. As I viewed the bloody landscape, I began to realize how many of our own had been killed. The wreckage of the news chopper smoked in the middle of the carnage. I felt sick with anger and sadness.

Nausea squirmed up my throat.

The millipede trundled toward my demon. The Abyssal gripped the creature's head, but couldn't stop its body from snaking around it. The tentacle creature rolled over to the fighting demons. A dozen of its appendages shot out and wrapped around the Abyssal's head.

"Justin, we can go now!" Ivy tugged on my sleeve.

"Are you okay, son?" Mom appeared before me. "You've got to release the demon. We have to go through the portal."

Unsummoning a demon was simply the reverse of what I'd done to bring it into this realm, but there was a huge difference between then and now. The pressure of maintaining control balanced on a razor's edge. If I tried to spare enough concentration to send it back, I'd lose my grip on the creature.

"Can't do it," I gasped. "I'd have to let it go, or let it die to the other demons."

"Let me fly the carpet," Ivy said. "I'll take us into the portal."

I shook my head. "No. We can't go through or I'll lose the connection." I peered behind Mom. The Abyssal was completely engulfed between the two demons. It couldn't possibly survive much longer.

I briefly considered relinquishing control. I'd been told that freed demons wouldn't last long in this world because their corporeal bodies would eventually fade without someone to mentally maintain it as Daemos did for the bodies of their hellhounds. If these other demons killed the Abyssal's body, it would automatically go back to Haedaemos.

I felt the Abyssal's presence fade. Relief flooded me and the weight on my mind lessened. *They killed it.*

The Abyssal's many voices spoke in a calm but very loud voice. "The Abyss is eternal. No less so am I." Its body of dark matter writhed and twisted like water, spinning free from the two demons. It flowed around the millipede. The Abyssal's red eye gaped wide. With a deafening shriek, the eye sucked a shadow copy of the millipede from its own body and drew it inside.

The weight in my head went from unbearably heavy to bursting with pain. I groaned. My bones seemed to crack. My mind screamed to be free. I couldn't take it any longer or I'd die. With frantic desperation, I severed the tether. The Abyssal was free. The tentacle demon tried to flee, but the battle mages controlling it fought back, forcing it to fight.

A deep voice echoed across the parking lot, speaking in a harsh, strange language I intuitively understood. *Once the greatest of demons, I now fall to the Abyss. Grant me mercy, dark one, and I will grant thee great power in Haedaemos.*

The Abyssal spoke with a thousand sonorous voices. "Well spoken, Holiblothinaal. Your journey ends." It plunged a fist into the mass of tentacles. The creature quivered and screeched. It exploded in a cloud of black energy. A spectral copy of its form hovered in the air before being drawn into the Abyssal's eye.

192

Daelissa's army had apparently figured out that the Abyssal was one badass they didn't want to mess with and flew into a full retreat. The dark demon ignored them and turned toward me, its single red eye seeming to gaze into my soul. "As foretold, my pattern emerges from the dark. A new consciousness consumes the old. A new journey begins."

"What does that mean?" Ivy asked in a frightened voice.

I wanted to shout something back at the monster I'd just unleashed on the world, but it was all I could do to keep my head from lolling forward.

The Abyssal spun until it turned into a dark vortex. It shrank down to a smaller humanoid form. In a blur, it vanished into the distance.

I had saved our forces, but unleashed hell on earth.

Chapter 23

The next few hours were a blur. When I woke up, I found Dad and Kassallandra sitting next to me, their eyes closed.

"Hello?" I said.

Their eyes blinked open simultaneously, sending creeptastic chills crawling up my spine.

"How are you feeling?" Dad asked.

I sat up, flipped my head to both sides, and cracked my neck. "Other than a little soreness and a slight headache, I feel pretty good."

"We had to help your soul repair itself." Dad pinched the bridge of his nose as if he had a headache. "It really took a beating."

"You almost lost yourself to that creature," Kassallandra said. "Did I not warn you to never summon it again?"

I pressed my face into my hands and groaned. "I didn't know what else to do. We were losing people left and right. I had to do something to save them."

Dad squeezed my shoulder. "I understand why you did it, Justin." He sighed. "We'll just have to send demon hunters after it, provided we survive this war."

"Won't it lose its corporeal body after a while?" I asked, attempting to pluck a bit of hope from this mess.

"Abyssal demons are a special breed," Kassallandra said. "It was rumored they once walked the realms, able to maintain a physical presence until they were banished to Haedaemos by powerful beings from one of those realms."

I felt sick to my stomach. "Will it consume more souls? Did I just kill the human race?"

She shook her head. "I cannot say. It is said they seek revenge on the beings who banished them. Perhaps it will content itself to search for them."

"It ate the equivalent of an entire Chinese buffet," Dad said. "I don't think it'll be hungry again for a while." He stood and stretched. "Besides, we have bigger things to worry about."

I thought about our staggering losses and felt even sicker. "How many did we lose?"

Dad met a gaze from Kassallandra and looked back to me. "Things are bad, son." He put a hand on my shoulder and managed one of his cocky smiles. "Before you dive into the bad news, I think you should enjoy a little good news."

"Good news? Good news?" I stood abruptly. A sharp pain spiked into my head and I winced. "There is no good news in the Overworld."

"It's good enough for me," said a familiar voice.

I turned to the door and felt my heart soar. *Elyssa!* Ignoring the pain in my head, I ran to my love and squeezed her in a tight hug.

"You saved me," she said. Her warm lips pressed to my cheek. "You saved me." Her kisses moved to my lips.

I felt hot tears sting my eyes and pulled away so I could drink in the sight of her.

"We'll leave you to it," Dad said.

Kassallandra touched us both on our shoulders. "Enjoy your time together. I fear what the future may bring."

With that chilling statement, they left the room, leaving us alone.

I closed the door to the room and realized we were in the healing ward in La Casona.

"I came to my senses when they were bringing you in here," Elyssa said. "Seeing you so battered and bruised snapped me out of my confusion."

"If I'd known that would work, I would've stabbed myself in the hand." I smiled. "Then again, I didn't have much blood left after you got your fangs into me."

Elyssa pressed her hands to my face and kissed me long and deep. "I was quite the hot mess, according to Meghan."

195

"Yeah, it was pretty painful watching you act like a wild animal."

She led me to the bed and pulled me down onto it. "Can we just lay here for a while? The world's falling apart, but all I want to do is cuddle."

Considering what lay ahead, it sounded like the best idea in the world. I squeezed her tight to me and felt her warmth, her smooth, creamy skin, her soft lips. I couldn't believe I had Elyssa back. Without her, I'd felt so lost. Without her, I'd felt hopeless.

Eden teetered on the brink of destruction. Our army had been brutalized. Our backs were to the wall. I should've felt inconsolable. But Elyssa had ignited a spark inside me. We weren't dead yet. We were just mostly dead. With the right chocolate-coated miracle pill, we could still defeat Daelissa.

An hour later Elyssa and I portaled to Queens Gate and met with Thomas and Ketiss in the war room at the mansion.

"Elyssa." Thomas hugged his daughter and kissed her forehead.

She seemed a little surprised by his affection, but smiled, tears sparkling. "Where are Mom and Michael?"

"They're here. I'll send for them." He reached for his pendant.

"I can talk to them after the briefing," Elyssa said. She wiped at her eyes. "I feel like I've missed out on a lot."

Thomas turned to the Darkling commander. "Legiaros Ketiss, this is my daughter, Elyssa."

He splayed his fingers toward her and nodded his head. "A pleasure."

Elyssa mimicked his greeting and nodded back. "It's very nice to meet you."

"He still hasn't learned to shake hands," I said with a smile.

"Apologies, Commander Slade." Ketiss saluted.

I dropped into a chair at the table. "How bad is it?"

Thomas sat down next to me. "We lost more than half our Templar forces. The Darklings took severe casualties as well—over four hundred soldiers."

"What about the lycans and the Blue Cloaks?" I asked.

"We lost three packs of combined shifter forces." He consulted his arctablet. "The Blue Cloaks were able to minimize their casualties. They lost thirty-two people. Fjoeruss informed me he lost a combined total of one hundred fifty-two golems. He returned to one of his secret bases to construct more, though he warned he would not have time to replace all of them."

I braced myself for the answer to my next question. "Overall?"

"We're at less than half strength." He went through a list. "The only silver linings are the performance of our revived Darklings. Joss and Otaleon have taken over command of those units, which we've codenamed UV."

I raised an eyebrow. "As in ultraviolet?"

"Precisely." Thomas leaned back in his chair. "They were able to shield many of our troops from attack. If not for them, the fight would've been over much sooner."

"Did Daelissa attack Atlanta?" I asked.

He shook his head. "The Abyssal demon caused them to retreat to Thunder Rock." Thomas scrolled down the screen on his tablet. "From the ASE recordings of the battle, we calculated that Daelissa lost about a quarter of her Brightling troops, including approximately thirty archangels. All goliaths were destroyed and her contingent of battle mages was decimated. There were some vampires in the fight, but no sign of Red Cell, the elite vampire army." He pressed his lips together. "We believe they're on guard duty somewhere."

"My people are now dual feeding on human volunteers," Ketiss said. "A sera—I mean, woman—by the name of Katie told me they had procured several hundred more from veteran hospitals in exchange for proper medical care."

"What's the nom political situation?" I asked Thomas.

He set the tablet aside. "Your father informed me that Daemos agents are having success countering Exorcist moles in nom governments. So far, they have stopped several assassinations. Unfortunately, it appears that Russia was already under the control of Daelissa's minions. She is using them to forcibly take Ukraine so she can reinforce Chernobyl and protect the Grand Nexus."

"She's in control of Russia?" I didn't want to think what kind of damage she could cause with nuclear weapons. "How did nobody notice this?"

Thomas shrugged. "The question is moot at this point. The real question is how do we proceed?"

I had no reply. Daelissa had nearly wiped us out today. Despite the loss of her goliaths, she still had several more in production. They would no doubt be involved in future battles.

Phoebe entered the room. "I'm here, Commander." She saw Elyssa and her face lit up.

"Phoebe!" Elyssa embraced her sister.

"I'm so glad you're back with us," Phoebe said, eyes moist. She pulled back and looked at me with a smile. "Justin has been impossible to deal with."

Elyssa laughed. "Nothing unusual about that."

Thomas cleared his throat. "Perhaps we should return to the matter at hand." He looked at Phoebe. "What did you find?"

Phoebe flicked her fingers on the arctablet and projected a holographic image of the battle as taken by dozens of ASEs. She zoomed to the back ranks of Daelissa's troops where Daelissa stood next to some of her closest advisors. Phoebe focused on an archangel I recognized immediately.

"That's the dude who attacked us at the Three Sisters." He was obviously a bigwig if he got to stand next to Daelissa. "His name is Primarion Arturo."

"Arturo is Daelissa's new strategist," Phoebe said. "She revels in employing overwhelming force even if it's not the best tactic." She grimaced. "As her former tactician, I often had to convince her it was wiser to split forces to achieve multiple objectives simultaneously."

"It would appear she had it her way this time," I said.

"Actually, it was more likely her fondness for extreme force fit nicely with Arturo's objectives." Phoebe zoomed to an overhead view. "Arturo's strategy baited our unprepared army to face his well-prepared forces. Even though the Brightling army has been here only a week or two longer than the Darklings, they've spent that time feeding."

"Do they know about dual feeding?" I asked.

She shook her head. "Unlikely. Even if they knew about it, Daelissa would never allow it." A troubled look crossed Phoebe's face. "She has an unusual aversion to Murk that I could never quite understand."

I snorted. "She's a Murkophobe."

Phoebe nodded. "She absolutely hates it."

I thought back to what Nightliss had told me about her family history. "Daelissa grew up with a Darkling family. When they were banished to Pjurna, she did everything in her power to get back to the Brightlands."

Ketiss looked at us with a somewhat bewildered look on his face.

"Are you okay?" I asked.

He nodded slowly. "I apologize. It is unsettling to hear of beings such as Daelissa spoken about so casually. All my life she and Nightliss were but legends and icons of evil in our religion."

"Stories can lose their original meaning as centuries pass," Thomas said. "I know this is a shock to your system, but we all have to adjust to the realities that face us. Nightliss would never aid Daelissa. In fact, she's the Clarion for our Templar forces."

"It is evident some of the teachings were perverted over the centuries." Ketiss looked at the image of Daelissa and Arturo hovering above the table. "The resemblance between the sisters is very unsettling."

"I feel like I've missed so much." Elyssa shook her head as if clearing it. "Why didn't we have any of Fjoeruss's battle golems in play?"

"Though we control the Obsidian Arch at the Grotto, it would be impossible to transport such large golems through Atlanta without detection." Thomas pursed his lips. "There's simply too much traffic congestion for a camouflage spell to work, and the constructs are too large to haul with a truck."

I knew Thomas was right and took a different tact. "We don't have the luxury of protecting the noms from our existence any longer."

Elyssa reeled back from my statement. Thomas gave me a long hard look.

Apparently, I'd just stepped on their toes. "I know it's in your job description to police the supernatural world and protect the noms from beings who might take advantage of them, but there was a news helicopter flying over our battle, in case you didn't notice."

"The civilian aircraft was destroyed by a goliath," Thomas said.

I winced. "What about all the bodies we left behind?"

"The Custodians are working on that problem right now." Thomas folded his arms. "We're fortunate the area is not heavily traveled, because the size of the task is monumental."

Just thinking about so many deaths roiled my stomach. "So, you're determined to stick to the rules even though Daelissa is on the verge of plowing through downtown Atlanta with giant golems?"

"We're looking for alternatives, Mr. Slade." Thomas's voice turned a tad frosty. "Daelissa still controls Kobol Prison, so the arch there is out of play. If it comes down to it, we'll use the Grotto way station. Until then, we have to do everything possible to play by the rules."

I posed a question I'd long wondered about. "Would it really be so awful if the noms found out about the Overworld?"

"That is not for us to decide," he replied. "I can tell you from experience, noms have little enough restraint as it is when it comes to their technological means of destruction. I have seen them commit atrocities with magic."

"I've seen them do good as well," Phoebe said. "Things would balance out then as they have now. I don't think the citizens of the Overworld have done any better of a job behaving with magic than noms would."

"The citizens of this world are not allowed to use magic?" Ketiss looked befuddled. "Why would you rob them of such a gift?"

"They use *science*." Thomas loaded the word with disdain. "Perhaps once you get to know this realm better, you'll understand. Until then, suffice it to say I will not willingly reveal the Overworld to the noms."

"What if I command it?" I hated to pull rank, but this was ridiculous.

The tension in the room thickened considerably. I felt Elyssa's hand tighten painfully on my arm.

Thomas gave me his legendary ice stare for several long seconds. The man didn't even seem to breathe. His eyes narrowed.

I remained stoic before his glare even though I desperately wanted to bust out with an irreverent comment to break the tension.

Thomas took a deep breath and released it, as if he were pushing the frost from his lungs. "You are ultimately in command, Mr. Slade. If you truly think it's necessary, we will trample on centuries of secrecy and reveal ourselves, to hell with the dire consequences."

I maintained my own steady gaze, unwilling to lose this staring contest. "I respect your judgment and beliefs, Commander Borathen. If I make such a decision, it will not be done lightly."

No one spoke for a moment. Ketiss's eyes flicked back and forth between my face and Thomas's as if he were watching a mental tennis match.

"It's settled, then," Phoebe said, using her own command voice. "Let's continue."

Thomas looked at his daughter. "Agreed."

"Okay," I said.

Elyssa squeezed my hand a little more gently this time. "Yes."

Phoebe resumed the playback of the battle. The video remained focused on Daelissa and Arturo. Daelissa swept her arm in an arc as if indicating the surroundings on several occasions. Arturo nodded and said something. Unfortunately, the ASEs had been unable to record whatever was said over the roar of battle.

"Why does she keep doing that?" Elyssa paused the video.

I looked at Daelissa caught in the act of scratching her hand.

"What do you mean?" Phoebe asked.

Elyssa rewound the video and pointed out several instances where Daelissa scratched at the palm of her hand. "See how she grimaces? Her hand must really be bothering her."

"Interesting," I said, "but I don't think we can rely on a hand rash to end this war."

"That is her feeding hand," Ketiss said. "Perhaps she has overindulged."

I shrugged. "I wouldn't put it past her."

"During my time with her, I recall several instances where her hand appeared to be bothering her." Phoebe tapped a finger on her chin. "It was usually after she expended a great deal of power and drained several noms to replenish herself."

Ketiss grimaced.

"Aether overload?" I asked.

Phoebe waggled her hand in a so-so gesture. "Do you remember Montjoy?"

I blew out a breath. "How could I forget that pompous ass?"

"He procured what he called pure specimens for Daelissa to feed from." She looked down and fiddled with the arctablet, as if still ashamed that she'd once served under the former leader of the Exorcists. "Supposedly these noms contained very little dark soul essence and were able to limit Daelissa's mental episodes to a minimum. Once she began binge-feeding on those types of noms, her hand started to ache."

Thomas turned to his eldest daughter. "While this sidebar is intriguing, I don't see how it's pertinent to the current discussion."

"I'm just highlighting a possible weakness in the enemy, Commander." Phoebe met his gaze. "Right now our army is in no condition to fight Daelissa's, at least not in a head-on fight. Perhaps it's time to consider covert options."

Elyssa caught on to her meaning. "Like assassination?"

"That's one possibility." Phoebe clasped her hands together. "We have specialized personnel like Kanaan who might be capable of infiltrating Thunder Rock and taking out either Arturo or Daelissa."

"Removing them from the equation still gives us no guarantee the war would end," Thomas said. "Another Brightling might simply take their place."

"It buys us time," Elyssa said. "It might even sow confusion and chaos."

Phoebe's plan wasn't ideal, but it seemed to me the best way to push the enemy off balance long enough for us to gain strength. "Isn't Kanaan on another mission?"

"Yes." Thomas consulted another arctablet. "I'll speak with Captain Takei. Perhaps he has another Magitsu master who could actually pull this off."

Kanaan was amazing to see in action, but deep down inside, I knew even he might have a problem killing Daelissa. Getting close to her might not be a problem for someone with his particular talents, but summoning enough power to finish her off would be the trick. Then again, I'd seen him detonate a seraph's head by shooting a spell up the poor dude's nose. If he stuck his wand up Daelissa's nose, I hoped he'd record it because the look on her face would be priceless.

It occurred to me there was another eminently qualified individual for such a job—someone I hadn't heard from in quite a long time.

"You just got that look on your face," Elyssa said. "Don't tell me we're going to recruit the tragon again, because the Darklings are in Colossus Stadium and there's nowhere else big enough to keep it."

I couldn't deny the idea held a lot of appeal for me, but we simply didn't have the logistical capability to transport an unruly dino-dragon to Atlanta without using the Grotto way station. I wasn't that ready to run roughshod over Thomas's desire to keep the Overworld secret.

"No, I have something else in mind." I leaned back and let the suspense build for a few seconds.

Elyssa punched me in the shoulder. "Will you spit it out already? This isn't a television drama."

Despite the awful situation, I smiled. *It's great having my baby back.* "I'm going to talk to Underborn."

Chapter 24

Ketiss was the only person who didn't look shocked by my idea. Technically, Thomas didn't look shocked either, but I figured he just repressed it as usual.

"Is that a person's name?" Ketiss asked.

"Underborn is an assassin," I said.

Thomas scowled. "He's not to be trusted."

"He's the master of all assassins in the Overworld," Phoebe added.

Elyssa topped it off with her opinion. "He's a dirt bag."

"All true." I stood and stretched. My brain still felt a bit fuzzy from whatever Dad and Kassallandra had done to heal me. "But if anyone can kill Daelissa, it'll be him."

"You're probably right," Thomas said. "However, I must note that he's probably been aware of Daelissa for quite some time and has never, to my knowledge, taken direct action against her."

"He has his own agenda." Elyssa shook her head slowly. "I don't think he'll help us."

"Maybe he will, maybe he won't." I shrugged. "Even if he doesn't agree to kill Daelissa, he has access to artifacts that might help us defeat her."

Elyssa tilted her head. "The Relics of Juranthemon?"

"Precisely." I paced away from the table. "According to Underborn, there are seven relics. The key, the map, and the Chalon are the only three I know of, but it stands to reason he might have more."

"What about Jeremiah's vault?" Thomas said. "Have you searched in there for anything that might help us?"

Thinking about the vault reminded me of the snow globes. The snow globes made me think about how Nyte's father had broken his leg in a snowstorm Elyssa and I had made. I pushed the thought from my mind. *Now isn't the time.* "No, we haven't been back."

Thomas nodded. "Perhaps you should exhaust that option before seeking the help of Underborn."

I held up a finger. "Before we go down that road, hear what I have to say." I put my hands on the table and leaned forward. "If we procured the key and the map from Underborn, we'd have the ability to transport even our largest assets wherever we needed them."

Elyssa scrunched her forehead. "But the key only works on doors, Justin. We'd need a massive door on both ends."

I grinned. "Exactly."

Ketiss tapped me on the shoulder. "Could you explain this key and map?"

"Sure." I pushed back from the table and walked around to the other side so they could face me without having to turn in their chairs. "The map is used to link a door anywhere in the world with another door. Once linked, the key can be used to open either door for instant travel from one location to the other."

"Could you link a door from this realm to one in another realm?" Ketiss asked.

I shrugged. "I don't know if the map only works in Eden, or not."

"What about giant doors?" Elyssa challenged me with an eyebrow.

"Simple. You know those siege platforms your Arcanes use?"

Her other eyebrow joined the first. "Now you've completely lost me."

Phoebe gave me a similar look. "Your mind works in weird ways."

I held up a hand. "Bear with me." I grabbed the arctablet and projected the video of a siege platform in its compact shape—roughly the size of a small wooden plank. "This platform goes from being just a couple of feet long." I advanced the video as the platform unfolded into a large tower about fifty feet tall and ten feet wide. "To a structure with cubic dimensions nearly sixty times larger." I hadn't really done the math for a complete answer, but figured making it up on the spot wouldn't hurt anything. I could've sworn I saw light bulbs blinking on above the others' heads.

"You want to create unfolding doors." Elyssa seemed shocked that I'd come up with something so clever. "We could link the doors and transport them anywhere."

I smacked the back of my hand into the other's palm. "Precisely. We could use omniarches to place them anywhere."

"Provided the key and map work with this little hack of yours," Elyssa said. "For all we know, the door might not even show up on the map, or moving the door might destroy the link."

I shrugged. "There's only one way to find out."

She narrowed her eyes. "Didn't Underborn extort the map and key from us so you could save Felicia from the vampling curse?"

"He did, indeed. I don't think there's any way I could convince him to let me borrow it." I smiled in the way I imagined a con artist would smile after assuring everyone that his plan to rob a bank couldn't possibly go wrong. "If diplomacy fails, we're going to steal them."

Everyone spoke at once, except for Ketiss who still didn't seem to understand who this Underborn character was or how dangerous it was to piss him off.

I held up my hands. "Simmer down, everyone."

"Putting yourself at such risk is unacceptable," Thomas said. "While your idea to use the map and key might be sound, I suggest we open a dialogue with Underborn."

"Maybe there's something in Jeremiah's vault we could trade him for the relics," Elyssa said. She snapped her fingers. "We still have the original Chalon and the Chalon from the Shadow Nexus. Maybe we could trade him one of those."

"You'd give him the very key to the Grand Nexus?" Phoebe shook her head vehemently. "Not a good idea."

"The Chalon is redundant." Thomas touched his chin in a thoughtful manner. "Since Daelissa is using the Chalon she gained in Seraphina and she controls the Grand Nexus, we can't use either Chalon in our possession."

Elyssa nodded. "They're useless."

Phoebe gave her a warning look. "Unless there's something about them we don't know."

"I studied the Chalon with Jeremiah and he didn't seem to think it had any other use besides attuning the Grand Nexus." I exchanged my sly expression for something professorial. "The Chalon enables a gateway between realms while the map and key operate similarly to an Obsidian Arch. Since the Chalon requires a very specific arch to operate, I think we can safely trade one to Underborn." *I just hope he actually wants it.*

"Sounds a lot safer than trying to rob an assassin," Elyssa said with a relieved look.

"We should thoroughly examine Jeremiah's vault to be sure there's nothing else of value there," Thomas said. "Perhaps the answer to our logistical problems lies within."

"The vault is huge." Elyssa widened her arms as if to encompass the room. "It would take us weeks to search it, and that's provided we even understand what we find."

"We sure as hell don't want to cause any more snowstorms." I made a sour face. "For all we know, Jeremiah stored certain items in there to make the world a safer place."

"We're going in circles." Phoebe looked exasperated. "I'll speak with Captain Takei about having some of his most knowledgeable Blue Cloaks catalogue Jeremiah's vault while you two open communications with Underborn and find out if he's willing to trade. That will be the most efficient plan of action."

I had to agree with Phoebe. Thanks to Daelissa's "blessing," Elyssa's sister was exceptionally smart and would be a good person to lead this effort. "Okay, you're in charge of that operation."

Phoebe smiled. She looked so much like Elyssa, I had to glance at my girlfriend again to see the differences.

"Thank you for trusting me, Justin." Phoebe stood. "I'll get on this right away."

I nodded. "Elyssa and I will move on the Underborn angle." I took out my arcphone and transmitted an image of the vault to

Phoebe's phone. "There's no other way into the vault except using that picture with an omniarch."

"Understood." Phoebe looked at me for a long moment before clearing her throat and glancing at her sister. "I'll be on my way then." She hurried from the room.

I turned to Thomas. "Can you can coordinate with Fjoeruss and find out what sort of assets he has? We'll need a count of his battle golems and their capabilities."

"I'll speak with him." Thomas stood and turned to Ketiss. "Please check on your troops and make sure they're having no difficulties feeding from noms or using the prisms. Their health is vital."

Ketiss nodded. "I will do so immediately."

There was so much to do if we wanted to survive. Despite the dire circumstances, I couldn't wait to be alone with Elyssa again. Every part of me ached to touch her.

Elyssa and I left the war room, took a left, and went up the main staircase in the large common room. We walked quickly without saying a word. She and I looked at each other. The intensity of her gaze flushed my body with heat. The moment I got her inside our bedroom, I slammed the door and attacked her lips with mine. She wrapped her arms around my waist and pressed herself tight against me.

"I missed you so much." The words trembled in my throat.

She wiped a tear from her eye. "You went to the ends of the earth and back for me." Elyssa kissed me gently on the lips. "I don't ever want us to be without each other."

"Promise me you'll never die or almost die again." I smiled and kissed her forehead.

She rolled her eyes. "I can't promise you that, but I can promise something else?"

I raised an eyebrow. "What would that be?"

"How about I give you a calisthenics workout you'll never forget." She pulled off my T-shirt in one fluid move and ran kisses up and down my chest.

I shivered. "Best workout ever." I assaulted her clothing and before long, we were under the bed sheets and working out like it was our last day on Earth.

A couple of hours later we showered, put on fresh Nightingale armor, and ate.

I idly formed a gray ball of Stasis and stared at it while I waited on Elyssa to finish off her food.

"Any luck figuring out what Clarity does?" she asked.

I shook my head. "It's really bugging me too." I turned toward her. "I keep thinking about the vision I had when I made the choice."

"The one where you saw the rivers of Brilliance and Murk?"

"Yeah, and the sky was like a fountain of gray Stasis."

She pursed her lips. "You said an inner voice told you the choice was clear and you realized you could choose everything."

I noticed the gray sphere I'd channeled was fading, and blew it. It scattered like smoke. "If choosing this clear magical element was so important, why doesn't it do anything?"

"Maybe you haven't been testing it correctly." Elyssa took my hand. "Try it out on me."

I shook my head vehemently. "Are you kidding me? I just got you back. I'm not about to risk killing you."

"Just use a tiny bit of power." She regarded me seriously. "This is really important, Justin."

I ran a hand through my hair and considered it. It would be safe if I kept the energy level really low. Besides, Clarity didn't seem to damage anything. I pressed my lips together. Nodded. "Okay."

Elyssa kissed my cheek. "Take your best shot, babe."

I conjured a small orb of Stasis and let it hover between us. "Hold out your hand."

Elyssa put her hand in front of the gray ball. She winced as if preparing for a shock.

Using my fingers, I channeled a trickle of Murk and Brilliance through the sphere. A stream of clear rippling energy emerged from the other side and flowed into Elyssa's hand. Her body stiffened. She gasped, eyes flaring, mouth forming a wide O.

209

"Elyssa!" I stopped channeling immediately and gripped her.

Her eyelids fluttered. Her forehead pinched. "That was so strange."

I inspected her hand. It looked a little pale, but otherwise undamaged. "What happened?"

"It was like an out of body experience." Her violet eyes flashed. "I don't know how else to explain it."

"You left your body?"

Elyssa looked at her hands and flexed the fingers. "For an instant, I was floating on a perfectly clear lake. At the same time, I hovered over my naked body and looked down on myself." She turned a confused gaze on me. "It was like a dream where you see yourself as another person. I looked happy and content. If I stared long enough I thought I'd be able to see through my body and into my soul."

I groaned. "Just great. If I ever want to make somebody trip balls, I'll just dose them with Clarity. It must be the magical equivalent of LSD."

Elyssa giggled but a frown quickly stole her smile. "I'm sorry. I wish Clarity was more useful."

My legs abruptly turned to jelly. I dropped into a seat as the world blurred and a heavy weight seemed to fall on my shoulders.

"Are you okay?"

I leaned on a hand. "Yeah, I guess channeling Clarity into a person is a lot more exhausting than inanimate objects or animals."

Elyssa's eyes widened. "You've been testing it on animals?"

I gave her a sheepish look. "Just Cutsauce."

She glared at me. "Justin Slade, you leave that poor hellhound alone."

A text from Phoebe buzzed on my phone and saved me from further chastising. *I'm onsite at the vault with several of Takei's people. I closed the omniarch portal in case you need to open one here.*

Elyssa read the text and gave me a look. "I think my sister is sweet on you."

I flinched like she'd slapped me. "Say what?" I shook my head like a dog shaking off water. "Look, even if that's true, I don't want to talk or think about it."

Elyssa took a sip of water and gave me a serious look. "When you thought I'd die, did you ever consider her as a replacement?"

"Never." I mustered some energy and slashed a hand through the air to underline that statement. "I also never thought you were going to die—not if I could help it."

"I'm not trying to trick you."

It's a trap! "Can we move on to something worth talking about?" The bone-deep weariness retreated, leaving only a faint background fatigue behind. I stood and picked up my plate so I could take it into the kitchen.

Elyssa smiled. "I'm sorry. I was just curious."

A lone figure emerged from the foyer and looked at us with inhumanly large eyes the color of green seawater. Her light blue hair writhed as though it had a life of its own. A diaphanous gray dress that resembled fog enveloped her form.

I almost dropped my plate in shock. "Melea?"

"Is it true an Abyssal walks the Earth?" Her mellifluous voice belied her very young appearance.

I hadn't actually spoken with Fjoeruss's adopted sister. She'd only been reborn for a short time so it was very surprising to see her physical age was that of a teenager. Rather than answer her, I gave myself a moment to overcome the surprise of seeing her here. "I'm glad to see you're in good health." I stepped closer to her and tried not to gawk at her strange hair. From a distance, she seemed to have a headful of sea anemones. Up close, I saw that her hair flowed and billowed almost as if she were underwater.

"Why do you not answer, Justin Slade?" Melea seemed to sing when she spoke. Her large eyes blinked.

"I'm curious why you came all the way from El Dorado and asked me that question without so much as a 'hello.'" I gave her a suspicious look to underscore my statement.

She blinked again. Her hair flowed back to reveal long pointed ears. "The Abyssal are a grave danger to all the realms."

211

Elyssa stepped forward. "Are your people the ones who banished the Abyssal to Haedaemos?"

"So it is sung." Melea tilted her head slowly and her hair flowed back as if in a gentle water current. "Oddly, I do not remember all the songs I should."

"Because you've only recently been revived," I told her. "Most of your memories should return before too long." I decided it wouldn't hurt to test her memories since she was a member of the race that built the arches. "I'll answer your question, but I'd like to ask you a few questions as well."

"If they are within my power to answer, so shall I." Melea nodded her head like a queen granting a favor.

I repressed a sigh. "Yes, an Abyssal escaped my control."

"What was his true name?"

My mouth opened, but I didn't have an answer for her. As Daemos, I had far more control over summoning demons than Arcanes who required protective circles to contain the powerful beings. Having the true name of a demon meant you could have complete control over a demon without most of the other prerequisites—or at least that's what my father had taught me.

I shrugged. "I'm sorry, but I don't know."

"By now, those in the Abyss have changed their names." She looked sad. "We will require new songs to send them back."

"I didn't realize demons could change their names."

"Even those in the infernal plane can change a name if given thousands of years to do so." She pressed the palms of her hands together and nodded. "You have answered. I shall return the favor if I can."

I decided not to beat around the bush. "Are you familiar with the Relics of Juranthemon?"

Melea's eyes lost focus as if gazing into the past. "I am familiar with the name Juranthemon, but cannot attach significance to it."

"What about a map which can connect two doors anywhere in the world and a key which can open the connection between those doors?"

She thought for a moment. "I am familiar with your language's meaning of key and map."

Her answer confused me at first, but my recent adventure in Seraphina clarified her meaning. Even though many words in Cyrinthian were easily translatable to English, there had been times when the translation spell had chosen words that made no contextual sense. Simply put, there were some things that existed in Eden that didn't exist in Seraphina and vice versa. Arcphones were a good example, although the gems the Seraphim wore operated in a similar manner.

Remembering what Underborn had told me about the key and the map, I knew there might be a better way to describe them. "The key is an analogue based on perception. If I think it's a normal metal key, then it appears as such. In its most basic form, it is simply an object that unlocks or gives access to something closed."

"Ah, as in an opener." She pursed her lips as though she'd just solved a great mystery.

"Uh, yeah, an opener." I'd expected a much cooler name than that.

Melea continued with another brilliant revelation. "The map is a locater."

Elyssa quirked an eyebrow. "And you would be considered a knower of stuff."

The siren didn't seem to realize Elyssa was being snarky. "I am a knower, among other things."

Despite the lack of cool names, I pressed on with my line of questioning. "What do you know about the opener and the locater?"

"They were once used to chart the realms and facilitate easy travel." She tapped a slender finger against her arm. "Only the explorers were allowed such powerful tools, lest someone without proper knowledge create a rift to the Void."

Jeremiah had told me about the Void and a supposed Beast which lived there. He'd considered unleashing the creature on Seraphina as revenge for the loss of his wife. "How much more can you tell me about these relics?"

"That is all I remember." She stopped tapping her finger and traced it down her arm. "Should I recall anything further, I will tell you. For now, I must find a way to send the Abyssal back where it belongs."

I stopped her as she turned to leave. "Wait, one more question." She regarded me patiently.

"Can the Chalon do anything besides attune the Grand Nexus?" I couldn't think of a better way to word it. "Does it have any other abilities?"

Her eyes once again lost focus for several seconds. "No. The Chalon, as you call it, aligns the resonance of one realm's magical energy with that of another. The aether separates the realms and makes them distinct." Her next statement was almost a murmur. "It was not always so."

I looked at Elyssa. "Looks like trading a Chalon for the map and key are our best bet."

Melea's gaze focused on me with razor-sharp intensity. "You possess a Chalon?"

"We have two of them." I instantly regretted my decision to open my mouth.

"Perhaps if you allow me to study them, I will discover something useful." The pitch in her voice altered ever so slightly.

I got the distinct feeling she was lying. "Why do you want them?" I stepped closer and narrowed my eyes. "What aren't you telling me?"

She didn't seem fazed by my aggressive posture. "I was simply offering my help." The song in her voice once again sounded enigmatic, but innocent. "I must go plan my next moves against the Abyssal. May the song guide you, Justin Slade and Elyssa Borathen." She turned and seemed to glide rather than walk out of the front door.

Elyssa gave me a troubled look. "I don't trust her one bit."

My stomach knotted. "There's a lot more going on with her than she's letting on."

If the fate of the world hadn't been in the balance, I would've gone ninja stealth and followed Melea. Unfortunately, we didn't have the time.

We had to visit the most dangerous assassin in the world.

Chapter 25

Elyssa and I stood outside the doors to the Grotto, a place I hadn't visited for some time. The way station looked virtually empty. The stables to the right of the Obsidian Arch, usually full of animals from all over the world and the steaming piles of dung to prove it, remained silent, aside from a small black goat bleating maniacally and running circles around a pile of hay. A smattering of travelers, most of them Templars or Arcanes, judging from their appearances, populated the vast space. It was as if the population of the Overworld was in hiding until the dust settled.

Even though Underborn didn't live in the Grotto, this was the only place I might have a chance of contacting him. Elyssa and I had discussed how best to talk to the man and approach what we needed. Trying to outthink him was beyond me, but we weren't entirely defenseless. If he agreed to see us, it meant he wanted something. If he wanted something, I had to negotiate the best price for it. Now I just had to hope we could find him.

Jeremiah had possessed a gold ASE with a direct line to Underborn, but that device had been lost when Daelissa killed the ancient Arcane. That left me with no choice but to rely on a method of contact I'd used once when Underborn marked my father for death.

The entire event had been a ruse by the assassin to test my mettle and see what I was made of. My appearance on the Overworld scene had been prophesied by Foreseeance Forty-Three Eleven, but Underborn liked to know everything about everyone.

I opened an email sent months ago from one Buzz Masterson. The account was fake, created by Adam Nosti during his more reclusive days before he'd become a part of the gang and started dating Meghan Andretti. Back then, he'd gone by the alias of Smith. It seemed like all of that had been so long ago, but it hadn't been much more than a year since I'd been a mega nerd at Edenfield High School.

The email read:

1. *Go to The Laughing Dog in the Grotto.*
2. *Purchase a Mr. Nutter's Angel Biscuit.*
3. *Go to Grotto Park.*
4. *Sit on the northeast bench facing Orange and MagicSoft.*
5. *Wait. Wait some more. Keep waiting.*

P.S. You can eat the Angel Biscuit if you get hungry.

Elyssa chuckled glanced at the email. "Wow, talk about a flashback."

"Except this time we shouldn't have an army of gray men waiting to ambush us." I took Elyssa's hand and led her toward the double doors guarding the entrance into the pocket dimension where the Grotto existed.

"G'day, guvnah!" said a peppy British voice.

Elyssa and I spun to see Oliver, the pooper-scooper boy walking toward us from the stables.

I smiled at the kid. "I guess job security isn't what it used to be, is it?"

"No animals, no dung." He shrugged. "Not a lot I can do about it." He pointed at a donkey who was watching the crazed goat. "At least Rachel enjoys the time off."

"Cute." Elyssa gave him a curious look. "Were you here when Daelissa controlled the Grotto?"

"Of course." Oliver motioned at the cavernous place. "Plenty of places to hide around this place. I even came out and did my work, but nobody notices or cares about the stable boy." He gave me a pointed look. "By the way, Underborn said you can skip buying the Angel Biscuit this time, unless you're hungry."

I almost choked on my own tongue. "Say what?"

Oliver smiled apologetically. "He's a right bastard if you ask me. Always knowing what everyone is up to and all that."

Elyssa looked at Oliver suspiciously. "How in the hell did he know we were coming to visit him?"

"If I knew that I wouldn't be the stable boy."

A sudden truth dawned on me as I regarded the young lad. He hadn't aged a day since I'd first met him, even though he was definitely of the age where growth spurts weren't uncommon. Even Shelton had been using Oliver as an informant for quite some time and couldn't explain why the kid didn't age normally. "Number one," I said, "you're not just a stable boy." A smile stretched my lips. "Number two, you're in a perfect position to snoop and eavesdrop on people."

"Are you about to say he's Underborn?" Elyssa said.

I shook my head. "Heavens no. Oliver works for the man. If anything, I think he's somehow related to Phissilinth."

Elyssa tilted her head. "The teeny tiny man assassin?"

"Or whatever he is."

Oliver grinned. "You're more of a doer than a thinker, Justin Slade, but you eventually figure things out."

I shot him a sarcastic smile. "Whatever, smartass. What do I need to do to see Underborn?" I looked at the prancing goat. "Do I need to scratch the goat behind the ears and then walk on my hands while reciting *Mary Had a Little Lamb*?"

Oliver pursed his lips. "That would be quite amusing, and I'm awfully tempted to say yes." He ran a hand through his thick mop of hair. "Unfortunately, it would just waste your time." He jabbed a thumb over his shoulder in the direction of the stables. "Underborn is in there."

"Let me guess. We showed up here. You eavesdropped on me talking about visiting Underborn." I folded my arms and tried to look smug. "Then you called him, he used the Key of Juranthemon to get here super fast, and then you got my attention."

"Someone is on top of their game today." Oliver motioned us to follow him. "You must be taking plenty of fish oil supplements, Mr. Slade."

I resisted the urge to pop him on the back of the head. "Yeah, yeah. I'm really appreciative to see how much trouble Underborn went through to make himself look omniscient all for little old me."

Elyssa squeezed my hand. "I always knew you were special, honey."

I rolled my eyes. "Yeah, special in the head."

A very small man whose height barely reached Elyssa's waist stepped from within the stable and regarded us with a pleasant smile. He wore a dark green suit with a red bowtie and matching bowler. Auburn sideburns hinted at the color of hair beneath the hat. "It is a pleasure to see you again, Ms. Borathen and Mr. Slade." Phissilinth's baritone voice didn't fit with his small stature, though it definitely fit with the confident way he carried himself.

Oliver gave a curt bow to the short man and went inside.

"Hello, Phissilinth." Though I'd seen him on a couple of different occasions, I hadn't exactly been thinking clearly. Then again, when did I ever think clearly? The small man's appearance reminded me distinctly of a mythical little creature who didn't want children eating his marshmallow cereal. "Are you a leprechaun?"

Phissilinth gave me a haughty look. "If you'll notice, sir, my accent is markedly British and not Irish."

Elyssa laughed. "Justin, there's no such thing as leprechauns."

"How am I supposed to know that?" I threw up my hands. "I mean, there are vampires, werewolves, werecats, and demons. Why not leprechauns?"

Phissilinth gave me a dour look, turned, and entered the stable. "Bloody leprechaun, indeed."

Despite the promise of Underborn, the stable was empty. I knew better than to open my mouth and ask where he was. The assassin might have heard me divining his sneaky ways and decided to leave just to spite me. Phissilinth produced a small skeleton key. Even though it looked like a key, I knew it was the opener, as Melea had so eloquently named it.

The small man walked toward a closed door that had no lock, only a sliding plank, which held it closed. The key seemed to melt into the wood. He twisted the key and pulled open the door. A carpeted hallway lined with paintings and candlelit sconces waited beyond.

I managed to mask my surprise at how the key had worked with solid wood. "Looks like you've mastered the key and the map."

"We've become quite familiar with them," Phissilinth said. "It took us only a matter of minutes to use the map and form the link between this door and the hallway." He waved us toward the door. "After you."

Oliver sat atop a bale of hay. "Have fun, mates."

I looked around dubiously. "Yeah, you too, kiddo."

Elyssa entered the doorway. I followed behind her and waited for Phissilinth to close it. He continued on his way down the hall. The last time Elyssa and I had been here, he'd made us sit in a waiting room. This time, however, he took us straight to the library where we'd first met Underborn.

The assassin himself stood before a round wooden table, a confident smile on his handsome brown face. A black outfit lined with small, shiny scales similar to snakeskin hugged his lean, muscular build.

Shelves of books lined the room behind him, vanishing into the distance. During my tenure at Edenfield High School, Underborn had posed as an English teacher named Mr. Turpin. If he was to be believed, he'd actually been a Templar serving under Thomas Borathen and survived an ambush at Thunder Rock that had claimed the lives of Templars and Daemos alike. In truth, the man was far more than an assassin. He was a center of information. Like Fjoeruss and Jeremiah, he was extremely powerful in his own way, and focused on an agenda all his own.

"I'll inform Pressley that we have guests," Phissilinth said. "Shall I have him bring you any tea?"

I assumed Pressley was the butler. "I'm fine."

"I'd like some oolong tea," Elyssa said.

Underborn nodded. "Have him bring me a fresh pot of Earl Grey."

"I'll inform him," Phissilinth said in a clipped voice.

I got the feeling he didn't enjoy being a messenger boy for the butler. I pulled out a chair from the table and took a seat. Elyssa sat next to me. Even though I wanted to bring up the reason for my visit, I was curious to see if Underborn had divined my intentions.

He sat across from us. "Mr. Slade, you have changed since the last time you visited this place."

I leaned back and clasped my hands behind my head. "Yeah, it's great. My pubic hair finally started to come in, and my voice is changing."

"Your sense of humor, however, has not." Underborn settled back into his chair. "I suppose we should get to the point." He paused, apparently waiting for me to commit by revealing my intentions.

"Sounds good." I looked at him expectantly. "What do you want?"

A look of surprise flashed across Underborn's face and just as quickly vanished. "How interesting." He looked from me to Elyssa. "I can see you've put a great deal of thought into this conversation."

"When meeting someone like you," Elyssa said, "it's important to discuss the options."

"Indeed." He rubbed his hands together as if this fresh challenge excited him. "Events have reached a critical juncture and it would seem Eden's fate dangles by a thread. You have helped me realize my goals beyond my wildest dreams, Mr. Slade."

I couldn't hide my surprise at his statement. "Does so much death and destruction make you happy?"

Underborn shook his head. "On the contrary. I am an advocate of precisely controlled violence. Despite my reputation as an assassin, I would describe myself as a—"

"Puppeteer?" Elyssa said.

He shrugged. "More accurately, as an adjuster. It is one reason I collected every foreseeance I could get my hands on. Knowing what we may face has made it easier to change the course of events."

"If that's the case, why haven't you killed Daelissa?" I blew out an exasperated breath. "A little bit of your precise violence could have prevented this war."

220

Underborn's forehead creased into a sad look. "I'm afraid the war is necessary. If not for the war, certain events would not have taken place, and other avenues would not have opened for us to pursue."

"Us?" I gave him a confused look.

"All of us." He smiled. "Now, let us get back to what I want."

Here it comes.

Elyssa's hand tightened on my leg.

Underborn seemed to relish the dramatic tension and milked the pause a little longer.

"You must not get out a lot," I said as the seconds ticked past. "Seriously, if you find this sort of thing so amusing, you need to get a girlfriend or a pet goat."

"Apologies, Mr. Slade." Underborn pressed his lips together and shook his head slowly. "I'm rather proud of the man you've grown into. I'd like to think my guidance from afar has helped."

"Guidance?" I snorted. "The godfather every kid wishes he had."

"Indeed." His expression turned serious. "Now, back to the point. In the most general of terms, Mr. Slade, I would like you to put an end to this war as efficiently as possible." Underborn's facial expression remained serious. "Unfortunately, I cannot assassinate Daelissa."

A pshaw exploded from my lips. "Can't or won't?"

"I cannot." For once, he looked mildly humbled by this statement. "I have tried several times to manipulate her into a position which would facilitate my ending her, but all attempts have failed." He leaned his forearms on the table. "Daelissa is always surrounded by her army and by battle mages skilled at warding against assassins. Even if I were to bypass all this security, Daelissa is now simply too powerful for me to kill." Underborn looked down. "She has snowballed out of control."

I threw up my hands. "Great! There goes my idea for cutting the head off the snake."

"There is more troubling news." The assassin looked back up. "Daelissa has recalled the Second Battalion from the front lines on Seraphina. They will be here by next week."

221

The next smartass comment I'd prepared died on my lips. "Another army?"

"The future is quite dire." Underborn slid a piece of parchment across the table to me. "After your first crushing defeat at the Grand Nexus, no less than thirty individuals with the gift of sight foresaw only one possible outcome of this war. Though this came from many sources, nearly every one of them says virtually the same thing. Rarely have I ever seen such agreement among foretellers."

What I read chilled my soul. *The bright one surges to victory crushing all before her. For Eden, for the Cataclyst, there is no hope save one. An act of pure love, a true willing sacrifice, will be the only path to victory.*

Chapter 26

I crumpled the parchment and threw it away. "I'm done with foreseeances. Four-three-one-one didn't predict what everyone thought it meant. This one is no different." Despite my desperate attempt to disregard the foretelling, my stomach tightened.

"Whether you believe it or not, it is very specific." Underborn glanced at the wad of parchment.

"No, it doesn't come out and say, 'Justin must kill himself to save the day,' does it?" I speared the parchment with Brilliance and watched it burn. "Just because Daelissa is, as you say, snowballing out of control, doesn't mean we can't beat her." *Who am I kidding?* Underborn himself admitted he couldn't assassinate Daelissa. I was one of the few people who might stand a chance at solo killing her. To get that close meant I wouldn't survive.

Sweat trickled down my face. My stomach impersonated a contortionist.

Elyssa squeezed my hand. She took my chin and turned my head to face hers. "Justin? Are you okay?"

I shook my head. "No, I'm not okay." I glared at Underborn. "Do you think we're doomed?"

"Not entirely." Underborn's expression regained some of its lost confidence. "I have some tools which might make your quest easier."

"Like the map and key?" I scowled. "If you hadn't taken them from me in the first place, we might have won a long time ago."

He waved his hand. "Water under the bridge, Mr. Slade. You and you alone possess the raw power and determination to stop Daelissa. It would appear your army, however, could use some help if we are to prove wrong this foreseeance."

"Are you offering your services?"

"I am." He looked at me as if I should fall to my knees and thank the heavens.

Instead, I narrowed my eyes with suspicion. "Does that include the entire guild?"

"Indeed." He clasped his hands on the table. "Most of us are not accustomed to fighting as part of a coordinated unit. We are, so to speak, weapons calibrated for independent operations."

A knock sounded on the door. The butler entered, and without a word, placed oolong tea before Elyssa and a cup of Earl Grey in front of Underborn. "Will that be all, sir?"

Underborn took a sip of tea and nodded. "Yes, Pressley."

The butler left.

From the time the butler entered to when he left, I couldn't stop trying to figure out how in the world a bunch of lone wolf assassins could help fight a war. I picked up the conversation where we'd left it. "If you and your people don't coordinate, how will you contribute? Do you plan to sit back and snipe enemies?"

"We can do far more than that." He took out an oval stone made of obsidian. "This is one of the Relics of Juranthemon we have found. It would appear there are many more than I had first surmised."

I looked at it curiously. "Is it a paperweight?"

Underborn chuckled. "I call this a blink stone. It enables the wearer to transport themselves instantly across short distances."

My interest abruptly doubled. "Does it make the user nauseous at all?"

"At first, yes." He shrugged. "After a number of uses, the wielder's body adjusts." Underborn rubbed the smooth surface of the stone. "It operates much like your innate ability to blink."

How the hell does he know I can do that? I tried to keep surprise from registering on my face. "What good will one blink stone do?"

"Who said we possessed only one?" One side of his mouth curled upward. "We found dozens of them at Thunder Rock in the same room with the portal-blocking statues you so cleverly used."

"Was this before or after I killed the horde of scorps protecting the place?"

"Some time after." He pressed the blink stone against his outfit. It stuck in place. "One must simply look where one wishes to go and will it." He vanished in a puff of shadows. "And you will appear there an instant later."

I turned in the direction of his voice and saw him behind me. "Wonderful. Are you offering these to me?"

Underborn blinked back behind his chair, pulled it out, and sat down, this time a little unsteadily. "No, I am simply showing you some of the capabilities we now have thanks to the relics. We can blink into the midst of our enemies, kill someone, and blink back out before they know what happened." He massaged his forehead. "Unfortunately, the more blinks you chain together, the more disoriented you become."

"I'd like one of these for Elyssa."

Underborn nodded quickly as if he'd anticipated this request. "Of course." He removed one from a pouch at his waist and slid it across to her.

Elyssa looked at it suspiciously before picking it up and pressing it to her Nightingale armor. "I'll test this out later. I don't feel like puking in front of everyone."

Underborn chuckled. "I'm sure one of your physical caliber will have no difficulties adjusting, Miss Borathen." He swung his gaze back to me. "Now, why don't you tell me how else I can help you?"

"Before we move on, I need to know the price." I motioned at Elyssa's blink stone. "What do you want in return for that?"

"Only that you allow us to remain autonomous."

I shrugged. "As long as your efforts aren't counterproductive to mine, that's fine with me."

"I assure you, we will mesh quite well."

Despite how forthcoming he was being, I still felt we were beating around bush. I decided to tell him what I really wanted. "Since you're in such a generous mood, I'd like to have the key and map back. We need it for logistics."

Underborn's eye twinkled as if I'd broached the very thing he expected. "I am willing to let you borrow them. In exchange, I only ask for the Chalon you took from the Grand Nexus."

By now, I'd decided that trying to figure out how he knew what he knew would only make me extremely paranoid. On the other hand, he didn't seem to know we had the original Chalon as well. Since Jeremiah had stolen it right from under our noses, it made me think that the old Arcane had been better about keeping secrets.

I countered with a question. "Why do you want the Chalon?"

"As you well know, it's useless since the Grand Nexus already has another Chalon, albeit on the Seraphina side of the gateway." He shrugged nonchalantly. "I'd simply like to study it."

"So, we get to *borrow* the map and key but have to *give* you a Chalon in exchange?" I shook my head. "I don't think so. I thought you wanted to help. Instead, you're up to your old games."

Elyssa leaned forward. "Borrowing the map and key is acceptable. We'll happily return them after the war. Why do you really want the Chalon?"

"I believe the symbols on it may offer clues about other realms and locations of other Relics." He tapped a finger to his chin as if giving a great deal of thought to something. "How about this—you may borrow the map and key for as long as I borrow the Chalon?"

That sounded like a reasonable arrangement, but his willingness to negotiate only made me more cautious. He knew something about the Chalon we didn't. I was about to pepper him with more questions when I realized what he'd just said confirmed my hunch. Only someone who'd seen the Chalon would know about the tiny symbols etched into it. Even Jeremiah hadn't known about those until he'd studied it at length. That meant only one thing.

I nodded as though Underborn's proposal was entirely reasonable and then said, "You already have a Chalon, don't you?"

Underborn blinked a couple of times. A smile slowly stretched across his face. "What makes you suspect that?"

I gave him a stern look. "Yes or no, Underborn."

If he was exasperated he didn't show it. "Yes."

Elyssa pressed for the kill. "If that's the case, why would you need a second one?"

"I would like to test some theories, nothing more." Despite our badgering, he remained calm. "Surely, it will do you no harm to let me borrow the Chalon."

"If you know of anything the Chalon could do to help us, you need to tell me now." I felt my fists tighten at the man's enigmatic posturing. Even with our backs to the wall, he was still intent on wringing out a deal for himself.

"I know nothing for certain."

I almost slammed my fist on the table, but resisted the urge. "I have the feeling you know exactly what you're looking for." I shook my head and stood up. "You know what? Keep your map and key. Just stay home and wait for us to lose this war. I'm sure you'll do just fine when Daelissa is running the world."

Underborn held up his hands, palms out. "No need to be melodramatic, Mr. Slade."

"I wish I was just being melodramatic." I pressed my knuckles on the table and leaned toward him. "If you can't be forthcoming with me, I have no use for you."

Elyssa took the blink stone off her armor and dropped it on the table. "I hope you find what you're looking for in life. I think the quality of living is about to go to hell once Daelissa takes control."

Underborn pinched the bridge of his nose as if a horrible headache had just tightened a vice on his cranium. "You two are simply intractable."

A spiteful laugh burst from Elyssa. "We happen to care about the world, not our own personal gain."

"I can't believe you used to be a Templar." I snorted with as much disdain as I could cram into a snort. "I'll bet your mother would be proud, *Kevin.*"

Underborn reeled back as if I'd slapped him in the face. He stood and greeted us with stony silence, though his right eye twitched as if he wanted to murder us on the spot. "I can see now why I decided never to have children. Were you anyone else, I would kill you on the spot for your insolence."

I suffused my body with Brilliance until I glowed. "I'm not the same boy you toyed with before, Underborn. If you truly think you're a match for me, then let's get this over with right now."

The anger in his face smoothed over. "Just because you could kill me in a direct fight doesn't mean I couldn't end you by my own means."

"Then maybe I should just kill you right now so you're no longer a threat."

Underborn backed up a step. "I bear you no ill will, Mr. Slade, but you are very tiring to deal with."

"Right back at you." I flashed a grin. "Now, why don't you tell me what having a second Chalon can do?"

The assassin dropped into his chair, an air of resignation hanging about him. "There are two differences between the Grand Nexus and the other Alabaster Arches."

My curiosity was piqued. "The Grand Nexus is much larger and has a socket for the Chalon."

"Correct." Underborn clasped his hands and placed them on the table. "As you may know, Serena, Daelissa's pet Arcane, has been able to attune the Chalon using recordings of your mother singing. I managed to procure a copy of these recordings and used them with the Chalon in my possession."

I was confused. "You used your Chalon on the Grand Nexus?"

"No. I took the Chalon in my possession to the Three Sisters Alabaster Arch. Although it has no socket for the Chalon, I discovered that it will bind itself to the same area on the Alabaster Arch that it normally would on the Grand Nexus."

I ran through the possibilities in my mind. "You mean we could change the alignment of the Grand Nexus and all the other Alabaster Arches by attuning a Chalon on another arch?"

"Incredible," Elyssa said. "We could seal off the nexus from Seraphina. We could stop the Second Battalion from ever reaching Eden!"

"Ah, but there is one problem," Underborn said in a cautionary tone. "I was unable to wrest control from the nexus. The Chalon focuses and channels the power required to open a portal between

228

realms. I believe if I placed two of them on the same arch I could overpower the Grand Nexus and assign control to a different Alabaster Arch."

I tried not to let hope override my common sense, but it was hard not to see how cutting off Daelissa from Seraphina and her new troops could help us win this war.

Elyssa's eyes shined with renewed faith. "I can see why you didn't want to tell us this, Underborn. If you pulled it off, you'd control the new Grand Nexus."

He shrugged as if it were of no concern. "Perhaps."

I stood. "You can borrow the second Chalon on the provision that you return it once the war is over."

Underborn stood and offered his hand. "I accept, Mr. Slade."

I rose from my chair and accepted his hand. "The map and the key, please?"

"Of course." He reached to a shelf behind him, withdrew a book, and removed the map and key from behind it. "I will show you how to operate them."

He knew what I wanted all along. "Good, I'll need instructions."

"You'll need much more than that, Mr. Slade." Underborn took out an arcphone and projected an image showing Daelissa standing before an army of battle golems, each one every bit as massive as the five we'd fought in our first battle. She appeared to be inspecting them with Serena. "I'm afraid Daelissa showed you only a fraction of her capabilities in the last battle. Even if we prevent her reinforcements from arriving, she has more than enough might to crush you."

The surge of hope I'd felt drained like melting snow in a fire pit. My forces would be hard pressed to stop her next attack. Without some kind of reinforcements, we weren't going to last long.

Elyssa took me aside and spoke in a low voice. "Justin, I'll retrieve the Chalon. You stay here and find out how to operate the map and key."

I nodded. "Bring both Chalons."

She gave me a dubious look. "Are you sure that's wise?"

"What if two aren't enough to overpower the nexus?" I slashed a hand through the air. "We don't have time for games."

"We just have to hope Underborn feels the same way." I kissed and hugged her tight. "I'll be waiting here for you." I walked to Underborn and told him the plan.

"Phissilinth will escort you back to the Grotto and wait for you to return with the Chalons." Underborn pursed his lips and looked at me. "Two Chalons, Mr. Slade? It appears I've underestimated you yet again." He picked up the blink stone from the table and handed it to Elyssa. "Don't forget your gift."

She regarded it uncertainly for a moment before taking it and pressing it to her uniform. "I'll be back soon." She and Phissilinth left.

"Now, let's get to the map." Underborn smoothed the parchment open. A myriad of crisscrossing black lines covered the tan surface. I could hardly make heads or tails of it. Underborn stared at it for a few seconds. Most of the lines faded away until all that remained was a three-dimensional drawing of a door.

"Did you clear the map?" I asked.

He nodded. "I find it easier to scroll the map to a desired location first. Once there, I focus on a smaller area until I find the door I want to use. In this case, I've selected a closet door in a highrise condominium in downtown Atlanta."

"No wonder the lines were so dense." It had been like looking at a blueprint of the structure.

"Precisely. The map will draw every detail unless you direct it to simplify the illustration." He touched the drawing of the door and narrowed his eyes. The door glowed a dull yellow. "I've now selected the first door." He pinched his fingers on the map and zoomed out much like a person did with the map on an arctablet. "This is how you zoom out." Outlines of the Atlanta skyline appeared. Underborn tightened his fist and twisted it sideways. The map rotated to an overhead view. "That is how you shift the orientation."

I watched as he zoomed in on a house in the northern suburbs and selected a closet door. A glowing yellow line connected the two doors.

"To confirm the connection, you simply pluck it." Underborn pinched the line with two fingers and pulled at it like a guitar string. The line actually lifted from the map and vibrated when he released it.

As it grew still, the yellow glow faded and left a light blue line behind. "The connection between the two doors is now established."

He continued with the lessons, showing me how to break a connection, how to form multiple connections between doors, and how to select a specific one with the key. The map didn't require a door to have a handle or even a lock to work. If a person wanted it to home in on their location, they simply had to think about it and tap the map twice. Underborn refused to let me do it, however, lest I discover the location of his secret hideout.

Thirty minutes into the lesson, Elyssa texted me to let me know she'd gone into Jeremiah's vault and was procuring the Chalons. I was texting her back when I heard a cry of pain from somewhere outside the library. Underborn and I exchanged concerned glances. He folded the map, placed it and the key in a small leather pouch, and handed it to me.

"Keep it safe." Underborn opened the door and crept into the hallway.

Another agonized shout reached our ears. Quick as a cat, Underborn raced down the hallway, his feet making no sound. I followed him. The Nightingale armor masked most of my footsteps. He stopped at the portrait of a devilish-looking man dressed in all black. Underborn slid the picture to the side and waved a hand across the stone wall. The wall turned transparent to reveal the waiting room.

"Illusion," Underborn whispered.

I was too busy staring at the bizarre scene on the other side of the wall. The source of the screams was a man dressed in butler livery. A doughy white blob encased his right leg. A humanoid figure with sickly pale skin watched with a smile.

"Where is the entrance?" the doughy man asked in a gurgling voice. "Tell us now and we'll make your death quick."

A grinning tooth-filled mouth formed in the blob around the butler's leg. It opened wide and then clamped down. The man clenched his teeth, but the pain was too much. He screamed.

An army of spiders seemed to crawl up my body as the identity of the attackers dawned on me. They were beings I'd hoped never to see again.

Flarks.

Chapter 27

Mr. Bigglesworth, Ivy's shape-shifting protector, had been the last and only Flark I'd ever encountered. The creatures were nearly immune to direct magical attack, and could shift like putty into virtually anything.

Even Underborn looked unsure how to proceed. "I wonder where Daelissa found more Flarks," he murmured in an offhand manner. "It would seem I underestimated Serena."

"It would seem underestimation is your strong suit." His last statement bothered me. "What does Serena have to do with this?"

He shrugged. "I had some dealings with her. It would appear she somehow located this place."

"So much for your hideout."

"This is one of many." He shrugged.

The butler shrieked in pain again.

I gave Underborn a troubled look. "What about your man in there? We need to save him."

"Yes, I suppose Pressley would appreciate it." Seemingly in no hurry to rush in, he put a hand on his chin and pondered the situation.

"The last time we killed one of those things, it was with a magical drain ward." I shuddered as Pressley cried out again. "Do you have wards like that around here?"

"No. I suppose we'll just have to grab Pressley and run for it."

I remembered Elyssa and sent a quick text to keep her and Phissilinth from returning here. *Flarks are in Underborn's hideout. Wait at Queens Gate.*

Her reply came seconds later. *I'm coming to help.*

No, we're okay. Just wait.

I tucked away my phone. "Is this illusion solid?"

Underborn nodded. "I'll remove it for you. After that, I'm not sure how to free Pressley."

"Let me take care of that."

"Very well." He traced a pattern on the wall. The illusion on the other side must have vanished quickly because the humanoid Flark turned toward us quick as a snake.

Channeling Murk with one hand, I shot strands around Pressley's torso. With the other hand, I dug a molten furrow in the stone floor just next to the blob around the butler's leg. Lava bubbled onto the mass. Flarks might be immune to direct magic, but they were vulnerable to indirect attacks. The blob writhed. The mouth around Pressley's leg howled in pain and the mass retreated as fire bit into it.

The second Pressley was free, I jerked him toward us. The skin on his leg was blistered where the Flark had touched it. The creatures liked to consume their prey live and the experience felt like swimming in acid.

"Underborn!" one Flark gurgled as his companion flowed into a bipedal form next to him.

"The Slade boy is here," Flark number two hissed.

Underborn traced a pattern, presumably to close the wall again, but the Flarks reacted with lightning speed. Tendrils of their doughy bodies zipped through the opening and jerked their amorphous masses forward like rubber bands. The disgusting creatures blocked the opening and kept it from sealing.

"Let's go." Underborn ran down the hallway toward the door I'd used to arrive here. "I need the key."

I pulled it from the pouch and handed it to him. He twisted it in the lock and opened it.

"Good heavens," Pressley said.

I spun in time to see the Flarks springing down the hallway after us, sticky tendrils of pale flesh jerking them along.

We leapt through the door and into the stable at the Grotto. Before I could slam the door closed, the Flarks thrust into the opening and jammed it.

Oliver leapt up from a bale of hay, eyes wide as we ran past. "What is that?"

"Run!" Underborn shouted over his shoulder.

Pressley huffed and puffed. "I'm in no condition to be running around like this, sir."

We ran from the stable and into the parking lot. Aside from an electric green Maserati with purple racing stripes, the area was empty. I didn't want to lead the Flarks up the ramp to the shopping mall above. Unleashing them on the nom population was unacceptable. I stopped and turned to face our pursuers.

Underborn touched a pouch at his side. "I must admit I have no idea how to kill a Flark."

The two shape-shifters emerged from the stable. One flowed into humanoid form. The other took a hybrid shape with a human top and snakelike bottom. Neither looked nearly as skilled in shifting as Mr. Bigglesworth had been, which led me to believe they hadn't been in Eden for long, or were freshly revived from a husked state. One hissed; the other gurgled as they walked the few yards separating us.

"What do you want?" I said, hoping to stall for time.

"Two deaths: yours and his," Gurgles said. "One was planned, the other providential."

Not the answer I was hoping for. I shifted to another line of questioning. "Why do you work for Daelissa?"

"It matters not." Gurgles's empty black eyes regarded us as he drew inexorably closer.

"I will take Slade," the other one hissed. "She will be pleased."

I pshawed and put on a little bravado. "Don't make me laugh, Hissmeister Pro. I'll give you a choice. Retreat now, or die."

Gurgles made a sound like a man hawking up a loogey. "There is nothing you can do to harm us."

"No?" I traced the floor with destruction and sent flecks of molten stone flying at them. The Flarks zipped with lightning speed away from the magma. Gurgles flew at me, his body spreading open like a net. Hissmeister Pro slithered toward me from the other side.

I threw up barriers on both sides. Gurgles splatted against the shield. His buddy flowed around it.

235

"Get back!" I shouted at Underborn and the others.

"I wish I could help," the assassin said. "If I had access to my weapons—"

"If ifs and buts were candy and nuts, we'd all be fat as pigs," I muttered through clenched teeth while adjusting my barriers to delay the Flarks. "Now get back."

Gurgles flowed over my barrier, just yards away and sprang forward.

I tried to leap out of the way, but the Flark was just too fast. His doughy white flesh wrapped around Underborn and me. The Flark seemed to seep through the Nightingale armor, completely bypassing it like liquid. Agony erupted from every molecule of skin. There was pain, and then there was *PAIN*. This sensation was squarely in the latter category. I couldn't stop the scream tearing from my throat. My vision went blurry from tears. I heard a growling noise and realized it was Underborn trying to be a tough guy.

I had no such concerns about proving my manliness and let it go. I had only seconds to do something before the pain completely overwhelmed my senses and knocked me unconscious. My survival instinct suggested something I'd used to escape death before. Squeezing shut my eyes, I fought past the pain, channeled Murk from every inch of my body, and pushed the energy outward. The pain abruptly abated as the barrier pushed the doughy flesh away from me.

I knew I wasn't out of the woods just yet, though. The creature's magic resistance was already weakening the barrier. Frankly, I was surprised a shield worked at all. When I'd fought Bigglesworth, any direct attacks simply splashed off or flowed around him with no effect. Then again, a barrier was rigid and couldn't splash or flow around something unless I allowed it.

That gave me an idea.

Using the shield like a giant spatula, I scraped Gurgles off Underborn. Once the assassin was free, I delivered a swift kick to his backside and sent him skidding across the polished stone surface toward Oliver and Pressley.

Hissmeister slithered toward my feet. I leapt backward and released the barrier. Gurgles splatted on top of his buddy, but both quickly reformed. Before they could separate, I enclosed them in a sphere of Murk. The two Flarks squirmed inside the trap. The more they moved, the more they weakened their prison. I funneled more power into the bubble, but I knew it wouldn't last.

Think fast, Justin!

Whereas humans were made up mostly of water, Flarks were comprised almost purely of magical energy. That was what made them so resistant to it and allowed them to change shape so easily. It was also why Bigglesworth had died to a magical drain ward. I didn't know of any way to drain their magical energy, but I did have something that might neutralize it.

I wove Brilliance into the Murk bubble, infusing the two together. The Flarks shrieked like banshees. They thrashed and flailed as the ultraviolet bubble grew grayer and grayer. As they vanished from sight, I sensed them slowing until they became absolutely still. Breathing heavily from the effort, I released the weave. The gray bubble dissipated like fog leaving the contorted shapes of the Flarks standing like frozen statues. I couldn't tell if they were dead or simply petrified, but their usually pale white flesh looked blue-gray and completely still.

"You continue to impress me, Mr. Slade." Underborn stood by my side. "It behooves me to thank you for saving my life."

I wiped sweat from my forehead and gave him a long steady look. "Remember that the next time you want to deal with someone like Serena."

He paced around the Flarks. "Are they dead?"

I shrugged. "I don't know. If they're not, I don't know how to get rid of them."

"I believe I have just the thing should they reawaken." He motioned to Pressley. "Go back to the lair and retrieve one of the extra-large diamond fiber body bags."

"Get me tea, he says," the butler mumbled. "Bring my dinner, he says. Pressley, good man, fetch me an extra-large body bag." He turned a dour look on Underborn." I shall return shortly with them, sir." The butler seemed a bit frayed at the edges, but had somehow maintained a slippery grip on his professional dignity even if his butler livery was torn and bloody. He headed back to the stables at a brisk pace, his injured leg giving him a limp.

"I remember old Bigglesworth," Oliver said in a quiet voice. "Never thought I'd see another bloody Flark after him."

"I, too, thought he was the last of his kind." Underborn inspected a raw patch of skin where Gurgles had touched him. "Unfortunately, I don't know enough about these creatures to say if Daelissa retrieved them from another realm, or revived them here."

"Let's hope these are the only two she has." My body itched like crazy all over as if I'd rolled around naked in a patch of poison ivy. The charms in the Nightingale armor tried to soothe the irritated skin, but the magical injuries resisted treatment.

Pressley returned a few minutes later with a large black body bag. "Here you are, sir."

Underborn ran a finger down the front to unseal it. "Diamond fiber is nearly impervious to magic, and is non-porous. I believe it should hold them should they awaken."

The gray tumorous-looking mass of Flarks quivered.

"I think we'd better do this in a hurry." I gripped the other end of the bag and helped Underborn slide it over the creatures. Using the diamond fiber like a glove, I pulled the Flarks completely inside it, tilted them to the ground, and sealed the bag.

Underborn produced a dagger and held it out to me. "Perhaps you should seal it with blood to be safe."

I took the knife, nicked a finger, and ran blood down the closed seam. Only I would be able to open it now. "I find it rather interesting that you have diamond fiber body bags."

"The supernatural world is full of surprises." The assassin seemed amused. "There have been times when a target decided it wasn't ready to die just yet."

His statement reminded me of his grim profession and I was already in too grim a mood. I texted Elyssa, *All clear,* and sent her a picture of the fabulous Maserati for a reference. A portal opened a moment later. She and Phissilinth stepped through.

The small man looked at the body bag on the floor and raised an eyebrow. "It seems I missed a spot of excitement."

Elyssa assaulted me with kisses. "What happened? Are you okay?"

I held her against me. "I'm fine, babe." I told her about our little adventure. When I was done, I gave Underborn a stern look. "Looks like playing both sides only put you right in the line of fire."

"It is a calculated risk," the assassin replied.

I gave him a suspicious look. "What I'd like to know is why the timing coincided with my visit."

"Coincidence." Underborn wiped the blade of his dagger with an oiled cloth. "Daelissa knows she has your back against the proverbial wall. She must have reasoned that you might turn to me for help and sent Flark assassins to dispose of me before you made contact. I suspect if they'd been successful, one of them would have assumed my identity and tried to kill you when you came to visit."

I turned to Pressley. "What did they interrogate you about?"

"They wished to know Master Underborn's location." He tilted his nose up. "I, of course, refused to comply with their questioning. I may not be an assassin, but I have sworn the oath and would die before betraying the guild."

"Did they ask about me?" I asked.

He shook his head. "No. They seemed rather surprised to learn you were already here."

My eyes went to the body bag as it shuddered. "I guess we can bring along the Flarks and question them if they revive."

Underborn gave me a gold ASE. "Contact me with this when you're ready to move on Daelissa."

I rolled my eyes. "Look, enough with your special ASEs and sneaky ways. Just give me your stinking phone number so I can text you." I held out Nookli to him with the number pad on the screen.

He seemed to wrestle internally with the idea. Apparently, the idea pinned him to the mat because he finally entered his digits. "Do not give this out to anyone."

"Wouldn't dream of it." I planned to write his number on bathroom stalls and give it out to telemarketers once the war was over. I grabbed one end of the body bag and dragged it toward the glimmering portal Elyssa had come through. "We'll be in touch."

Underborn reached into his pocket and withdrew the key. "I almost forgot to return it to you." He regarded me with a curious look. "How do you plan to use it to transport an army?"

I took the key and flashed a confident grin. "If my plan works, I'll be sure to let you know." With that, I left the assassin with a disgruntled look on his face.

We stepped through the portal and into the omniarch room in Queens Gate. I closed the portal.

Elyssa burst into laughter. "I loved the look on Underborn's face when you left him hanging."

"It was the least I could do after all the crap he's put us through." I exited the room, dragging the body bag behind me. The movements inside it became more frequent.

Shelton stood outside the mansion watching the construction golems as they put the finishing touches on the roof. He turned as we drew near and flinched back a step when he saw the body bag.

His upper lip curled back. "What in the blazes is inside that?"

"Flarks," I said.

Shelton jumped back. "Are you crazy? There's no way—" He stopped midsentence and narrowed his eyes at me. "You're just kidding, right?"

I shook my head. "This is diamond fiber, though, so they shouldn't be able to get out."

He opened his mouth and shut it several times. "I don't even know what to say, but I sure as hell want to hear the story."

I gave him the short version and held up the map and key. "Mission accomplished."

"You've got balls, I'll give you that." Shelton shuddered. "The Brotherhood of Assassins ain't no pansy organization to be screwing with."

"The Assassins *Guild*," Elyssa said.

I tucked away the map and key. "I need those giant unfolding doors as soon as possible."

"I'm on it." Shelton took out his arcphone and tapped on it. "Adam is going to come over and assist me."

"Not that you need the help, of course." I grinned.

He returned a knowing look. "Nah, I figured he could learn something by hanging out with a pro."

Elyssa snorted. "You two have fun."

My smiled faded as I thought about the terrifying images Underborn had shown me of Daelissa's army. "Even with Fjoeruss's battle golems, I don't know if we can win this." I told Shelton what I'd seen.

"Holy butt macaroons," Shelton growled. "We can't catch a break, can we?"

"Our timeline just got a lot shorter. We need more help." I sighed. "The Brotherhood—"

"The Assassins Guild," Elyssa said. "How many times do I have to remind you that they're equal opportunity?"

Usually I would've enjoyed joking around with her, but my mood was growing more sour by the moment. "What good will assassins do against an army? Daelissa has an army of giant battle golems. I doubt even Fjoeruss has numbers to match hers. If we don't cut her off from the nexus soon, she'll have another battalion of archangels and infantry too."

Shelton grunted. "We need bigger and badder guns."

I completely agreed. Unfortunately, we'd been soundly turned down by the only people who might be able to help. Without Science Academy, I didn't know how we could win.

Chapter 28

The next few days felt like the calm before a massive storm. Nom volunteers flooded Queens Gate, eager to lend a helping hand to angels who could not only save the world, but also cure the volunteers of illnesses and disabilities the nom medical system had been unable to treat. With the prisms provided by Fjoeruss, the Darklings dual fed and grew stronger. I tried to find new allies, even going so far as to beg Altash and Lulu for their help again, but the leviathan dragons once again ignored my pleas. Slitheren and the smaller dragons were nowhere to be found.

Underborn began experimenting with the Alabaster Arch at the Three Sisters to see if he could indeed wrest control from the Grand Nexus. For some reason, the recordings of my mother singing didn't work as well with three Chalons. Mom and a crew of Arcanes who specialized in arch operations joined his research.

I met with the leaders of allied factions and went over different scenarios that might help us win the next fight. Fjoeruss informed us that he had only four battle golems—far fewer than half the units Daelissa possessed. He'd seen little utility in creating such monsters with an army of gray men to rely on. By the end of the meeting, he admitted that even if he committed all his time to building more battle golems, he would need months to match Daelissa's current numbers. By then, her own army would likely have outpaced his efforts.

The political situations in nom governments were also growing more unstable. Russia had already invaded Ukraine and increased tensions across all the Baltic nations and Europe. The nom news stations were filled with stories about a new cold war. Daemos operatives were doing all they could to keep the larger governments from destabilizing, but Russia was a lost cause.

I spent as much time with Elyssa as possible. Every day with her was a gift I didn't intend to squander, especially since the next battle with Daelissa might end the war with us on the losing end. We set up a massive movie screen in Colossus Stadium and showed the Darkling army the *Princess Bride*. Flava absolutely loved the movie and began referring to Daelissa as a warthog-faced buffoon. Ketiss and many other Darklings mistook the movie for a historical documentary and wondered if we might enlist the help of the Dread Pirate Roberts.

As for our mortal enemy, Daelissa—well, she seemed to be content to wait. What little information our spies brought from Thunder Rock indicated the Seraphim forces were feeding from humans and growing stronger every day. Her battle mages were working on more battle golems and other magical weapons. But the most troubling news came at the beginning of the following week when one of Underborn's spies hand-delivered a small scroll to me.

Elyssa and I had just returned from a nice dinner at the Copper Swan in Queens Gate. I opened the parchment and held it so we could both read it.

The Brightling Second Battalion is three days away from entering an Alabaster Arch in Seraphina and arriving in Eden. There is also talk in Daelissa's camp of another unknown ally coming through the portal. Suggest we move up the timetable for taking control of the Alabaster Arch network. Send word through my messenger.

-Underborn

"Unknown ally?" Elyssa grimaced. "I don't like the sound of that."

"Or the Second Battalion." I incinerated the parchment with Brilliance and turned to the spy. "Tell Underborn to meet us at El Dorado first thing in the morning. We'll use the Alabaster Arch there."

The spy nodded and sped away without another word.

"Why El Dorado?" Elyssa said. "What if Daelissa figures out which arch we're using to bypass the Grand Nexus?"

"There are several good reasons." I hooked an arm around her shoulder and headed down the path from the ferry dock toward the Dark Forest. "The Three Sisters is still under siege. If it weren't for tons of rocks and debris, Daelissa's people would have already broken through. If we convert another Alabaster Arch into the new Grand Nexus, we can more easily control and defend El Dorado."

"We would be fighting aboveground, I assume."

I nodded. "The caverns would be too cramped."

She pursed her lips. "If the dragons change their minds, at least they're not far away."

"Exactly." I was so sick of them ignoring me, but even I couldn't bully one of those monsters into a conversation. "Daelissa forced the last fight by attacking the city we call home. Now she seems content to sit back and build up her forces. I have a feeling that once the Second Battalion reaches Eden, she'll attack again."

Elyssa wrinkled her forehead. "I agree, but what would her next target be? Queens Gate?"

I shook my head. "She has no easy way to get her troops here. Even if she hijacks the Obsidian Arch in the way station or Colossus Stadium, she'll be faced with a bottleneck. Funneling her troops through one of those arches while under attack would only lead to staggering losses on her side."

"True." She thought about it for a moment. "She has an Obsidian Arch in Thunder Rock, which means there are hundreds of different places she could attack."

I booted a rock out of our path as we reached the walkway near the dorms at Arcane University. "I don't know much about her new tactician, Arturo, but from my conversations with Ketiss, it sounds like he's the sort of seraph who sticks with what works."

"You think he'll attack Atlanta again?"

I nodded. "The information Underborn gave us indicates that the only reason Arturo didn't commit all their battle golems was because they weren't fully weaponized. Daelissa probably pushed him to finish the war, so he finally attacked with what was available, drew us out, and did his best to annihilate our army."

"I'd concur with that assessment," Elyssa said in her military tone of voice. "It would also explain why goliaths Bronze, Ash, and Quartz were underpowered. Some of their weapon shards weren't fully functional. I'll bet they were rushed through production."

"Exactly." I directed us down a walkway leading to the left of the dark dormitory buildings. Aside from occasional patrols, the campus was like a ghost town. "Arturo has probably convinced Daelissa that the best option is to bring all their unconventional forces fully online and wait for the Second Battalion to arrive."

"An army of goliaths and nearly two thousand Seraphim sounds like Daelissa's wet dream come true." Elyssa stopped walking and faced me. "We can't let her wait, Justin."

"Exactly. We need to force a fight somewhere." I rested a hand on her hip. "I've considered trying to force a confrontation at El Dorado, especially if we can take over the Grand Nexus. It's far away from nom populations, and Daelissa couldn't transport her goliaths there very easily since there's no Obsidian Arch within hundreds of miles."

"But would she attack without her prime assets?"

"If we cut her off from Seraphina before reinforcements arrive, there's a good chance it would leave her with little choice."

Elyssa bit her lower lip and thought it over. "Fighting on our turf, our army versus hers, we might have a shot at winning this." Her eyes brightened. "I think it's worth a try."

"My main concern is Arturo. He might convince Daelissa to simply proceed with another Atlanta attack."

The excitement faded from her face. "What will we do if he does?"

I shook my head. "I know this sounds horrible, but I don't think we can afford to respond. Without a counter to their goliaths, I don't see how our forces could survive another encounter."

"In other words, we have to make sure Daelissa doesn't listen to him." A slow smile spread across her lips. "Daelissa has a horrible temper and she hates you with a passion. If we take control of the Alabaster Arch network, maybe you could rub it in her face. I'd be willing to bet that would make her come to El Dorado."

"I think you're right." I kissed her on the nose. "Maybe I'll call her a warthog-faced buffoon."

Elyssa rubbed her hands together. "I can't wait to see the look on that bitch's face."

"Let's go home and compile a list of insults. I want to be prepared for this."

She giggled and wrapped her arms around my neck. "You really know how to show a girl a good time."

The next morning, we met Underborn at El Dorado. My mother was already there with the assassin, inspecting the Alabaster Arch. She gave me and Elyssa warm hugs.

Underborn didn't give us hugs, opting instead to nod briefly in our general direction. "I can see why you've chosen El Dorado, Mr. Slade. Should Daelissa discover which Alabaster Arch we've used to take control from the Grand Nexus, she might think twice before attacking here."

"Actually, I'm hoping she'll attack us here." I outlined my plan to force a fight we might win.

"She won't bite," Underborn said without hesitation. "If there's anything stronger than Daelissa's ego, it's her sense of self-preservation. You might anger her, but unless she feels confident of victory, she won't attack."

"I'd have to agree." Mom quirked her lips into a sad frown. "I've seen Daelissa so angry she was literally foaming at the mouth. Somehow, she bottled up that rage and saved it for later. I don't think you can goad her into such a risky attack."

"But, Justin and I stayed up late making a list of insults," Elyssa said. "We came up with some pretty funny ones."

"I had it all planned out." I blew out a breath of disgust. "It all started with calling her a miserable, vomitous mass, and ended with telling her to stick her head in doo-doo."

Underborn blinked a couple of times. "You obviously put some serious thought into this, Mr. Slade. I fear you'll have to come up with something better."

"I'm not giving up on the idea." I turned to the Alabaster Arch. "What have you found out so far about taking control from the nexus? We have less than a day before her troops reach the gateway."

"It has proven considerably more difficult than I thought." Underborn withdrew the three Chalons. Each sphere was small, white, and etched with tiny lines. "We've tried individually aligning the orbs with Seraphina, and then affixing them to the arch, but the Grand Nexus resists our attempts to remove it as the primary arch."

"I can sense our Chalons overpowering the nexus, but just when they're about to take control, the nexus take the arches offline and resets." Mom threw up her hands. "I don't know what else we can do."

"I know just who to call." I sent a text to Adam Nosti. *Need help hacking an Alabaster Arch at El Dorado.*

He responded a moment later. *I can be there in an hour. Helping Shelton with your magic doors.*

"Magic doors?"

I flinched and saw Underborn standing behind me. "Snoop much?"

He didn't seem the least bit embarrassed. "Do these doors have something to do with the map and key?"

"They're making giant doors that can fold into compact form for easy transport."

"Interesting." He narrowed his eyes. "That would solve a great many logistics problems should your unconventional idea work."

"Exactly." I put away my phone. "Now if only we had an army of battle golems to transport with them."

"Given the lack of time before our next conflict, I don't believe constructing more battle golems is the answer." Underborn idly rolled the Chalons between his fingers like a street magician manipulating marbles. "You've made ample use of flying carpets, but have you considered rocket sticks and flying brooms? They're much faster."

"Flying carpets are more stable," Elyssa said. "Arcanes find it easier to cast from them."

"Perhaps, but what about Seraphim?" Underborn gave us a sly smile.

"Flying brooms?" I'd never even considered such a thing. The more I thought about it, the more I liked the idea. "Are they hard to fly?"

Underborn waggled his hand in a so-so gesture. "The learning curve is a little steep, but it just so happens that you have a resident flying broom expert."

I knew the answer immediately. Underborn seemed intent on making me wait for the answer so I decided to ruin his fun. I folded my arms. "I'm totally over your dramatic pauses. You're talking about Bella."

Disappointment flickered across the assassin's face. "Indeed. Your friend Bella used to be in one of the underground boomstick leagues here."

"Boomstick?" My forehead pinched. "Isn't that a shotgun?"

"It's Arcane slang for highly modified broomsticks and rocket sticks, especially those used in racing," Elyssa said. "The Templars bust racers who decided to take their sport into nom cities."

"Sweet!" It seemed there was always something cool I hadn't known about the Overworld. I'd seen flying brooms around campus during my first days at Science Academy and Arcane University. Heck, I'd even seen frat boys riding flying vacuum cleaners, mops, and those rolling floor sweepers used in restaurants. I'd never considered them viable for combat operations, especially the one Bella wanted to pack for our trip to Seraphina. I took out my phone and called Bella. I didn't waste time explaining what I wanted when she answered. "Are you a boomstick expert?"

She paused as if the question caught her off guard. "Dare I ask why you want to know?"

"Underborn suggested flying brooms might be more effective for our Seraphim combat operations than flying carpets," I said. "What do you think?"

She made a squealing noise. "I think it's a wonderful idea. We'll need modified broomsticks. Do you know where we can get them?"

I turned to Underborn. "Where can we get boomsticks?"

He took out his arcphone and tapped on it. "I have an excellent contact in the underground league who can supply them. Give me a few moments and I'll make the arrangements."

I put the phone back to my ear. "I'll let you know once we have them."

"This will be fun, Justin." Bella sounded super-excited. "I can't wait."

I wanted to feel optimistic about this venture, but a part of me decided I was desperately grasping at straws, or more specifically, straw brooms. The other Seraphim and I might be more mobile, but would we be any match for the archangels? More importantly, would we have time to train with them?

Chapter 29

Underborn's contact came through, but he wouldn't deal with Templars, so I had to leave Elyssa behind. Shelton, Bella, and I took a flying carpet down into Queens Gate. The meeting place didn't show up on the map, so we used directions given to us by Underborn. After twisting through countless alleys, we finally arrived at a dead end.

"Son of a monkey's ass," Shelton said as he regarded the red brick walls on three sides. "I'll bet Underborn is having a good laugh."

"Did we miss a turn?" Bella waved her wand around the alley, casting revelation spells intended to highlight illusions. Her spells fizzled on the walls and failed to find anything.

I looked at my notes and recounted the trip in my head. Despite the complex instructions, I felt positive we hadn't missed any steps. I examined the last few sentences.

Turn right into Blind Wizard's Alley.
Take a bow.

When I'd first read the last sentence, I thought it was telling us to pat ourselves on the back for getting here. Now I felt certain it was literally telling us to nod our heads. I lowered the carpet to the cobblestone road, looked at one of the walls, and bowed.

With a loud grating noise, the red brick wall at the end of the alley slid down into the ground, revealing a dark passage.

"Thank heavens," Bella said. "I think Harry was about to lose his temper."

Shelton grumbled something about kicking mysterious assassins in the rear end and walked into the dark passage. He vanished from sight the instant he stepped inside. Narrowing my eyes, I peered into the pitch black, but Shelton was nowhere to be seen. I stepped through after him. The second I crossed the threshold, I stood inside a large well-lit garage instead of a pitch-black tunnel.

Bella bumped into me. "How interesting. It would seem this place doesn't hide behind illusion. It uses some kind of pocket dimension magic."

"Underborn set it up for me," said a young Asian man as he came around the corner. He sported thick black hair and wore tight-fitting black jeans and a light-blue T-shirt with a yellow lightning bolt on the front. "I'm Rai."

Shelton snorted. "You sure as hell don't look like an underground racer to me."

Rai shrugged. "What did you expect? A nom grease monkey?"

"I sure expected more after traipsing all over the blasted city looking for this place." Shelton scowled like a hungry man who'd just dropped his last jelly-filled donut into the gutter.

I glanced around the garage. One side held racks upon racks of brooms. Stainless steel pedestals resembling the kind of stands used to repair bikes held broomsticks in various states of construction. A large bin in the back contained what looked like straw and next to it were stacked bins of wooden rods, each one labeled by the type of wood. Some of the other containers held exotic-looking materials I didn't recognize.

I walked to the proprietor and held out a hand. "Nice to meet you, Rai. I'm Justin."

He grinned and gripped my hand firmly. "It's an honor to meet you. You look a lot younger than I'd imagined."

"I moisturize daily." Not wanting to waste time on idle conversation, I waved a hand toward all the brooms in the back. "Are those the boomsticks?"

Rai rubbed his hands together as if I'd just asked him his favorite question. "Yes, they are. Each one of them handcrafted by me or one of my skilled apprentices."

"You look awfully young to have apprentices," Shelton said.

Rai arched his eyebrows. "You look awfully young to be so grumpy."

251

"You'll have to forgive Harry," Bella said sweetly. "He doesn't know much about the sport." She ran a finger along one of the brooms clamped into a broom stand. "I see you're using Bavarian straw and wood in your construction. Do you prefer it over Italian?"

Rai's eyes brightened. "Now that is a debate I could go on and on about." He cast a sideways glance at me. "I don't think Justin wants to wait that long, though."

"I used to be a boomstick racer back in the day," Bella said. "It looks like things haven't changed much since then."

"A lot has changed if you're talking about gadgets," Rai said. "But if you want pure power and speed, you'll still find the same old arguments about wood quality, the kind of straw used, and the best aerodynamic design."

"How much more aerodynamic could a broom be?" I asked, examining the slender rod of wood.

"Magic doesn't completely free us from physics," Rai said. "That's why all the novelty crap like flying mops and vacuum cleaners handle like pregnant pigs saddled with bathtubs." He looked proudly at the racked brooms. "Nothing handles quite the same as a hand-crafted broom."

"How hard are they to fly?" I asked.

Rai glanced at me. "Ever flown one before?"

I shook my head. "Flying carpets only."

"These things will run circles around even the fastest flying carpets." He winked. "Why do you think the Templars have so much trouble catching us?"

I was glad Elyssa wasn't around to argue the point. "We need as many brooms as you can spare."

"What exactly do you plan to do with them?" Rai actually looked a little worried, like a father dropping off his kid for the first day of kindergarten.

"We're up against flying Seraphim," Shelton said. "Maybe even goliaths."

The proprietor's eyes grew wide. "I've heard rumors, but it's still hard to imagine these Seraphim actually exist, much less fly."

I put a hand on his shoulder and looked him directly in the eye. "We absolutely need these brooms and the training to go along with them. We can pay you whatever you want."

"I have fifty-eight completed brooms. I usually sell them for around three thousand or more, depending on the mods." He looked up as if performing some quick calculations in his head. "I'd be willing to let them go for a hundred thousand tinsel."

Shelton whistled. "What the hell are these things made, of, gold?"

I gave Shelton a warning look. "Money isn't an issue."

Shelton pshawed. "Tinsel ain't gonna be worth squat if Daelissa wins."

"My people and I will also help with the training," Rai said.

I gave him a curious look. "Why are you being so helpful?"

He crossed his arms, a grim look on his face. "Cyphanis Rax's enforcers killed some of my friends after that joke of a vote by the council to make Rax the Arcanus Primus. I want payback."

Rax's enforcers had nearly taken out Elyssa and me not so long ago. Thankfully, we'd chased those thugs out of town when we'd taken control of Queens Gate with the help of the tragon.

I gripped Rai's hand and shook it. "Welcome to the team."

He grinned. "I hope you kick their asses back to the Stone Age." Rai called his people so they could inspect the broom inventory and fine-tune any stale stock.

I called Cinder once we left. A text from Elyssa popped onto the screen as the phone rang. I swiped it aside to answer later when Cinder answered. "How many combat-worthy revived Seraphim do we have?" I asked.

"Seventy-three, Justin." He made a loud grunt. "Unfortunately, we lost many people during the last battle." Cinder grunted again, but softly this time.

"Why are you grunting?"

"Ah, Shelton told me that by interspersing grunts throughout a conversation I could sound more natural." As if to underline the point, he unleashed a rumbling grunt. "Do you agree?"

"Maybe you should hold off on the grunting until you study how people use it." I gave Shelton a dirty look. "Shelton grunts a lot because he's always in a foul mood."

Shelton snickered like a kid who'd just given someone a wedgie and said in a loud voice, "Don't listen to Justin. You keep on grunting, buddy."

I groaned. "Really, Shelton?"

He shrugged. "How else am I gonna entertain myself?"

Bella tweaked his ear. "Harry, you can be so mean sometimes."

I returned to more important matters. "Cinder, I need at least thirty candidates for broom flying school ready to assemble on the main back lawn behind Arcane University tomorrow. Do you think you can pick the best ones?"

He grunted. "I believe my close work with the reborn qualifies me to handle such a task, Justin."

"Excellent, thanks." I bid him farewell and ended the call. "Grunting, eh?" I shook my head. "That poor golem is never going to fit into society."

"Grunting is an important part of daily societal nutrition." Shelton shrugged. "Besides, he freaks me out sometimes when he goes completely still and silent while he's thinking something over. I like a person who makes some noise."

We got back on our flying carpet and took it up to Arcane University. I caught Shelton staring at the silvery organic curves of Science Academy across the way.

"Have you come up with any brilliant ways to change their minds?" I asked.

He shook his head. "I did some digging, though. Turns out Frankenberg and Newton met with Cyphanis Rax right after he locked down Queens Gate. My instincts tell me they reached some kind of non-aggression treaty."

"Yeah, but Rax fled Queens Gate when we took it over. For all we know, he's hiding in Thunder Rock."

Bella made a sour face. "Perhaps speaking with *the man* is counterproductive."

Shelton snorted. "Did you really just call Frankenberg the man?"

"He is the man." Bella gave him a fierce look. "Thinking back on my racing days has certainly revived my rebellious side. I think we need to subvert the academy council and go straight to where the levitation spell hits the road."

"The students?" I asked.

She replied with a brisk nod. "I'm sure you could convince them to help, Justin."

"Yeah, but after the show he put on for the council, they've probably got his face embedded in the recognition software of every battle bot on campus." Shelton frowned. "Even if they couldn't harm him, the fireworks and destruction would probably scare off any potential recruits."

"I'm don't want to put students at risk," I said.

Shelton waved away my concern. "Bah. They've got as much a stake in this as anyone else."

"I think I know who can help." Bella took out her arcphone and tapped on it, her face screwed up with intense concentration. After several minutes, she grunted in satisfaction.

"See?" Shelton said with a grin. "Everyone grunts when they're thinking."

Bella rolled her eyes. "I was texting someone." She regarded her phone as someone might regard a venomous snake they'd managed to grasp by the tail. "I still don't quite like these techie things, but they have their uses."

"Who'd you text?" I asked.

She flashed a bright smile. "Lina Romero."

I steered the carpet over the sparkling diamond dome of the massive library at Arcane University and gave Bella a confused look. "She didn't go to Science Academy. She was going to Arcane University like me."

"True, true." Bella gave me a smug look. "But her boyfriend attends the academy."

"What does that get us?" Shelton said. "One student isn't gonna convince all of them to join us."

"Do you remember the last Grand Melee?" she asked.

I snorted. "How could I forget? I let the tragon chase me into the arena so it could take out a rampaging battle golem. Elyssa saved me from the tragon, I almost died from the vampling curse, and Ivy decided to save me." A shrug. "Just another day in the life of Justin Slade."

"I suppose it was rather memorable," Bella said. "Lina met a young man who was with the battle bot team from Science Academy. He may have the connections to help you."

"I'm willing to try anything," I said.

Shelton nodded sagely. "More grunting."

I grinned. "I'm gonna shove you off this carpet."

"*Madre de dios*!" Bella jumped as if something had bitten her. A sheepish look came over her face and she withdrew her phone from within her pink robes. "I did not realize it was set to vibrate."

Shelton and I burst into laughter.

Bella muttered something in Spanish and looked at her phone. "Ah, Lina replied. She said she and her boyfriend can meet with Justin at the Science Academy ferry dock."

"Why there?" I held out my hand. "Can I see your phone?"

"Of course." Bella handed it over.

I texted Lina. *This is Justin. Can't we meet in town? I'm not sure SA is the safest place to meet.*

Ryan can't leave campus. Under lockdown. He can temporarily disable robot guarding ferry dock. Meet there ten PM.

I didn't like the arrangement, but didn't have much choice in the matter. *OK. CU then.* I gave Bella her phone and told them about the meeting.

"We'll come watch your back," Shelton said.

I shook my head. "No. If things get ugly, it'll be best if it's just Elyssa and me. Maybe you could take a flying carpet and keep watch from a distance."

"You got it." He flicked his wand as if blasting something. "I hope Frankenberg shows his ugly mug. If he's really consorting with Rax, he's gonna go down."

I landed the carpet at Colossus Stadium and found Ketiss in his command tent. After filling him in on the broom plan, I asked him to choose thirty candidates for training.

He gave me a dubious look. "I am not familiar with this broom thing you speak of. Can you describe it?"

It took me a moment to remember that the Darklings probably didn't know much about the more mundane items that played important roles in everyday life in Eden. "Well, brooms have long wooden handles with stiff straw on the end. We use them to sweep debris off floors." While I didn't know much about the real origin behind flying brooms, I told him what I knew. "In my culture, flying brooms were used by witches."

"Oh, brother." Shelton gave me a disgusted look. "I hope Zagg gave you an F in history."

Ketiss looked extremely confused. "Why should anyone wish to ride a cleaning implement? It sounds undignified."

"My friend Zagg can give you all the history you want on flying brooms," Shelton said. "At least they're a lot more stylish than flying plungers."

"Believe me, if we can train some of your soldiers to ride properly, they'll be able to take on the archangels in the sky." I grunted and gave Shelton a pointed look. "They might even be better since our Seraphim won't be using their own power to fly."

Ketiss nodded. "Commander Slade, you are, of course, right. I will choose my most skilled fighters for this new airborne unit."

We left the tent and headed toward the hidden tunnel to the mansion.

Shelton chuckled. "Angels on flying brooms. I'll bet the Christians would throw fits if they heard about this."

I imagined winged beings in white robes flitting about on brooms while holding onto their halos to keep them from blowing off. An amused smile touch my lips. "It would certainly liven up Halloween."

I just prayed flying angels would be enough to overcome Daelissa's superior forces.

Chapter 30

Elyssa was waiting for us in the main hall of the mansion. "I've been worried about you. Why didn't you reply to my text?" Planting hands on hips, she tapped her foot while waiting for an answer.

Cutsauce stood by her side and yipped at me.

"Uh, we'll see you in a few." Shelton took Bella's hand and hastily led her upstairs.

I tried to look sheepish, but probably only managed something goatish. I remembered the text she'd sent to me while I was on the phone with Cinder. "I forgot?"

"You forgot." Judging from the stern look on her face, that answer wasn't going to fly. She strode right up to me. "I know this shady underworld contact of yours refused to do business if you took me along, but dammit, I have a right to know you're okay." A tear trickled down her cheek.

Cutsauce growled.

I felt absolutely awful. "Babe, I'm sorry. You texted me when I was talking to Cinder. Then I had to coordinate stuff with Ketiss, and I completely forgot to text you." I took her hands and kissed them. "Forgive me, please."

She took a deep breath, nodded. "It's okay. I'm just on edge."

I hugged her. "We all are."

"Everything is so uncertain. We don't know what Daelissa is planning. We don't know if the next attack will take us all out." She pulled away, closed her eyes. An intense look of concentration overcame her face. "I don't feel like I'm in control of my own emotions right now. Ever since I came back, I've been deathly afraid that you're going to die and leave me alone."

258

That once sentence brought all my fears rushing back in. The faces of the people I loved flashed in my mind. "There was a point in my life where I had nothing to lose. Then I met you, Ash, Nyte, Stacey, Shelton—the list goes on. Now I have so much to lose I have to force myself not to think about it, or it completely paralyzes me." I brushed a strand of raven hair from her face and tucked it behind an ear. "I just have to keep remembering that if I don't fight, I'll lose everything anyway."

She cast her eyes at the floor and nodded. Her fair cheeks blushed pink. "I'm sorry. God, I can't believe I said something so stupid."

I gave her a gentle smile. "You are my greatest treasure, Elyssa. I almost lost you twice. Once because Daelissa wiped your mind, and another time because Qualan blew a hole in your chest. You're my greatest reason to fear the war and my greatest reason to fight it." I gripped her shoulders. "I use the fear to fuel my determination. I won't let Daelissa deny me a happily ever after with you. I will fight her, and I will win."

Her violet eyes met mine. "Then we can ride white horses into the sunset?"

I kissed her long and hard before answering. "Then we can explore everything together from the Cliffs of Insanity, to the Fire Swamp; and we'll do it all together."

"I like the sound of that." She snuggled her head into the crook of my neck. "I can't wait to start our happily ever after."

"Me either."

Cutsauce whined and looked up at us as if he wanted in on the loving. I sent him a mental command. *Go bother Shelton!* He barked once and took off upstairs.

Elyssa sighed, kissed me, and took on a business-like attitude. "I think it's time you filled me in on the broom situation."

"Let me sweep you off your feet, babe."

She groaned and rolled her eyes.

We went upstairs to our bedroom. Once there, I brought her up to speed and told her about the late-night rendezvous with Lina and her boyfriend, Ryan.

"I hope he can give us some help," Elyssa said.

I nodded. "You and me both."

Elyssa twisted her lips. "More importantly, we have to come up with a name for our airborne angels."

"What do you mean?"

"Daelissa has the archangels, so we need something badass for our people."

I snorted. "It just so happens I'm the master of naming."

"Let me guess, your idea of a wonderful name would be sky angels." She raised an eyebrow as if daring me to contradict her.

I had to admit, I liked the sound of it, but I wasn't about to let her know that. "No, that's an awful name. How about the Valkyries?"

"Now you're just stealing names." She frowned. "I'm actually a little disappointed hearing that from the same person who named a hellhound Cutsauce, and calls their arcphone Nookli."

"Don't forget Captain Tibbs."

She wrinkled her nose. "What poor creature did you call that?"

"That's what I called Nightliss in her cat form when I rescued her from a dog." I shrugged. "I thought it was a cool name."

Elyssa giggled. "Poor Nightliss. I'm glad that name didn't stick."

I rubbed my hands together. "Back to business. What's a good moniker?"

"Let's call them skydevils."

I scrunched my forehead. "I'm the only one who'd fit that description. I want something to make enemies fear our wrath. We need to up the poop-in-the-pants level."

"Hmm, I like the sound of that."

I raised an eyebrow. "The poop in the pants part?"

"No, silly." Elyssa tapped a finger on her chin. "We need a scary name."

One thing I'd always found frightening—besides clowns, of course—were ghosts. I imagined flying ghosts trailing tattered clothing, their skeletal hands coming for the throats of our enemies. That was when the name hit me. "Skywraiths."

Elyssa looked at me in stunned silence. "I can't believe it."

"What?" I winced in anticipation of her scorn. "Does the name suck?"

She shook her head slowly. "No. It's actually the coolest name you've ever come up with."

"Really?"

She nodded. "Totes, babe."

I pumped a fist. "Woot!" Unfortunately, I had no idea if our new Skywraiths would stand up to the archangels. "I just hope we can get them off the ground."

Elyssa made a dorky face. "Oh, you're so punny."

I tickled her until she threatened to karate chop me if I didn't stop, then we curled up together and made out like it was our first time, though this time she didn't pin me to the ground and hold a knife to my throat.

I felt so relaxed, so at peace. Deep down, I knew that every second of idle time with Elyssa was a luxury. A part of me argued I couldn't afford it. I put that part of me in timeout and ignored it. I'd been so busy over the past few months I'd almost forgotten what it was like to be bored. People who had that much time on their hands didn't know how lucky they were.

After a few more minutes of bliss, we grunted, groaned, and got up. I typed up a quick report on the day's events and sent it to Thomas so he could disseminate it as necessary.

At ten o'clock sharp, Elyssa and I arrived at the Science Academy ferry dock. Shelton and Bella flew to a position just beneath the cliff, their carpet hidden by a camouflage enchantment.

The bipedal robot guard for the dock was slumped over, its single, unlit eye facing the ground.

The air flickered, and suddenly Lina and a tall male appeared. Ryan lifted his finger from a button on his belt and nodded at us.

"Neat camouflage belt," Elyssa said under her breath.

I landed the carpet next to the dock.

"It is so good to see you." Lina gave me a firm hug and kissed me on both cheeks, Colombian style before repeating the greeting with Elyssa.

I shook her boyfriend's hand. "Ryan, I presume?"

"That's me." He was tall, thin, and geeky, but handsome in his own way. "We don't have a lot of time. I can only disable the robot here for twenty minutes before someone notices it."

"I'll get straight to the point, then." I looked around cautiously and then launched into my mini-speech. "Daelissa has massive battle golems. We don't have much to counter her and were hoping Science Academy might come through. I have to admit I don't know everything you all are capable of, but any help might turn this war around."

Ryan pursed his lips and nodded. "It just so happens that we have several brand-spanking new battle bots that could probably help."

I felt my hopes rise. "That's great."

His face darkened. "When we first started working on them, we thought they'd be for defending the academy in case the war spilled over here. One of my friends overheard Frankenberg talking to Newton recently and it turns out that's not the case at all."

"What do you mean?" Elyssa asked.

Ryan frowned. "I think Frankenberg is waiting for both sides to wipe each other out while he forces us to build an army."

"This campus isn't just on lockdown," Lina said. "It's become a prison."

"They keep us working like slaves." Ryan gazed longingly across the valley at the lights shining from Arcane University. "I could escape, but I wouldn't be able to get everyone out." His jaw tightened. "Frankenberg told me that if anyone leaves, he'll take it out on the other students. He's keeping some of my friends in an undisclosed location." Ryan's face screwed up in disgust. "He showed us video of his people threatening a girl. Even if we could escape, we can't leave anyone to suffer."

I briefly thought about using the map and key, or even a series of omniarch portals to help the students, but since I didn't know where the hidden students were being kept, that approach wouldn't work. "How is he maintaining control?"

"The council controls the security drones and bots." He regarded me. "From what I heard, they're no problem for you, but we can't handle them."

"How many?"

"Fifty airborne drones. They look like small flying saucers, and they pack a wallop." He jabbed a finger toward the disabled bot. "They have approximately thirty security bots."

"What about the battle bots?"

"Thankfully, they aren't powered." He looked around nervously and continued. "They use a hybrid aether-nuclear core that won't start without an Arcane. The students at the School of Magical and Scientific Synergy escaped before lockdown occurred, so Frankenberg has no way to ignite the power cores." He nodded his head toward Lina. "They don't know she sneaks in to see me."

I felt relieved. "So if we mount a rescue operation, we won't have to fight them."

"Exactly." The wind rustled nearby trees, causing Ryan to scan the area once more. "But there's another problem. Frankenberg claims that he has a failsafe. If he dies, or if he activates a trigger, he'll set off a series of explosives and take out everyone on campus."

My stomach knotted. "Like a nuclear bomb?"

Ryan shook his head. "No, I think it's more conventional. From what I understand, the Arcane Council set up wards to prevent Science Academy from detonating weapons of mass destruction after the Einstein Crisis."

"Well, we got that going for us, which is nice." I bit my lower lip in thought. "In other words, we have to do this quickly and covertly."

"There is no other way," Lina said. "I wanted to come to you for help sooner, Justin, but you've been so busy with the war."

"We tried to escape before the lockdown." Ryan looked down. "We're all supposed to be so smart, but everyone is too scared to do anything. I'm just ready for this to be over."

"We've all been there before." I thought about our options. "I'll need a complete list of Frankenberg's supporters, drone patrols, etc."

Ryan handed me an ASE. "This all-seeing eye has everything you need. We've been collecting the data ever since the campus went into lockdown. If you can help us, we'll get those battle bots online and do everything we can to win this war."

"We'll get you out of this," I promised. "You should get back to wherever you need to be before you're missed."

Ryan shook my hand. "Thank you, Justin."

I looked at Lina. "Is it safe for you to be here?"

"I'm sneaky." She smiled. "I can take care of myself."

Elyssa hugged her. "Be safe."

We headed back to the university.

"I always figured Frankenberg for a dumbass," Shelton said as we flew over the sparse lights of Queens Gate in the valley far below. "If he thinks he can mop up the winning forces after the war, he's gonna be in for a nasty surprise."

"I know who'd be perfect for this job." I looked at the others. "Underborn."

Shelton wrinkled his forehead. "Isn't he busy screwing around with the Alabaster Arch?"

"My mom can handle things there." I rolled the ASE around in my hand and tucked it into a pocket. "If he lives up to his reputation, he should be able to take out Frankenberg and his failsafe without raising an alarm."

"I agree," Elyssa said.

Elyssa and I parted ways with Shelton and Bella back at the mansion and went through the omniarch portal to El Dorado. We found Mom, Underborn, and Adam Nosti working intently on the Alabaster Arch.

"We're extremely close to a solution," the assassin said.

Mom nodded. "I think this might actually work."

Adam Nosti flicked a hand across his arctablet. "Serena probably knows we're up to something, so she opened a portal to Seraphina and has been keeping it open. That's why we can't take control of the Alabaster Arch network." He looked up from the screen. "We're going to bind the Chalons into one big Mega Chalon to concentrate their energy and send a power surge through this arch and into the nexus. That should cause it to reset and sever the connection to Seraphina. Then we'll have at least a minute to take control."

Mom's forehead wrinkled with worry. "We don't have long before the Second Battalion reaches the gateway in Seraphina. This has to work."

"I have complete faith in you." Worry tried to wedge itself into my chest, but I couldn't let it—not now. I turned to Underborn. "I have an important matter that requires someone of your particular talents." I led him to the far side of the room, explaining the situation at Science Academy. Elyssa walked by my side, but said nothing.

Underborn frowned. "I don't believe I'm best suited for such an operation."

I felt my eyebrows climb. "What do you mean? You're a stealthy assassin. Taking out some bureaucrats shouldn't be an issue for you."

"You're right. I could easily take them out and escape unharmed." He shrugged. "I am an expert at precisely nullifying a target or small number of targets. I can infiltrate just about any location. I might even be able to save a few people." He shook his head. "What you're asking me to do is carry out a complex rescue operation. Even though I could get past the drones and security bots, I would also have to neutralize this failsafe Frankenberg has and find the hidden hostages. To accomplish that, I'd likely have to capture this man and interrogate him for information."

"I never said it would be easy." It was hard not to feel disappointed. "After all the hype about you, I figured you'd be a shoo-in. Now you're telling me you can't do it."

Underborn smiled. "I never said I couldn't—I simply said I wasn't the best suited for such an operation." He sighed and looked at the Alabaster Arch. "Truthfully, I don't want to leave this project. We're so close to a solution, I can taste it."

I countered his assertion. "If we don't get those battle bots on our side, this project might not matter."

He pursed his lips. "Can you confirm if Kanaan is back from his mission?"

I almost asked him how in the world he knew Kanaan had even been on a mission. Even I didn't know all the details. Then again, Underborn probably knew how many times a day I used the bathroom. "I don't know. I can ask Captain Takei."

He nodded. "Ideally, his help would be invaluable. While I am skilled at extracting information, Kanaan has an uncanny ability to get straight to the point. He's also an excellent fighter."

"That's an understatement," Elyssa murmured.

I put in a quick call to Takei and asked him about the Magitsu master.

"As a matter of fact," Takei said, "Kanaan returned just last night. I'll have him report to Underborn immediately."

"Thanks, Captain." I disconnected and looked at Underborn. "Kanaan is on his way. Do you need anything else?"

"I'd like Michael Borathen on the team."

Elyssa's face registered shock. "He swore he'd never work for you again after you made him lie to me."

Underborn smiled. "Nonetheless, I need someone with expertise in rescue operations."

I squeezed Elyssa's hand. "Is it okay if I ask him?"

She took a deep breath and nodded. "Of course." She took out her arcphone. "I'll let him know."

I handed the ASE to Underborn. "This has all the information we have."

A loud thrumming noise filled the control room and a Klaxon wailed. I spun around to see Adam and Mom watching the Alabaster Arch. Magical energy crackled up and down the surface. The three Chalons, bound in a triangular formation, hovered between the columns. Adam slammed his staff against the floor. Brilliant energy cascaded from his staff and into the Mega Chalon. The three orbs soaked up the energy until they glowed.

Underborn trotted across the room toward the arch.

I glanced at Elyssa. "I'm gonna wait at a safe distance just in case."

She seemed unable to break her gaze from the arch. "Good idea."

The thrumming crescendoed into a whine. A gateway opened within the arch. The Mega Chalon unleashed a torrent of energy into the portal. Thunder rumbled and, with a blinding flash, the portal closed. The arch went dark without even the usual humming noise as it wound down.

The Mega Chalon dropped to the floor. Mom ran into the binding circle around the arch, scooped up the bound orbs, and pressed them to the arch. She sang a familiar tune—one that she'd used to attune the Chalon to an arch. The Mega Chalon clicked against the arch, and emitted a sullen glow.

Mom closed her eyes and pressed a hand to the Mega Chalon. She remained that way for only a moment, but it felt like forever. If this failed, Daelissa's army would soon outnumber us even more.

Mom's eyes blinked open. She backed away from the arch, a smile lighting her face. "We did it! We control the Alabaster Arches!"

Chapter 31

I sagged with relief and a lump of fear melted away. "All your base are belong to us."

"Yes!" Elyssa clapped her hands and cheered my mother. "You go, girl!"

"Daelissa's reinforcements are trapped in Seraphina." Mom breathed a sigh of relief. "We just have to hope they can't reverse the process."

I wasn't ready to celebrate just yet. If Adam was right and Serena knew what we'd done, she might be able to divine our location. Even without the battle golems, it would be a formidable army. We had to lock down this facility ASAP. "Are all the portal blockers active?"

"Everywhere except designated zones," Elyssa said. "Daelissa won't be getting in here that way. Slitheren and the other ley worms blocked most of the surface tunnels. She'd have to march her army down the same dangerous path we took the first time we came down here."

A hulk of a man entered the control room and approached Elyssa. "I hear you need me, Ninjette."

She smiled at the nickname, but it quickly faded. "Underborn requested your help on an urgent mission."

Michael wasn't one to emote very often, but this drew a scowl. "Explain."

Elyssa told him about Science Academy. "It's imperative we secure their help."

Underborn approached from the arches looking like the cat who swallowed the canary. "Good to see you again, Michael."

Michael looked at the assassin with a dark expression.

A hooded figure appeared in our circle. He lowered the hood to reveal a face of mixed Caucasian and Asian descent, and a head of thick black hair. "I am here as requested," Kanaan said.

A loud pinging noise echoed in the control room, causing some of us to jump. I looked toward the Alabaster Arch and saw Adam, a concerned look on his face, tapping away on his arctablet. He jogged over to us.

"Serena pinged the arch network before I could get a portal blocking statue in place." He ran a hand down his face. "If she wasn't sure where we hijacked the nexus from, she knows now."

"That means we don't have long." I turned back to Underborn and the rescue crew. "Free Science Academy. We need all the help we can get. Underborn has all the intel on the situation."

"I'll put Phissilinth in charge of our military operations," Underborn said. "He should be able to hold the fort until we return."

I nodded. "Good luck. Keep me informed."

"It was nice to see you again, if only for a moment." Kanaan nodded his head at Elyssa and me. "May fortune favor you."

Underborn flourished a bow, turned, and led his merry trio away.

"I texted my father," Elyssa said. "He's mobilizing all our forces, but it'll take time to transport them via omniarch portals."

"Does that include Ketiss and the Darklings?"

She nodded. "The army will gather in El Dorado on the surface."

"Shouldn't we set up the army below ground?" Mom asked. "It might be easier to defend the tunnels." She looked toward the main chamber. "Plus, we have the dragons out there."

"The cavern is too small for all our forces, and he has valid concerns about trapping our army in an enclosed space." Elyssa motioned us to follow her out of the control room. "If Daelissa somehow deployed a malaether crucible in here, it could kill us off in one blast." We stepped into the main chamber and looked across the vast space. Large as it was, I'd seen a malaether crucible, the equivalent of a magical nuke, explode. Thomas was right. It'd be like a firecracker exploding in a bottle.

I looked toward the dragons. They appeared to be sleeping. "I wonder how long we have until Daelissa's army arrives." Using omniarch portals, she could have the bulk of her troops here in hours if she so desired.

"Let's just hope she takes her time."

It was almost midnight. I figured we'd done all we could do at the moment so we returned to the mansion. I tried to sleep, but the dreams of war and battle kept shocking me awake. I must have finally stayed asleep because the next thing I knew, my alarm was going off.

After showering, Elyssa and I went downstairs for a quick breakfast. Surprisingly, Bella and Shelton weren't there.

Elyssa received a text on her phone and read it. "Templar scouts report no signs of the enemy mobilizing." She looked up. "Maybe we have more time than we thought."

"I hope so." I put my dirty dishes in the sink like a good boy and headed for the front door. "Guess it's time for me to learn how to fly a broom."

Elyssa's phone chimed again. She looked at it and grunted. "While you're doing that, I'm going to work with my father on the defenses at El Dorado."

I hugged her tight, kissed her nose, each ear, and went for the grand finale on her lips. "I love you. Be careful."

She sighed longingly. "You too, Prince Charming." Elyssa headed for the omniarch room. I took the tunnel to the surface and jogged to the large grassy field behind the university. As promised, Darklings from Ketiss's army were there. Another group of revived Seraphim were also present. The Tarissan uniforms made it easy to differentiate Ketiss's people from the revived Darklings in Templar armor. Mom, Ivy, Nightliss, Joss, Otaleon, and other familiar faces were also present.

I spotted Flava near the front. She made eye contact with me, but quickly looked away. I wondered if I'd offended her at some point. Ever since she'd healed Elyssa, Flava hadn't spoken to me.

"We get to fly brooms!" Ivy clapped her hands and jumped up and down. "I've always wanted to fly one."

I almost told Ivy she couldn't be here. I didn't want my little sister flying into combat on a broom, but she'd proven powerful in the first battle. My heart clenched at the thought of anything bad happening to her.

"You sure about this?" I asked Mom.

She returned an uneasy look. "No, of course not." She glanced around at the young faces of revived Seraphim. "Just the thought of Ivy in danger makes me sick to my stomach." She sighed. "Unfortunately, we need everyone for the next battle, and if anyone is capable of learning to fly a broom, it's her."

"I promise I won't let you down," Ivy said, her blue eyes big and pleading. "Just let me try. You saw how good I fought already."

I ruffled her hair. "I know you can fight, sis, but I don't want to lose you."

"They won't be able to touch me. I'll be zooming all over the place." Making flying noises, she zig-zagged with her hand.

I squeezed her in a tight hug. "I'll give you a chance, but if I don't think you fly well enough, I'll have to find somewhere else for you to be."

She snorted. "I'll be one of the best. I promise."

"I think she will do very well," Nightliss said. "I just hope I can rise to the challenge."

"You and me both," Mom said. "I've never been a fan of brooms. They're nothing like flying carpets."

"Hello, Justin."

The question jerked me from the conversation. I turned and saw Lanaeia standing behind me. Having seen her in battle, I knew she was quick, agile, and powerful. She could prove a valuable asset. "Think you can fly one of these things?"

"Bella seems to think these brooms are much better than flying carpets." Lanaeia pursed her lips doubtfully. "I decided to see if this was true." She looked toward Colossus Stadium. "It would appear the brooms have arrived."

I glanced across the field and saw a wide floating platform with racks of brooms making its way toward us. Figures on flying brooms circled the platform. A couple of them broke off and zipped toward us. It didn't take a genius to see that they were moving a lot faster than even the swiftest Templar flying carpets.

271

The leader wooshed overhead. He pulled into a steep climb, performed a loopty-loop, did a couple of barrel rolls, and then skidded to a stop at the top of a small rise in the middle of the field. Grinning, Rai landed the broom and stepped off it, leaving it to hover next to him.

I walked up the small rise and greeted him while his apprentices landed their brooms behind him. I spotted a pink blur racing over the university. Magnifying my vision, I realized it was Bella, her face flushed with excitement. She went into a steep dive, pulling up just feet from the ground, and performed the flying broom equivalent of a hockey stop next to the other brooms.

"What a rush!" she exclaimed, her Colombian accent thickening with her excitement.

By now, the Seraphim volunteers had gathered into a crowd at the base of the hill, their formerly bored, uncertain faces now lit with interest. I could hardly blame them. I was dying to try out a broom myself.

First, I had to get through the introductions. I raised my hand for quiet. "Welcome, volunteers. You have been invited to train for a new airborne unit called the Skywraiths."

"Ooh, cool name," Rai said.

Murmurs went up from the crowd. Most of them nodded as if they liked the name.

"Elyssa must have come up with that," Bella said.

I looked over my shoulder at her. "Believe it or not, I'm the one who did."

She gave me a scrutinizing look. "I find that hard to believe."

I turned back to the crowd. "With me today are Rai and his apprentices. They will break you into groups for training."

"Me too," Bella said.

I nodded. "Yes, and Bella too."

Lanaeia raised a hand. "Can Bella be my instructor?"

"We'll get to that in a minute." I turned to Rai. "Why don't you say what you need, and get started?"

He raised a hand in greeting. "Welcome to flight school, everyone! Let's get started with the basics." Rai held his broom over his head. "From now on, you will not refer to this as a flying broom. A finely crafted work of art like this is called a boomstick."

I watched as some of the Seraphim practiced pronouncing what was probably a very strange word for them. I pressed my lips together to keep from grinning.

Rai lowered the broom so it hovered waist high and ran his hand over the black leather seat. It resembled the kind of sleek saddle favored on racing motorcycles with a small, cupped backrest. "As you might have guessed, this is where you sit." Metal rods ran from the sides of the seat and ended in stirrups. Rai gripped one of them. "This is not only where you put your feet, but also where you control the yaw and roll."

Several hands went up. Rai pointed to Joss. "Yes?"

"What do those terms mean?" Joss asked.

Rai pointed the broom toward the crowd and slid the front of the broom from side to side. "Yaw is the left to right movement of an aircraft." He barrel-rolled the broom. "This is the roll." He then angled the broom up and down. "This is the pitch." Rai went through a few more examples until the candidates seemed satisfied with the answers.

Rai continued the orientation. "How many of you have flown a flying carpet?"

Several hands went up.

"For those of you who aren't familiar with them, you control the speed of a flying carpet by willing it to go fast or slow." He backhanded the air. "That approach is crap. You lose precise speed control, and it limits the top speed." Rai gripped an indentation in the boomstick handle. "This is the throttle. To go faster, you twist it right. To slow, you twist it left." He pulled back on the throttle. "Pull toward you for the emergency brake. Unlike magic carpets, you're not bonded to the seat, so if you brake hard, squeeze your legs tight to the seat to keep from flying off." He looked around. "Any questions?"

Nobody raised a hand.

Rai folded his arms. "Excellent. Let's divide into groups."

We broke into groups of five. I joined Rai since Ivy, Mom, Nightliss, Lanaeia, and Flava hurriedly joined Bella's group. Rai let

273

each of us take turns sitting on a broom. The first student flipped upside down and couldn't get it upright. The next student accidentally revved the throttle and planted the handle into the ground. When it came to my turn, I prayed I didn't do anything to make myself look stupid.

I hopped onto the boomstick and put my feet in the stirrups. The broom tilted to the right, so I gingerly pressed down with my left foot.

"The trick is not to overcompensate," Rai said as I toppled to the left.

Using pressure from my feet, I managed to keep the broom upright. It was like balancing a plank centered on a rail. "Why is it so hard to keep it centered?"

"It's like riding a bicycle. When you're moving forward, it's easier to stay balanced." He gripped the end of the broom to steady me. "Standard brooms use stabilizing charms, but those take precious aether power from the speed enchantments." He released the end of the stick.

I shifted my feet back and forth, somehow managing to keep upright.

"Excellent," he said. "Now I want you to do a barrel roll."

Gulping, I released pressure on left and pushed down on the right stirrup. My view rotated. Falling back on my demonic physical enhancements, I used hyper reflexes to slow my sense of time and stopped the roll at the perfect moment.

Rai looked surprised. "Wow, I rarely see anyone get that right on the first try."

I gave a nonchalant shrug. "Beginner's luck, I guess."

The other students didn't fare quite so well and took turns rolling out of control. Thankfully, the revived Seraphim and their supernatural reflexes allowed them to catch on more quickly. Ketiss's soldiers took longer, but by lunchtime, it seemed most of the candidates had the basics down.

After lunch, Rai produced a two-seated broom. "I don't usually start assisted flying until a couple of weeks into training, but since we don't have a lot of time, we're going to have to jump ahead."

One of the other trainees gulped loudly.

Rai chuckled. "Don't worry. Most of my students don't have the lightning reflexes of Seraphim."

There were a few nervous chuckles at that statement.

I saw Bella hopping on the back of her two-seater with Lanaeia driving. The broom jerked forward, stopped, and jerked forward again, nearly throwing the two women off. Bella touched Lanaeia's arm and pointed at the throttle. The Brightling gently twisted on the throttle and the broom glided forward smoothly.

"Ready, Justin?"

I flicked my gaze to Rai and nodded. "Ready as I'll ever be."

I took the broom, tapped a symbol above the throttle, and activated the levitation spell. Once it rose to waist level, I climbed on and steadied the roll with my feet while Rai hopped on the back.

"Ease open the throttle," Rai said.

Using Lanaeia's example, I very slowly twisted my hand on the throttle. Even though there were no moving parts, it felt as though the wood moved under my hand. The broom slid forward. As we gained momentum, the need to keep it balanced with my feet diminished until I didn't even have to think about it anymore.

"Pretty neat, huh?" Rai tapped my right shoulder. "Steer us in a circle."

I pulled the handle to the right. The broom turned to the right in a very wide arc, taking us right toward the forest. I pulled harder, but that didn't make it turn any faster. Just as we closed in on the tree line, I twisted the throttle back down and pulled toward me. The broom jerked to a stop.

"Not bad," Rai said. "Have you ever driven a bicycle?"

I nodded. "Used to be my only mode of transport until high school."

"You went to a nom school?"

"Yeah. That was before I found out my parents weren't exactly human."

He laughed. "Wow, that's really cool. I always wanted to try the nom lifestyle." Rai cleared his throat. "Anyway, my point about the bicycle riding is this—how do you make sharp turns?"

It only took a second of thought before his point hit home. "You lean the way you want to go."

"Exactly. You only turn the wheel a little bit." He motioned to the left with his head. "Spin us around by pulling left and gently pressing on the left stirrup."

I did as instructed. The broom tilted to the side and swung in a swift arc. I over-steered a few degrees, but managed to stop the turn without toppling us over.

Rai whistled. "Dude, you're a natural. Give me a couple of days and I'll have you ready for the pro scene."

I grinned. "I just hope we have two days."

Lessons continued until darkness claimed the field. The brooms had illumination orbs—the magical equivalent of headlights—but Rai didn't think it would be safe to continue lessons. I got together with him and the other instructors after dismissing the students.

"How are they looking?" I asked.

"I have two who'll take a bloody month just to teach throttling," said a young man with a red Mohawk and Cockney accent. "I grounded them after the assisted flight lesson because it would've been a waste."

The next few instructors chimed in with reports. Most had at least one incompetent student, but were satisfied with the bulk of their students.

"Every one of mine picked up on the basics very quickly," Bella said. "Ivy caused me quite a scare when she performed a looping barrel roll." She tittered. "I must say she's the best student by far."

"Impressive," Rai said. "I'd have to say Justin one-upped that, though. He did a three-sixty spiral tail-whip."

"Oh?" Bella pursed her lips. "Ivy did a moon-shot reverse roll with a one-eighty endo."

"Not bad." Rai grinned. "I forgot to mention that Justin also—"

Part of me was ecstatic that Ivy was doing so well, while another part of me tightened with apprehension. I threw up my hands to stop their one-upmanship. "Look, I get that you're proud of your students, but just because me and my sister are better than average doesn't mean squat. We can't form a fighting unit with just two of us."

276

Bella and Rai looked like I'd just slapped their hands for reaching into the candy jar.

"I'm sorry, Justin," Bella said.

Rai shrugged. "Yeah, dude. We'll get everyone up to par."

"Bloody right we will," said the Mohawk dude.

By the end of the little pow-wow, I felt better about our chances. I decided to replace the poorly performing students with fresh recruits. Rai assigned an instructor to teach them and split that group among the others.

After planning out the next day of training with the others, I returned to the mansion. Elyssa was there with a grim look on her face.

Dread crept up inside me. "What's wrong?"

She showed me a report on her phone. "Our scouts report that Daelissa is mobilizing."

"Destination?"

She shook her head. "We don't know."

Wherever Daelissa was going, we were out of time.

Chapter 32

Shelton showed up for dinner with good news. "The doors are ready. We made three of them just in case." He took me outside and displayed a thick piece of wood, which he set flat on the ground. "Just trace this symbol, and"—the wood unfolded into a massive door—"voila! A big-ass door."

Constructed of dark mahogany with thick support columns to either side, the door was tall and wide enough to admit battle golems. Strange runes painted in silver and gold adorned the surface. I pointed them out. "What are those?"

Shelton leaned back on his heels and nodded. "Enchantments for structural stability and other crap so this thing doesn't topple over and smash into a thousand pieces."

The doorknob and lock assembly was situated low and on the right. Compared to the size of the door, it looked woefully inadequate. "Is it hard to open?"

He shook his head. "It's enchanted."

I walked around the thick support columns. "Show me how it works."

He snorted, touched the doorknob. With a faint creaking noise, it swung open. "Complicated, I know."

Elyssa gave him a slow clap. "Nice work."

He bowed. "Thank you." Shelton touched a small fob on the doorframe and the door swung shut with a click. He traced the symbol again and the door compacted, making a series of wooden clunking noises until it was once again a thick plank.

I gave him the Map and Key of Juranthemon along with instructions for linking the doors. "Test them out and make sure they work even after you compact and move them."

He saluted. "I'm on it, boss."

I left him to his work and contacted Thomas. "Any word on Daelissa's troops?"

"We've scouted the area around El Dorado, but the jungle makes it hard to see if there's any activity." He made a thoughtful noise. "Our Arcanes have established wards up to a mile around the perimeter of the city. We should know if anyone breaches it."

"Do you think she'll make another play on Atlanta?"

"Entirely possible. With her reinforcements trapped in Seraphina, she might want to draw us out." He paused. "I would advise against responding in such a case. Better to make her come to us."

I'd had the same thought myself, but hearing Thomas say it made it plain just how bad our situation was. "Just sit back while she rampages through the city? The city could be destroyed and the noms would know about the Overworld."

Thomas sighed. "I think this war is beyond containment. Atlanta holds no strategic value for her other than a way to bait us into a fight we'd be hard pressed to win."

I paced in a circle, trying to think of a way we could fight her in such a situation, but unfortunately, Thomas was right. We had to win the next battle, or the war was over. "I really hate this, but I don't see any alternative. Maybe the nom military can put a dent in her."

"Daelissa is not the brightest strategist, but if Arturo knows anything about nom military capabilities, he might advise against attacking the city if we don't respond." Thomas grunted. "The noms far outnumber us. In an all-out war scenario, they would likely win. This world is far different than the one Daelissa ruled thousands of years ago."

"There's a reason the Overworld Conclave didn't want to stir the bee hive."

"Precisely. A smart strategist would advise her to win the magical war first, and then use subversion to take over the nom governments. After decimating us, they could take control of the Alabaster Arches again and bring through more troops." Thomas's voice sounded unsure. "We just have to hope Arturo respects how dangerous the noms could be if attacked."

"Let's hope so." I told him about Shelton's doors. "Once we confirm they work, we'll move Fjoeruss's battle golems into position at El Dorado."

"That's good news, at least. I'll keep you apprised of further developments. In the meantime, I suggest you get some rest. Tomorrow could be the day."

My stomach knotted. "You too." I ended the call.

Elyssa put her arms around my neck and leaned on my chest. "We're not ready, are we?"

"Ready as we'll ever be." My words sounded hollow. Even without the battle golems, Daelissa's Brightling army would be extremely hard to beat.

Tense as I was, I knew that we had to get some sleep. I put my phone next to the bed and prayed that nobody called with news of an attack.

I slept fitfully, but was relieved to wake up and find out that there was still no information on Daelissa's next target. No news might be good news, but it still left a gut full of uncertainty weighing heavily in my abdomen.

After breakfast and a short talk with Thomas about preparations, I met Rai and the other instructors for more lessons. Everything went much more smoothly, and the replacement candidates mostly proved better than their predecessors. Within a few hours, we were able to take our first solo flights. Rai took our group on a flight over the Dark Forest and had us practice formations. Then he took us down into the trees to learn maneuvers in tight quarters.

Two students crashed into each other while trying to avoid the same tree, but quick action on Rai's part kept them from falling off their boomsticks. Later, I caught a branch in the face and barely managed to hold onto the limb while my broom glided on without me. It was embarrassing and my nose hurt for a while, but I climbed back on the broom and pressed on. A broken nose was the least of my worries at this point.

Late in the day, we received word that the enemy had vacated Kobol Prison and Thunder Rock. According to the report, our scouts were unable to get close enough to the Obsidian Arches in either location to determine where the army had gone. That set everyone's nerves on edge.

There were no sightings of troop movements near Atlanta, or near El Dorado.

We barely had two days of training, but I felt it was time for us to go to El Dorado so we could be there just in case. I texted Underborn for information on the situation at Science Academy.

Still assessing the situation, was his reply. *We cannot act until all variables are accounted for.*

I almost texted him a terse reply telling him to hurry up, but resisted the impulse. I could practically hear a countdown ticking away in my head toward the next inevitable showdown. Stress swelled like a knot in my stomach. I felt completely blind to Daelissa's intentions.

"I just wish she'd do something already," I said as Elyssa and I prepared for bed that night.

She massaged my shoulders. "You know what they say—be careful what you wish for."

"I know, I know." I dropped into bed and closed my eyes, but my stomach hurt too much to sleep. "I feel like I just ate a little bit of everything on a spicy Indian buffet."

Elyssa cuddled up to me and kissed my cheek. "Have faith, Justin. After everything we've been through, I actually feel optimistic."

Optimism wasn't high on my list of feelings right then, but I tried to find the silver lining anyway. It proved as elusive as sleep. "We don't know where her army is, or what she's doing. What if she attacks Atlanta? What if she attacks some other city?"

Elyssa was quiet for a moment. "There's nothing to be done by worrying about it. She will do what she wants to do, and we'll have to decide how to respond. Until then, we have to prepare the best we can and hope for the future."

I brushed hair from her face and drank in her beautiful eyes, her full lips, and her creamy skin. "When I look at you, I see our future, Elyssa. More than anything else, I'm scared to death of losing that time with you."

Her face flushed as a broad smile spread her lips. "Why fear for the future when we have each other right here, right now?" She traced a finger up my bare back and I shivered with pleasure.

By constantly thinking about what lay ahead, I'd forgotten one thing. *There's no time like the present.* I pulled her in for a deep kiss.

She moaned softly and pressed her body against mine. Fire burned in my stomach. I nipped her neck and traced my tongue around her ear. We fell into each other and came up for breath sometime later. As we lay there tangled in each other's arms, I felt the worries of the world slide away. The tempo of her breath against my neck lulled me into a deep sleep.

When I woke up, I saw Elyssa propped on her elbow watching me. She rewarded me with a beautiful smile.

"I like watching you sleep." She brushed my cheek with her hand. "You're so peaceful."

"No demonic snoring?" I asked.

She giggled. "Not yet. I think you have a few more years before the snoring and hair loss kicks in."

I made a face and ran a hand through my hair. "It would be awful to lose this magnificent mane."

"The world would mourn." Her phone buzzed. She rolled over and picked it up. "Since you'll be leading the Skywraiths into battle, my father wants me to be a coordinator on his command platform."

Knowing she wouldn't be at the front lines warmed me with relief. "That's an excellent idea."

Elyssa rolled out of bed. "We'd better get moving. It's already six-thirty."

I groaned. "Whoever invented morning should be locked up."

"I love getting up early." She headed into the bathroom. "There's nothing more refreshing than waking at the break of day and watching the sun rise."

"Good luck with that since we're hundreds of feet underground."
I forced myself out of bed and joined her for a shower.

After breakfast, I walked her to the omniarch portal so she could
travel to El Dorado.

"Love you." She smiled, but her eyes looked worried.

"I love you too." I narrowed my eyes. "Is everything okay?"

Elyssa nodded. "I don't like knowing that you're flying into battle
without me." She bit her lip and frowned. "As a matter of fact, I hate
it. Can't you get one of those two-seated boomsticks and let me ride
with you?"

"I've thought about it, believe me, but those are for training.
They're nowhere near as fast as the single-seaters." I gave her a
reassuring smile. "If anything, the boomsticks will be safer than flying
carpets since they're so much faster."

She shook her head. "I don't care." She took a deep breath and
closed her eyes, opening them a moment later. "I know this is what's
best." Elyssa motioned to the omniarch operator. He opened a portal
to reveal a large stone pyramid located near the center of the ancient
city of El Dorado.

I kissed her goodbye and watched her walk away until the portal
winked off. The operator opened a portal to the practice field. I
stepped through and met with Rai, Bella, and the others. The students,
now officially boomstick pilots, stood in their flight group formations,
brooms in hand.

"We need to practice flying while fighting today," I told the
instructors. "Once we get the basics down, we'll join the main army at
El Dorado."

"Sounds good," Rai said. "We've organized the strongest flyers
into groups, which should help."

I raised an eyebrow. "Won't that put some of our groups at a
serious disadvantage?"

"Every unit is only as strong as its weakest link," Bella said. "We
talked about this quite a bit last night and think it's for the best."

I gave her a doubtful look. "I hope you're right."

"The better flyers will be able to stick together more easily but
perform more complicated maneuvers," Rai said. "The less-skilled

groups will probably fly more conservatively and get into less trouble that way."

His argument made sense. If I took my group on a dangerous run, I didn't want to lose anyone because they couldn't make a sharp turn, or even worse, slam into someone else and knock them off their broom over the enemy forces.

"Okay, we'll do it your way." I looked out at the groups. "Which one is mine?"

Bella pointed to a formation with Mom, Ivy, Flava, and Lanaeia. "You've got the cream of the crop." She sighed. "I wish I could fight with you, but my spells are no match for Seraphim magic."

"It'd be a bloody trip to fight from a boomstick," Seth, the Mohawk-haired instructor said. "Can you imagine the rush?"

Rai gave him a fist bump. "It'd be epic." He looked to me. "We have enough brooms for us instructors to fly. Is there any way we can help?"

I gave it some thought and came up with an answer a moment later. "How would you like to be bombers?"

Seth whooped. "Hell yeah, mate! Where do I sign up?"

"What will we bomb with?" Bella asked.

I grinned. "Aether crucibles."

"Ooh, I like the sound of that." Rai gave my hand a firm shake. "We're in."

One of the female instructors raised a hand. "I'm not that crazy. Count me out."

"Anyone else?" I asked.

Three others raised hands, expressions ranging from shame to relief.

I nodded. "Looks like there are six of you. Once we arrive at El Dorado, I'll inform Thomas of your new assignments." I looked back at our pilots. "In the meantime, let's start practice."

Rai motioned toward the assembly. "We've done our part and gotten them flying, but we obviously can't teach them the magic bit." He showed me a list of names on his phone. "I've assigned leaders to each group. Coordinate with them from now on."

It all felt very rushed. Hell, it *was* rushed, but this entire exercise had been a crash course. I spoke with the group leaders, told them what exercises we'd be doing, and joined my flight group.

"I can't tell you how glad we are to have you as our captain," Mom said.

Lanaeia took my hand in hers. "We will not let you down, Justin."

Ivy pumped a fist in the air. "Yay, Justin!"

Nightliss offered me a wan smile. "Rai told me that Josh and Otaleon were better than me, but there was only one slot left in your group and they wished to remain together, so he placed me with you."

I gave her a thumbs-up. "You're gonna do great."

The others chimed in with their agreement, though Flava seemed lost in her own world. I wanted to take her aside and ask if everything was all right, but now wasn't the time for dealing with personal issues. I took us up in flight formation and led the group over the Dark Forest.

Once there, I swung around and hovered in front of them. "I don't want you using full power on these exercises. For now, I want you to concentrate on aiming."

"At what?" Ivy asked.

I hit a tree with a weak shaft of Brilliance. Dozens of spider bats burst from the foliage, their screeches deafening as they swarmed into the air. With wide, leathery wings and several spindly legs covered in fur, these things lived up to their name.

Flava shrieked as one swooped over her head. "I do not like these creatures!"

"They are beautiful in their own way," Lanaeia said in a calm voice.

Judging from Mom and Nightliss's expressions of disgust, they seemed to lean more toward Flava's point of view.

"Freaky-deeky." Ivy's eyes shined with delight. "They're so cute!"

Mom grimaced.

I spotted a bat with white fur flapping furiously in a wide circle. "That's our target." I gave them a warning look. "Don't hurt it. Just use enough power so it's like hitting it with a beam of light."

We streaked after the bat. Keeping my left hand on the throttle, I hit the bat with a low-level burst of light. The others each took turns firing at it. Due to the chaos of the swarming bats, most of our shots missed or hit other bats. We flew out of the bat cloud and prepared for another run. Just as we were turning, I saw someone in the practice field waving frantically at me.

Shelton.

I nodded toward the ground. "Come with me." Swooping in low, I screeched to a stop in front of Shelton. "What's wrong?"

He must have been running, because he spoke between gulps of air. "I just got an alert from El Dorado. I think they're under attack."

Chapter 33

Using an Arcane spell Shelton had taught me, I shot a flare into the air to signal the other flight groups to come in. Within minutes, they were all hovering nearby.

I guided my boomstick a little higher so they could all see me. "El Dorado is apparently under attack. We'll depart immediately to aid them."

Though some people looked at each other with concern, nobody seemed particularly shocked. This was the news we'd all been expecting.

I turned to Shelton. "Are the doors ready?"

He nodded. "They're working great. One is set up at El Dorado and another is in Colossus Stadium. It's already open and waiting."

"What are you doing after we leave?" I asked.

Shelton shrugged. "I don't know yet. Thomas asked me to wait here for further instructions."

I drifted lower, got off the broom. "Take care of yourself, Shelton."

He gripped me in a tight hug. "Justin, be careful. I know we've been through some hairy situations, but I have a bad feeling about this."

I had to admit I was a little surprised, but returned the hug. "Don't get all emotional on me now, okay?"

He chuckled. "You know me. I'm Mr. Calm."

Ivy got off her broom, stood on her tiptoes, and kissed Shelton's cheek. "Just in case we all get blasted, I wanted you to know that I'm glad you're my brother's friend even though he stinks."

Shelton squeezed her in a hug. "You be careful, okay?"

Blue eyes shimmering with an inner light, her lips spread into a wicked smile. "Daelissa is the one who'd better be careful." She skipped back to her broom, humming "Ring Around the Rosie."

Bella parked behind Shelton. "I'll be along shortly," she told me.

Shelton's forehead wrinkled. "Where do you think you're going?"

"I'm going to be a bomber, Harry."

"A what?" Shelton exclaimed.

I could tell they needed a little time to talk, so I hopped back on the boomstick and lifted off. "Skywraiths, form up!"

The other pilots guided their brooms into the air and joined their flight groups. Lanaeia and my group formed up behind me.

I pumped a fist into the air. "Skywraiths, go!"

We streaked toward the stadium. I couldn't help but look back and feel a sense of awe. Fearful as I was, this was probably one of the coolest things I'd done. *I'm leading a squadron of flying brooms into battle!*

Once we cleared the top of the stadium, I spotted the giant door sitting just outside the range of the Obsidian Arch in the center of the field. I swooped low, veered around, and aimed for the open door. A gray stone courtyard waited on the other side. I was glad Shelton hadn't set it up next to a pyramid or other obstacle. When we burst through, humidity hit me in the face like a wet sponge. The sky was overcast with thick clouds, casting the land into a surreal gray twilight.

I heard explosions and pulled up to gain altitude. An immense tract of flattened jungle lay in smoking ruins, leaving a path at least a mile long into the city. I saw hundreds of enemy troops marching toward us from the north.

Large stone pyramids, each one with massive mosaics dedicated to the Seraphim who'd enslaved the ancient citizens of El Dorado, lined the edges of the huge stone plaza. Our forces gathered outside the pyramids where we'd clear-cut hundreds of yards of jungle for the perimeter.

I saw Fjoeruss drifting nearby on a flying carpet and realized Cinder was with him. The seraph spotted me and flew to my position.

"I am teaching Cinder all there is about golem making and strategy. He has proven an apt student."

"It is fascinating," Cinder added, real emotion penetrating his typical deadpan voice. "What do you think of the battle golems?"

Fjoeruss's Battle golems, five in all, stood in a line before the troops. A static sheen hung in the air before them indicating a camouflage screen masked their presence. The golems stood far taller than the trees around them. Two humanoid versions, constructed of some kind of volcanic rock like basalt, had cylindrical heads lined with white, black, and gray gems. They rivaled the height and size of Daelissa's battle golems though their weaponry seemed less impressive.

In the middle stood an ornately crafted replica of an Egyptian sphinx, its body gold and shiny. A blue-striped nemes headdress with a striking cobra completed the impressive ensemble. Red gems shimmered in the cobra's eye sockets. The eyes on the human head glowed azure blue. Although the golem stood only waist high to the humanoid versions, it was still nearly two stories tall.

The last two golems were oddities. Half of a sphere with the flat side facing up perched atop three round legs with massive domed feet. Gray men manned—golemed?—shard turrets lining the wide platform. Several large weaponized gems protruded from the front. They were, in essence, walking battle platforms.

"They look awesome." Despite the threat of imminent death, my inner nerd was awed and excited to see Fjoeruss's monstrous creations. I had to hand it to the seraph—he made golems right. I had a feeling the Brightling soldiers would wet their pants the second we dropped the camo screens. I turned to Fjoeruss. "Will they hold up to Daelissa's goliaths?"

He shrugged. "The megaliths are the closest ones I have to hers."

"The humanoid ones?"

"Yes." Fjoeruss turned his gray eyes toward his monstrous creations. "I believe their offensive capabilities match the goliaths, but since I don't know the specific enchantments Daelissa's golem makers use, all I can offer is pure speculation."

"They should be sufficient for fighting conventional troops," Cinder said.

I was glad we didn't have to worry about fighting goliaths this battle, but unless we captured or killed Daelissa this time, we might still have to fight them.

Our other troops were arrayed similarly to the first battle. The Darkling army formation stood in front of the tripod golems on the right flank while the Templars massed to the left in front of the humanoid golems. Blue Cloaks on flying carpets filled the air, and Arcanes manning catapults filled the back ranks. I couldn't help but notice how much smaller the army seemed. The last battle had taken a tremendous toll on us.

The lycan and felycan contingents were noticeably diminished. Though the Daemos had summoned fresh hellhounds, their numbers also seemed reduced. I spotted my father and Kassallandra waiting near the front lines, their massive hounds pacing restlessly nearby.

"We'd better report in," I said.

Cinder stepped to the edge of the carpet and shook my hand. "Good luck, Justin."

"Stay safe, friend." I released his hand and offered a nod to Fjoeruss. "Perhaps we can end this today."

"Perhaps." He gave me a discerning look. "I must admit that your ability to draw together such a diverse array of individuals into one cohesive unit is impressive. Even Underborn and his assassins have joined the fight."

My eyebrows almost flew from my forehead in surprise. "Was that a compliment?"

Fjoeruss shrugged. "Merely an observation." He turned back to Cinder. "We should inspect the final preparations." With that, the two flew toward the neat square formation of gray men standing near the tripod golems.

I led the Skywraiths to the Templar command platform hovering in the center of the back lines and held up a fist. The flight groups behind me stopped while I dove down to speak with Thomas.

"How long ago did the enemy arrive?" I asked.

"Perhaps twenty minutes. They tripped our outer wards. Before we could respond, they launched a series of destructive spells that laid waste to a long stretch of jungle." He tapped on his arctablet. "We suspect they portaled in and then rushed to clear a path."

As I watched, it seemed more and more enemy soldiers appeared from thin air in the distance. "Why don't I see their portals?"

"Camouflage screens." He waved around the city. "We have several such screens around the city so they can't see in."

"Won't they think it's kind of strange that they can't see El Dorado?"

He shook his head. "The spell makes it appear as though the city is empty. I just hope none of their scouts have penetrated the perimeter."

The enemy lines grew closer and closer. The tension in the air felt as thick as the humidity. I felt like prey lying in wait for the hunter to draw near, hoping by some miracle to kill him before he killed me. I repressed a shudder and regained my composure. "The Skywraiths are ready to go on your command," I told Thomas. "Hopefully we can make a difference."

He reached out a hand. I grasped his and gave it a firm shake.

"Good luck, Justin."

"Same to you, sir."

Elyssa approached from her station and took my hand after Thomas released it. "I love you, Justin." She swallowed hard. "Please, be careful."

I got off the broom and squeezed her to me. "No matter what happens, I will always love you." I kissed her, not even the tiniest bit ashamed to do it in front of her father and everyone else. But time was fleeting and I had to go. Trying to push back the fear clenching my heart, I released her. "Be safe, my love."

She took a deep breath, nodded. "Kick Daelissa's ass, baby."

I gave her a toothy smile. "As you wish." I hopped on the boomstick, rose into the air, and zipped across the army toward my father.

He grinned when he saw me coming. "Nice ride, son."

291

"I know, right?" I dropped down to his eye level. "Are the Daemos ready to kick some booty?"

"We are ready to end this war," Kassallandra said in a cold, hard voice. "Without goliaths, I predict Daelissa's forces will fall more easily."

Dad didn't look quite as convinced. "We've got a couple of contingency plans in case things get hairy."

"House Salomon stands ever ready to advise," Godric said from his perch on a flying carpet. "Victory through wisdom."

How about victory through a punch to your face, you pompous asshat? I wondered if he would fight this time or hang back as usual.

Yuuki, also on a carpet, drifted toward us. "The infernal hands of Haedaemos stand ready to aid our cause." Members of House Wakahisa burst into cheers.

I wasn't really sure how to respond to her declaration so I kept it simple. "Excellent. We need all the infernalness we can get." I turned to my father. "Now, if only I could get the dragons to help us."

Dad put a hand on my back and leaned closer. "They're stubborn, Justin."

I lowered my voice to match his. "They fought alongside you centuries ago. Why not now?"

"Back during the first war, Moses had problems getting them involved." He looked around, but the other Daemos were distracted by Godric as he launched into a soliloquy proclaiming his wisdom. "I don't know what Moses did to make them change their minds."

"He didn't tell me anything before he died." I growled with frustration. "It's too late to do anything about it now."

Dad nodded. "I'm sorry." He gave me a firm hug. "I-umm…" He cleared his throat. "Just want to say, I love you, son. I just needed you to know…in case."

I blinked back the mist in my eyes. "I love you too, Dad." I backed up a step and gave him a stern look. "You'd better survive this. Mom will never forgive you if you die."

That brought his smile back. He looked toward the Skywraiths. "She and I said our goodbyes last night."

I squeezed my eyes shut for a moment. "Don't talk like that. We're all going to live long and prosper, okay?"

Dad's face grew serious. "I want you and Elyssa to have a happy future. No matter what happens, remember that you have a gift more powerful than all the armies in the world." His hand gripped my shoulder. "You have true love, son. It will get you through the darkest days and the coldest nights." Dad gazed at the encroaching army. "It'll get you through this and whatever comes next."

A terrible feeling gripped my heart and I wondered if this might be the last time I saw my father alive. "The love you have for Mom is no less strong," I said. I looked him straight in the eyes. "Don't ever forget that."

His serious expression vanished behind a smile. "I never do." He cracked his knuckles. "You'd better get back into formation. We don't have a lot of time before the enemy reaches us."

I nodded, rose into the air, and headed back to the Skywraiths. The Brightling army was perhaps ten minutes out, but every second seemed to tick past slower than normal, like the cook timer on a microwave when you're starving and waiting for your food to heat. An advancing army was, unfortunately, a bit more frightening than the mystery leftovers in the back of the fridge.

I swung my broom into position just above the Skywraiths so they could hear me speak. "This is the moment we've all been waiting for," I shouted. "Today is the day we take down Daelissa. Her tyranny ends here!"

The Skywraiths roared with cheers.

"That's my big brother," Ivy declared proudly.

I smiled though inside I felt grim. The army on the near horizon easily outnumbered us. We had to make every person count. There could be no retreat today.

I heard shouts and screams from the ranks of the catapult operators below and dove closer so I could see what was happening. Soldiers in the back ranks dissolved into doughy white globs and sprang onto the Arcanes. A white-hot shock of horror stabbed into my chest.

"They have Flarks!" I shouted. I spun to the nearest person on a boomstick. "Fly to the Templar command platform and tell them we're under attack by Flarks. Daelissa already knows we're here!"

The seraph streaked away.

I circled a hand above my head to gather the others closer and thought furiously about what to do. "Who here can dual channel?"

Several hands went up, including Ivy, Mom, and those in my group. "Attack the Flarks with Stasis, but try not to hit our own people."

"That requires channeling with both hands," Mom said. "How are we supposed to control the broom speed?"

"You'll have to take your hand off the throttle while you channel," I said. "The broom will maintain the same speed. If you're not comfortable with that, don't come." Not wasting another second, I dove toward the bubbling tide of Flarks. How so many of the creatures had infiltrated our ranks, I didn't know. That was when I realized some of them were seeping from cracks in the stone and from holes in the sides of the pyramids. I suddenly realized why Daelissa had taken her sweet time attacking. She'd sent Flarks to spy on us. By now, they had to know everything.

Fleshy blobs leapt from one target to the next. Many of the catapult operators lay deathly still while others rolled on the ground screaming after contact with the Flarks. I released the throttle. Took aim at the closest shape-shifter. Weaving together Murk and Brilliance, I channeled a wave of gray Stasis as the creature leapt for more prey. The beam struck it in midair. The Flark shrieked, but its screams were short-lived. It froze into a solid gray lump and thudded to the ground like a rock.

More screeches pierced the air as Ivy and the others struck down more of the shifters. Unfortunately, I knew the things weren't dead. Without a drain ward, I didn't know what else to do but confine the monsters. But how could we imprison them on such short notice? We had diamond fiber containers in the caves below, but they were too large to fit through an omniarch portal. I knew from experience Flarks could squeeze through anything that wasn't magic resistant.

What else could contain them?

The answer slapped me in the face with its simplicity. Flarks were creatures of almost pure magic. The one thing that could, without a doubt, contain pure magic was a containment circle. I waved to the troops below me. "Clear this area!"

I had to shout several more times before they heard me over the din of battle. Abandoning their posts, they ran back until I had a wide space to work with. Channeling a thick beam of destruction, I carved a circle in the stone plaza. I parked the boomstick, hopped off, and pressed a thumb to the circle.

Willing the circle to let magic in, but not allow it back out, I closed it. The air within the container thickened with the static feel of aether. I heard a shriek and looked up in time to see a Flark leaping for me. I dove out of the way. The blob passed over the circle and thudded to the stone tiles.

Figuring this was a good time to test my theory, I hopped over the blackened groove in the stone and prepared to hit the Flark with Stasis. The creature shifted into a giant mouth with sharp teeth and flung itself at me. The instant it reached the circle, the air flashed with a bright light and threw the Flark back inside.

I touched the communication pendant on my collar and set it to transmit to the squadron. "Put the Flarks inside the big black circle I made. If you can't channel Stasis, use a bubble of Murk to trap them temporarily."

As I ran back to my broom, I heard a whooping noise and looked up. Ivy flashed past, dragging a massive gray blob trapped in a sphere of Murk. She flung it toward the circle. The ultraviolet bubble vanished and the gray blob separated into four Flarks, which plopped to the ground.

I got on the broom and zipped back into the air. The other pilots had trapped many more shifters, though we had no way of knowing if any had escaped and blended back into the crowd. Within minutes, the ground inside my impromptu circle was littered with white and gray blobs. The Darklings who weren't adept enough to channel Stasis were skilled with Murk and able to trap the shifters.

Unfortunately, the damage was done. Dozens of Arcanes lay dead or severely wounded, and many of the catapults had been destroyed. More Arcanes came forward to man operable catapults, but we'd lost over half of them.

Bella, Rai, and the other instructors who'd volunteered for bomber duty swooped down and gathered two crucibles each, placing them into satchels attached to the sides of the boomstick saddles. With the catapults gone, we'd need her crew more than ever.

Thomas's voice sounded through my comm pendant. "What's the situation?"

"The Flarks are contained." I told him about the catapults.

"We just lost most of our long-distance offensive capabilities." Thomas's voice was grim. "That puts more pressure on the Skywraiths."

A low rumbling noise reached my ears. I spun the broom to face the oncoming horde. The forest behind the waves of enemy troops flickered and vanished, revealing a wide clearing. In the middle of the clearing stood the unmistakable form of an Obsidian Arch. My stomach twisted into knots. Even more troubling than the arch was what walked through it.

Goliaths.

Chapter 34

I could've sworn I heard a collective gasp rise from our army. I couldn't blame them. I felt like throwing up.

"Daelissa must have used a cube to grow another arch," Mom said.

Bella nodded. "The ley lines near El Dorado are certainly powerful enough to support one."

"Crap, crap, crap!" My vocabulary had become as limited as my ability to think. "How are we supposed to fight that?" Four of the lumbering behemoths had already emerged from the arch. The rest of Daelissa's army halted and cleared a path for the goliaths. It didn't take a military genius to figure out what would happen once they reached our front lines.

I focused my gaze on the threatening horizon. We had at least fifteen minutes before the goliaths made it to the enemy lines. "I have to talk to the dragons. They're our last chance." I signaled a halt and called the omniarch operator in the caverns below El Dorado.

A moment later, a portal opened in the courtyard. I ducked and flew the broom through the opening. Without pause, I spun left and guided the boomstick out into the main cavern. The dragons were there, but they weren't sleeping as usual. Lulu was growling at Altash. The big red dragon turned his head away from her as I rose to his level. His large, parietal eyes settled on me.

"We need your help," I shouted, trying to project over Lulu's ruckus. "There are over a dozen goliaths bearing down on us. Without you we don't stand a chance."

Altash made a thoughtful rumbling noise. The pupil in his eye narrowed to a slit. *WE CANNOT. IF WE ENTER THIS FRAY, SO WILL THE ANCIENT NEMESIS.*

His voice rang loudly in my head. If I'd been standing, I would have staggered. "Ancient nemesis?"

The image of a massive black serpent filled my mind. It was larger than even Altash. The serpent slithered toward me, massive body racing cross an obsidian plain. With a hiss, it reared up on four legs. Its head split into dozens of smaller heads, each one hissing and striking. Massive wings sprang from its back and launched it into the air. It reminded me of the dragon I'd seen flying over the ocean in Seraphina.

I was suddenly back in the cave, Altash's eye only feet from me. "If you join us, that creature will fight for Daelissa?"

THE TRUCE WILL BE BROKEN. HE WILL STRIKE. OUR MIGHT WILL MATTER NOT.

"In other words, if I get big ass dragons to fight for me, this dude will even the odds for Daelissa." I threw up my hands in disgust. "Why didn't you just tell me this before?"

IT IS NOT OUR PLACE TO FIGHT FOR THIS REALM.

I knew there had to be a lot more to this than just a big evil dragon looking for an excuse to fight. In the vision, I'd seen him on a plain of obsidian. That place looked exactly like the siren realm.

I had one more question for Altash. "What happens if Daelissa wins?"

The dragon turned away from me, apparently unwilling to answer. Lulu growled and moved her massive head toward me. A commanding female voice filled my head.

IF EDEN FALLS, SO FALL THE OTHER REALMS. A rumbling sounded deep in her throat. *YOU MUST PREVAIL.*

"Wow, thanks Captain Obvious." I had nothing in my arsenal of wits that could convince these creatures to help us. The only things I had plenty of were questions. What was that giant black dragon's deal? Where did the dragons come from? What had happened to the other giant dragons? So many questions, so little time.

I spun the broom around and headed toward the floor so I could go through the control room door. A hissing noise caught my attention. A ley worm the size of a large truck slithered over to me. One side of its snakelike body bore scars where an evil Arcane named Dash Armstrong had used him as a power source before I rescued him.

"Hey Slitheren." I looked toward the back of the cavern and saw several more of the small earth dragons waiting there. "Are you guys just here to watch us get our asses handed to us?"

He hissed and gave me a dirty look. Then again, with his long toothy muzzle and reptilian eyes, most of his facial expressions seemed angry. For all I knew, he was smiling.

Altash has forbidden our direct help.

I jerked my head back in surprise. He'd never spoken to me before. "Look, I understand. Your hands are tied." Considering the dragons didn't even have legs or arms, the idiom might have been lost on him.

We have tunneling duties. It is possible we might stray too close to the surface. It is possible we might accidentally open a fissure up above. Be careful not to fall in.

I felt a trickle of hope drip into the hollow pit of despair where my guts had once been. "Thank you, friend."

I owe you a life debt. The others feel you have brought meaning back to a dreary existence. We will do what we can. Slitheren's mouth parted into a crocodile smile. It was frightening enough to make a grown man cry. He slithered back to his comrades and they vanished into one of the tunnels.

I hadn't recruited the big guns, but with the help of the smaller dragons, we might actually stand a chance. Alternatively, I might just be deluding myself. On the way back to the control room I passed by rows and rows of weapons where the Templars had set up an impromptu armory after evacuating the Ranch. It all looked like so much useless junk now. None of them could take down giant battle golems. I passed by swords, shields, and even diamond fiber grappling hooks. I'd considered using soggers to make the ground a muddy mess, but we'd used every last one of them defending the Ranch from Daelissa.

"We are so screwed." I was just about to head back to the omniarch portal when an idea struck me in the back of the head. It seemed kind of ridiculous at first, but the more I thought about it, the more viable it seemed. I gathered all the supplies I'd need and went back through the omniarch portal to the surface.

The hopeful look on Mom' and the others' faces faded when they saw me.

"We'll have no help from the big dragons," I said. "But I have a plan." I'd found enough supplies to make six sets of gear for my diabolical plan. I distributed them to Mom, Ivy, Nightliss, Flava, Lanaeia, and kept one for myself.

Circling a finger over my head, I gathered the entire squadron together. "I'll test my plan on the first goliath. If it works, we will move to the next one. The rest of you must keep enemy soldiers on the ground occupied while I go in." I tapped on the comm pendant and informed Thomas of my plan.

"It just might work," he said in a grim voice.

"We have to do it while the goliaths are still far enough out, though."

"Understood. Proceed."

I raised an open hand over my head. "Skywraiths, form up!"

Everyone glided into position. I swung my arm forward and moved out.

Bella flew in next to me. "We're ready to commence bombing."

I nodded. "You'll have the perfect opportunity in a moment." I pointed toward the first rows of Brightling soldiers. The closest goliath was still about two hundred yards behind them. "Fly high and drop the crucibles. That should disorient them so the rest of us can attack the first golem."

"Good luck, Justin." Bella blew me a kiss and rocketed away toward her squad.

Our troops were a blur beneath us. I heard cheers as we soared over them. Their shouts of encouragement chipped away at my doubts little by little.

We can do this!

Bella's group broke formation and gained altitude to begin their bombing run. Battle mages on flying carpets rose to meet us. Blazing wings flashed in the distance and archangels soared into the air. A group of them streaked higher on an intercept course for Bella's group.

I touched the comm pendant. "Zeta Squadron, break off and escort the bombers." Glancing over my shoulder, I watched the five flyers streak after the bombers.

Mom drew even on my right. "There must be fifty flying carpets in our way."

"And a whole bunch of flying Seraphim," Ivy said from my left.

The Brightling infantry below launched arrows of pure white energy toward us. They fell well short of reaching our height. The enemy battle mages formed a line with their flying carpets and hurled curses at us. Malignant energy sprang from their staffs. Yellow spheres whizzed past. Green lightning bolts exploded in the air. An azure beam exploded against a shield channeled at the last second by Nightliss. A flaming red skull screamed past me and narrowly missed Lanaeia's head.

"They must be really mean to know such awful curses," Ivy said as she blocked a coil of venomous green vapor.

The mages unleashed another volley of spells. They streaked through the air like fireworks, exploding and filling the air with burning ash. The heat burned my lungs and choked me. I touched the neck seam of the Nightingale armor. It flowed over my head, protecting my eyes and lungs. Slashing an arm through the air, I channeled a gust of wind, clearing a hole through the blinding soot.

"Masks on," I croaked into the comm pendant. A quick glance showed me that most of the others had already done so.

We burst through the ash cloud and were met by a flock of archangels, their lightning-wreathed vjaltis swords extended before them.

A battle cry sounded from above. I looked up as a seraph swung his vjaltis toward my neck. His cry turned into a scream as a thick beam of Brilliance punched through his chest.

301

"Leave my bro alone!" Ivy shouted as she watched the stricken Seraphim spiral to the ground, blood and black smoke trailing from his wound.

I didn't have time to thank her before another archangel came at me. I leaned hard right to dodge. Threw up a hand and caught his arms just below the wrist before he could complete the downward swing of his sword. Forming a spike of Murk on my left hand, I swung the broom around the seraph and punched him hard in the face. Bone crunched and blood sprayed. He went limp. I released the energy and let his body fall into the morass of infantry far below.

As I turned to find the next enemy, I saw the other Skywraiths weren't faring as well. Several were fighting for their lives, or dodging the enemy. Most of us had swords, but we hadn't practiced sword fighting from the seat of a flying broom.

An archangel beheaded one pilot and kicked the body from the broom. Another plunged his vjaltis into the chest of a female Darkling. His eyes lit with bloodlust as he watched her topple from her perch.

"No!" I screamed as another swooped in behind Ivy while she fought two enemies. I throttled to full speed and slammed into the seraph before he could stab her in the back.

An explosive grunt burst from his mouth as the end of the boomstick rammed him. Rage burned into me and flames flickered on in my eyes. I gripped him by the throat. "That's my sister you're messing with." My voice was a low furious growl. Encasing my hands in Brilliance, I wrenched off the archangel's sword arm. He screamed. His wings puffed away as his concentration shattered.

I bared my teeth at him and let him go. His screams faded into the distance. I flew behind the next closest enemy and locked an arm around his neck. My inner demon surged with bloodlust. *Destruction! Brilliance!* An animalistic roar tore from my throat and mingled with the hysterical screams from the seraph in my grip. With a savage twist, I wrenched his head so hard, it nearly came off.

When I spun to find the next target, I saw Nightliss and Mom staring at me with huge, horrified eyes.

302

Ivy laughed and clapped her hands. "That was so cool! Can I break their necks too?"

Mom came to her senses and blasted a nearby archangel out of the sky with destruction. "Justin, we need to get to the first goliath!"

I'd been so enraged with bloodlust, I'd completely forgotten the primary objective. Once again, my demonic side threatened to rip away all control. Now wasn't the time for a therapy session. The first monstrous battle golem was nearly upon us. Explosions lit the ground beneath us as the bomber squad's first volley hit the Brightling army. I threw up a shield to block a death beam from one of the archangels. Nightliss flew in behind the attacker and punched a hole through his neck with an ultraviolet spear.

I looked toward the goliath, but a blockade of battle mages on flying carpets flew in to protect it. "The battle mages are in the way!"

Bella's voice spoke through my comm pendant. "Justin, we're about to create some space for you."

Several glass crucibles sparkled in the air as they fell toward earth. I suddenly realized most of them would never reach the ground. The battle mages realized the same thing too late. One of them looked up and managed to shout, "Watch ou—" before the first crucible hit him right in the face.

Explosions blossomed in mid-air, sending battle mages and carpets flying. Smoking bodies spiraled to the ground. The battle golem rocked back on its heels from the shockwaves and seemed as if it might fall over. Much to my chagrin, it managed to stay upright.

"Retreat!" One of the archangels shouted. "Let the goliath destroy them all!"

Cheers rose from the other Skywraiths, but I knew it was too early to be celebrating just yet. As if in answer to my cautionary thoughts, the weapon shards on the goliath began to glow. The low hum that meant they were charging reached my ears. The weapon design on these behemoths looked slightly different from the ones we'd fought in Atlanta. Instead of crystal shards jutting in all directions, these bore four swiveling shards on the chest, enabling them to aim the death rays more accurately.

We were still a hundred yards out from the goliath when the hum turned to a high-pitched whine.

"Evasive maneuvers!" I shouted over the comm pendant.

Each group broke off into different directions. I took Alpha group low and lined up for my attack run. The goliath's weapons fired. One massive death ray made contact. Two boomsticks exploded into flames. Only a cloud of ash remained where once living pilots had been. Flashbacks of the first battle raced through my head, leaving a trail of bile down my throat.

I bared my teeth. "Not again, you bastards."

Aether arrows streaked past us like lasers as the infantry on the ground took aim. The other groups of Skywraiths unleashed attacks of their own. Beams of destruction carved through the army below. Smoke boiled where the attacks lit crushed foliage on fire. The enemy soldiers ceased fire and shielded themselves.

The sound of the shards powering up reached my ears again just as I reached the legs of the goliath. I threw out a diamond fiber grappling hook. It caught in the rough gray stone just below where a knee would be on a person. Leaning hard right, I looped diamond fiber rope several times around the golem's legs until I ran out of line.

The monstrous creation lifted its foot but was unable to move it. It tried to recover, but stopping the forward momentum of tons of rock proved impossible. The goliath toppled. Shouts rose from the Brightling infantry and they swarmed to the sides to escape the impact. The shards, now full of energy, exploded on impact. Dust and rubble flew in all directions. The goliath crumbled to inert stone.

"Ivy, get the next one while they're disorganized!" I shouted.

"I'm on it!" Ivy jetted toward the next objective about fifty yards behind the first with Mom and me to either side of her. Ivy's eyes flashed with inspiration. "I have a better idea."

I didn't have time to ask what it was before she zipped past the second golem and headed toward the third. "What are you doing?"

"Two stones with one bird." She flashed a grin.

Several archangels flew in to intercept. Lanaeia raked the first one with a searing white beam. Nightliss encased the next in a bubble of Murk and let it drop to the ground. Mom and I hit the same attacker in the chest, blasting the seraph like a burning meteor through the air.

I saw Ivy zipping around the goliath's legs. Like the first one, it couldn't beat physics and lost its balance. I suddenly realized what Ivy's brilliant plan had been when the granite leviathan tripped headfirst into the goliath in front of it like a giant domino. Both crashed to earth, sending a tidal wave of dirt and vegetation flying to either side. The giant golems broke into pieces on impact, the enchantment binding them together unable to withstand the incredible force. Their sparks burst free of the wreckage and winked out, unable to maintain cohesion.

A small ravine opened beneath some of the enemies and they vanished into the dark earth. I thought I saw one of the smaller earth dragons diving beneath the surface. *Good job, Slitheren!*

The Brightling infantry recovered their wits. Hundreds of light arrows streaked toward us. I took us up to a safer altitude, but several more Skywraiths fell. As I looked around and took a count, I realized we'd lost nearly fifteen pilots. We'd downed three battle golems, but I counted at least ten more coming our way.

Our small victories amounted to little more than a dent in Daelissa's juggernaut.

Chapter 35

The odds were against us, but we couldn't quit now. "Form up," I commanded. "We're going to try the same thing on the fifth goliath."

"We might not have a chance," Mom said.

The other goliaths fanned out, their massive feet trampling virgin jungle. The first one had stopped walking so the others could catch up. A dark cloud of leathery winged beings rose from the ground and encircled it like bats.

"Flying vampires," Lanaeia said. "So long as they are not the ancient ones, they shouldn't pose a serious threat."

With the goliaths changing formation and the swarm of vampires in our way, we stood a slim chance of taking down another battle golem. "We've lost too many people to risk it," I said. "We have to pull back and let our army engage them."

Bella, Rai, and the others in the bomber squadron glided to a halt near us.

"I think they're onto the plan," Bella said. "And we're running low on crucibles."

Despair squeezed my throat. Perhaps a hundred of the Brightling infantry lay dead. Others had fallen into small ravines just large enough for a person to fall through. Archangels and battle mages added another sixty or so to the body count. We'd killed so many, but it wasn't nearly enough. Daelissa's reinforcements were already on the way. A large contingent of vampires clad in the crimson armor of Red Cell marched behind the oncoming goliaths. A horde of flightless vampires thronged behind them. I even spotted the remnants of the Synod Templar army and Exorcists. Daelissa had pulled out all the stops. She was throwing everything including the kitchen sink at us. We'd done all the damage we could for now.

In a hollow voice, I gave the command. "Retreat."

We flew high and raced toward the outer edges of El Dorado where the bulk of our army still waited. The camouflage screen was gone, revealing Fjoeruss's megaliths and tripods. I saw no sign of the sphinx. Since the Flarks had already infiltrated our ranks, Thomas had probably decided it was no longer worth maintaining the illusion.

Brightling infantry hurled spears of light and shouted curses at us as we flew over them, but we were out of range of their spells. I took us back to the Templar command platform, parked my broom, and hopped off.

"Good work," Thomas said.

I shook my head. "Not good enough."

Elyssa rushed over and hugged me. "I was so worried."

I squeezed her hands. "I'm fine, babe." I turned back to Thomas. "What now?"

"We stand and fight." He cast a grim look toward the horizon.

The enemy forces had resumed their march with the goliaths in a triangular formation in front of them. They no longer marched down the clearing where the troops were, remaining at a safe distance so if they fell, they wouldn't kill their own people. The great crackling of massive trees echoed. The thuds of their footsteps vibrated the air like miniature earthquakes.

Thomas checked the screen of his arctablet. "Once we engage, I'd like the Skywraiths to bomb and harass enemy forces."

"We'll be ready." I looked at Elyssa. "I guess this is it."

Elyssa's hands tightened on mine. "We'll make it through this."

Thomas looked at his daughter. "Templar, please resume your post."

She stiffened and backed away. "Yes, sir."

Thomas pulled me to the other side of the platform. "I have a failsafe should this battle not go our way."

"A failsafe?"

He nodded. "Two malaether crucibles Jeremiah left in his vault."

My jaw went slack with surprise. "I didn't realize we had any more of them."

"Neither did I until our people found them." He glanced at Elyssa, but she was busily tapping away on an arctablet. "If worse comes to worst, I will take a malaether crucible on a camouflaged flying carpet straight at Daelissa. If I'm lucky, I'll reach her and detonate it."

I gave him a startled look. "I can't let you do that."

"You will take my daughter away from here and keep her safe." Thomas's hand tightened like a vice on my shoulder. "Understood?"

"No." I narrowed my eyes. "If it comes down to that, I'll take a crucible to Daelissa. The brooms are much faster than the flying carpets."

"Unacceptable."

"I will not let you kill yourself." Thomas squared his shoulders as if readying for a fight.

I crossed my arms and stared him down. "Who's in command here?"

"You are," he said in a stony voice.

"Correct." I chose my next words carefully. "I'm one of the best flyers. I could probably get close enough to Daelissa to deliver the explosive. I also have the best chance of surviving the blast. After all, I shielded myself and others from a malaether blast during the defense of the Australian Templar compound."

Thomas's shoulders loosened a little. "That might be true, but it's still a suicide mission."

I put an arm on his shoulder and managed a smile. "It's not suicide if I survive." I glanced over my shoulder at Elyssa and back to him. "Believe me, I want to survive this, but if it comes down to surviving or stopping Daelissa, I will do what I must to save Eden."

"You seem to have fully grasped the meaning of duty, Mr. Slade." He didn't look entirely happy about it. "I hold no illusions about this battle. This is everything we have against everything she has." The low rumbling march of the goliaths drew his attention. "Unfortunately, Daelissa has a great deal more."

The enemy was close. *Time to fight.* I caught Elyssa looking at me with worried eyes and blew her a kiss. It wasn't much, but it was enough for now. She knew I loved her to infinity and beyond, and I knew she felt the same way. There was nothing more to be said. All that remained was victory or death.

"We'll see this through, Commander." I hopped back on my broom and flew back into formation. Trumpets sounded and our front lines met the enemy forces.

I threw up a hand. "Skywraiths, attack!"

We flew toward the front line. Deadly beams streaked back and forth between the two armies. Blue Cloaks and revived Darklings on flying carpets engaged archangels. The Darkling infantry, now supercharged by feeding on humans, channeled gouts of Murk at the encroaching Brightlings. In response, the Brightlings fired back focused beams of destruction through their swords.

Our front lines buckled under the assault. I swooped low and shouted in Cyrinthian, "Remember, you can dual channel! Use everything you have!"

One of the Darklings shielded himself with Murk and fired a beam of white energy from his right hand. He caught a surprised Brightling in the face. Other Darklings followed the example and unleashed Brilliance against their adversaries. Shocked Brightlings staggered backward. Their armor had been designed to neutralize Murk, not Brilliance.

I took the Skywraiths toward the flying vampires. Ivy knocked several from midair with precise blasts as the creatures came for us. I punched a hole through the wings of two more, sending them to their deaths.

"Don't let them swarm us," I said. "They're slower than us, so stay just away from them and keep firing."

We strafed back and forth, knocking vampires from the sky. They shrieked with impotent rage, unable to fly fast enough to catch us. I glanced down and saw our front lines pushing back the enemy. Small holes opened up in the ground beneath Brightlings, sending the surprised soldiers plummeting into the darkness. Even the Templar lines were doing well against the Brightlings. The weapon improvements had obviously made a difference. One could never underestimate the power of duct tape.

A low humming noise signaled that our advances would soon be at an end. The goliaths were in range of our troops.

Fjoeruss's monstrous creations responded. Sometime during the battle, the megaliths had moved far out to the left flank while the tripods had done the same on the right. The sphinx was still nowhere to be seen.

The gem arrays on the megaliths blasted chunks from one of the enemy units. Their focused fire reduced the goliath to rubble within seconds. They turned their fire on the next target, but the enemy units responded. Torsos swiveling, they aimed crystal shards toward this new threat. The goliaths unleashed everything at the first of Fjoeruss's megaliths. It buckled under the assault but fired back. The lower torso of the closest goliath shattered. Unable to maintain its balance, it crashed into the jungle.

The concentrated fire from the goliaths pierced the basalt megalith. Its spark exploded in a dark cloud. The other megalith ignored its inert companion and pressed the attack. The gems on its cylindrical head blazed with energy. When they fired, the beams converged, forming a solid gray beam, which struck the leg of the next goliath. The stone froze in place, but the marching goliath kept moving forward. Its leg broke free. Massive arms flailing for balance, the goliath thundered to earth.

Before the megalith could open fire again, three goliaths discharged everything on it. Fjoeruss's creation cracked apart. The gems fired as the golem toppled backward, casting a gray beam up into the sky. I watched in horror as it enveloped Joss and sliced through the flock of flying vampires. Frozen figures plummeted toward the ground.

"No!" Otaleon cried out. He dove for his friend and caught him with strands of Murk. Another Skywraith assisted him, and the two pulled the statue-like body up to them.

"Get him back behind our lines!" I shouted as the surviving vampires surged toward us, eyes filled with fury.

"Is he dead?" Otaleon asked.

"I don't know." Chances were, he was simply frozen for a time and would revive. "Take him to Fjoeruss."

I signaled our formation to fly further out for another pass at the vampires. Below us, Fjoeruss's tripods opened fire on the enemy's left flank. A cutting beam sliced the leg from one goliath. It tumbled to the ground, breaking apart and crushing the jungle around it. Daelissa was down to six of the monstrous things.

A flash of white caught my peripheral vision. I looked left and saw Arturo leading a large group of archangels toward us. We couldn't possibly take them and the vampires at the same time. With the megaliths destroyed, the goliaths turned their focus on the tripods. A very dangerous idea took hold of me. I touched my comm pendant. "Alpha, Bravo, Charlie, Delta, with me. Everyone else, continue your attacks on the vampires."

Less than half of the remaining Skywraiths broke off from us. The less-skilled pilots had taken heavy casualties. There were only seventeen of us remaining from the first four groups, not including Joss and Otaleon who were effectively out of the battle for the near future. Bella and the bombers were too far away to assist. I counted perhaps thirty-five archangels on an intercept course.

I spoke into the comm pendant. "We're going to fly into the crossfire between the goliaths and the tripods. If you don't think you can cut it, break off now."

Ivy looked with wide eyes at the brilliant lightshow ahead. Sizzling beams of destruction large enough to incinerate elephants crisscrossed the sky as the massive golems tried to destroy each other. She looked at me, eyes full of excitement. "This will be so much fun!"

Mom groaned and Nightliss gasped.

Lanaeia raised an eyebrow. "Alysea, your child has an interesting perspective on life."

"I have never been so frightened in my life," Nightliss said. "This is not fun at all!"

Ivy's face screwed up with confusion. "Grownups just don't understand, do they, bro?"

I snorted. "It's called a sense of self-preservation, sis." I winked at her. "Maybe you'll develop one someday." Despite my light-hearted response, I felt deathly afraid for her and the others. This felt like a no-win scenario and I was all out of cheat codes to win the day.

The archangels adjusted course to come at us from behind the goliath closest to them. We dove beneath a flurry of fire from a goliath as it battled the second tripod. A gray beam from the latter froze the leg of the goliath seconds before a large sphere of Brilliance shattered it. The goliath's massive arm swung out for balance causing a gust of wind to scatter our formation. I spun out of control, desperately pulling left to counter the spin. I recovered, dizzy and disoriented. Someone cried out. I looked back and saw tons of stone falling toward me, massive arms swinging in a downward arc to crush me.

I twisted the throttle to full speed. The instant acceleration dislodged my feet from the stirrups and nearly threw me off. I held on for dear life, feet and body flapping in the breeze. I heard a tremendous roar and saw a shadow displace the meager sunlight that penetrated the dense clouds. A shout of pure fear escaped my throat. I glanced back and saw that I wouldn't make it. There was no way I'd clear the falling goliath in time and with my feet off the stirrups, I couldn't steer or roll to the side.

Something streaked toward me from the left. At the last second, I saw Flava, teeth bared, her face tight with absolute concentration.

"No!" she screamed long and loud. She pulled left at the last second, ramming me in the side. I careened out of harm's way.

The falling goliath's body roared earthward only feet away to my left. A blast of wind knocked me into a spinning roll and I lost sight of Flava. Everything became a gray blur. I felt myself diving to earth, completely out of control. Something wrapped around me. Despite my daze, I realized it was a strand of Murk. I slowed and came to rest atop blasted, barren earth, the broom hovering a few yards away.

"Justin, get back on your broom!" Ivy released the Murk strands she'd used to rescue me. "Hurry, they're almost here!"

I pushed up, stumbled forward, my senses scrambled. Broken limbs from downed trees, broken rock, and clumps of dirt did their best to trip me. I saw a broken broom near mine and heard moaning.

Flava lay nearby, arms and legs twisted. Blood welled from cuts in her skin. I ran over to her. "Lie still, I'll get you to safety."

She sucked in a harsh breath. "No. Go. You must fight."

I knelt down and inspected her wounds. There were too many to count. "You saved me," I said.

Flava managed a weak smile. "You are so strong. So courageous. All I admire in a person." She coughed up blood. "It is…honor to die for—" another cough racked her body.

"Tell me how to heal you." I pressed my hands to the side of her face. "Tell me what to do!"

A tear trickled from the corner of her eye and across my thumb. "I envy Elyssa."

I didn't understand why she was saying that. "Why?"

"Because…I love you." She coughed again and crimson foamed at her mouth.

Grief locked its cruel fist around my heart. I could never return her feelings, but in the short time I'd known her, she'd proven to be selfless and caring. She was the kind of person the world needed more of, and that cruel bitch, Daelissa, was about to take her. I heard shouts overhead and looked up. Arturo and his minions were closing the gap.

I sent a picture to the omniarch controller with an urgent message. *Open a portal here now!* A split second later, a gateway appeared. More shouts echoed behind me. I looked back and saw Brightling infantry crossing the rugged terrain, eyes fierce, and swords drawn.

Encasing Flava's body in Murk to make her broken bones immobile, I lifted her and set her on the other side of the gateway. I stepped through and saw the Templar controlling the arch. "Get her medical help now!"

He saluted and raced away. I released the Murk from Flava and knelt next to her. "I command you to live! Do that for me!"

She blinked, but seemed unable to reply. I had no time left and raced back through the portal and onto the battlefield. With a thought, I willed the portal to close. Arrows of Brilliance arced toward me. I threw up a barrier to intercept them and hopped on my broom. The wave of destruction crashed against my shield even as they loosed another salvo. Holding firmly to the broom, I twisted the throttle and launched myself toward the still-standing trees.

I twisted through the labyrinth of foliage for a hundred yards and then pulled back on the boomstick. I shot through the canopy and into clear air, aether arrows sizzling into the greenery around me. I saw Mom and the others firing toward the infantry on the ground and jetted toward them.

"Justin!" Mom cried out. "Are you okay?"

Panting for breath, I nodded.

"Flava?" Nightliss asked.

My throat locked with pain, but I managed an answer. "I don't know."

"They are almost upon us," Lanaeia said.

The archangels had moved past the goliath closest to the first tripod and were closing in fast. We were out of time.

Chapter 36

The first tripod listed to the side as two goliaths crippled it. The second tripod turned to assist. I made a quick calculation. "We can still make it." *But it'll be close.* "Go!"

We launched toward the enemy. I glanced back. The other three goliaths had changed course and were headed toward the tripods. As I was about to turn around I saw the sphinx lunge from a behind one of the massive pyramids in the plaza and race toward a goliath. Its four massive legs pounded like giant sledgehammers as it crashed through the jungle. Three goliaths turned to face it. The huge gems on the sphinx's head blazed to life, blasting the goliath closest to it, but doing little damage. The goliath opened fire but missed its relatively fast prey. The sphinx rammed the battle golem hard enough to rock the air with thunder. The goliath's torso shattered. Its upper body fell onto the sphinx and a huge cloud of black dust rose into the air.

I didn't have time to see what happened and faced forward. The two tripods were in a battle for their unlives. The first had lost a leg and was barely maintaining balance. Huge blackened holes were all that remained where its weapon gems had been. The goliaths were heavily damaged, but still able to move and fire.

Arturo closed within range. He and his archangels extended their swords.

"Well fought, Slade!" He cried. "But we are mightier. We have won this day!" With that pronouncement, he and his comrades fired a massive salvo of Brilliance from their vjaltis.

"Dive!" I shouted.

We dove. One of the Darklings didn't move fast enough. He screamed as the beams burned his body. The archangels dove after us

315

just as the crystal shards on the goliath behind them opened fire on the second tripod.

I veered between the moving legs of the tripod at the moment it responded to the goliath. Arturo, hell-bent on killing us, realized his mistake too late. He cried out a command. A massive gout of Brilliance from the tripod ripped a hole through the center of the archangel formation. The goliath's discharge struck several more Brightlings from behind. The archangels scattered in confusion.

We looped up and over the tripod, rolled, and came at the enemy from above. I balled my right fist and gathered a sphere of Brilliance. "Ready."

The others followed my example.

I targeted Arturo. "Aim."

Everyone picked an archangel.

"Fire!"

We unleashed everything we had. Arturo dodged at the last minute, but other archangels weren't so quick on their feet—um—wings. Seraphs screamed and died. Their comrades returned fire and streaked toward us. Arturo swung his vjaltis as he passed by me. I barrel-rolled beneath the blade, narrowly avoiding the loss of my head and dived out of the way of another attacker. When I spun around, I saw that several Skywraiths had fallen.

Ivy engulfed an archangel in a gout of Brilliance. Pulling up hard and looping backward, she blasted another enemy with a constant beam while flying upside down. I looked back and saw Arturo chasing right behind me, murder blazing in his eyes. I whipped my broom in a one-eighty and reversed course toward him. His eyes flared with surprise, but his warrior's instinct guided his sword in a downward arc to intercept me.

Thanks to Elyssa's training, I'd anticipated his response and jerked the broom right. His sword slashed empty air. My fist impacted his face so hard I felt my bones crunch. Arturo's sword fell from a limp hand and the leader of the archangels dropped like a rock. His subordinates dove after him. Two caught his arms while the others flew interference to keep us from finishing him off.

The high-pitched whine of weapon shards pierced the air. Mom's eyes flew wide. She pulled up hard. Ivy dove. A massive blast of light incinerated three Skywraiths and two archangels. Ivy cried out as the blast singed her hair. I heard a shriek and turned toward the sound in time to see Nightliss falling from a burning broom.

I dove after her. I shot a strand of Murk, but fatigue took me in its grip and my aim faltered. I took aim again and missed. "Nightliss!" I shouted.

She blinked her eyes as if coming out of a daze.

I screamed her name one more time and fired Murk. The strand gripped her leg but snapped. I was running on fumes. I had almost nothing left. Nightliss extended her arm. A strand of ultraviolet shot out and smacked me in the face. I felt all her weight settle on my head and neck. I couldn't breathe. I couldn't see.

I didn't care. I was the only thing keeping her alive.

Using all my physical strength to keep my neck from breaking, I pulled up on the broom. The sensation of falling stopped and I managed to level out.

"I've got her," Ivy said.

Vision returned and the weight vanished. I gulped in a breath of humid air and shook my head to clear my senses. What I saw chilled my heart with horror. The tripods were in smoking ruins. Four goliaths remained and were heading for our army, or the scattered remnants of it. The Brightling infantry had taken heavy casualties, but Red Cell and the vampire horde were plugging the gaps and killing our exhausted soldiers.

Fjoeruss's gray men had engaged the Red Cell, but the elite vampire warriors were handling them with ease. The normal vampires weren't especially skilled at fighting, but their numbers made up for it. Some carried swords while others fired automatic weapons. Synod forces flanked our Templars, fighting them from all sides while the Daemos and their hellhounds tried to fight back.

Infernal forms sprang from the earth as Daemos summoned mightier beings to war with their enemies. A four-legged demon with a flaming skull for a head pushed back at the Synod. Other bizarre demon forms sprang up next to it. The Exorcists joined the Synod and began purging the demons.

No matter what we did, Daelissa's army had an answer.

The archangels had retreated, but the remaining goliaths turned in pursuit. We'd claimed minor victories, but we were going to lose the battle.

I felt absolutely sick to my stomach. We'd reached the end game Thomas and I had discussed. Looking behind us, I saw Daelissa on a cloudlet drifting a couple hundred yards behind the goliaths. With my supernatural vision, I saw her gloating face. Saw her laughing with glee. She knew we were on the ropes.

I would use her overconfidence to my advantage.

Nightliss hung unceremoniously beneath Ivy's broom since there was no space for her on the seat. Mom, Lanaeia, and the others looked as exhausted as I felt.

We were done.

"Retreat to the Templar command platform," I told them.

We gained altitude. Ivy's broom struggled with the extra weight. Mom lined up her boomstick so Nightliss could grasp it with her other hand to distribute the burden. We flew high enough to stay out of harm's way from the battle below. Bullets zinged past as vampires took potshots at us with their rifles.

From above, the battle looked like a mosh pit. Bodies and blood hindered the movements of both sides. Many Blue cloaks had abandoned flying carpets to fight on the ground with swords. I assumed they'd exhausted themselves magically and were putting in a last-ditch effort.

Once we reached the back of our lines, Mom and Ivy landed to let Nightliss get off.

I halted the squadron. "We've done all we can. I want you to rest for a few minutes. You're going to need it."

Several Darklings collapsed to the ground. Even Ivy looked ready to drop. I got off the broom and gave my sister a hug. "I'm so proud of you, Ivy." I kissed her forehead. "You were amazing."

She kissed my cheek. "You too, bro." Ivy sighed. "I have so much fun with you. I can't wait to beat Daelissa so we can go get more ice cream."

I mussed her blond locks and forced a grin. "Me either." I turned to Mom and squeezed her tight. "I love you, Mom. Thanks for everything."

She managed a tired smile. "We gave it our best, didn't we son?"

"Yeah." My voice cracked as emotion tried to break through the façade. "We're not done yet. I need to talk to Thomas."

"We will fight to the death," Nightliss said. "We will never give up." She gripped my hands. "Thank you for saving me. I owe you my life once again."

I kissed her forehead. "I could never let someone so cute splat on the ground."

She laughed. "It is a rather undignified way to die."

"I could think of worse," Lanaeia said. "You could end up head-first in a mud bog with your legs protruding in the air like Qualan."

"No less than he deserved," Mom replied.

"Agreed," Lanaeia said, silver eyes flashing bright.

I wearily got back on my broom and headed toward the Templar command platform. Thomas met me with a grim face when I stepped off. I caught a glance from Elyssa and held up a finger so she wouldn't rush over. I didn't want her to hear this.

I took Thomas aside. "I think it's time."

"Are you certain?" For the first time since I'd known him, he sounded tired, defeated, and unsure.

I nodded. "There's no other choice. I need to go now while I still have the strength."

"You may be no man, Justin, but you are a better man than most." The person who had once been my adversary, the father who once abhorred the thought of me dating his daughter, gripped me in a short but very manly hug and stepped back. "Godspeed, son."

I swallowed the lump in my throat. "Thank you, sir."

"The malaether crucibles are in the blue container over there." He pointed to the box where it innocently sat next to several other crates on the ground. "You can take one or both."

I looked toward the vicious battle. "You might need to use one on them if it comes to it."

He sighed. "It is what I had planned for that contingency."

"I thought you might have." I looked toward Elyssa and caught her concerned look. "I'm going to say goodbye to Elyssa, just in case."

"She'll know you plan something drastic. She might not let you go alone."

"I can't just leave without saying it."

Elyssa stalked over to us. "What is it? What's going on?" She narrowed her eyes at Thomas. "Justin is about to do something stupid, isn't he?"

I caressed her shoulders. "I have to stop Daelissa."

She threw off my hands. "You are *not* leaving me, Justin." Tears welled in her eyes. "You are not riding off on a suicide mission." Elyssa gripped my hand painfully tight. "If you go, I'm going with you."

"Elyssa," Thomas said in a commanding voice.

She jabbed a finger in his face. "Don't you dare Elyssa me, Father. You'd better tell me right now what you have planned."

I sighed. "I'm going to take a malaether crucible and detonate it in Daelissa's face."

A fierce grin stretched her lips. "I'm going with you."

"But, I'm taking a broom—"

"Do you really think I wouldn't secretly practice broom riding so I could show you up later?" Elyssa showed her teeth. "I made Bella teach me." She looked me up and down. "You're exhausted. You need me."

"Elyssa," Thomas said again.

"Father, this is my decision, not yours." She glared at him as if daring him to contradict her.

Thomas stiffened. "You're right. Together, you have a better chance at getting back alive." He crushed Elyssa in a bear hug. "I love you, daughter, and I'm very, very proud of you." He pulled away, an uncertain look on his face as if he couldn't believe he'd just shown so much emotion. He quickly masked it. "Please come back in one piece."

She kissed him on the cheek. "I will do my best." Elyssa turned to me. "Justin, when I say I love you, it means I'm *all* in, for better or worse. Maybe one day you'll get that through your thick skull."

Some of the anguish melted away. I didn't want her to die if things went wrong, but just knowing she'd be there gave me the extra hope and determination that might get us back alive. "I love you so damned much."

She punched me in the shoulder. "I know. Let's go. I want to see the look on Daelissa's face when I smack it with a malaether crucible."

I touched my comm pendant. "Lanaeia, I need your broom on the command platform, stat!"

"On my way," she replied. Seconds later, she drifted to a halt next to my broom. "Here I am."

I headed toward her. "Excellent. Elyssa needs your broom. Can you stay and help here?"

"Of course." She gave me a curious look. "What are you planning to do?"

"Something drastic." I hopped on the broom and zipped down to the blue crate.

True to her word, Elyssa kept up without a problem. She got off and opened the crate to reveal two glass orbs about twice the size of my head, each glowing with malignant light. She took a cloth sack and secured it to the back of her broom.

"Maybe we should take a flying carpet with a camouflage spell," I said. "We could get it right next to her and detonate it."

"Too slow." Elyssa rummaged in one of the other chests and withdrew two silver bracelets. She tapped them together once and tossed one to me. "These light-benders will conceal us. I linked them together so we can see each other while they're on. They only hold about a twenty minute charge, though."

"It won't take us that long to reach her," I said.

She snapped the bracelet on her wrist. "I can throw the crucible about a hundred feet. Can you detonate it from that far out?"

"Maybe." I gave her a serious look. "Elyssa, I might be too tired. Even if I detonate it, I can't shield us from the blast. I'm practically useless."

"In other words, I have to literally hit Daelissa or someone near her hard enough to crack this crucible open." She swung into the boomstick saddle. "I guess that's what I'll have to do."

"That means once you throw it, we'll have to fly for our lives before it hits."

She bit her lower lip, nodded. "I know." Elyssa glanced toward the front lines as the goliaths began to open fire on our besieged troops. "We've got to do this now before everyone is dead." She activated her bracelet and shimmered out of sight.

I tapped mine. Light rippled around my body, turning it into a blur. Elyssa's shape became visible a few seconds later as the linked bracelets recognized each other. I got onto my broom and gripped the throttle. "Let's go."

We sped low across the ground keeping behind the giant pyramids and then hung a left where the sphinx had carved a valley through the jungle. I spotted Daelissa's cloudlet several hundred yards away, high in the air behind the goliaths. Setting my sights on her, I angled up so we could approach from below.

A formation of archangels left another of the large cloudlets and looped outward. One of them suddenly pointed at us.

I looked back to see if there was something behind us, but saw nothing except the smoking remains of the sphinx and a goliath. "He can't see us, can he?"

Elyssa peered at him. "Not unless—"

The archangels unsheathed their vjaltis. One of them threw a glowing blue orb. It detonated, sending an electrical shockwave hundreds of yards in all directions. Our camouflage flickered away.

I realized the lead archangel wore a strange pair of rose-tinted spectacles. Since Seraphim didn't typically need eyeglasses, that could only mean the spectacles enabled them to see through magical camouflage.

"So much for Plan A," Elyssa growled.

"Give me the crucible," I said. "I'm going to ram it down Daelissa's throat."

"You're not doing this alone!" Elyssa gave me a sad look. "I guess this is it, isn't it?"

I choked up with sudden grief. It took everything I had not to turn the broom around and run, if only to save Elyssa. "Underborn's stupid foreseeance was right. Maybe we can run for it."

"We can't run, Justin. If we do, she'll hunt us and those we love for the rest of our lives."

I swallowed the hard lump in my throat and nodded. "For the people we love. For family. For Eden."

"For Bella, Nightliss, our parents, our siblings, and even Harry Shelton." Elyssa bared her teeth in a fierce grin. "We have plenty of people worth dying for."

"That's for damned sure." Purpose surged through my veins. "Let's go put the *Die* in Daelissa."

Elyssa narrowed her eyes. "I'm with you to the end."

I extended my middle finger toward the oncoming archangels. Their numbers had grown as reinforcements closed on our position. "We'll have to dodge these jackasses."

"Are we fast enough?"

"They're fast, but they can't juke a flying broom."

Two of the goliaths turned toward us and the odds suddenly grew worse. We had no choice but to duck into the jungle and try to lose pursuit, or fly high enough to avoid the goliaths. A flock of black-winged vampires flew up from one of the cloudlets and came toward us. My supernatural vision recognized the skeletally thin vampires at once.

"Those are the ancient vampires." Confidence abandoned my voice.

Elyssa shouted a filthy word. "I know for a fact they're as agile as our brooms."

There was no way we could reach Daelissa. We were done.

Chapter 37

"I don't think we can punch through them." I slowed my broom and stared at the encroaching enemy.

Tears filled Elyssa's eyes. "No! We can't let everyone die." She stared daggers at these new obstacles. "We have no choice but to try. Even if we don't kill Daelissa, we'll take out everything she's throwing at us. Maybe we can get close enough to hurt her."

I turned toward her. "Is it worth it?"

"If we do nothing, we die." She wiped the moisture from her eyes. "I won't let her take us without a fight."

I looked at the jungle below. "Okay. Let's do it smart though. We'll dive into the jungle and—"

My comm pendant crackled and Shelton's voice came over it. "Justin, you idiot! Stop!"

"Where are you? How did you know—" I looked around in confusion.

"Everyone knows! They saw you the minute the archangels blew your camo." Shelton sighed. "You're really lucky you have a friend like me." He started laughing maniacally. "You ready to see Daelissa crap her pants?"

Elyssa and I shared a confused look.

"Yes?"

"Then look behind you."

I looked back toward the destroyed sphinx and saw an open portal. Shelton stepped out, set something on the ground, and backed away. One of his huge doors unfolded. Despite the trampled trees, it managed to stay upright.

"Oh," he said, "you might want to scoot to the side."

The door swung open to reveal a gargantuan battle bot. Chrome body gleaming magnificently, it stepped through the door, huge feet quaking the ground. Massive guns jutted from its arms. Missile turrets sprang from its shoulders the moment it cleared the door. Behind it marched another battle bot, and behind it another. They were shorter than the goliaths, but proved more agile as they raced through the doorway.

After eleven of them emerged, another five giant spider bots scuttled through. Behind them came a squadron of people on shiny silver rocket sticks, all armed with a variety of intimidating weapons.

"Let me introduce Science Academy, bitches!" Shelton cried through the comm pendant.

I was still in shock. "Underborn did it?"

"That he did." Shelton whooped.

I felt an evil grin stretching my lips and turned toward the enemy. The vampires and archangels held position, shocked looks clear on their faces. All four goliaths rotated toward us.

Shelton cried a command. "Battle bots, engage!"

"By your command," the bots replied in their cybertronic voices. Every one of them launched a salvo of mini-missiles at airborne enemies. The archangels fled, but couldn't outrun the projectiles. Explosions rocked the air. Smoking bodies plunged earthward. Only the vampires remained unaffected.

"Must be heat-seeking missiles," I said. "The vampires aren't warm-blooded."

The battle bots fired brilliant yellow lasers at the vampires, turning some of them to ash. The ancient creatures scattered in panic. The spider bots crawled with the fluid grace of their organic counterparts toward the oncoming goliaths, firing missiles and lasers. The projectiles slammed into the behemoths, rocking the nearest back so hard, it collapsed. The battle bots joined the fight. Two of them sprinted to the next goliath. Each gripped a leg and jerked. The goliath crumbled at the crotch and fell apart. Another leapt high with the aid of a jetpack and tore the head from a third behemoth.

The squadron of rocket-stick pilots streaked toward the ground forces and began pummeling the enemy from behind and above with a lightshow of lasers and death rays.

"Daelissa is getting away!" Elyssa shouted.

I looked skyward and saw her cloudlet fleeing. "After her!" I jetted forward.

"Are you strong enough to fight her?" Elyssa shouted over the roar of the wind.

I hadn't even thought about it, but there was no doubt in my mind about the answer. "No. I'm too tired." We grew closer and closer. I saw Daelissa red-faced and screaming at a short blond woman I recognized as Serena.

"If you feed off of me, would that help?" Elyssa asked.

Magical exhaustion couldn't be completely sated by feeding—even it required sleep—but if I drew from Elyssa, I might have a small chance of fighting Daelissa to a stalemate until help arrived.

I looked at her. "I'll have to suck it in fast. You'll feel very drained."

Black hair flying wild in the wind, she held out her arms. "Take what you need. I am your dark light." Her words echoed a foreseeance I'd long forgotten.

I extended both hands and opened myself fully. Inky black and brilliant white shot from her fingers and into mine. I tensed hard and drew on her soul essence like a thirsty man sucking on a straw. Elyssa gasped, but maintained her balance on the boomstick. After a few more seconds, I sensed her weakening and released the connection.

Elyssa slumped forward, white-faced. She gripped the broom with both hands and managed a weak smile. "Kick her ass, baby."

Strength surged in me. I grinned. "As you wish." We were within fifty yards of the fleeing cloudlet. A torn flap of my Nightingale armor flapped in my face. I retracted the torso so I could see. Daelissa wasn't alone. From here, I made out Serena, Arturo, and two other archangels.

A shimmering gateway opened in the air and I realized with horror that they were about to escape. Daelissa might go into hiding for another two thousand years until she figured out how to raise another army.

I leaned forward and put up a thin shield of Murk in front of the boomstick for better aerodynamics. My velocity increased ever so slightly. Just as the cloudlet reached the gateway, I leapt off the broom and flew through the air. A startled archangel shouted as I slammed into him. His body bounced off Daelissa and sent her careening to the left and toward the edge. I saw a seraph standing in a cave on the other side of the gateway, presumably in Thunder Rock. I blasted him in the chest with Brilliance, focused on the gateway, and willed it to close. It vanished.

Serena gave me a curious look from the other side of the large platform. "You are very persistent." She jotted something on a notepad, looked over the side of the cloudlet, and promptly jumped off. A second later, she flitted away on my broom with the malaether crucible still inside the saddlebag. My boomstick must have drifted there after I jumped off.

Arturo and his remaining companion drew swords and advanced on me. Their wings briefly flared behind them but soon sputtered out.

"Looks like you're too tired to fly."

Arturo spat. "You are still no match—"

I didn't give him time to finish that sentence. Using all my demonic speed, I blurred between him and the other seraph. I knocked his buddy off the edge with a roundhouse, ducked, and slammed Arturo in the chest. He staggered backward. A quick blast of Murk gave him enough momentum to fall screaming off the other side to the ground far, far below. Without wings, he was in for a hard landing.

I spun to see the biggest threat to my existence pulling herself up over the edge of the cloudlet after the seraph's body had nearly knocked her off. Daelissa's eyes blazed with Brilliance. She scratched furiously at her right hand. "You have doomed yourself, boy. Have you forgotten how powerful I am?"

I pinched my forehead. "I don't remember. On a scale from kiss my ass to arrogant bitch, how powerful are you?" As I spoke, I drew

in aether. Experience had taught me well what to expect from
Daelissa.

She didn't disappoint.

With a scream of rage, she unleashed a massive torrent of
destruction so bright, it nearly blinded me. I dodged left and wove a
beam of gray Stasis, meeting her attack in the middle. Her energy
shattered like ice. Unfortunately, Daelissa was rested and full of piss
and vinegar. I couldn't maintain the same level of energy. She
scowled and redoubled her efforts. Even as her sizzling death beam
broke into shards against Stasis, it slowly gained ground.

Mom, Ivy, someone, I need help! I hoped Elyssa had contacted
someone who could come to my aid.

"You are weak, boy." Daelissa's scowl turned to a smile. "You
cannot hope to destroy a goddess. Nothing can defeat the light." She
pushed back the Stasis until only a few feet remained between me and
incineration.

I decided it was time to rely on something besides magic. I
released the channeled energy and dove right. My hyper instincts
engaged and time seemed to slow. Sprinting at top speed, I blurred to
her side. Most humans would have appeared in slow motion to me,
but Daelissa hardly seemed affected and raked the death beam toward
me. I reached her just as the heat from it began to singe my arm hair.

My fist connected with her jaw.

Blood sprayed. The channeled Brilliance vanished. I didn't let up.
Putting everything I had into the next blow, I socked her in the
temple. Daelissa spun like a top and went down in a boneless heap.

I hated hitting women, but Daelissa was one of those people who
made it easy to break that rule. I despised her so much I didn't even
pause when I raised my hands over my head for the killing blow. She
lay supine, eyes rolled into the back of her head, hands splayed to the
side. She looked so much like Nightliss, that it caused me to pause
half a heartbeat. Her right hand twitched, and I noticed a strange
bulge in the palm where the flesh looked as if she'd scratched it raw.

I grabbed her hand and looked closer. Something was lodged in
the flesh. Manifesting into part demon form, I extended a sharp black
claw and sliced open the skin. A bloody crystalline object sparkled as

if lit with an inner light. Using my claws, I tried to pry it loose, but it wouldn't come out. It looked familiar, but with so much blood seeping into the wound, I couldn't make it out.

Daelissa screeched and punched me hard in the stomach. Before I could react, she threw me several feet away and climbed to her feet.

"You have violated me!" She raised her bleeding hand in the air. "You profane, despicable speck! I am divine! I am a goddess! You cannot win!"

Bracing for her next attack, I bared my demonic teeth. "Goddess?" I spat. "You keep using that word. I don't think it means what you think it means. A goddess doesn't bleed, you warthog-faced buffoon."

She screamed and blasted a wave of death toward me. I leapt high, channeled my angel wings, and levitated. The barrage narrowly missed my lower extremities. The remnants of my Nightingale armor couldn't keep out the heat. The soles of my feet felt flash-fried. Almost without thinking, I retaliated with a blast of Brilliance. My inner demon roared with ecstasy and lunged for sole possession of my consciousness.

Insatiable hunger filled me, buttressed by deep red rage. The demon drew on Brilliance like an infant sucking on a bottle of milk and channeled everything at Daelissa. The attack threw her backward. I roared with pleasure.

Get out of my head, you idiot!

I'd had an internal dialogue with my demon side a while back and figured we'd settled things once and for all. Apparently, it had no intention of ever passing up a chance to be the boss of me. My inner demon tried to draw on more Brilliance, and suddenly realized that it had screwed up big time. As a Seraphim, I could directly channel aether without storing it, but burning through the rarified soul essence gained from feeding on humans diminished my power. My demon side had burned through nearly everything in one go.

I used the moment of confusion to take back control and slammed it back into its cage. My body morphed back to human form. Daelissa climbed to her feet, a maniacal gleam in her eye. She had the power to finish me off right here and now and there wasn't much I could do to stop her unless I leapt off the cloudbank.

Daelissa laughed. "Pitiful. You attacked me with everything and failed. You cannot kill an immortal, boy. My light outshines yours." A misty wall of Brilliance formed in front of her. "You have nothing left to fight me with. I will make your final seconds long and painful."

There was nothing I could channel to counter her next blow. I couldn't manage enough Stasis to ward it off, or enough Murk to shield myself. A stiff wind rose and the steel gray sky rolled overhead like a fountain of Stasis. To either side of cloudbank, black and white smoke from the raging battle flowed past like rivers. Daelissa and I stood at the center, her facing me with victory shining in her eyes.

"Finally my time has come." She burst into insane laughter. "I will end you and come back stronger than before. In a few years, I will have another Seraphim army at my back and proceed unhindered to conquer Eden. The mortals will bow before me and I will claim all that is mine."

I heard everything she said, but found myself captivated by the surreal scenery. It reminded me so much of the vision I'd had with rivers of Murk and Brilliance to either side of a tiny island while overhead, a fountain of Stasis roared past. I'd made a choice during that vision. Instead of the light, dark or the gray, I'd chosen all of them.

The choice is clear.

I thought back to my earlier attempts at channeling Clarity. At what it had done to Elyssa.

Run or fight.

If I leapt, I'd fall hundreds of feet and possibly die. Daelissa would get away and eventually form another army. If I fought, death was almost guaranteed, and the results would be much the same. Something told me neither of those was the right choice. Fear grew palpable in me. I didn't want to die. I wanted to live a long happy life with Elyssa and my family. But if I ran, if Daelissa survived this and escaped, my cowardice would pave the path for another war. The next time, it might be even worse. She might subvert more nom governments and use them in her conquest, causing a nuclear holocaust in the process.

But I was drained physically and magically. In short, I was out of options.

Daelissa released the translucent wall of energy. "Enjoy the sight of me for your last few moments on this earth." She blew the pulsating energy as if blowing me a kiss. Moving at the pace of a walk, it was too wide to dodge or leap over, and I hadn't the energy to levitate. The malicious smirk spreading on her cruel face told me that she knew how weak I was. Prolonging my death by fueling my fear and despair as I looked on powerless seemed to fill her with joy.

Everything grew quiet, as if the world were holding its breath while the fate of Eden hung in the balance. Then again, I might have just been scared senseless.

"Justin, I love you!" Elyssa shouted from somewhere behind me. "Don't die!"

I looked back and saw her, pale-faced and tired, still in pursuit. Her broom smoked and flew erratically. She wouldn't catch up in time. In that instant, I knew I wouldn't run. I'd do as I'd always done—cling to the last shred of hope and fight. Daelissa was powerful, but she was missing the most powerful element that not even death could stop.

Love.

Elyssa put her hands to her mouth. "Justin, Clarity is truth!"

In that instant, everything became clear. Destruction, creation, and Stasis were all different forms of change. Clarity didn't change anything. It simply laid bare something's true nature. That was why it didn't do anything to inanimate objects. That was why Elyssa had seen herself floating naked in a lake of clear water.

I knew what I had to do. Unfortunately, doing it meant I had no chance of escape.

I will always love you, Elyssa.

I channeled Murk from every finger of my left hand, and Brilliance likewise from my right, weaving the threads into gray. I channeled beams of creation and destruction from my eyes and into the gray. Clear energy rippled the air around me like a stone in a lake.

"Daelissa, I think the universe wants you to have a good hard look at yourself." I grinned. "I don't think you're going to like what you see."

A crystalline beam speared from the gray sphere and toward Daelissa. It did nothing to stop the deadly energy inexorably burning toward me and went through it. But that didn't matter.

Clarity found its target.

Daelissa stiffened, arcing as if someone had stabbed her in the back. She screamed. "No, that isn't me! That isn't me!" Tears poured down her face. She dropped to her knees. "I hate you! Hate you!" Her voice was raw with agony. "You're worthless!" Oily dark light and brilliant white poured from her in all directions. A horrific shriek tore from her mouth. "You are nothing!"

Exhaustion claimed me. I took one faltering step back and felt open air beneath me. Daelissa's magic wouldn't kill me, but gravity would.

The rush of wind filled my ears. It was almost a pleasant last sound to hear. I wondered how long it would take before I hit the ground.

My arm jerked painfully in its socket as someone grabbed it. I heard Elyssa cry out in a long, agonizing scream. I opened my eyes and saw her tear-filled eyes looking at me. Saw her slumped over the broomstick, arm hanging unnaturally from the shoulder. Her fingers somehow clung to me in a white-knuckled grip.

"Grab the broom!" Elyssa sobbed. "Help me save you!"

Moving my other arm was like moving dead weight. The broomstick seemed too far away to reach.

"Damn it, Justin, do you love me or not?" she screamed. "Grab the broomstick!"

Out of nowhere, I felt a tiny jolt of extra energy inside me. Putting everything I had toward moving my arm, I flung it upward. My fingers scraped the bottom of the stick and missed. Elyssa cried out as my momentum jerked on her arm. I dully realized I should have gone for the stirrup instead of the handle since it was much closer, but no matter how hard I tried, I couldn't summon the energy to move my arm again.

"No, no, no!" she shouted, eyes clenched shut with concentration. Her sweaty hand slipped down my forearm to my wrist, wrenching Elyssa's arm again. Her tears rained on my face. Her hands slipped to my fingers. For an instant, they hooked together.

"It's okay," I said. "I love you."

Elyssa's eyes opened wide as she lost her grip.

I plummeted to earth.

Well, about ten feet or so. Don't get me wrong, the impact still hurt, especially since my back landed perfectly on a broken tree branch. I shouted in surprise at the sudden impact.

Elyssa's boomstick levitated lower until she was right over me. She groaned. "I guess it's a good thing I headed straight for the ground while I was holding onto you."

I snorted. "I guess so." Unfortunately, I was too tired and hurt to move. "I'm just going to lie here forever. I'm exhausted."

"Me too." Elyssa toppled off her still-smoking broom and landed next to me with a loud grunt. "Lying here with you forever sounds wonderful." The riderless broom rose a few feet and spun in a lazy circle.

"What happened to your broom?" I asked.

"Serena hit it with a spell when she stole your broom." Elyssa groaned. "I really hope we can capture that over-analytical little imp, because I'd like to punch her in the face."

Daelissa's cloudlet, probably damaged by her attack on me, lost altitude, drifting lower and lower as it diminished in size. It finally settled down not far from us. I heard moaning and sobbing.

"Help me up," I said.

Elyssa pulled me to my feet. We staggered to the cloudlet. Daelissa huddled in the middle. Dark veins laced her alabaster skin. She looked up at me, bloodshot eyes filled with tears. Her hand reached for me. I hesitated, but took it.

Something amazing happened. Daelissa smiled. It was not a cruel smile, or an evil smirk, but a genuine smile. She looked nearly identical to Nightliss in that single, perfect moment. "Thank you." Her voice was a faint rasp. "I was lost, but you found me." She shivered violently. "The truth is too much to bear." Daelissa's grip grew weak.

The curve of her lips relaxed, and the light left her eyes. I released her hand and let her body recline on the cloudlet.

I dropped to my knees and stared at her. My eyes wandered the destruction all around us. Bodies piled on the ground, the forest flattened and smoking. How many people had died because of this woman—this Seraphim? Why hadn't I known how to use Clarity before? I could have stopped her sooner. I could have prevented this. None of this should have happened!

Grief welled in me until I couldn't take it anymore. I leaned into Elyssa and cried. She hugged me and shook with sobs of her own.

We had won. We had survived.

The cost had been staggering.

Chapter 38

Someone shook me awake.

I opened my eyes and found Shelton and a group of Templar healers hovering over us. *We must have fallen asleep.* For a moment, I thought everything had been a dream. I turned and saw Daelissa's body not far from us. *It's real. The war is over.*

Shelton whooped. "I can't tell you how happy I am to find you alive." He chuckled. "Man, you two look awful." He glanced at Daelissa. "The queen bitch looks even worse."

The healers loaded us onto flying carpets and began treating us.

"I'm not feeling so hot," I said in a scratchy voice. Actually, I was feeling very hot thanks to baking in the sun for much of the late afternoon.

Elyssa winced as the healers reset her dislocated arm. "What's the situation?"

Shelton grinned. "Daelissa's army surrendered a couple of hours ago. We've been combing the area for you and other survivors, but digging through all the wreckage and destroyed trees has taken hours of family fun." He glanced at Daelissa again. "What did you do to her?"

I followed his gaze. "I hit her with Clarity."

He raised an eyebrow. "The clear magic that didn't do anything?"

"Yeah. Elyssa figured out what it does."

Shelton gave me an expectant look. "Well, spit it out."

"It reveals the absolute truth to whoever I hit with it." I thought back to Daelissa's last words. "The truth was too much for her to bear."

"Uh, promise you won't ever hit me with that stuff." Shelton grimaced. "I ain't too sure I want to see the absolute truth about myself."

I chuckled. "That's something none of us want to see." We were silent for a moment, then I asked, "How's my family?"

"They're fine." He motioned with his head. "Your parents and sister are out looking for you. I'll let them know you're here." He touched the comm pendant on his Arcane robes and sent the message.

Within an hour, Elyssa and I felt well enough to walk. We went through an omniarch portal to the caverns beneath El Dorado where the Templars placed Daelissa's body in a preservation spell. The large cavern was filled with the wounded and dead.

I found Nightliss staring at the body of her sister, a deeply troubled look on her face.

She looked up as we approached. "My sister is truly dead."

I couldn't tell what she was feeling, so I asked. "How do you feel?"

Nightliss bit her lower lip. "Relieved. Sad. I wish I understood what drove her to be the person she was."

I looked closer at Daelissa's body. She looked like a white marble statue that had cracked from age and weather. I noticed crusted blood on her right hand, and curiosity drew me toward the wound. I motioned to a nearby healer. "Can you remove the preservation spell for a moment?"

The woman nodded. "Of course." With a wave of her wand, the shimmering field around the body flickered away. The healer left to tend to other wounded soldiers.

I examined Daelissa's hand. The wound had closed, but not fully healed before death. "Sorry about this," I told Nightliss.

She peered closely at it. "What is that beneath her skin?"

Elyssa handed me a small dagger. I sliced open the skin, feeling a bit ill as I did so. Once I cleared away the muscle, I found something that made us gasp in surprise.

"Kiddo!" Dad came up behind me and gripped me in a bear hug.

I groaned as sore muscles protested. "Ow."

He pulled away, a huge smile on his face. "Sorry. I kinda forgot you just saved the world."

Ivy latched her small arms around my waist. "Oh, Justin. I was so worried about you."

"When they broke your cloaking spell, everyone saw you headed for Daelissa," Mom said as she stepped beside Ivy. She kissed me on the cheek. "Thomas told me you planned to detonate a malaether crucible." Her eyes reddened. "I was sick with worry but powerless to help."

Despite my bloody hands, I returned Ivy's hug and Mom's kiss. "It had to be done."

Mom embraced Elyssa. "I can't tell you how happy I was when Shelton told us you were okay."

Dad looked at Daelissa's still form. "Wow. After everything we've been through, I can't believe it's over."

"It is surreal," Nightliss said in a soft voice.

Elyssa nodded toward Daelissa. "Maybe you should show them what we just found, Justin."

I took Daelissa's hand and exposed what was fused inside her palm. Mom gasped.

"Is that what I think it is?" Dad gave me a disbelieving look. "All her notions about Brightling superiority and—wow."

"When Nightliss told me about her family and told me about the odds of a Brightling child being born to two Darklings, I didn't think much of it." I touched the tip of the crystal prism embedded in Daelissa's hand. "She didn't want to be a Darkling so much, she figured out how to implant a prism inside her hand so she could channel Brilliance and look like a Brightling."

"That would explain why we saw her scratching her hand," Elyssa said. "She must have been using so much power lately that it began to irritate her skin."

I shook my head in disbelief. "Daelissa was a Darkling all along."

"Now I understand what Daelissa meant," Elyssa said. "The truth was too much for her."

337

The realization made me feel awful. "When I hit Daelissa with Clarity, it made her face her own worst nightmare. She saw her true nature."

Elyssa's face saddened. "More than anything else, Daelissa hated herself. Facing every terrible thing she'd ever done in a single moment of lucidity killed her."

Tears trickled down Nightliss's face. "Channeling only Brilliance in a body with an affinity to Murk must have driven her mad." She wiped her eyes. "If only I had known, perhaps I could have convinced her to stop. Perhaps my sister never would have become the monster she turned into."

Dad gave us a sage look. "Well, kids, the moral of the story is this—just be yourself." He chuckled at his own joke.

"*David!*" Mom gave him a disappointed look.

Ivy giggled. "That's funny."

Nightliss seemed lost in her own world as she stared at the body of her sister. "I could have saved her," she murmured. "I just didn't see the truth."

I hugged the petite sera to my chest. "There was nothing you could have done. It's not your fault."

She backed away and managed a small smile. "She is at peace now. I should take solace in that, at least."

Thomas, Leia, Michael, and Phoebe appeared from the direction of the control room a few moments later. Elyssa cried out with happiness and ran to them.

Shelton and Bella came in behind them, broad smiles on their faces. I showed them our discovery.

"Well I'll be a vampire monkey's uncle." Shelton's mouth dropped open. "What a hypocrite!"

Dad chimed in with the moral of his story again and Shelton guffawed. I had a feeling Dad would be using this joke for centuries to come.

Bella sighed. "Sometimes I wonder who the real children are."

Looking around at the people I called family, a deep joy radiated in my heart, melting the fear, tension, and drama of the past few months. *We did it!* I could finally have something approaching a normal life. Despite the prophecy, I had somehow survived.

I spotted Ketiss across the cavern talking to his wounded soldiers and excused myself so I could talk with him. He knelt next to a still female form. My throat constricted when I saw it was Flava.

She blinked and tried to smile, but her face showed deep, purple bruises.

I knelt next to her. "Are you okay?"

"Not dead yet," she said in a raspy voice.

Ketiss stood and saluted in the Darkling way. "You have saved the Promised Land, Destroyer."

"Please, just call me Justin from now on, okay?" I glanced over my shoulder at Nightliss. "Is she off the hook for being a bad guy?"

He nodded. "Our religion was mistaken about her affiliation. Nightliss has proven beyond doubt that she is not to blame for the sins of her sister."

I turned back to Flava. "What you did was so brave. If you hadn't saved me, Daelissa might have escaped. You are directly responsible for me being able to end this."

Flava managed another smile, but talking was apparently too hard for her right now. She had nearly sacrificed herself to save me. She'd told me she loved me. I suddenly wondered if her sacrifice had been the one mentioned in the foreseeance.

"She will be awarded many honors," Ketiss said. "Unfortunately, Cephus's sins against our people have left us with a great deal to sort out when we return." He looked at me uncertainly. "Do you intend to come to Seraphina and aid us in driving back the Brightlings?"

I had nearly forgotten about that, but a promise was a promise. "After I've seen to the recovery here, we will try to solve the problems of Seraphina, starting with Cephus and working toward the Brightling Empire. I would like to see everyone as equals under your law."

Ketiss looked uncertain. "Would it not be better to destroy the Brightlings?"

I realized I had a lot of convincing to do if his feelings were indicative of the greater population. "Everyone has a purpose, Ketiss. We should seek to heal the old wounds caused by millennia of misguided elitism. By uniting the Brightlings and Darklings, all Seraphim will thrive."

He still didn't look convinced. "Perhaps you are right, but it will be a long and difficult journey."

That's an understatement. "Difficult, but worth it in the end." I kissed Flava on the forehead. "Rest well. We'll talk again soon."

She managed a word. "Yes."

On my way back to Elyssa, Underborn and Fjoeruss intercepted me.

"Mr. Slade," Underborn said in a rather smug voice. "It would appear my efforts paid off just in time."

Fjoeruss arched an eyebrow. "What is curious to me is that many of the students from Science Academy claimed they were ready for the assault nearly an hour before they deployed."

Heat rushed to my face. "An hour?"

"It took time for logistics to take shape," Underborn explained. "We had to wait for Mr. Shelton to arrive with one of his unfolding doors."

"With omniarches, that should have taken only minutes to complete." Fjoeruss clasped his hands behind his back and gave Underborn a long look. "Do not think I'm unaware of your fondness for orchestrating events."

"Sometimes life does not imitate art precisely enough," the assassin said, not a hint of shame in his voice.

It took everything I had not to strangle the man. "You could have sent reinforcements earlier?"

"Truly, not much sooner, Mr. Slade." Underborn folded his arms across his chest. "At the most, perhaps fifteen minutes. Once I heard about your attempt to fly straight at Daelissa with a malaether crucible, I thought it the perfect time to launch our attack."

"You were saved by an army of robots at the last minute," Fjoeruss said. "Quite literally, *Deus ex Machina*." His voice sounded cold even by his standards. His gaze shifted back to Underborn. "I believe you spent too much time as a literary teacher at that high school."

I took a step toward Underborn, my anger rising to the boiling point. "If I find out you could have come to our aid sooner, I promise there will be no last-minute intervention from a god to save you."

"I can assure you the timing was merely coincidence." Underborn shrugged. "Interview all the academy students you want. You will find that we were moving things along as speedily as possible." A small smiled touched the corners of his lips. "Perhaps one day I will tell you how you ended up going to a high school with the name Edenfield, or how the name of the foreseeance which told of your coming was designated as four-three-one-one."

I resisted the strong urge to punch him in the face. "Are you saying you somehow engineered it so I would go to a high school with the name Eden in it?" I took a deep breath to ward off the anger. A few questions with people from Science Academy would help me decide what to do about Underborn.

The assassin shrugged at my question. "A bit too providential, wouldn't you say?"

"And what in the world does it matter what the number of the foreseeance was?"

"Perhaps if you imagined the numerals." Underborn took out an arcphone and put the numbers on the display. *4311.*

At first I didn't see what he was talking about. Just as I opened my mouth to retort, my nerdy side made the connection. "Those numbers spell the word 'hell'." I didn't know whether to roll my eyes or backhand him across the cave. I vaguely remembered getting this reference before, but it certainly wasn't at the top of my most memorable occasions. "You went through all the trouble of having the foreseeance assigned those specific numbers."

"It was no great trouble. I simply switched the real four-three-one-one with four-four-six-three."

"You've got serious problems, man." I'd originally come here to thank him for his help, but with all the meddling he'd done in my life, I had a feeling there was quite a bit more he wasn't telling me. "Maybe you should see a psychotherapist about your OCD."

"Fjoeruss is no less guilty of tampering with events," Underborn said. "You have proven your worth, Mr. Slade. You are exceptionally intelligent when you put your mind to it, and gifted in rare and unusual ways. We wish to open communications with the powers that be in Haedaemos. As of yet, that realm has remained largely untouchable by our physical standards. We believe you are powerful enough in the spiritual sense to gain the attention of Baal himself."

"Whoa there, Nellie!" I backed away palms out. "Are you trying to recruit me into one of your secret little cabals?"

"It is a business opportunity," Fjoeruss said. "Also, with Daelissa gone, there is a power vacuum to be filled here in Eden and Seraphina. Should you so desire, you could take advantage of the political situation and gain a great deal of influence in the new order."

It wasn't surprising to me in the least that these two were already scheming for power. Choosing me to help them was surprising. "If you think I'm going to replace one dictator with another, you really don't know me all that well."

"On the contrary," Underborn said. "We know you quite well. You would be an excellent leader of the new Overworld Conclave—a chancellor or president, perhaps?" He tapped his chin thoughtfully. "The title really doesn't matter. Thomas Borathen, soon to be the new Supreme Commander of the Templars, can help you gain whatever power you desire."

I shook my head. "Not interested."

"Indeed," Thomas said from behind Underborn and Fjoeruss.

Though neither of them jumped or looked the least bit guilty, I saw Underborn flinch.

Thomas stepped around them to my side. "If you two have any useful input on the new ruling body of the Overworld, perhaps you could set up an appointment. I would be happy to take your suggestions."

I stepped closer to Underborn. "If you ever get the notion to mess with my life again, maybe I'll use my Haedaemos connections to mess with your life. I guess you don't know this, but I have spoken to Baal and he's pretty happy with what I've done so far."

Underborn's face actually went a bit pale. "You have truly spoken to Baal?"

I hadn't, of course, but that didn't really matter. "Yep. He's a scary son of a gun, but he said he owed me for containing the Daelissa threat." I put an arm on Underborn's shoulder and squeezed hard enough to make the assassin wince. "You'd better hope I don't find out you intentionally delayed reinforcements from Science Academy either. I know you like to pretend you're a genius mastermind, but you're probably just compensating for something else." I glanced down at his crotch.

Fjoeruss's lips turned up at the corners just a fraction. I had the feeling he enjoyed seeing Underborn in a bad spot.

I released Underborn's shoulder and nodded at Thomas. "I leave them in your capable hands, Commander Borathen."

Remaining here another minute would drive me crazy. I wanted to go someplace nice and quiet with the only person in the world I wanted to see right then. I found Elyssa and we sneaked away through an omniarch portal to a deserted island beach with a nice sunset.

Elyssa in my arms, we lay in the sand listening to the water lap the shores.

"This is perfect," I said.

She ran kisses up my neck. "More than perfect."

"The war is over, but I can't stop thinking about how much we have to do to get things running again."

"It's almost like we're starting over from scratch." Elyssa groaned. "I don't want to think about it. Can we get back to enjoying quiet time?"

I jumped up off the sand and proceeded to remove my tattered Nightingale armor.

"What are you doing?" She gave me a mischievous smile.

"What does it look like I'm doing?" I winked. "Get out of those clothes, Miss Borathen. That's an order."

She slid out of her uniform to reveal her shapely athletic curves and fair skin. "As you command, Mr. Slade."

I looked at the water about a hundred feet away. "Race you."

She nodded. "On the count of three. One—" Elyssa lunged toward the water.

I'd anticipated something like that and paced her. "Nice try."

343

She stuck out her tongue and promptly tripped me. I recovered my balance, but she hit the water first. I took her in my arms and swung her around.

"I suppose you win a prize."

Elyssa giggled. "And what would that prize be?"

"Let me show you."

Chapter 39

By the end of the week, most of the wounded were back on their feet and the cleanup process at El Dorado began. An entire committee was assigned to handle the delivery of bodies to families located all over the world. It sickened me to look at the list of the dead, but it also put into perspective the cost of the war.

Ketiss decided to keep his troops in Eden a while longer so they could feed and grow strong enough to counter Cephus and his people when they returned. He also requested that more of his troops be brought to Eden so they could dual feed. Since I hadn't given a lot of thought to handling the new situation in Seraphina, I wasn't keen on giving him a huge advantage, so I told him we needed to wait until everything here was settled. The last thing I wanted was a supercharged Darkling army committing genocide on the Brightlings.

Thomas sent scouting parties to Thunder Rock and the Grand Nexus. Daelissa had left little in the way of security at either place since she'd truly sent everything she had against us at El Dorado. The Templars were able to secure both locations without resistance. Mom removed the Mega Chalon from the Alabaster Arch at El Dorado and reassigned control back to the Grand Nexus to be certain their hack wouldn't destabilize and cause another Desecration.

Nightliss and many of the revived Seraphim who'd fought on our side, both Darkling and Brightling, began to interview the revived Brightlings who'd fought for Daelissa. They already knew who many of her inner circle were, and those who'd committed atrocities during Daelissa's initial rule. We decided it unwise to let those Seraphim live free and put them in special prisons until we decided how to handle them in the long term. In the meantime, Cinder continued reviving the remainder of the husked Seraphim, starting with the Darklings first.

During this process, I came upon an idea that might soothe the problems back in Seraphina, namely the religious conflict that threatened to destabilize the Darkling nation. Any revived Darklings who were willing would return and tell their descendants the truth about the Seraphim War. While I fully wanted Cephus and his people punished, I needed the other believers and non-believers to coexist peacefully. I still had a feeling it would be difficult to overturn thousands of years of religion even if we had incontrovertible evidence that the history behind it was flawed.

Ketiss had a very hard time dealing with this prospect, but Flava convinced him that it was necessary. I asked Nightliss and some of the revived Darklings to start with the Darkling troops from Seraphina as their test subjects.

I also promised Ketiss that once the rebuilding was underway here, I would return with him to shut down Cephus and his base of operations. Once that was done, we would find a way to end the war between the Brightlings and the Darklings. Solving a conflict that was nearly as old as mankind itself wouldn't happen quickly, but it would definitely happen.

I left Thomas in charge of rebuilding the Overworld Conclave. We agreed that it should remain similar in structure. While it wasn't perfect, it was much better than a descent into anarchy. The Custodians already had their hands full reintegrating into society the new vampires unlawfully drafted into military service by the vampire elders. Many of them had been forced to fight by compulsion, so we couldn't hold them liable for the war. Most of them also wanted to go back to their old lives, only to discover that they couldn't. Some of them did it anyway, forcing the Custodians to arrest them.

I knew it would take a long time to fully clean up this mess.

I finally got to keep one promise I'd made. Elyssa, Katie, Ash, Nyte, Shelton, Bella, and I all went out for pizza at Antonio's.

"Is this for real?" Ash said as he took the first bite of a thick slice of pie with all the works. "I thought this day would never come."

Katie laughed and wiped his mouth with a napkin. "Don't talk with your mouth full, silly."

"I can't believe we made it." Nyte took a sip of his drink. "The three of us had to help clear the wounded off the field since the healers were so busy." He blew out a breath. "It was awful, man. I never thought I'd see so many hurt and dead people."

"I never could have imagined I'd be in a war like that," Katie said. She leaned her head on Ash's shoulder. "I know there's a lot to do, but now we can finally catch a break."

"Amen to that," Elyssa said, holding up her drink for a toast. "Here's to rest and relaxation."

"Hear, hear!" Shelton said a bit too enthusiastically.

"As if you'll be doing much relaxing," Bella said. "Have you told the others what you'll be doing?"

"Please, god, tell me he's not going back into bounty hunting," Elyssa said. "I think he's caused enough emotional trauma to innocent families."

"Ha, ha." Shelton said in a deadpan voice. "I plan to start causing emotional trauma on a whole new level." He grinned. "I'm going to be a teacher at Arcane University."

I slapped him on the back. "Congratulations, buddy!"

Bella lifted both eyebrows. "They asked him to be the Grand Chancellor over both Arcane University and Science Academy, if you can believe that."

"Who is 'they'?" Elyssa asked. "Someone in an insane asylum?"

"Professors from both institutions who were cleared of sympathizing with Daelissa voted on it." Shelton wiped his hands on a napkin. "Just so happens Zagg and a few other friends of mine are now in the new Ministry of Education."

"As I recall, Zagg tried to kill you not long ago," Elyssa said. "You have a funny way of making friends."

"Yeah, turns out collecting the bounty on someone's girlfriend isn't the best way to go about it." Shelton shrugged. "At least things got sorted in the end."

"Why didn't you want to be the chancellor?" I asked.

347

"Too much responsibility." He picked up another slice of pizza. "Besides, a position like that requires using diplomacy. You know I'd be the first person to tell them to kiss my ass if they pissed me off."

The table burst into laughter.

I gave him an amused look. "You realize you're going to be one of those people whose friends can't believe you're a teacher, right?"

"Meh, it's a living," Shelton said with his mouth full.

"Is this seat taken?" a familiar voice said.

I looked up and saw Dad, Mom, and Ivy. Behind them I saw Elyssa's entire family plus Felicia and Adam Nosti, Meghan Andretti, Nightliss, Stacey, and Ryland.

Stacey planted a big kiss right on my lips before I could utter a word and pulled back. "You marvelous man! I knew you were destined for greatness from the moment I met you."

"You mean when you used your felycan wiles to feed on me when I was clueless?" I couldn't suppress a huge grin as I stood up and looked at everyone.

"We heard there was a pizza party," Dad said, pushing together several tables while a waiter tried desperately to control this new unexpected situation.

"Is it my turn?" Felicia Nosti stepped up next to Stacey. She kissed me and then gave me a big squeeze. "I've been wanting to do that for a long time."

"He's an incubus," Stacey said. "You know how they are."

Elyssa rolled her eyes. "I'm going to let this slide just this once, okay, ladies? Next time, you're going to answer to me." She grinned as if she were joking, but the flash in her eyes indicated otherwise.

I shook hands with Thomas and Michael.

Elyssa's mother, Leia, kissed me on both cheeks and hugged me. Before she pulled away, she whispered in my ear. "I couldn't be prouder of you if you were my own son. Perhaps one day we'll be able to call you that."

I felt a blush coming on and said softly, "There's no 'perhaps' to it. That's a definite."

She smiled and backed away.

348

Phoebe hugged me next. "I wanted to thank you again for rescuing me. Without your help, I might have died with Daelissa."

Shelton stood up and banged his fork against his plastic cup. The room grew silent. "I hear a lot of people saying thanks to Justin." He put an arm around me. "If you think about it, everyone here has probably had their bacon rescued by him at one point or another."

My face warmed and I felt acutely uncomfortable as murmurs went up among everyone.

Shelton didn't give me a chance to speak. "Raise your hands if you ever tried to kidnap or kill the poor guy at some point."

Felicia, Shelton, Elyssa, Ivy, and several others raised their hands. Leia nudged Thomas and he grudgingly raised his as well.

Shelton chuckled. "I don't know about the rest of you, but I'm glad he saw the best in us. I'm glad he believed in us. When I met Justin, I wasn't a very good person. I'm proud to say that he gave me something in life I thought I'd never have again." Shelton choked up a little at his next words. "A best friend."

Everyone broke into applause. I felt hot tears in my eyes and saw quite a few others wiping their faces. I slung an arm around Shelton. "Here's to best friends." I held up my soft drink.

Not everyone had a drink yet, but those who didn't pretended they did. "To best friends!" they shouted.

I wiped my eyes and smiled like a fool. So many awful things had happened to get us to this point, but I felt happy. "There was a dark time when I felt lost and alone. If it hadn't been for Elyssa, I might have given up. Since then, I've gotten my family back." I motioned toward Dad, Mom and Ivy. "And I've extended my family by quite a bit." I waved a hand around the room. "You're all an important part of my life now, until the end."

The room broke out into applause. Even some of the other patrons who didn't have a clue about the nature of my family joined in the applause and cheers. I idly wondered if a video of this would end up on the internet.

More pizza arrived. I waved to the tables. "Now, let's enjoy the food and the time we have together."

349

The rest of the evening was amazing. We laughed, we reminisced, and there were plenty of tears.

The recent past had been incredibly painful, but it had brought us to this moment. The future would be full of hard work and uncertainty. But for now, I had the present to keep me happy.

The world was safe for the time being. I had a big family to rely on. I had Elyssa, my one true love, by my side.

Life was good.

"Saddle the white horses," I told Elyssa. "It's time to ride off into the sunset."

She beamed a beautiful smile at me. "As you wish."

###

I hope you enjoyed reading this book. Reviews are very important in helping other readers decide what to read next. Would you please take a few seconds to rate this book?

Go to http://www.johncorwin.net to join my newsletter for information on upcoming books.

Section A
MEET THE AUTHOR

John Corwin is the bestselling author of the Overworld Chronicles. He enjoys long walks on the beach and is a firm believer in puppies and kittens.

After years of getting into trouble thanks to his overactive imagination, John abandoned his male modeling career to write books.

He resides in Atlanta.

Connect with John Corwin online:
Facebook: http://www.facebook.com/johnhcorwinauthor
Website: http://www.johncorwin.net
Twitter: http://twitter.com/#!/John_Corwin

CPSIA information can be obtained
at www.ICGtesting.com
Printed in the USA
LVHW052130160123
737280LV00018B/126